When Duty Calls...

When Duty Calls...

J.L. Kramer

CAPPUCCINO BOOKS LTD
Copyright © 2002 J.L. Kramer

Published in Ireland by Cappuccino Books Ltd
Galway Technological Centre
Mervue Business Park
Mervue
Galway
Ireland

ISBN 0-9542546-0-0

Printed and bound in Ireland by
Betaprint, Dublin

For Stu

About the Author

J.L. Kramer was born in Kildare, Ireland. He holds a degree in Public Administration and is a qualified Accountant. His experience of the international trade scene is the inspiration for this book. He has created a board game *Mandarin – The Game of Leadership in the Forbidden City*. This is his first novel – he is currently working on his second. He lives in Brussels with his wife and three children.

J.L. Kramer is a pseudonym.

Prologue

November 1999
Brussels

THE CELLAR WAS BARE, apart from a bench and trolley in the centre. A single fluorescent strip above the bench was the only source of light. The walls were a faded white, relieved, at one corner of the room, by six or seven stone steps leading to a metal door.

The door opened and a woman was carried down the steps by four shrouded figures. Her head was covered by a hood and her arms and legs bound but she was resisting furiously. The shrouded figures, their eyes barely visible through slits, hauled her onto the steel bench and busied themselves strapping her down.

They wasted no time. Legs first, then her arms, and finally a leather restraint was placed across her throat. One of the figures picked up a scissors from the trolley and moved towards the bench. Starting with her blouse he cut freely until it was in shreds, throwing the bits to the ground. In one quick movement he pulled the remaining piece of material from under her. She tried to wriggle her body but it was impossible. She could just about arch her back.

The shrouded figure now moved down towards her skirt, cutting methodically. In seconds it was gone. Just her underwear to go. He snipped again until that, too, lay in shreds on the floor.

She was now naked, constantly writhing but it was impossible to break free. The four white figures stepped back and the door opened again. This time a figure, shrouded in red, walked down the steps. He was followed closely by a second figure carrying a case about half a meter long and a quarter wide. It was placed on the trolley which was now wheeled closer to the bench. The assistant opened the case, bowed and stepped back.

The master returned the bow and moved towards the trolley. He studied the neatly arranged knives and then,

1

averting his eyes, he observed the woman for a few moments. He drew the smallest blade from the case, held it up to the light to inspect it and then moved towards the bench.

Immediately he began making tiny incisions in the soles of the woman's feet. Moments later he was working on her toes, drawing the razor sharp edge across from one to the other. These cuts were deeper. The blood came quickly and started to trickle onto the bench. The woman jerked involuntarily, the hood covering her head moving noticeably as she groaned, the pain excruciating. He quickly stepped towards the trolley and selected another knife. It was his favourite - a scalpel - and he didn't want to waste time. Starting below the throat he made multiple tiny incisions on her chest and along her abdomen. The blood ran freely as she again tried in vain to escape.

One of the figures stepped from the side and removed the hood. He then cut the masking tape that covered her eyes, abruptly yanking it away with one quick movement, stopping short of removing the gag on her mouth. Her pupils were dilated, her eyes bulging with fear, with terror. They were red and watery and darting rapidly in all directions. Their deep blue colour had almost vanished.

As the master craftsman held another knife up to inspect it she lost control of her bodily functions, wetting herself. Without faltering, he brought it down quickly, making a triangular incision on her forehead. The woman's face contorted in pain as she tried again to wrestle herself free. The blood oozed out, forming a perfect triangle. The figure stood back, taking satisfaction from his artistry. Moments later he recommenced his work, this time the butchery almost indiscriminate as veins along her arms and legs were lacerated. Blood rushed out in rivulets and began dripping from the steel bench. He picked his step to avoid the blood now gathering in pools on the floor beneath as he moved around to finish the task.

Just like the nine hundred and ninety-nine that went before, he raised the knife and, without faltering, ceremonially made the final cut. The razor sharp blade was swiftly drawn across her throat with precision, the blood gushing out in pulsating spurts for about five seconds and then dropping to a mere trickle. He had made the thousandth incision.

He sloshed the knife around in the bucket of water beside the bench to clean it of bloodstains and then placed it back in the case. He would be called on to use it again, he was sure.

The job was finished. He showed no emotion - no feeling - no remorse. He was very professional, having done it many times before. The only difference this time was the victim. She was Caucasian and she was beautiful. But that didn't matter.

He stared at the row of knives and took satisfaction from the fact that he had used all six this time.

All six knives.

A record.

He turned and stared. Yes, she was tall, unlike his usual oriental victims. It gave him scope to use all his skills and all his knives.

He closed the case and walked towards the door. His assistant stepped forward, picked up the case and followed him. The other men keeping vigil also followed. Their job, too, was complete.

The woman would not need to be restrained anymore; she was dead.

Death By One Thousand Cuts.

MORE THAN TWO YEARS EARLIER

Chapter One

January 1997
Beijing

A *YIN* HAD ARRIVED.

For more than three weeks the harsh Siberian winds had swept down from the north, blanketing the city in snow. Despite the sub-zero temperatures, Beijing Airport was functioning normally on Saturday morning and the flight from Hong Kong had landed on schedule at eleven o clock. The passengers lined up in the main terminal to clear immigration.

"Next." the Immigration Officer thundered in Mandarin.

A small, swarthy man stepped forward and handed over his passport. The official scrutinised it. He compared the features of the passenger – the combed-back, black hair, receding at the temples, the weathered skin tautly covering the bony face and the few wrinkles rippling out around the eyes – with a photograph in his cubicle. They perfectly matched. They also agreed with the passport details. He pored over the papers for a second time, but again found nothing inconsistent. This man was definitely Zu Wong. The official stamped the page, handed back the passport and dismissed him with a curt nod of his head.

Slipping the document into an inside pocket, Wong made his way to the arrivals area where he lit up and inhaled deeply, taking comfort from the smoke now filling his lungs. He still could not come to terms with the fact that he was in the place he had vowed never to visit, but he knew that, when he had received the 'invitation' one week earlier, refusal was not an option. As he flicked the first ash to the floor, two policemen stepped forward, motioned to get rid of the cigarette and escorted him in silence to the waiting government limousine parked directly outside the arrivals-area.

Wong climbed into the car and began to search the faces of the military officers in the front seats. *What could the Communists possibly want to discuss with a small-time lawyer from Hong Kong?* He shifted uncomfortably on the back seat and allowed that question to occupy his mind once more. He was no friend of the Communist regime; in fact, he had happily pursued a capitalist lifestyle in the tiny enclave, indifferent to the excesses of the regime across the border.

Sirens blared as the Mercedes 500 moved off from the airport and headed towards the city, the red Chinese flag fluttering on the left front fender. Forty minutes later, the convoy swept onto Chan'gan Avenue, ushering the black limousine past Tiananmen Square straight to the red-walled leadership compound. Tourists queuing at the entrance to the Forbidden City turned and stared, eager to catch a glimpse of the dignatory through the tinted windows, but the 'visitor' sitting on the back seat would not be displayed for public view.

The seat of Communist Party power - the old imperial grounds at Zhongnanhai – was the destination. The cavalcade whisked past the fifteen-foot-high perimeter wall, through the gates, coming to a halt outside the forbidding entrance.

A sentry moved forward to open the door. Wong stepped out and was ushered up the steps, leaving him no time to observe the landscaped gardens and glistening lakes nestling within the walls of the compound.

The door closed. The visitor was led by his uniformed hosts down a corridor to a spacious room. Shards of sunlight streaked through two windows directly behind three men who sat at a table. A life-size terracotta warrior stood in each corner and gold-gilded scrolls hung on every wall. The ceiling and walls were in need of decoration; the atmosphere suffused with a musty smell.

Zhou Feng beckoned to him to take the only chair - strategically positioned in front of the table - and immediately introduced himself in Mandarin, the official language of the Communist Party, as the chairman of the Central Military Commission. He then introduced the corpulent figure sitting to his left as Hu Biao, the general secretary of the Party, his gray Mao suit contrasting against the neatness of Feng's military attire. The chairman now gestured towards the narrow-faced figure of Zhang Yinchu, the secretary of the National People's Congress, who also dressed in the unrefined garb of the Mao era.

Wong squeezed the Zippo lighter in his palm, an uncertain smile barely parting his lips.

"Like Chairman Mao's long journey to Beijing in 1949," Feng started off, "you too, Comrade Wong, have made a long journey today."

"I have indeed," came the reply in flawless Mandarin. Wong's linguistic skills allowed him to slip from English into the official language or the main dialects used in Hong Kong as the occasion demanded.

"Have you studied China well?" Biao enquired.

"It is almost my homeland," Wong answered, the vagueness of the question puzzling him. He had often thought that he could have been a politician or businessman in Beijing if Mao had not thrown his father into a labour camp after the revolution in 1949. In the early fifties, Yan Wong had established a clandestine network of sympathisers to fight the corruption and abuses of power by the fledgling regime but was eventually betrayed by a friend. He survived the hunger and privations for ten long years in the north-western corner of China close to the Pakistan border before eventually succumbing to the deplorable conditions of cold and grime. With no possibility of ever seeing her husband again, Li Wong had taken the young Zu to the safety of Hong Kong.

"Well then, you will know that China has five thousand years of history behind it. It is the greatest civilisation on earth, a culture we can all be proud of."

Wong bowed respectfully, but did not speak. He was searching their words for a meaning; something to reveal their intentions.

"The Middle Kingdom had a written language," the Communist Party official continued, "and had invented paper and silk-weaving and even the compass long before the imperial West. We knew about the movement of the heavenly bodies thousands of years ago."

"Our culture is the greatest," Wong said proudly, displaying his patriotic colours for the first time to test their reaction, but still determined to remain neutral until he knew which way the wind was blowing through the corridors of power. *Maybe these mandarins are plotting to oust Ziang Zemin*, he thought.

"Yes, Comrade Wong," Yinchu interjected. "The greatest -

but now Mother China must make progress and become great again."

"Yes, great again," the visitor agreed stolidly.

"And this time we will not repeat the mistakes of the Great Leap Forward when eight million of our people died."

"No," Wong replied, but smiled inwardly since he knew that not eight but almost thirty million had died because of Mao Zedong's crazy Leap Forward scheme in the fifties and sixties. It was Hong Kong that did the leaping while China took a great step backwards.

"We will make a great leap forward into the twenty-first century."

"Indeed," Wong said. "A great leap forward."

"Yes Comrade, with your help."

Wong was now baffled. What could he possibly do to help the communists? In a way they were ideological enemies, but he would listen. After all patience was a Confucian virtue and he had plenty of it. Feng was back in charge. "It is time for us to put in practice our communist philosophy: *'From each according to his ability, to each according to his need'*. And now Comrade Wong your ability is great, but Mother China's need is greater."

They were talking in riddles. He studied their faces for a clue, but was met with stony-faced, deadpan expressions.

"I do not understand."

A hawking sound came from Yinchu's throat and suddenly he craned his neck and spat into a spitoon beside the chair, immediately rubbing his mouth with the coarse material of his sleeve. "Comrade Wong," he crackled, "All we ask is that you serve Mother China according to your ability. As the most powerful Triad leader in Hong Kong you have proved your worth."

"But how may I help?" he asked almost involuntarily, shocked that they seemed to know about his covert exploits. "I'm a lawyer. I just deal in …" He hesitated for a moment still unsure whether they were setting him up.   "…just deal in property."

Feng nodded towards the three-inch thick manila folder on

the table. Wong had heard about those dossiers. The Communist government kept a *dangan* - a secret personnel file - on every dissident and businessman in China. The brief downward glances of Biao and Yinchu towards the bulging folder made explanation almost superfluous.

"We have watched you for more than ten years now," the chairman said. "…in fact, since Thatcher sold out Hong Kong in that Sino-British deal in 1984. It seems the achievements of your Yangtze Triad over the last three decades have been spectacular. You have poisoned America and Europe with China White and illegal immigration. Your empire has infiltrated the highest levels of government and commerce around the globe and usurped the forces of law and order at every opportunity."

Wong was startled by their knowledge, but he maintained eye contact. His operations were obviously not that secret after all.

"Yes, Comrade Wong," Yinchu now added, his intervention a well-orchestrated display of Communist leadership unity. "You can be a great friend to Beijing and your organisation can now help to make the *one-country-two-systems* deal for Hong Kong work."

"But," the lawyer protested. "Hong Kong is to remain capitalist…that was the deal with the British or did I misunderstand?"

"No, you didn't, Comrade Wong. That was precisely the deal and that's where you play your part…for China. You will play capitalist and we…we will continue to play communist."

Wong blinked in disbelief. Here were the communists talking capitalism. *Why didn't they talk that language fifty years ago,* he thought. *Before they took my father's silk factory and left him to rot in squalor.*

"Your Yangtze Triad may continue its existing businesses from Hong Kong but by Chinese New Year in the year of the Dragon you will have found ways to make China technologically superior."

"But Comrades…"

"You have three years," Feng interjected vehemently. "So remember the words of encouragement from Mao Zedong: *Let a thousand flowers bloom, let a thousand thoughts prevail.* Three years to prove your credentials. When China takes over in July we will station a garrison of the Peoples Liberation Army there. We can and will be as vicious as your organisation. Honour the deal and you do not have to worry. If you fail to help Mother China in her hour of need you will be met with *mei juizu.*"

This was the communist process of wiping out entire clans, even slaughtering distant relatives. Wong's lips quivered. He had always dished out *mei juizu,* never thinking for a moment that he might be at the receiving end of such barbarity.

"But-"

"Comrade Wong," Yinchu snapped. "You are hesitating but you must understand that China wants to change...so you must heed the saying of Deng Xiaoping. *'It does not matter whether it's a black cat or a white cat, so long as it catches mice.'* We no longer have any ideological hang ups, but we cannot tell our people that. China will never become great if we continue the old iron rice bowl policy. *'If you pretend to pay me I will pretend to work'* – that system has failed. We want the fruits of economic progress for our people but *we* must, and will, firmly maintain political control."

Wong felt pressurised to say something. "I understand," he muttered.

"So," Feng concluded, lifting the *dangan* off the table. "You will bring us a yang from the south...a new spirit of generosity to share with the mainland. You will practise naked and corrupt capitalism for us just like you've done for decades, but we will disavow any knowledge of it."

This was not a deal, at least not in the sense that Zu Wong, Supreme Lodge Father of the Yangtze Triad had become accustomed to. It was an ultimatum, making him distinctly uncomfortable, but there seemed no way out. Play the game the Beijing way or else. Ever the realist, he decided it was time to curry favour with the evil empire. He stood up and cleared his throat.

"China will awake and shake the world," he called out arrogantly in Mandarin, echoing the immortal words of

Napoleon. The apparatchiks nodded in unison, a clear signal that they accepted his commitment. Wong responded with a bow, turned and walked towards the door.

LESS THAN A MILE AWAY, but a world apart, Laura Harrison stood in Tiananmen Square. The snowfall had raised the temperature a few degrees but the penetrating cold lingered. Impatiently she paced the Square, eventually turning her attention to the picture of Mao Zedong hanging above the entrance to the Forbidden City.

Her visit to the city had not been planned – at least not until two days earlier. Before then she had known little of the traditions and culture of the ancient kingdom and even less about Beijing. She had been in the Far East on business, intending to return to Europe after the legal conference in Seoul had ended. Instead she had met Marc Schuman, an investigator from the European Trade Bureau, at the after-conference drinks bash in the Hilton Hotel and found out that a group of lawyers had decided to spend the weekend in China's capital. After a two-hour conversation over cheese and wine in which there was no lawyer talk, no replaying of European Court cases and no arguing arcane legal points of a recent judgment, her appetite was whetted by his enthusiasm for China. He suggested that she change her ticket and join them for the sightseeing trip to the oldest civilisation in the world. With nothing exciting waiting back in Europe, she thought 'why not' and by late Friday evening found herself on a flight to the Chinese capital.

Suddenly Laura's attention was drawn towards a figure bounding in her direction. As it came closer she realised that it was Marc. He now slowed and came to a stop, panting in the dry air like a dog.

"…I almost got arrested. Just as I was about to exchange the dollars the police swooped and arrested the black market dealer and an American…took them away in police vans. I vanished into the crowd."

"That was close."

"Tell me about it. Not worth it for twenty per cent more."

11

"So you'll just have to queue in the Bank of China."

"We'll do that later," he said as his breathing eased. He pulled a map from his pocket and unfolded it.

"Let's just see where everything is. This is the largest square in the world."

Laura held the upper part of the crumpled map.

"See that gate, the New China Gate at the north-west corner. You know that leads to Zhongnanhai where the Government buildings are."

"We'll hardly get an invite there, will we?" she asked jokingly.

"Unlikely. It's called the new Forbidden City - only high-ranking mandarins and government guests are allowed to enter there."

Marc studied the map and then nodded towards the Great Hall of the People on the western side. He turned his head and pointed to the Monument of the Martyrs.

"I think you'd make a good tourist guide," she teased. "Maybe you should give up your job at the Trade Bureau."

He smiled. "I'll take that as a compliment. Now let's make the most of our time here."

He passed the map to Laura and said, "Remember I told you on the flight that one of my ambitions was to ride a bicycle around Tiananmen Square. I reckon now's my only opportunity because we'll be with the group tomorrow on that bus trip to see the Great Wall."

"Be my guest, I can read or do some sight-seeing," she said, waving her hand in approval. As Marc moved away, she tried to settle back into the book that he had given her on the contemplative life of Tibetan monks. Concentration eluded her as the surroundings kept vying for her attention. She knew that she should be absorbing the sights and sounds, the colours and smells, the real life in this great place. Eventually she put the book back into her bag and pulled out a camera.

As she was ready to take a photograph of the entrance to the Forbidden City a bicycle bell tinkled behind her. Marc jammed on the brakes, forcing the back wheel to skid sideways, just stopping short of her toes.

"I've longed to do this," he said thrusting defiant hands in the air in a mock gesture. "Look, I'm liberating China. Nobody can stop me - no tanks, no guns. I feel as powerful as that student in 1989 standing in front of the tank. All the world saw it. Maybe big brother is watching - me on my bicycle against the sleeping might of the Chinese state."

Laura giggled. "Now that you've hired the bike, go cycle it around the Square, over towards the Forbidden City, around by that centre piece statue or whatever. Stick your nose up at Mao, salute Confucius. I'll take the photo."

"Let's away trusty steed," he shouted as he pedalled hard in the direction of Mao's tomb. Laura again stood alone in this frenetic place watching the rapid movement of cars and bicycles and the throng of people. *This is the essence of China,* she thought, *Tiananmen Square made particularly more symbolic by the democracy movement snuffed out by the awakening giant in 1989.*

Marc continued around the Square. He could now see the detail on the façade of the Great Hall of the People. Cycling closer for a better view, he put one foot down to balance himself and stopped for a moment in solitude while at the same time enveloped in the frenzy of it all.

The modern day Marco Polo, he thought, as he pushed on the pedals and headed back towards the 'Rent-a-Bike' stall. It was situated in a *hutang* (side street) off Chan'gan Avenue. When the bike was safely returned to its owner, Marc opened his wallet and thrust two dollars into the wrinkled hand of the old Chinese man. The man's eyes sparkled and he bowed profusely as the European moved away and headed back to rejoin Laura.

They made their way further down the Square towards an obelisk. "It seems to be made of granite. Mao put this up to commemorate the Revolution," Marc said as he scrambled to mount the raised plinth on which the obelisk stood. Laura's eye caught the illustrations at the base of the platform depicting scenes from before the Revolution but was soon distracted by the orator.

"Pay attention all you Chinese," Marc started off, cupping his hands as if speaking through a microphone and loudspeaker, "burn Mao's little red book - buy my little green book. It's cheaper and more environmentally-friendly."

"Get down off that platform or the People's army will come and take you away, especially for mocking Mao," Laura called out, concerned about his safety especially standing on the spot where so many were massacred only a few years previously.

"I wonder if you started shouting protests in English would they arrest you?"

"I wouldn't try it - you're not going to be an orator today...come down and we'll go to see the Forbidden City," she pleaded.

Minutes later they were at the entrance. Marc queued at the ticket kiosk. Laura stood a few metres back, allowing her eyes to observe him. Athletic and broad-shouldered, he stood about six feet tall.

Yes, attractive, she thought. *And he has a sense of humour.* On the night they had met, she found out that his father was German but had come to work for Philips Electronics after the war, married a Dutch woman and settled in Eindhoven in Holland. Marc had studied law in Utrecht and later received his doctorate from the University of Leiden. He turned around and walked towards her with the tickets and cassettes in his hand. She reminded herself that this was just a sightseeing trip to Beijing.

Once inside the walls of the Forbidden City the Peter Ustinov commentary on the audio cassette was their guide.

"It was the Ming dynasty which bequeathed the splendour of these palaces to us," Ustinov started off. "The orderly layout conformed to the idea of harmony between the elements and human life."

Laura found the detail hard to absorb, the cold air making it unappealing to linger on the words and observe the detail. She moved on towards the Hall of Supreme Harmony, the largest building in the Forbidden City. The skilfully-carved, gold-covered Dragon Throne caught her attention. The image created in the mind's eye by the cassette was as visually impressive as the actual scene before her eyes.

"The Palace has 9000 rooms," the commentary declared,

"housing around 10,000 inhabitants, a substantial number being eunuchs, maids and concubines."

She paused for a moment reflecting on the vastness of it all. *How did they survive in the freezing cold winters with no visible heating system,* she wondered.

She turned around to find Marc studying the intricate wooden carving on the eaves of a building. Laura quickly made her way to the Inner Apartments and weaved through the labyrinth of pavilions, doors, gates, courtyards and gardens, eventually reaching the home of the imperial family. Just as she expected, it was a palace given to male dominance as the Ustinov tape confirmed that the emperor was the only potent male to enter these chambers.

An hour later they reached the northern extremity of the City.

"Did you enjoy that?" He didn't wait for a reply. "It was fantastic, don't you agree?"

"Yes, but I didn't spend time absorbing all the detail."

He threw a smile at her as they continued walking. "The Ming dynasty really left something wonderful to the world with this city. The complex of temples, palaces and ceremonial halls on such a grand scale is hard to comprehend. Imagine these were built with manpower alone under the watchful eye of Yung-lo, the fifteenth century emperor."

Laura acknowledged with a nod. Her mind was fixed on something else but Marc was oblivious.

"The golden dragons perched on the roofs must have taken years to carve," he continued, "not to mention all the little ceramic pieces on the pavilion's eaves. You know, Laura, this is the largest complex of wooden buildings in the world. Ustinov described it well."

She nodded her agreement. As dusk fell they walked around by the purple cloistered walls of the Forbidden City.

"Let's have a quick coffee," he said, interrupting her thoughts. "Remember we're meeting the others in the Friendship Hotel at seven to plan the trip to the Great Wall."

"Let's just do that," she replied, slightly mocking his Dutch accent.

Chapter Two

January 1997
Boston
NOBODY IN THE STEEL-AND-GLASS building ever challenged the president of Kimble-Sinclair Inc. He had grown accustomed to more than thirty years of deference, making all around him grovel or flinch and always compromise. And the morning of the seventh of January was no different.

"Gentlemen, now that we've got a dominant position in the US market your challenge is to take Falcon Tech to stage two – make it a global multi-billion dollar corporation within three years. That's your mission!"

The words were brusque and businesslike, tinged with arrogance. Leaning back in his leather chair he continued, "It's my ambition to see our computer subsidiary listed on Wall Street and I will not countenance failure."

Howard Sinclair III was the quintessential president of a large East Coast corporation; a patrician from the Yankee Establishment in his early sixties, six foot four, one-hundred-and-seventy pounds with silver hair and gold-rimmed glasses. He reeked of money - old money - seven generations of inherited money.

Kimble-Sinclair was his corporation. An annual turnover of thirty seven billion dollars ranked it number two in the worldwide healthcare business. And over the past three decades, it held an enviable record in drug delivery innovation, making it a much sought-after stock.

Sinclair had been riding the crest of a wave but one ambition remained. It was burning deep within him, demanding release. And it was imperative that it be satisfied before he stepped down as president of his blue chip corporation. On that morning his dream was coming closer to reality, his pet project was entering the final stages. Sitting behind his walnut desk in his plush office on the twentieth floor of the Pioneer Tower Building, every word was carefully chosen to let his new management team from the Valley know the power he wielded. Surrounded by his personal collection of priceless paintings, the ritual he played out was a well-measured display of prestige and position.

"If anyone among you is not up to the challenge of taking Falcon Tech global, then opt out now before I make the formal announcement later today."

Batista, the newly-appointed president of the Falcon Tech subsidiary, flashed a confident smile across the table.

"Look, Howard, we're fully committed. We wouldn't be here if we didn't want a challenge," he said as he glanced at his two colleagues. "After all, there's a lot riding on this for us too."

Batista wore a sober grey suit and bright red-striped tie making him the classic corporate executive, staid and upright. Tomorrow he would be back in the Valley and, more importantly, back in casuals.

"We wouldn't miss a dog fight like this for anything - global dominance of the computer market. We all know it's going to be a *winner-takes-all* roller coaster ride over the next few years," Dylan Lindell, the new hot-shot chief executive officer, echoed the same commitment to Sinclair's challenge.

Sinclair eyed Lindell's blue jeans and sweatshirt and wondered for one awful moment whether he had made a big mistake. There was a dress code on the twentieth floor and it had not been breached in twenty years.

Tom Newman's enthusiasm for the assignment didn't need to be confirmed, at least not in Sinclair's eyes. He was, after all, a Kimble-Sinclair boy moving across from the parent company to run the finance function of the emerging star in the global computer business. A safe pair of hands that would help make the subsidiary a trophy and the envy of competitors.

"I hear your commitment but let me remind you what's expected over the coming months. Your mission is to take Falcon Tech to Europe and Asia and make it a household name. And in three years' time you walk through that door and tell me that you've got the company ready for the stock market. Gentlemen, remember your prize is around one hundred million apiece depending on the share price at launch. That's not counting stock options. I'm committed to ensuring that good management will be rewarded."

A smile lit up his otherwise austere face. "Any questions?" he asked.

The three Falcon Tech executives looked at each other and then at the president. Lindell tapped the table with his fingers. "Questions! Well, I've got one. We've got to achieve the targets. That's fine but what about reporting to you and the level of detail?"

Sinclair peered over his glasses, irritated. The operational details were for the new executives, he stressed but suggested that they come over regularly to headquarters for an oral presentation on profitability and progress generally. Finally he said, "the success of Falcon Tech means a lot to my board members. They will be keeping a close eye on your performance, a very close eye."

Lindell glanced across at Batista who nodded fractionally. "Okay, agreed," he said.

A faint smile now broke across Sinclair's face as he echoed his previous admonition. "*Remember* you were hand picked for this assignment. Responsibility for the success of *this* whole venture lies with you."

Batista fixed on Sinclair's eyes. "Yes, Howard, but the computer industry is cyclical. There will be losses when we go on a discounting drive to win market share. I know it well 'cause I've seen it happen in the Valley over the last twenty-five years."

Sinclair looked irritated again but managed to disguise a hint of contempt in his voice. "Look Albert, that's your challenge…don't come here with quarterly losses. It simply won't look good when they are combing over the company for the launch…you know what those due diligence things are like. It's not beyond your intellect to ensure that losses don't appear. Anyway, the market is expanding at an explosive rate. Make it happen."

Batista felt a surge of anger welling up, his face reddening, but he remained calm. An uncomfortable silence ensued. Newman cleared his throat and said, "I think that's fairly clear. We just go out there and bring back a scalp."

"That's about it. And Albert, my family has been in business for many generations. We know what it takes to stay at the top. I accept the computer industry is different but that's precisely why I've picked you," he said, wagging a finger across the table. "You people...you've got a freer hand. Make the best of it. Sell to anyone who wants a computer. You know the technology. The information revolution is here to stay. It's a golden opportunity. Now go out there and do it."

The new team nodded in unison. The president of Kimble-Sinclair muttered as he stood up, walked towards the credenza behind the desk, turned and started off again. "One final word," he said pointing the index finger of his right hand across the desk at the new executives, "remember how I will play it later today at the press launch. Well, you follow suit. A small bit of wining and dining can do much more for the profile of a company than a big advertising budget. Make no mistake on that one."

"We get the drift," Lindell said.

"Right gentlemen, I expect you all back here in the conference room by eleven-thirty for the press briefing."

Sinclair perfunctorily shook their hands and slid back into the chair behind his antique desk. Batista led Lindell and Newman towards the door.

THE FALCON TECH EXCUTIVES rode the elevator to the ground floor sharing a joke about Sinclair's penchant for good publicity.

"And the paintings! It's a gallery, not an office," Lindell exclaimed.

"Yes, I was surprised too," Batista agreed. "I thought his precious paintings were kept at the Sinclair Foundation."

Newman affected an *arty* voice. "I like to keep a Monet or two at the office."

The two West Coast guys snorted. Newman raised his right hand. "Listen, you guys are totally new to the K-S corporate culture. This is Sinclair's swan song and he badly wants to shove it down the throats of the press. He's never really recovered from that magazine article a few years ago that called him a caretaker relying on his top managers. He's determined to prove them wrong and go out in glory...the American dream and all that. And Falcon Tech's the way it's going to happen in his eyes."

"Doesn't surprise me. He knows damn all about our industry for a start. Look, wining and dining is hardly the way to run our business?" Lindell asked.

Batista was distracted, evaluating the bald spot on the crown of his head in the ceiling mirror of the elevator. He was now craning his head at all angles. "It's getting bigger," he muttered. He then drew his eyes away sheepishly. "Sorry Dylan, you were saying...all this wining and dining...oh yes I'm with you. He has to do it in his business. It doesn't mean we have to follow suit. It simply won't sell more computers. But telling every household that they need them certainly will. And there's only one way to do that! *Advertising*. We'll sponsor sporting events to get to the younger generation. The Internet...that kind of thing. Nothing surer."

"I guess Albert's right, Tom. What do you say?"

"I agree. Howard likes to court the right people...to be seen in the right places. Down in Washington and the rest. For him connections are everything and that's how he runs the healthcare business. I've seen it for more than seven years now. He just wants to act like a big shot all the time."

"Yeah," Lindell agreed, nodding eagerly and then continued. "And this crazy scheme of his to parade us in front of the press. Step out on the catwalk for the camera-clicking journalists. No way."

"Me too," Batista echoed. "But we must play along. Whatever it takes we'll have to do it."

"Yes," Newman said. "He just wants a champagne launch in a few years."

Batista punched the air with his fist. "I think we're goin' to make a great team. We'll beat the ass off the competition and steam roll our way to the top."

The executives clasped each other's hands in a pact, and, moments later, stepped out of the elevator. They exited the corporate headquarters and emerged into the crisp sunshine of Boston, headed for the car park and drove downtown to the financial district.

IT WAS PRECISELY NOON when Sinclair ascended the podium in the conference room of its headquarters. He flicked a switch, dimming the lights. Voices became hushed. To his left the executives of Falcon Tech Corporation sat at a table. Immediately behind them a large screen displayed the instantly recognisable K-S logo.

Sinclair put on his glasses and started to read from a prepared script.

"Good afternoon ladies and gentlemen. The purpose of this gathering is to inform the business press of our plans for the future of this very successful subsidiary. I trust that we will receive the same fair and balanced coverage that we have grown accustomed to from your articles over the past years."

He paused and looked towards the front row of seats where his favourite business correspondents were installed. Sinclair spoke eloquently about the wisdom of diversifying into the computer industry in Silicon Valley, emphasising that the company was purchased for twenty million dollars back in 1989. A glowing list of achievements followed and when the journalists' questions came, he brushed over the technical details, preferring instead to talk about the future. Places like China with a market of one billion. Sinclair was setting a vision for the twenty-first century. After all, he was a visionary of sorts. Finally, he said,

"We've put in place the best team of talent to be found out in the Valley. These are the people who will make it happen. Let me introduce them to you."

He stretched out his left hand towards the table and spoke about Batista's track record.

The spotlight shone brightly on his silvery hair. Batista acknowledged the clapping with a smile and then nodded across to Sinclair who turned around to face the audience.

"And Dylan Lindell who has made a name for himself with a prototype hands-free computer. Some of you may have read about his breakthrough which means that the computer of the future will be commanded directly by our thoughts. Kimble-Sinclair is, of course, funding the whole development phase. Well, we've now got Dylan on board. Real entrepreneurial spirit and just the kind of CEO to drive our plans."

Sinclair again looked over his left shoulder and nodded towards the table.

"We welcome Dylan to Falcon Tech."

The dark-haired, athletic figure to Batista's right contrasted sharply. Lindell was in his early thirties, the ultimate techie. He looked uncomfortable in the limelight but managed an open smile, his pearl white teeth shining brightly.

The president of Kimble-Sinclair again faced the audience, introduced Newman, and then continued reading from the script. He tilted forward on his feet, clasping the sides of the podium and leaned towards the microphone. He raised his left arm and stretched it out with fingers pointing towards the table.

"In a short three years we want Falcon Tech to be a household name around the world, just like Microsoft and Intel."

He again paused for effect. The message was clear. Falcon Tech's rightful place was up there with the big guys.

"It's a real challenge for our new team but they, ladies and gentlemen, are the people who will make it happen. Thank you."

The briefing lasted no more than thirty minutes. Questions were not invited at this stage nor were any asked. The president stepped down from the podium and shook hands with his new team. Camera lights flashed and people began to shuffle about. The staff of Kimble-Sinclair and Falcon Tech filed out of the room. A couple of the business correspondents came up to the table to ask clarifying questions. The president saw them approaching and immediately switched to his avuncular role. He placed his arm over one of the journalists' shoulders in a friendly gesture and boomed, "Gentlemen, let's move downstairs to our executive dining room. You are our guests today and your searching questions are easier to answer over a good claret."

With that, the bemused journalists were ushered towards the elevator.

BY THREE O' CLOCK the wining and dining was coming to an end. Two waiters in starched white livery hovered around the table, picking up a dessert bowl here and a wineglass there. Nothing was said but it was the president's way of ensuring that his satisfied guests eased their way into the valedictories. Expressions of appreciation echoed around the executive dining room as chairs were pushed back and the thirty-eight journalists got to their feet. Sinclair nodded warmly to each as they filed past his position at the head of the table. His secretary accompanied the visitors to the ground floor and then saw them off the premises. He leaned back in his chair and looked down the table at his new Falcon Tech team.

"I think our business correspondents enjoyed our hospitality. Let's hope they give us the right spin for those Wall Street analysts."

"Have no worries on that score, Howard. It's all damn good news. And you portrayed the right image. They enjoyed the lunch and were impressed. No doubt they'll give us the right coverage," Batista answered.

"That's the plan. I'm certain that we have whetted the appetite of the press. Give them a whiff of a launch and they'll watch us closely."

"Yes, particularly a technology stock. It's the flavour of the decade," Lindell said as he nonchalantly thumbed the pages of the press release. Sinclair pointed at the document in Lindell's hand.

"Strange thing about a stock launch," he said. "It's more about creating the right allure than hard and fast financial figures. It's vital that we keep drip-feeding them over the next year or so. By launch date the institutional investors will be in a feeding frenzy. They'll have their fat cheque books ready to snap up the stock."

"They will, Howard… they sure will. I've seen it happen so many times in the Valley. Wall Street has a love affair with technology companies…it simply can't resist them. You can be sure of that," Batista said reassuringly.

Sinclair chose to ignore Batista's last comment. After all, the Silicon Valley executives were merely means to an end, instruments to fulfil a burning ambition. The last thing the president of Kimble-Sinclair needed was advice and technobabble from the Valley.

"Gentlemen, it's time to get to work in earnest."

With that, he stood up and waved a dismissive hand in the air.

Chapter Three

THE ARRIVAL OF THE EUROEAN UNION headquarters in the sixties transformed Rond Point Schuman - a roundabout linking several arteries to Rue de la Loi, the main thoroughfare to the city centre - into the nucleus of a European quarter. A relentless invasion of concrete-and-glass buildings to accommodate the burgeoning European administration gradually eroded the Horta-style architectural streetscape around the area. In its wake came a wave of law firms, international institutions and lobbyist organisations all eager to physically juxtapose themselves as close as possible to the heartbeat of the Union's administration.

International trade and competition law was the staple for many of the law firms though the environmental agenda had become more lucrative in the nineties as the corpus of legislation expanded rapidly. However, the latter area did not appeal to *Erik* Verbiest. He had no time for the tree-hugging environmentalists and even less interest in defending large corporations against pollution law suits. Besides, after more than twenty years as an international trade lawyer, he had carved out an enviable reputation and, in the process, become a legend. He loved the status that came with being successful.

The invitation to speak at the World Trade Organisation conference did not surprise him. In fact it made him very happy. He slapped into his leather reclining chair, bounced his feet onto the mahogany desk and re-read the speech for the second time, grunting approval at parts that particularly pleased him. When he would ascend the podium in Geneva on Wednesday afternoon, his peers would again sit up and take notice. Verbiest would be polemical and provocative, leading the charge that total liberalisation of trade was the way to go in the twenty-first century. Those people in Geneva wanted him back for the fourth year in a row; everybody wanted to hear Verbiest, it seemed.

He was, after all, a lawyer doing what lawyers do best - one day arguing for, and the next day against. And it came easy to him, keeping his profile glistening on the international conference circuit. He started to study the pages once more. A couple of minutes later a red light flashed on the telephone console, breaking his concentration. His nostrils flared and wrinkles formed around his eyes as he leaned forward and grabbed the hand piece with his right hand, still holding the sheaf of papers in his left.

"V'biest," he snapped, the irritation bestowing a vaguely simian appearance to his countenance.

"Good morning, Mr. Verbiest. Could you hold for a call from Mr. Greenwood, Trade Attaché at the American Embassy?"

His annoyance dissolved. "Certainly."

Moments later the attaché came on the line. After exchanging the usual pleasanteries Greenwood got to the issue.

"Say, Erik, I've got a computer corporation from Silicon Valley coming over in two weeks. They're looking for a law firm to help set up operations in Europe. Would you be interested in talking to them?"

Verbiest slid his feet off the desk and leaned forward attentively. "Interested is an understatement, Ron."

"So I'll put you on the list but I must warn you they will want to speak to the usual branches of American law firms here."

His pulse quickened. "Ron, tell them if they want the best it's got to be Petersson Knightley Verbiest & Saatchi."

Greenwood chuckled down the line.

"We're impartial here at the Embassy. You know that, Erik. It's not our call."

"Sure, I understand. Look could we do lunch next week? It's been a while."

"I'll have to take a raincheck. Secretary for Commerce is coming over next week. The European-American trade dialogue thing is hotting up again over bananas."

"You guys are really making a big fuss about that right now."

"We can't let the monkeys starve, you know."

Verbiest stifled a laugh. "Well, whenever you're free just give me a call."

"Thanks for the invite."

Verbiest dropped the phone and sprang from the chair, scattering the bunch of papers on the desk. Mounting the stairs, he headed for the managing partner's office. As he entered, Roger Knightley was standing close by a small table pouring tea. He nodded in acknowledgement without taking his eyes off the task in hand. Verbiest began to bounce around the office like a child.

"You're not going to believe this but I've just had Greenwood on the phone. A Californian computer company wants to set up in Europe. Greenwood's put us on the list of firms to talk to."

As Knightley walked across the office towards his desk he sighed audibly. "Ah Erik, you're wasting your time. I'm sure they'll give the business to one of those Ivy League firms across the Avenue. Look at our record. We've never managed to snare a US multinational in ten years of trying."

"I think it may be worth fighting for…at least this time we can use Harrison. I'm going to talk to Petersson. I need her to bait the client."

Knightley brought the cup towards his lips and sank deeper into the high-back. "Per won't let her out of the Intellectual Property Rights department. Her work is starting to earn big fees there. He'll go ballistic."

"Roger I must have her to win that client."

"Okay, if you must. Talk to him."

Verbiest vanished through the door and banged the lift button. Half an hour later he returned.

"Damn him. He won't budge. Roger, I want you to call a meeting of partners tomorrow. I want Harrison at all costs. She's the cream of the Brussels Bar right now. Everybody's still talking about that intellectual property rights case she won at the European Court in Luxembourg. She's the hottest thing we've got around here. I need her."

"Calm down and be reasonable for a minute. Petersson's department doesn't have enough associates to service its clients at the moment."

Verbiest groaned. "Ah don't listen to him. He's always the same."

Knightley's face became taut. "Seriously, he's doing a lot of complaining about your *modus operandi* lately…and frankly, I'm inclined to agree with him. You always seem to get your way."

Verbiest moved towards the window and watched the traffic on the Avenue below him for a long moment.

"Look, I'm trying to run this practice like a business, making sure we acquire and keep the best deep-pocket clients. What's wrong with that?"

Deep down Knightley was happy to let Verbiest do the hustling. "Okay, okay I'll arrange a meeting tomorrow but I'm making no promises. You hear me, no promises."

PETERSSON KNIGHTLEY VERBIEST & SAATCHI was probably the top notch Brussels law firm and the most prestigious to work for. The partners considered themselves *primus inter pares* of the Brussels Bar and held the richest portfolio of clients – state monopolies and pharmaceutical corporations across Europe – and generated the biggest fees per partner. They paid their staff above the going rate and never lost a client to their competitors. In fact *'never-lose-a-client'* was the mantra of the firm and it always worked out that way.

The boardroom reeked of old-world opulence, the large centrepiece Nepalese rug giving it a hushed appearance. The silver coffee service sparkled from its once-a-week polishing ritual. Two large oil portraits of former partners hung on the wall, facing the windows overlooking Avenue Louise. Both were a carryover from the old firm of Brussels lawyers who had sold out the practice in the early seventies. The new owners quickly re-focused on lucrative European Union work.

The partners' meeting was scheduled for three o'clock. It was not billed as a management meeting nor was it a discussion to consider issues of principle in the normal meaning of the term. Only Verbiest saw it as an issue-of-principle meeting but, in the other partners' eyes, it was just another arrogant attempt to paddle his own agenda.

Knightley eased himself into the leather chair, careful to avoid a crease on the charcoal grey bespoke suit from Savile

Row, and thumbed a sheaf of papers. Although his demeanour was relaxed, his mannerisms were English, very English. As managing partner, he enjoyed chairing partnership meetings where the hum-drum affairs of the firm were discussed.

Knightley kicked off the proceedings. "It's a one-item agenda. You've got the floor, Erik."

Verbiest leaned forward and spoke firmly.

"I think you're all familiar with the situation. I want Harrison to be at the presentation. She's the only one who can create the right impression...the right allure. With a bit of luck I'm sure we could win that American client."

"No way. Harrison's busy right now," Petersson answered resolutely.

"We'll never expand the business with that attitude, Per. All I'm asking is that she sits in on the first meeting...maybe make a presentation, if we get that far with them. It's for the greater good of the firm as a whole. She knows how those guys think and talk. She could help us to win the client with her 'have-a-nice-day' style."

Knightley shook his head.

"Maybe she is a real 'have-a-nice-day' girl as you like to portray her but just being American won't influence them."

"I don't think you're right, Roger. We've always lost out in the past because those Ivy Leaguers could talk their language. We just push Harrison out front this time. She's very competent. She...well...she can talk technology talk and she's attractive and articulate. I'm certain she could swing it."

Knightley leaned back into the chair. "Erik, don't get too excited yet. They're only coming to window-shop."

"I know that but all we need is one American corporation. Others will follow...I'm sure of it. If we crack that market the sky's the limit."

Petersson glowered across the table. Unmistakably Nordic, he was the conscience of the partnership and found it more and more difficult to tolerate Verbiest's self-centred approach. Today he bristled.

"Since when did you start thinking altruistically Erik?"

Saatchi grinned but said nothing. He thought about the

impression Harrison had made at the interview the previous year. *A good-looking, articulate young lawyer around the office could brighten things up. A curvaceous figure in a navy suit and a nice little ass underneath.* His bushy eyebrows twitched as he mused to himself. *And maybe at one of those parties or 'get togethers' who knows what could happen …*

Verbiest stood up and started to argue, hands outstretched. "It's a competitive market out there. We *have* to capitalise on any advantages we've got. All our different cultures and languages in Europe faze those Americans. They need to feel comfortable and well…all I'm saying is that she's the best one to do that."

Saatchi came to life. "Erik's right you know. Those Silicon Valley people just talk computer talk. The last thing they need to hear is fancy lawyer talk."

Knightley swung around to face Petersson. His job was chairman and peacemaker, balancing the fragile minds of arrogant lawyers. "Erik's really only speaking about you lending her for the introductory meeting. Could you live with that, Per?"

Petersson sighed. "If I could believe him. That's the problem. Then he'll want her to stay on to mind the client. And then more clients. It's the same old game Erik's been at for fifteen years…poaching all the good associates."

"Per, you have my word on that. Just give me a chance to expand the business."

Knightley pushed for agreement. "More business on the international trade side will take the pressure off all of us. Well, Per, what do you say?"

Petersson stared at Verbiest and then turned towards Saatchi. The Italian grinned mischievously. "She's a good looker…could influence clients. Sexual chemistry and all that!"

Petersson averted his eyes in disgust. "I don't trust him. If it works out I'm sure he'll try to keep her."

"He's given his word," Saatchi said.

The boardroom fell silent for a few moments. The other partners waited. Eventually Petersson stabbed a finger in Verbiest's direction.

"Just as long as it takes to win the client - no longer."

Verbiest nodded agreement. Knightley started to write in a book laid out in front of him. "That's settled then," he said as he closed the book and recapped the fountain pen. Verbiest had once again got his way and it was now time to concentrate on other things. He stood up and made for the door. After all, the cream of the world's lawyers and academics was waiting to hear what Erik Steffan Verbiest was going to say in Geneva tomorrow. And he was not about to disappoint them.

Hong Kong

ZU WONG HAD three passions in his life. As Supreme Lodge Father of the Yangzte Triad, exercising the power of life and death came first and still gave him the greatest adrenaline burst. In his younger years the sensuous dissipation of the girlie bars in Wanchu figured a close second but as the years passed, Mah Jong had taken its place. He would start at eight am, immediately after returning from his Tai Chi exercise routine in Kowloon Park. When his legal practice was not busy he sometimes played the computer version of the game for the whole morning.

He lit a cigarette and studied the screen, the Beijing edict weighing heavily on his mind. He was now lost in thought, searching for inspiration. It was definitely not a partnership, as they liked to portray it. No, he was sure, this was nothing short of an outright take over. And then he wondered how he could have been so naïve as to think that the communists would have reoccupied Hong Kong but ignored the triad racketeering going on under their noses. After all it was the life-blood of the colony, making it a paragon of pure capitalism.

A tap on the door interrupted his contemplation. The Supreme Lodge Father's personal bodyguard - a thin and sinewy street orphan - opened it and stepped into the room. Standing about five feet tall, Hu Hei's size nevertheless belied his strength. He had been hired to run errands for the brotherhood but had, by his twenty-fifth birthday, been trained to kill in one hundred different ways, even with his bare hands when demanded. Sometimes he played the consummate assassin at a distance. For those assignments his weapon of choice was an AK 47.

Wong's protector now lived in Wanchu far from the piled-up garbage and fetid sewers of the tiny alleyways in the walled city of Kowloon where he grew up. He was trying hard to learn English and was granted the privilege of sitting in on meetings when property deals were being struck. Hu Hei waited to receive the command to speak, then bowed reverentially and said, "Missa Cheng…see you."

Cheng stepped into the room and the bodyguard backed out, pulling the door closed. Cheng's message was urgent but the Supreme Lodge Father in the most secret society in the world commanded absolute deference. He, too, would not dare to speak until he received the signal.

Wong stared intently at the screen for another minute and then relaxed into the chair, the slight movement of his right hand being the command to speak.

"Mr. Wong we have a crisis." Cheng started off in Chiu Chow. "The Customs busted our Laos shipment last night. Peng and Tong have been arrested."

Wong rubbed his chin with one hand, casually reaching for the packet of cigarettes with the other. "Where did it happen?"

"Just outside the harbour limits. Somebody informed. We…we think it was Chang Nu. He's been spending a lot of time down in the gambling halls of Macau."

Wong's eyes turned cold and distant. "A 438-er couldn't afford to gamble unless…"

Cheng fawned. "…Unless he's getting a payoff."

"How much did we lose?"

"Twenty million dollars down the sewer and into the bay of Hong Kong. The fish are on a high instead of well off Yankees and we're left with an empty sack."

"We can't take any chances. Have him washed in the South China Sea."

"Yes Mr. Wong."

"And spread the word around just in case others are tempted."

"Triad honour."

Cheng was a wiry man in his early forties with a heavily pock-marked face and discoloured teeth. He had left Guangdong province in the southern part of China many years before but continued to speak the region's nasal Chiu Chow dialect. In the last five years he had little choice but to become fluent in English to carry out sophisticated international drug deals for his triad society. His badge of honour – a deep scar running from his left temple across his cheek to his upper lip – was worn with pride. Ruthless and vicious, he was known for his organisational ability and so had attained the highest rank in his Yangtze Triad branch. The Supreme Lodge Father depended on him to carry out assignments where expertise was needed and muscle was essential.

Cheng edged closer to the desk.

"Something on your mind?" Wong asked.

"We have trouble in New York too."

"New York?"

"Our man has turned to Colombia for his cocaine."

The Supreme Lodge Father glowered. "Eliminate him. Why the hell not? If he's trading with the enemy get rid of him. We don't deal with traitors."

"Mr. Wong, we will win him back. He runs a tight ship in the Big Apple. Demands total loyalty from his underlings…and has payoffs to the DEA and cops down to a fine art."

"Just like Hung honour eh? Consider him for membership."

"Membership?"

"Yes. Tie him in to us. Make him part of the family. Why not?"

"But he *is* Caucasian."

"So?"

"He couldn't abide by all the oaths."

"Of course he could. We have half a dozen members in Europe, all of them Caucasian."

"If you say so Mr. Wong but I would have to tell our US lodge fathers."

"Don't consult. Make him a member of the Hong Kong lodge. After all, it is the leading lodge. Others have to follow its dictats."

Cheng smiled. "We will make him an offer he can't refuse."

"Do it immediately."

Another pause ensued.

"By the way," Cheng asked, "would you like to attend an initiation ceremony this morning? We have some new recruits to our Yangtze brotherhood."

Wong glanced at his watch. "Now?"

"Let me see."

Cheng took out his pocket diary and started to flick pages. "At noon."

Wong stared through the big glass window and fixed his eyes on a ship about to enter the harbour. He answered wistfully.

"New brothers in Hung-Triad. Yes, I can always make time for new blood especially with our friends in Beijing trying to enter our patch. But first we must have tea."

He gestured to Cheng to take a seat, leaned forward and pressed the buzzer. "Two teas in my office."

Three minutes later there was a tap on the door. Hu Hei entered, carrying a tray.

"Two tea, Missa Wong."

He dropped the tray on the desk and waited until Wong dismissed him. Cheng pulled out his cigarette packet, tapped one free and slid the packet across towards Wong. They both lit up.

"I've again been in touch with Beijing. They've agreed that I should expand the *one choppe shoppe* to help get foreign investment into China…also been in touch with our moles in the West. They will help to put business our way. So in helping Beijing we help ourselves. We cannot rely on extortion and racketeering anymore."

Cheng blew a ring of smoke in the air. "China is changing. Our brotherhood will have to change too."

"Yes. Anyway it's not a good life for our people, depending on our back street sweatshops to turn out plastic penises and blow-up dolls for the sex shops of Europe and America. All for a dollar a day. And with the China white business unpredictable, we have to think of other things."

"You're right Mr. Wong. We must do something different. And maybe we'll pay taxes too just like rest of world," Cheng replied cynically.

"We'll do many things Cheng, but taxes!"

They both raised the cups to their lips and nodded in unison. Wong took one big gulp, draining it. For the next few minutes they sat in silence surveying the high-rise buildings as the room became enveloped in smoke.

"Amazing how all of this was built on the back of the opium trade in the nineteenth century," Cheng remarked.

"Yes, Hong Kong, the bastion of free enterprise, built by the imperialist traders of opium." They both grinned superciliously.

Wong looked at his watch and jumped to his feet. Cheng followed him to the elevator in silence. Out on the street they strode in the direction of Kowloon Park, exiting at the Austin Road gate, crossed over and walked a few paces down Shanghai Street. They paused, glancing up at a fifteen-story building, and then entered through the glass doors. A display board listed the occupants – mainly export trading houses and property development companies as well as a few stockbrokers. The Great Wall Street Investment Corporation occupied the sixth floor but the occupants of the seventh were not listed.

On the seventh they stepped into a large room with a mahogany table in the centre. A bead of chairs circled the table and a large cloth tapestry hung from one wall. It depicted the Yangtze Triad emblem - a red triangle, inscribed with Chinese symbols. Around its edges ornate, coloured patterns were woven into the material. A scroll illustrating ancient Chinese proverbs - the foundation stones for the Triad oaths – was mounted in a glass case on the wall. Several banners hung from horizontal flagpoles, each celebrating a famous hero of the Triad legend. Wong took a seat. He had not been to an initiation ceremony in latter years. As the highest-ranking member he did not have to attend such rituals any more. Initiation of new recruits was the responsibility of the Branch leader.

The officials had already gathered, together with a peppering of ordinary ranks. Cheng, the lodge father, sat at the top of the table and gestured to the Branch leader that the ceremony should start. Five new recruits - three men and two women - marched through the door in single file.

The probing started immediately. Endless questions were asked. Sometimes the questions were repeated. It was designed to test the patience of the new recruits for if they should fail on this score they would not be admitted to the largest and most secret society in the world. After the questioning was complete they were invited to kneel in front of the incense master who administered the solemn pledge. Each had to repeat thirty-six oaths, a prerequisite to becoming a 49-er, the lowest rank of the Yangtze Triad Society.

Acceptance of these oaths by the recruits created a bond of fealty, a strict code of honour among all, its breach punishable by death. The first duty of the initiated was to swear loyalty to his immediate superior and faithfully obey instructions from higher-ranking 426-ers and 438-ers. Layer upon layer of command was built up until it reached Cheng, who was referred to as a 489-er. He took his instructions from the Supreme Lodge Father, the controller of the Society.

Finally, each, in turn, stepped forward and held the Branch leader's hand in a secret Triad handclasp, calling out his name at the same time. The Branch leader then ceremoniously entered the new names in a tiger-skin covered book bringing the ceremony to a close.

Wong rose to his feet and looked in the direction of Cheng.

"Still plenty of young men and women willing to serve our tradition."

"Yes, our Lodge is very proud of its record with new followers. This cell is still the powerhouse of the Society," he replied.

Wong nodded. "Yes, Cheng, you should be proud. I'm depending on this Lodge to meet the challenge that Beijing has thrown in our face. When duty calls…,"

"…always ready to serve," Cheng called out, a gleeful smile of anticipation contorting his scar to make it seem like a grotesque wink.

Chapter Four

March
Brussels
ONE WEEK OF frenzied activity followed the visit of the Falcon Tech executives. Verbiest spent his time on transatlantic phone calls trying to establish the company's requirements. Late in the evening he would brief his fellow partners and Laura on developments and by Thursday evening he assured them that he had the full picture. The company had started out in a garage or attic but was now on a fast track and a force to be reckoned with in the States.

"So, Laura I would like a comprehensive report and presentation. The usual stuff. Manufacturing location… corporate structure, regulatory compliance and product liability. I'll get Armstrong, Haase and Co to do some economic analysis. We must give this our best shot."

"Okay fine."

Verbiest turned towards her and drew in a deep breath. "There could be a lifetime of legal work in it. And fees…big fees."

Knightley's eyebrows arched in mild disdain. "It's not all about fees," he said in a low voice.

Verbiest ignored the rebuke and winked at her. "So when they come to Brussels say you've seen their computers in the States. It's reassuring for them."

"Hmm."

"Potential clients have to feel at ease with us," Verbiest continued with a weak smile. He lifted his head, scanning the office. "We give them centuries of tradition to make them feel comfortable."

"Huh yeah," she muttered and then asked, "You want me to sit in on the meeting?"

"Not just sit in, *contribute*." Knightley interjected emphasising the last word by tapping his index finger on the desk. "Now's your chance to impress them with your knowledge."

"So," Verbiest said. "I want that report on my desk on Monday morning."

EVEN THOUGH BRUSSELS has been traditionally bilingual, its daily temperament reflects the dominance of French over Flemish, at least in the commercial sphere. But the European quarter of the city stands apart as a *pot pourri* of ethnic identities and languages from the Arctic Circle to the Mediterranean, all coexisting and blending together through the use of English as the preferred language of communication. This mosaic of fifteen-plus nationalities making up the Union has become a true cultural cocktail, allowing the city to establish itself as the genuine capital of Europe.

The quarter gains its sustenance from an influx of ethnic restaurants, cafés and pubs in a network of streets radiating out from Rond Point Schuman. After office hours, the plastic money comes to life as the prosperous professionals seek out ways to spend their healthy income. As a prelude to the expensive restaurants, many prefer the comfort zone of the Irish pubs where newcomers or long-standing friends can meet for serious talk or light banter unfettered by the mores of their backgrounds.

One such pub – Kitty O' Sheas - had, of late, become Laura's favourite for a relaxing after-work drink. Flagstone floors, a polished hardwood décor with bevelled mirrors and decorative brass, gave it a relaxed atmosphere, the lilting Irish music in the background adding to the convivial ambience.

She had arranged to meet Marc there to show him the photographs of the Chinese trip. The short break in Beijing had left her with good memories and since then, she had thought about nothing else but him and now had the ideal excuse to meet him again.

Marc arrived early and made his way towards the bar. He leaned his elbow on the counter and watched the reflection of the other drinkers in the mirror behind the row of liquor bottles on the shelf. A few minutes later he saw Laura, spun around and gave her a *Brussels-style, three-kiss-on-the-cheeks,* greeting. He noticed the head-turning glances of male customers and felt his ego climb the scale. She looked even better than he had remembered. A chic navy business suit and crisp white blouse complemented her blonde hair and, at that moment, made her irresistible in his eyes.

"Hey, you look great."

She smiled diffidently. They ensconced themselves at the bar.

"What do lady lawyers in Brussels drink?"

"Baileys on ice, please."

He leaned on the counter and nodded towards the barman.

"Baileys on ice and a Guinness."

"The photographs. You made so much about them. Let's see them."

"Patience Marc. Patience."

Feigning irritation for a moment he smiled. Laura took the photographs from the envelope and Marc moved closer. They began rekindling memories of China.

"And there you are Emperor Schuman on the Great Wall of China. Genghis Khan of the European Trade Bureau."

"Very funny."

The drinks arrived. She swirled the ice around the glass with the swizzle stick, raised it and clinked it against his. He took up the Guinness and said, "Ganbei. Here's to China."

Creasing her forehead, she tilted her head. "What was that word you used?"

"Ganbei. It's Chinese for 'bottoms up'."

"Amusing."

Twenty minutes later the photograph display was finished. Laura raised the glass of Baileys to her lips and said, "So, I've been checking around with a few lawyer colleagues. I believe you've made quite a name for yourself with those trade investigations." She then asked, "...Should I believe them?"

He shrugged. "I do my job. That's what I'm supposed to do. Isn't it?"

Marc had built up a reputation of being one of the best investigators in the Bureau. He didn't just rely on his lawyerly skills; second-guessing the motives of the big market players was his forte.

"You're hardly going to stay as an investigator all your life?"

"I don't deny it, I'm ambitious...want to make it to chief investigator, get some experience in law-making and then jump ship to become partner in a law firm."

"Partner? Remember there are lots of associates out there in law firms with burning egos too."

"Speaking personally?"

"Let's say I'm not doing a twelve-hour for nothing. Maybe first female partner around this town...what do you say to that."

"I'll get there before you," he teased.

She snickered. "Not a chance. You've no experience of holding clients. You're just a pampered fat cat in that golden cage."

"Bet you I'll get there first."

"Done."

After a short silence Laura tapped the glass on the counter. She told him that a potential new client was coming to the firm and that the partners wanted her to sit in and maybe make a presentation.

"Should be a change from the intellectual property rights work you've been at."

"Yes...could be, but Petersson - the partner in charge - is furious because Verbiest convinced the other partners that my American background would help swing the day."

"Sounds like a good move."

"Possibly. I'd like a shot at international trade."

"Problem is the paperwork! That's something else. Remember those investigations have to be done to strict legal deadlines and to the rule book."

"I'm sure I could handle my clients' interests."

Marc raised the glass towards his lips. "So tell me, what's an American doing in a European law firm?"

"Working!"

"Seriously...how did you end up in Brussels?"

"My father works - I mean worked, for the military. We started out in Washington but he was transferred to a base outside Frankfurt. My father retired three years ago but he's still doing some contract work for the Pentagon."

"And how did you end up in Belgium?"

"After two years in Germany he transferred to SHAPE."

"SHAPE?"

"It's the Supreme Headquarters of Allied Powers in Europe based in Mons. Big brother stuff. Uncle Sam and his European helpers keeping the Soviets at bay. That's of course when there were Soviets."

"I've learned something new."

She smiled. "So now you know who's protecting you."

"That's really very comforting."

After a pause she asked, "So who is this guy, Marc Schuman?"

He raised the glass and winked at her. "That story is for another time."

LAURA SAT COMFORTABLY in front of the mirror in her apartment bedroom. The evening had gone well, in her eyes. Time spent with a man who made her laugh, rekindled something that had been missing in her life for a long time. She remembered her love affair in California and her mind compared Marc to Tom, her former American lover. Marc didn't seem to possess the all-consuming ego of the Californian. He appeared more fun loving but time would tell. She found it difficult to trust the glib words of men since Tom had walked out without explanation. She wondered for a moment if it could happen again but then quickly suppressed the notion.

We're not even lovers! She mused. *It must be the memories of that short stay in Beijing.* She pirouetted in front of the mirror more than once and then leaned across for the perfume bottle which she carried everywhere. Her ex-boyfriend had given it to her on her birthday in 1995. Yes, the fourth of July...*Independence Day*. Each time she used it memories came flooding back. Those long car rides along the Pacific Coast Highway, stopping off at Monterey or Santa Barbara. The freewheeling life-style of Tom seemed like a roller coaster ride that would never end.

Wham, was I wrong!... What I thought was commitment, always punctual in his convertible, was just an ego trip. Living in the fast lane. Boy, had he got it down to a fine art...the deception, the other girls. It was easy for him to be punctual - he had to be.

It was like a business and he was using the just-in-time principle. Drop one off and, wham, pick up another.

Many times she thought about throwing the perfume bottle in the rubbish bin but she could never quite bring herself to do it. Anyway, she liked it and maybe memories were better than nothing! But it made her suspicious about men's motives and yet tonight, after seeing Marc again, she did not want to be cautious.

RAYS OF EARLY MORNING sun streaked through the bare trees that lined the central median as Laura made her way along Avenue Louise, the uptown area of the city. A row of expensive shops on both sides, made it the premier shopping area and, further down, the offices of the professional classes dominated the fashionable thoroughfare. She moved swiftly in the crisp air, her attention briefly drawn to the birds as they swooped down, pecking hungrily at the inhospitable earth under the trees. Five minutes later she entered the law offices of PKV&S.

As she stepped into the reception area on the third floor Verbiest's secretary looked up. A matronly woman in her mid-fifties, Angeline Bowans had long forgotten how to enjoy herself.

"Hurry up. They're waiting for you," she said curtly.

"Sor-ry," Laura muttered as she made directly for the office. Immediately she could see Verbiest deep in conversation with his fellow partners. He spun around as she approached and snapped, "I see you're against China."

"Do you mind if I take off my coat before the firing squad starts?"

Petersson smiled. Verbiest muttered something under his breath and beckoned eagerly towards the conference table. Laura pulled out one of the chairs and sat down. She flicked back a strand of hair behind her ear, looked at him and then said, "You were saying Erik?"

"The China thing…" he growled.

"I've set out the pros and cons and, in the case of China, the stakes are too high. A trade case against Asian-made computers is a real possibility…could devastate Falcon Tech's business overnight."

"Well I happen to see things differently. What we're doing here is advising a company on the best environment for manufacturing. The economic analysis supports China."

"Erik, you only asked for their views on cost comparisons for manufacturing. What about a trade case for instance. A duty on Falcon Tech's computers would put them out of the European market. We're morally and legally obliged to give them the full facts."

Verbiest became agitated. "That's nothing to do with facts. It's pure conjecture." He jumped from the chair and threw his hands in the air. "We can't pencil in all the possibilities. I've heard those executives. They want a low-overhead, high-volume environment. And that means only one thing. Low cost, Laura. So we can't afford to omit any of the key locations. Besides I happen to think China's the best option for them."

Saatchi readily agreed. "Erik's right. I've already briefed my fellow partners on developments last week. You see I had a phone call from the leading law firm in Hong Kong. With the hand over of the colony to Beijing rule the Chinese government has appointed them to secure more investment into Southern China. They have Beijing's blessing to operate a *one choppe shoppe* where all the legal stuff is sorted out together, all with the objective of getting as many Western companies as possible in there. The Communists want the capitalist mentality to seep over the border, not the other way around. It would be ideal for Falcon Tech."

"But that's a high risk strategy. In my professional opinion a duty is a real possibility. Practically all high-tech products from Asia have been hit - photocopiers, fax machines, televisions, CD players," Laura persisted.

Saatchi never got excited about anything. That is, until this morning. His reply hit her like a bolt of lightning.

"Look they never hit the Japs with duties on cars and for computers it's the same. Politically it's a non-runner. Wong says that Beijing will facilitate foreign investment in any way they can. This could be a golden opportunity."

"Selling computers is different from selling cars," she shot back finding it difficult to understand how her report could generate such strong views. Verbiest got ruffled ten times a day but for Saatchi it was out of character.

Verbiest took charge to end the sparring. "Look Laura, the clock is ticking. These people will be here in a few days. We've all got to sing from the same hymn sheet. We're running with China and that's final. Just do as I say."

Laura was incensed. Six months ago she would have told him to go to hell and walked out but she could not afford to lose this job. Right now Jessica, her niece took priority over her principles. She was helping to pay the medical bills for her sister's child who needed twenty-four-hour nursing care after a car accident had left her paralysed and her parents dead. She tried to control herself and turning to leave the office muttered, "You're the boss Erik, you're the boss."

FRIDAY MORNING: Folders were neatly arranged beside the nameplates on the boardroom table and the computer was wired for the presentation by 8 o' clock. Laura flicked the switch and checked the animation on the screen. The rehearsal went smoothly, reassuring her that no gremlins were on board.

She remembered her argument with Verbiest earlier in the week. Today was another day however; she would toe the party line; endorsing China as *the* location.

She went downstairs to her office and pressed her voice mail. To her surprise, Marc had phoned to wish her well. She smiled, pleased that he had remembered.

Shortly before nine the full complement of partners was on alert in the boardroom, ready to impress. A few minutes later the American contingent was ushered in. Knightley moved forward to greet the visitors. "I'm Roger Knightley." He extended his hand to greet Batista. "And let me introduce Per Petersson and Lorenzo Saatchi."

They each nodded in turn and shook hands.

"Would you like some tea…coffee?" Knightley asked as he walked towards the table in the corner behind the door. Lindell asked for a Pepsi. A flurry of activity ensued as Knightley's secretary was despatched to buy soft drinks from the local shop. Laura became conscious that Lindell's attention had instantly focused on her. He weaved his way around the oval table and shook her hand firmly. His blue eyes caught her attention, the gleam contrasting with the tanned complexion. Seconds later Batista was at his side also shaking hands with the associate, exuding the kind of confidence that comes with having made it to the top of the corporate ladder. Newman trailed over last, a bulging briefcase in his hand. The receding hairline and slight paunch belied the fact that he was still in his twenties. He was the figures man - the balance sheet guru - to make sure that the numbers stacked up. Laura had guessed correctly from his appearance.

Here in front of her eyes were two sober business suits and one stone-washed blue jeans. The familiar cadence of the Californian accents pleased her. Verbiest pulled out the padded chairs around the table and beckoned towards the huddle of people now congregated around her. The soft drinks arrived as they took their seats, the usual small talk - a necessary prerequisite to the business of the day - easing the visitors into the comfort zone.

Knightley rested the china cup on the saucer, removed his glasses and began. "We're a small firm of four partners with a mixture of clients." He pointed around the table in quick succession. "Erik Verbiest handles Customs and International Trade issues as well as Taxation. Lorenzo Saatchi runs the Mergers and Acquisitions Department and the whole gamut of Competition Law. Per Petersson holds the Intellectual Property Rights portfolio of clients and Consumer Law. For my sins, I am the managing partner with Environmental Law thrown in to keep me busy."

"Excuse me but do you have ice?" Lindell asked.

"I'm afraid not," Knightley replied.

"It's not chilled. I can't drink warm Pepsi."

"Sorry," Verbiest said.

"In that case I'll have regular coffee."

"Certainly," Verbiest said grabbing the coffee pot.

"No doubt, you can see we're a multicultural firm," the managing partner continued. "Erik's from Antwerp. Lorenzo's

Italian. Per is Swedish and I'm British. We maintain strong contacts in the capitals of Europe."

Batista leaned back and said in a business-like tone, "Our schedule's quite tight. We've already talked to three branches of American law firms here and you're the final one. I understand your firm's independent."

"Absolutely," Verbiest replied eager to reassure the potential clients. "We pride ourselves on our independence. We find that we don't have *conflict-of-interest* problems. Some of the larger firms on this Avenue are linked up internationally and may not have the same freedom to give *independent advice*. Big powerful clients elsewhere in the network can wield a lot of indirect influence nowadays."

"Damn right," Batista agreed. "Okay, let's get this meeting on the road."

Lindell rose from his chair and pulled a bunch of brochures from his briefcase, walked around the table and placed a copy in front of each of the PKV&S people. He pointed to a brochure. "That's what we have in mind. Falcon Tech sees huge potential for a commodity personal computer. A low-cost machine without all the bells and whistles because nobody uses half those accessories anyway. We think that's what the market wants right now. Just a simple personal computer connected to the Internet."

The partners listened intently as Lindell went on to sketch out even more ambitious plans for the future. He described the revolutionary new technology - a brain-command computer - that would change the interface between man and machine. An early-stage prototype had been developed, he assured the partners that would give Falcon Tech a quantum leap in technological evolution leaving its competitors in the dark ages. Commercialisation was only a few years away. "We're betting it will change the way we live," he declared confidently.

"So," Batista said. "We're about to spend three hundred million dollars of Kimble-Sinclair money and commit to another three hundred in borrowings to go global. Simple question: Where should we put the manufacturing plant?"

Knightley noted the urgency in Batista's voice and shot a

glance at Verbiest. The managing partner had planned to make the usual formal remarks - blandishments about the possibility of being associated with the fastest-growing computer corporation in the world. But he read the signal well, abandoned his plan and nodded in Laura's direction to deflect the spotlight onto her.

"Let me introduce Laura Harrison, our associate who has done the core work on this report. She'll give an overview presentation. I think, Albert, it's better if she sets out the whole picture."

"Fine," Batista replied.

Laura stood up and walked towards the small table supporting the computer. She looked confident and self-assured, the kind of lawyer that might be seen on The Practice or one of the other popular American court drama television series. The beauty spot on her cheek gave her a model appearance. *A la Cindy Crawford!* She was most definitely attractive and she immediately held the attention of the Falcon Tech executives. Simultaneously she flicked the power button on the computer and dimmed the boardroom lights.

"Good morning gentlemen. The PKV&S report on all the aspects of establishing a manufacturing operation and penetrating the European market is in the folder in front of you. I want to concentrate on the key issues." She tapped a key but nothing happened.

Oh shit, she thought and then continued out loud, "I hope this technology doesn't let us down." Laura again tapped the key, raising her head to make eye contact. "It's not a *Falcon Tech* computer you know."

Batista snorted. "That's why we want to get into the European market."

The flash of humour broke the tension. Laura felt she was building a rapport with her audience.

"As we all know, the decision on where to locate is critical in order to minimise costs and thereby win a dominant market position."

She lit up the screen with a map of Europe.

"Europe is the place where money can be made right now.

46

But we have to bear in mind that the Far East market will eclipse it within the next decade. There are some disadvantages attached to manufacturing in Eur-"

Verbiest wanted absolute clarity. His hands were immediately in the air to attract attention. He waded in with all guns blazing. "What she's saying is locate in the Far East. Am I right Laura?"

She turned towards him. "Well, I'm just coming to that," she retorted, a note of annoyance in her voice. She slowly turned towards the screen, redirecting attention, and pressed the keyboard. The screen split and maps of two countries came from the left and right - Vietnam and China.

"So, let's look at each in turn."

She clicked on the keyboard and the map of Vietnam expanded across the screen.

"Even though it's communist, there's a rapidly developing assembly economy. As long as the current leaders maintain power, it probably will remain politically stable. Low wage rates and a ready supply of labour make it attractive. However, the infrastructure is not yet well developed. So we do not favour-"

Suddenly Batista shuffled in his chair. "Dead goddamn right. I'm a 'Nam vet and I'm not going back. Choose where you like but not 'Nam. Those guys still have some of our boys and our own asshole Government doesn't want to make waves about it any more. All you hear from our politicians on Capitol Hill is bullshit. That's all you hear from Washington." He wagged a finger at nobody in particular. "They're still commies over there, you know. As long as I'm in charge they'll get no Falcon Tech dollars."

Knightley was startled by the sudden outburst. He took off his glasses and began buffing the lenses with a soft cloth. Verbiest filled the silence, concurring readily, "We too tend to think that it is a second-best option."

Attention quickly turned back to Laura. She hit the computer keyboard and pointed the infra red beam at the southern tip of China. "Our preferred option is China. This is where it's all happening in the next century. A potentially huge market and a rapidly developing enterprise culture. It's the economy of the twenty-first century. At the moment, it is evolving from the old state-controlled system to a market economy, at least in the southern part. The biggest advantage is the availability of very cheap labour. The workers you get will be dedicated. Falcon Tech can pick them. They are used-"

Lindell interrupted, shooting a finger towards the screen. "What about Tiananmen Square? There's been a lot of sabre-rattling in the States about that. Washington is hanging tough with those guys in Beijing."

She shrugged. "Well, that's the political game. But here you're looking at pure economics. Or am I missing something?"

Verbiest rubbed his forehead trying to soothe an incipient migraine. He wished Laura would stick to simple concepts. Politics was a dirty word when it came to making clients comfortable. Batista raised his eyebrows and turned towards her.

"It seems you could be right. The politicians have made a lot of noise but done nothing about it. I read recently in *Fortune* or *Time* that China isn't afraid of a trade war anymore. They have just as much leverage as the West now because they import so much." He nodded towards her. "Please continue. I would like to hear the rest."

"They have been used to two generations of a tough communist regime. Give them an incentive and they will work day and night. The result: Falcon Tech can ship the best and cheapest computers to Europe and the rest of Asia."

The Chinese images dissolved. The screen darkened and then a bustling street scene from Hong Kong came to life.

"Ideal for locating your finance and marketing functions. Ship out through Hong Kong and when the local Chinese market opens up it will be there for the taking - on your doorstep. That means hundreds of millions of computers. Over a fifteen-year time horizon, it's unbeatable."

Laura had been on her feet for more than two hours. So far there wasn't a hiccup, everything she said seemed well received. At every opportunity she held eye contact with the potential clients. And she appeared knowledgeable and confident. The atmosphere was just about right. She was pressing all the right buttons. The Falcon Tech executives were nodding their agreement.

"China is another commie regime." Batista nodded towards Laura. "What if there's a revolution and some new leader takes over our factory? I'm sure they're still as Red as ever so can we trust them?"

Verbiest stepped in quickly. "We have quite a few clients with production units in China. The local administration and Communist Party hacks are very supportive. It's simply unbeatable for low labour-cost production and once you've got a foothold you'll be ideally poised to capture the Chinese market when it opens up."

Lindell was open-minded. "Certainly worth looking at."

Saatchi moved into reassurance mode to capitalise on the moment. "Look the best place to locate is in Shenzhen in Southern China. There's a 'fixit' lawyer in Hong Kong called Wong who specialises in this sort of thing...deals with the mandarins...sorts out all the paperwork. Every official document needs a chop like an official seal or stamp and he's best placed to do that. He can arrange the renting of a factory in Southern China and hiring and housing of the local workers. It cuts out a lot of messing and red tape. Sure there's a bit of bureaucracy - permits and licences - but isn't the world full of it."

Batista spread his hands on the table.

"As you know Falcon Tech's in the market to go public in a couple of years. We would have to read how the institutional investors might perceive a move into China...that's if we choose this option."

Laura came into the discussion. "It's a fine commercial judgement. A trade-off between political risk and harsh economic reality."

Verbiest glowered at her. "Look there's negligible risk in effect. What we're saying is keep the sales and finance etc, in Hong Kong so that Beijing can't expropriate your money should the political landscape change."

Batista leaned back reflectively. "Okay. I hear what you're saying. We'll have to check it out in Washington...get a full political-risks analysis from the State Department. And run it past the board of Kimble-Sinclair. That's probably the easiest part. I certainly know Sinclair is fascinated by the potential of the Chinese market. If it stacks up then we may go for it."

The Americans seemed to be happy. Verbiest shot a glance at Laura. A clear signal to say no more on the issue. Just let the idea of China seep into their minds. Lindell got up and walked towards Laura. He tapped the side of the computer.

"An excellent presentation."

"Thank you."

He now dropped to an almost inaudible whisper. "Continue like that and we might be interested in you as an in-house lawyer if we set up in the Far East. What do you say to that?"

"Hmm, don't know. I prefer to stay in mainstream legal practice for the time being at any rate."

Batista stood up.

"I must thank Laura for a very comprehensive presentation. So, if we get the political imprimatur from the State Department, so to speak, then I think China may be worth considering. We're working to a tight schedule on this one. Everything's gotta be in place by the Fall."

The signals suggested that the client was in the bag. Verbiest beamed. The next few years would be busy at PKV&S. Very busy and, of course, very rich.

Rainmaker let it rain, he thought. *Right now!*

Chapter Five

March 1999
Boston

ALL LIGHTS WERE GREEN in the twentieth-floor office, making the president happy. He leaned back in his leather chair, certain in the knowledge that his hour had come. The Falcon Tech strategy of producing cheaply in China and selling directly on the internet proved to be the winning formula. The subsidiary was powering ahead under his guidance – *a veritable behemoth* - and was now unstoppable. In a short few months he would join the billionaire ranks and, at last, be vindicated in the eyes of his peers. No longer could they whisper that *Howie the third* was just a 'caretaker' living off the business acumen of his forebears. He had steered his blue-chip corporation outside its core activity and, in the process, made that modest diversification into the computer industry ten years ago a multi-billion-dollar trophy.

Wall Street would sit up and take notice. He could step down at the pinnacle of his success. Howard Sinclair III would enter the hall of fame as another exponent of the American economic dream. A computer corporation spreading its tentacles to all corners of the globe and about to launch a breakthrough that would put the power of the human mind directly at the centre of the technological world. All achieved in ten years, all thanks to him - that East Coast business guru, philanthropist and, of course, patron of the arts.

One file lay neatly on his desk - just one file marked: 'Five-year profit projections of Falcon Tech.'

The silver-framed photograph close by caught his eye, allowing him a few moments of indulgence. He looked with pride at the tall young man standing beside his mother. *Yes,* he thought, *a befitting heir to pass the torch to.* Howard Sinclair IV would graduate from Harvard Business School in a few months and would immediately join the board. That was the wish of Sinclair III and that's what would happen. Just as it had happened thirty-seven years earlier. In 1962 Cyrus Sinclair moved aside having groomed his successor. The heir apparent did not have a choice then, nor would his son now. Life was neatly planned in the Sinclair dynasty - very neatly planned. Seven generations of planning since 1843.

After the successful flotation of the subsidiary, the press release would say that he would step down in two years to devote more time to the Foundation. He could see it unfolding before his eyes. Washington would want him; that much was certain. The President himself would call. He would be invited to sit as an advisor on one of those high-powered congressional committees on Capitol Hill, charting the economic dream well into the twenty-first century. *Time* or *Newsweek* would run a front-page profile. His opinions would be traded over the airwaves. He would be called on to address the prestigious World Economic Forum in Switzerland. And his old *alma mater,* the Harvard Business School, would want him as guest lecturer. He might even consider going out west to share his wisdom. Everything was now possible...

Brussels

LIFE WAS GOOD for the partners at Petersson Knightley Verbiest & Saatchi. They convened around the table in the managing partner's office and started the most important meeting of the year. The annual share out of profits was about to commence. Without uttering a word, Knightley slid folders across the polished table. They were opened and the contents studied in silence. The accounts for the previous year were impressive. Not just impressive – the best year yet. The partners smiled but said nothing. They didn't have to. The figures spoke for themselves. Three million Euros per partner was nothing to be laughed at. After taxes, they would each pocket just over half of that.

Knightley ceremoniously opened the box of Macanudo Vintage No 20, took one out and inspected it up close. It would be a good complement to the glass of Irish Mist standing on the silver coaster. The other partners also took a cigar except Petersson, who detested smoking. Knightley leaned over and pulled the silver clippers from the drawer. He now readied the Jamaican-made cigar for his lips. A moment later it was lighting and plumes of smoke eddied towards the ceiling. Verbiest and Saatchi fired up too and soon the office was enveloped in a haze of smoke. Petersson spluttered and coughed but he was in a minority. It was the only time smoking was allowed on the premises. He would have to endure it.

Another folder was opened and the contents passed around. It was the breakdown of fees for each department.

"As you can see Erik's department pulled in the biggest fees and so he's entitled, under the rules of the partnership, to an additional three hundred thousand," Knightley advised.

Verbiest beamed. Petersson glowered.

"So nothing remains but to carve up the bonus pot among the associates."

Verbiest wanted to keep Laura sweet and loyal. "Well, Roger, if anybody should be rewarded it's got to be Harrison. She's strong willed and opinionated I know but she was instrumental in securing those two American clients last year on the coat tails of FT."

"More like principled," Petersson chided.

Verbiest grinned. "Maybe a little too principled for my liking but the important thing is that she's consistently delivered."

"Erik, why don't you take the whole pot yourself. Harrison was my associate. You-"

"Hold on a moment Per. Sure, she was your associate but look what she's done for the firm in the last two years. We've all benefited from her playing those Americans."

Petersson lifted the glass and turned towards the window. He was going to huff for the afternoon.

"So," Knightley said, businesslike. "Who deserves a bonus?"

Saatchi leaned back in the chair swishing the liqueur in the glass. "I say we divide more or less equally with two exceptions. I'm for pushing Maratta out. Rumour has it he's snorting coke. Anyway his performance is only mediocre. No bonus and a stagnant salary will give him the message. He'll eventually go quietly without a fuss."

"Everybody agreed?" Knightley asked. "We've already discussed Maratta's weaknesses last November. He doesn't fit our profile."

Verbiest and Petersson nodded.

"And your other exception?"

"Erik's already made the case. Harrison deserves something more. Just in case she strays."

"Yes indeed," Knightley said. "And take clients with her. Got a figure in mind?"

Verbiest blew a plume of smoke in the air. "Say fifty for her and around twenty for the others."

The Englishman looked around the table for agreement.

"And the usual for the secretaries I presume?"

Assent came easy. The usual. By four o' clock they had emptied the bottle and filled the silver ashtrays. Petersson had now discarded his glum demeanour and joined in the backslapping bonhomie of the merry partners on the fourth floor. An hour later they would join the faithful servants of PKV&S in the boardroom for the annual party. Right now the firm had the happiest lawyers in town. That is except for poor Maratta who was not wanted anymore.

BY EIGHT O' CLOCK the pace of drinking had slowed and the chatter died down. Verbiest rounded up a few of the juniors and guided them across the road to his favourite local. They would be told how to make it to the top of the legal pyramid and make a pile in the process *a la Verbiest*.

Ten minutes later Marc's BMW swished up to the kerb outside PKV&S and Laura jumped in. He leaned across and kissed her, lightly at first and then a lingering one.

"You're beautiful," he said.

She smiled across seductively and pulled her hair behind one ear accentuating her beauty if that were possible. "Maybe not quite beautiful but rich," she mused, the cocktails she had drunk making her eyes glow and her body appear willowy and sensuous. "I got the biggest bonus in there tonight. And that means dinner's on me."

"Fantastic. Beautiful and rich. What a combination? Beautiful and rich," he repeated until she slapped his hand lightly. Marc felt really lucky to have found her. Everything about her was irresistible. He kissed her once more and then drew back to concentrate on getting started. As he accelerated away towards Louise junction Laura picked up the CD holder and found Eros Ramazzotti. She hit the volume button and moments later Piu' Bella Cosa beat out as they reached the inner ring.

"Eros Ramazzotti! Imagine a name like that! Some reputation to live up to," Laura said dreamily.

"I can just imagine his chat-up line," Marc chuckled as he switched effortlessly to his best Italian accent. 'Hi I'm Eros Rammazzotti' and the girl replies 'Yeah and I'm Cupid, stupid.'"

Laura laughed loudly. "Cupid, stupid. I like that."

"Sounds more like a name for an Italian stallion if you ask me."

"Jealous are we?" She teased. "They say latin lovers are the best so why shouldn't he flaunt it."

"The jury's still out on that one sweetheart."

"Let's find somewhere to eat and maybe I'll buy you a beer as well."

"No. I don't need Dutch courage to perform tonight. I just need passionate sex with a beautiful woman."

"In that case let's skip eating. Take me to a nice hotel bedroom Eros," she purred across at him. "Take me, Eros. I'm yours tonight."

THE HUM OF COMMERCE at PKV&S didn't kick in until late the following morning. It was the only day in the year when the rules were relaxed. Even so Laura was at the office by ten o' clock and, fifteen minutes later, she was in front of her computer pecking at the keys. The first assignment called for interpretation of a clause of the Uruguay Round of trade negotiations for a Vietnamese textile exporter. It took less than an hour to complete but in billable terms it was at least a ten-hour! She moved on to the company restructuring case which she had been putting off for a few days. It should have been handled by Saatchi's department but Verbiest had a long-standing relationship with the company. It was his client first and foremost and was not for sale to another department.

The work was painstaking. Worse than the intellectual property rights case for the music company she had handled last Autumn. Tax codes and double taxation agreements all piled high on the desk. Every little detail of tax law in several countries had to be gone through. And double-checking product-liability legislation. There was no margin for error. Misconstruction of an arcane piece of legislation was not a defence. If the client, particularly a large multinational, fell on the wrong side of the tax code then writs would fly and damages would have to be paid. Knightley often warned of the dangers of getting the advice wrong.

'Our insurance policy for negligence is getting more and more restrictive. Precision is what it's all about. Don't take any shortcuts. If something goes wrong, the partners will have to pay out of their own pockets. And that just can't happen.'

The advice kept ringing in Laura's head as she shuffled the heavy legal tomes from the library around the desk.

The phone rang. An agitated and crackling voice boomed out. She held the receiver back from her ear as the words came out in a machine-gun splutter. It was Verbiest, his breathing laboured.

"Laura, drop everything and come up…Roger's office immediately."

"What?"

"I said come up to Roger's office *now*."

"Okay. Okay." She calmly headed upstairs and entered the office. He was pacing the floor, his face flushed and a frown across his forehead. He motioned towards one of the chairs around the table and called out, "Come in. Take a seat."

"What's all the mystery about?" she asked.

"Big difficulty with Falcon Tech on the horizon," he said, rubbing his temples. "When Roger gets here I'll explain everything."

Saatchi and Petersson were sitting on the opposite side of

56

the oval table. Petersson continued to read from a folder laid out in front of him. Five minutes later Knightley came into the office, pushed the door closed with his foot and slumped into his high-back padded chair.

"So what's all the fuss about? Trying to oust me as managing partner?" he asked good-humouredly.

Verbiest started. "Listen, I bumped into Demitri Sakalis last evening …you know the shining light from Smeulders & Rozenstock. He had been drinking with a colleague celebrating Saint Patrick's Day. He told me that they've been engaged by the European Computer Manufacturers' Federation to bring a trade case against most of the Far East countries, including China."

Ridge lines formed on Knightley's forehead. "What! Duties on computers?" he asked in disbelief. "Make computers more expensive right now in Europe?"

Verbiest slid onto a chair and explained to his fellow partners how serious the situation was for the firm.

"The Europeans are making unsustainable losses and they are determined to get protection from cheap Asian-made computers. This will hurt Falcon Tech big time if it gets off the ground. They've sold over eight hundred million dollars worth of computers in the Union in the last twelve months. Thirty per cent duty would be…well, a complete disaster for them."

Knightley threw a quizzical look in Verbiest's direction. "Indeed it could have repercussions for our other American clients. This can't be true."

Laura just listened and smiled deep in the recesses of her mind. The chickens were coming home to roost - big time. Verbiest had well and truly impaled himself on his own sword.

Saatchi mustered a pragmatic comment. "Are you sure the Europeans can get a case together - get enough evidence of low prices? The market's so segmented they'll hardly succeed."

"According to Sakalis – yes. After I poured a few more Bushmills whiskies his tongue loosened and he started to wag and brag. I just listened. The Europeans want to screw our client. They see FT as the biggest threat to their survival. Claims they have captured almost thirty per cent of the market in just two years. And what's worse, they seem to know a lot about Falcon Tech's operation over there especially the assembly sub-contracting in those village set-ups. He even muttered something about child labour. He's going to allege social dumping."

Knightley rocked back in his chair. "Arguments like that will give it irresistible charm for the politicians and bureaucrats in the Commission. They'll probably buy into it straight away and immediately order an investigation by the Trade Bureau."

"That's definitely the kind of allegation they'll make. And he even suggested that Falcon Tech was getting some of their sub-assembly work done in the *laogai*."

Knightley raised his head and fixed on Verbiest, his eyebrows deepening. "The what?"

"The *laogai*, you know, the forced labour camps the Chinese state has operated for dissidents since 1949. Those places are run by the military. They call it re-education through labour."

Knightley's right hand swept out across the desk in disdain. "I take it our client has no connection with those camps?"

"Can't be sure. They do most of the work in the factory apart from the sub-contracting to those village set-ups. At least that's what they told us. I'm sure the Europeans are just bluffing to make the case look damning. They're trying to bring in the old slave labour argument again."

"Okay, so that's it as far as Falcon Tech is concerned. But what about those other two companies we represent from Vietnam? Will they be affected?" Knightley demanded.

"Yeah, Vietnam was mentioned. It looks as if the Europeans are taking no chances this time. They're going to implicate every manufacturer in the Far East."

Knightley gazed at some point in the distance.

"I suppose we don't have to concern ourselves with the Vietnam clients. But-"

"But, of course," Verbiest stuttered, "Falcon Tech is the more serious for us. That's where our fee income exposure is greatest."

Petersson clasped his hands behind his head and then turned towards Verbiest with a hint of sarcasm in his voice.

"Of course, *this firm* advised them to go into China for cheap labour."

Verbiest's eyes blazed. "Hindsight. Twenty/twenty vision. We're all not blessed with the foresight of a Hebrew prophet."

"Now hold it, Erik. I remember the argument well. You advised them to go to China." Petersson stabbed a finger at Verbiest. "*You*, Erik."

An uncomfortable silence descended around the office. Petersson nodded in Laura's direction. "Laura argued about *this* possibility in *this* very room two years ago. I remember it clearly."

"Look, Falcon Tech was looking for a 'cheap labour' home at the time. They didn't engage us to decide the manufacturing location on trade considerations. No way."

Knightley gestured soothingly with his hands. "Calm down everyone. What's important now is how we play it from here."

"We advised them to go there. Laura and I will have to come up with a solution."

She smiled. "What's this 'we' thing?"

Verbiest bristled. "Come on Laura, we... yes, *we*. It was a decision of the firm."

He jumped up from his seat and walked around the room, stopping momentarily beside one of the big windows facing out over Avenue Louise. He sighed and muttered, "Roger, we're going to have to plan how to handle this."

Knightley rubbed his hands together as if washing them. "Erik, the firm's not going to carry the can on that one."

"Remember, Roger, if I go down so, too, does the firm."

Knightley dismissed his attempt at spreading the responsibility. "It's primarily your call. You know the trade scene better than anybody in Brussels."

"I'll need time to come up with a solution."

"Let's not get the blood boiling on this one for God's sake," Saatchi interrupted. "We're lawyers. Surely we can examine the situation dispassionately?"

Verbiest turned away from the window and faced his fellow partners. "If we can convince Falcon Tech that this was impossible to foresee then there's a chance that we can hold on to them."

The Italian leaned back, rubbed his thumb and forefinger together and smiled.

"And earn even more fees into the bargain defending them in a trade case. I like it Erik."

"It's not a joke, Lorenzo. We're looking for solutions here."

Saatchi remained unperturbed. Knightley was anxious to get an action plan going. He brought his elbows up to rest on the desk, put his fingers together and slid his joined thumbs under his chin. Slowly, he tapped his fingers against one another and said, "Okay, it's time to get all your channels of communication open. Suck out as much information as possible from the investigators in the Bureau. Call in any favours owed. Spend a bit of money on lunches. Whatever it takes. We'd better make sure that we have all the facts before we talk to Falcon Tech."

Verbiest turned back towards the window and continued to survey the grey sky over Brussels. He rubbed his chin and said, "The European manufacturers have hired Smeulders & Rozenstock. That could leak out very quickly and straight back to Falcon Tech. It would be disastrous for us if they heard it from the Europeans. You know how people talk to each other in the computer business."

Laura remained silent, listening. She had been vindicated but now was not the time to crow – not in public at least. Verbiest would have to come up with a Houdini-like trick to get them out of it.

"Keep in touch with Sakalis. Find out exactly when the complaint might be lodged with the Trade Bureau," Knightley ordered.

"Well, Smeulders & Rozenstock are quite tight-lipped. Sakalis should not have told me about it. It was a classic case of *in vino veritas*. I doubt if he'll remember half of what he said last night. I'm not going to approach him."

"Okay, our best hope is in the ETB itself. Ring Hoffmann. Doesn't he deal with the acceptance of the complaints? Butter him up a bit - lunch or whatever."

In a few sentences Verbiest outlined that Hoffmann had retired and that his replacement - a lawyer called Kelly - played his cards close to his chest. With all the top-level changes made recently he made it clear that the new faces were more sympathetic to the European manufacturers. The foreign exporters are getting a rough ride in these investigations of late, he confirmed. He shrugged and recalled that it was not like the old days in the eighties when a good bottle of wine would secure as much information as needed. "All that's changed," he said ruefully.

Knightley looked towards Laura. "Have you any ideas, Miss Harrison?"

"Well, it seems we have no choice but wait to see if the complaint is accepted."

"No, Laura, that's naïve," Verbiest rasped. "The real world doesn't work like that. If we wait until it's officially announced - you know Lindell – he simply won't accept it. We're supposed to be looking after the client's interest."

Petersson came to her defence. "Erik, calm down. No need to bite her nose off. She was just saying how she read it."

Saatchi once again awoke from his musing state, raised his bushy eyebrows and agreed, "A client has to hear it from you first - be it good or bad news; otherwise all credibility is gone."

Verbiest was feeling the heat from his fellow partners. He tried to sound positive. "We'll run a few calculations on the impact a duty would have on Falcon Tech. Laura, would you mind looking at last year and a few years into the future. You remember those projections Lindell was throwing around the place last year?"

"But I've just started the corporate restructuring. It's going to take at least a week. Maybe more," she said firmly, determined to set the pace.

"Laura, this damn thing's priority right now."

"Well, we have to make sure that that end of the business grows too, Erik," Knightley interjected. "You never know how the Falcon Tech thing will work out."

"I know but we can't talk to anybody without an idea of the impact."

Knightley sighed resignedly.

"If you say so but you're going to have Van Leewe on the

phone screaming for a progress report next week. What kind of duty should we model?" Laura asked.

"Say thirty, maybe forty per cent. A commie country's involved."

Knightley got up from his chair, a signal that the meeting was terminating. "Erik, you've got to track what's going on over at Smeulders & Rozenstock and the Bureau. Our flagship client's at stake," he said. Verbiest turned and walked towards the door with his tail between his legs.

Laura waited for a moment and then headed out into the reception area. Just then the antique grandfather clock struck noon. Coffee. She went downstairs, filled a polystyrene cup at the machine and returned to her desk.

She modelled several duty scenarios on the Excel spreadsheet. The results were not pleasing. It would mean crucifixion in the European market. The cheapest computer could now become very expensive. Falcon Tech would be hit even harder than the other Asian producers, all because they were trading from a communist country. It would not be easy explaining to the Falcon Tech executives that they had located in the worst place if a trade investigation were to start.

Chapter Six

March 1999
Brussels
THE WEEKLY REVIEW of chargeable hours took place every Tuesday afternoon. Laura printed off her clients' time sheets and went to Knightley's office. His eyes were glued to the screen but he managed to motion her towards the silver service.

"Pour yourself a coffee. I'll be with you in a moment."

Laura walked over and began pouring. Verbiest rushed in, threw a document onto the desk and rubbed his hands.

"The game has started. The Commission has already accepted the complaint. The evidence looks pretty compelling with huge differentials in price. Believe me Roger, defending Falcon Tech's interest could be very lucrative for us."

Knightley nodded towards Laura. Verbiest spun around towards her. "Oh ... oh Laura, I was...," he said, his voice quivering but he managed to regain his composure. "...I was just saying how complicated this case's going to be."

In Laura's eyes what Verbiest was saying was definitely not lawyer talk. It was business talk, making sure that everything was done in the interest of the business - his *business*. The client was only a pawn in the process. *So it's all about fees,* Laura thought. *Damn the client once we get our fees. Professional ethics must be for law school.*

She acknowledged with a smile, letting his words drift past.

"Erik, would you like a coffee? You look as if you need it," she said dryly as she walked towards him. He took the cup and gulped down a mouthful. Knightley flicked through the fifty-page document, stopping occasionally to mark a price with his red pen.

"How did you get your hands on this?" Knightley asked as he looked up from the document.

Smiling, he placed his index finger over his lips. "Roger, I always have my contacts in an emergency."

He turned towards Laura with a look of censure on his face and said, "It's the big bad commercial world out there. Got to keep the finger on the pulse. You'll learn that too one day, Laura."

Saatchi appeared at the open door.

"I heard that. So Erik's keeping all his trade secrets to himself. Come on, did you get it from Smeulders & Rozenstock or the Bureau?"

"Well, let's just say the Bureau has more holes in it than gouda cheese. I happened to be in the right place at the right time."

"How serendipitous!"

Verbiest grinned. "You could say that." He quickly refocused the discussion towards the issue in hand.

"The European industry has a lot of political clout on this one. I've never seen anything being decided so quickly. Got to plan what we'll say to our friends in Hong Kong. You know Newman, the bean counter. He'll want the full impact of the duty on the retail price. Batista and the other head office boys in California are heavy hitters…they just look at the bottom line and if they don't like what they see heads will roll."

"Maybe even yours," Laura muttered with a mischievous grin to dissipate the tension.

Verbiest's face tensed.

"I could do without smart ass replies. You've got a big attitude problem."

She glowered. "No Erik, I haven't got an attitude problem. I've got an altitude problem. I won't descend to your level."

Knightley stared at the computer screen, his lips tightening to suppress a smile. An arctic silence followed. After a few seconds a thaw set in.

"Look we're all a bit tetchy at the moment," Verbiest declared. "PKV&S has never lost a client, especially not a blue-chip like this one. And frankly, I don't want to be the first. So we must work out our tactics carefully."

"Remember those calculations - did you do them?" Knightley asked Laura.

"As far as I could using 35 and 40 per cent."

"Roger, the whole China thing. I was thinking hard about that. I wonder should we tell them up front, about how tough the Bureau could be? If we don't it could all blow back in our faces."

"See how they react to the news about the duty first."

Verbiest rubbed his chin anxiously. "Looks like we'll have to jump on a plane to Hong Kong to explain everything."

Knightley came around from behind his desk. On the way to the door he patted Verbiest firmly on the back, an unmistakable signal to confirm where the monkey would be staying. "Erik, I'm certain you'll come up with a solution. Remember this one's your call."

THE BUSINESS OF INTERNATIONAL TRADE was done almost exclusively through English, making it the *lingua franca* for communication between the trade lawyers and the European Trade Bureau. The headquarters of the Bureau, a six-storey brown-bricked building on Avenue de Cortenbergh, housed close to one hundred investigators. Their mission was to carry out about fifty trade investigations per year.

At precisely eight thirty on the morning of the first of March, Kurt Kaufmann, the Director, convened the regular management meeting in his office. He had more than twenty years experience behind him and ran the Monday morning meetings with classic Germanic precision, displaying little tolerance for breaches of his punctuality rule. Kaufmann was tall and lean with thinning hair and spoke English with a clipped delivery, his words leaving little scope for ambiguity or misinterpretation. The mahogany desk was strategically placed at an angle in the corner office, dominating the room and, at the same time, giving him a commanding view of the Brussels skyline. Black and white photographic prints of castles and architectural ruins from the Middle Ages adorned the walls.

Charles Windsor, the deputy director, was already seated at the conference table well before the deadline as were Pierre Champenois and Peter Kelly. As usual, the Director kicked off with a review of the current cases on hand. Achieving the tight legal time limit for investigations was always top of the agenda. It sometimes meant reassigning investigators and removing any bureaucratic obstacles outside and inside the Bureau. The meeting quickly disposed of the only problem case, giving time to allocate the new investigations in the pipeline.

The Director closed his folder and nodded to Windsor. He picked up his glasses, rotated his chair through one hundred and eighty degrees and grabbed a bunch of folders from a small table behind him, placing them on the conference table. Windsor was a heavy-set Englishman with sandy hair who had spent his early career in the Foreign Service in London but, when the United Kingdom joined the European club, he caught the bug and went continental. He nevertheless still kept a line of contact to Whitehall.

The meeting quickly allocated the first three cases to investigators. "Next," Kaufmann ordered.

"A very messy textile investigation. Literally hundreds of producers in the Far East and about six or seven countries involved. Weak evidence but a lot of political clout involved, so we had to run with it."

Champenois was sitting at the other end of the table directly opposite Kaufmann. He had the task of making sure that the Bureau delivered a politically acceptable result that the Commission could live with. The role he played required an astute mind; an intellect that could handle scheming, double-dealing and straight talking, all in the same sentence. All at a moment's notice. And when a devious little behind-the-scenes twist was called for, it would be delivered with aplomb making the Frenchman a skilful buffer between the administration and its political masters. He played the role well, sometimes too well, to the chagrin of those around him.

But this morning he was not familiar with the new cases. He had spent the previous fortnight on holiday in the South of France and so was out of touch with the latest developments. Windsor purposely did not make copies of the petitions, precisely because he wanted Champenois to squirm at the end of the table. Eventually Champenois' curiosity became unbearable forcing him to ask for sight of the textile complaint. And immediately he ran his eyes down the list of complainants to see if a French company was involved.

Kaufmann peered over his reading glasses. "Any eager young investigators, willing to travel and put in long hours, around the place?"

Kelly smiled. "Hmm yes....I get your drift. You're talking about the hired guns. The temporary contract people."

"Precisely. And if they muck it up, we'll tell the Commissioner that there's a price to pay for having hired hands around the place."

"Sensible approach Kurt," Windsor concurred.

Investigators were chosen and the case disposed of. Windsor ceremoniously opened the cover of another file.

"*Ah bon,* the computer investigation," Champenois said with a devious grin, "I knew you would leave it till last."

"Well?" Kaufmann asked. "Who do we have in mind for this?"

Kelly leaned back on the reclining chair. He had responsibility for liaising with the European industry and ensuring that petitions had sufficient *prima facie* evidence before they were formally lodged with the Bureau.

"Duty on computers just when the Union agenda is for every kid in Europe to have one. The consumer lobby will mount fierce resistance," he warned.

"Indeed," Windsor acknowledged. "It's dynamite. Even within the Commission we'll have a big argument on our hands. The Competition people will fight us all the way to the Council of Ministers. There's no doubt about it if we restrict Asian imports it's not going to be good for the consumer."

"And what's worse all these platitudes from the Commission lately about gearing up for the information society...everybody networking with computers," Kelly added.

Champenois' expression tightened as he drew himself up on the chair, pointing the index finger of his right hand down the table for emphasis.

"That's fine in itself, gentlemen, but remember the business we're in...protecting European industry from unfairly-priced imports. That's it plain and simple. All the rest is only piffle for some university debating society. If we don't have industries in Europe then we won't have jobs. And those kids you talked about won't be able to buy computers anyway."

Silence descended. Windsor turned towards Champenois waving the document in his hand.

"You know, Pierre, you're an outright protectionist," he said making little attempt to conceal the irritation in his voice. "Just like the press articles accuse us of. You want to build a fortress around Europe with duties. Is that the agenda?"

"Come on. I wouldn't go that far but if these guys are trying to snuff out our manufacturers with low prices then we have to step in. That's what we're here for. Isn't it?"

"Okay," Kaufmann responded sharply, his right hand shooting into the air to pre-empt further discussion. "We are not, and I mean *not,* going to reopen the philosophical debate. The Commission has decided to investigate. So now we pull together and concentrate on getting the best team for the job."

That brought the sniping to a close for the time being. Kaufmann looked down the table. "Any suggestions?"

"We need the highest calibre for sure," Kelly said.

Windsor loosened his tie. "We don't have a great choice at the moment. Our technology experts, Kotler and Rousseau are still tied up with the microprocessor case."

"When will they finish?" Kaufmann asked.

"End of the month," Kelly answered.

Kaufmann reflected for a moment. "We simply can't wait. The Commissioner won't tolerate any delay. Give me some suggestions for chief investigator."

Kelly drew in a deep breath. "Why don't we give it to Schuman...Marc Schuman. He's just finished that chemical case. He's got enough experience under his belt at this stage. Let's make him chief and let him get on with it."

"Sounds like a good choice. He wrapped up that investigation neatly," Windsor agreed.

Champenois quickly added, "And we didn't hear a murmur from any side. I'll go for him."

The Director was ready to take advantage of the general agreement around the table.

"He seems to have got your votes of confidence. Okay let's make him chief investigator."

Kaufmann walked to the door, leaned out and asked his secretary to call Schuman up to the sixth floor.

Two minutes later Marc was in the ante room. Janet

Wachter, Kaufmann's secretary, was on the phone. She pointed a finger, gesturing to him to go straight in.

"Please take a seat," Kaufmann said nodding to the soft padded seats circling the low informal table. "Well Marc," he started off. "I'm not going to beat around the bush. We want you to do the computer case. We're very pleased with your work and think you'd be able for the responsibility of leading a case."

"You'll need plenty of energy," Kelly emphasised as he picked up the document from the table. "Look, there are six countries involved." He paused, trying to find the page listing the countries in the fifty-page document.

"Yes,...eh South Korea, Japan, Malaysia, Thailand, Vietnam and China and fifteen or sixteen manufacturers in all. A lot of travel and a lot of work. Of course, you can pick your team...we don't expect you to do it all on your own."

Kaufmann leaned back on the chair. "We're confident that you can deliver a result."

"Yes," Champenois added. "A good outcome for the European computer industry."

"I would be happy to do it."

Champenois stared down the table. "You're our key man. There's a lot at stake here. It would be political dynamite to mishandle this one. Remember if we lose it Europe's technology sector could be decimated and the Bureau could be blamed. We just can't let that happen."

Kelly looked around at his colleagues and added, "Pierre's right. It's highly sensitive politically."

There were nods of agreement around the table. "Sure, sure."

Champenois leaned back on his chair waving a copy of the European manufacturer's complaint.

"Your job will be to re-establish fair competition in the marketplace. Ball-park figure of, say thirty-five per cent duty, maybe forty, depending on what you find. These guys are predators - they will just hook customers with low prices until they snuff out the European competition and then shoot up the prices when they have a monopoly."

"Pierre, don't try to dictate the outcome," Windsor snapped.

Kaufmann leaned back on the chair and took off his glasses.

"I hope you have no commitments that would make it difficult? The hours will be long."

Marc shook his head.

"Another thing," Champenois said tapping the table with his index finger. "These Asian companies are cash rich and competitive. I mean *very* competitive. They play a tough game in the market place and sometimes they play dirty - you know back-handers, under-the-counter-payments, holidays in exotic places for their marketing people. They try to influence anyone who can help them to gain market share and increase their profitability. So be very careful. No compromising your position, you understand."

Marc drew back, half offended at the thought. "Of course not."

Kelly grinned. "And remember one thing," he said, "In the Far East, masturbation is your only man."

A suppressed chuckle filled the room. Marc stifled a laugh. Kaufmann was unamused. He flipped the folder closed to show that the meeting was over. "Well, I think you have the picture. Peter will give you the documents and the names of the contact people in the industry. And, by the way, Smeulders and Rosenstock are the lawyers for the Europeans. Remember they have a lot of political connections."

"Chalk up a success as chief investigator with this one, Schuman, and your future will be bright here in the ETB," Windsor confirmed as he rose from the chair.

The Director stood up and walked towards his desk. He sat down in his high back chair and looked across at Marc. "You have nine months to deliver results. Nine months. That's your target. Full duties in place by year-end. A nice Christmas present for the European computer industry, a happy Commissioner, and a promotion in the pipeline for you."

Marc stood up. "Yes sir," he said and headed towards the door. Just then Champenois called out in French, *"Allez les gars. Il faut trouver quelquechose."* Get moving. You've got to bring back a good result.

LATER THAT AFTERNOON Marc reclined the chair, propped his feet on the desk, crossed his ankles and accidentally hit the keyboard causing an array of letters to jump across the screen. He picked up the phone and punched some digits.

"Hi Laura. You'd better prepare your client's case well!"

"Only the best from this firm. We're the leaders in defending our clients' interests, didn't you know."

"Well you'll be facing a formidable foe."

"What the heck do you mean?"

"The computer case."

"Fantastic. Congratulations you got it. Now I will be privy to, you know, helpful information for my clients," she taunted.

"No, no, baby. Strictly professional during office hours. You know what…they've made me chief."

"Great but come on, that's no way to treat your lover," she purred down the phone.

"It's the only way – I've got my professional standards."

"I'm joking Marc. Don't be so serious."

"Well I'm just teasing you too. Are we meeting after work, for a celebratory drink?"

"Is that an invite?"

"You could call it that – say, six thirty."

"Too early for me. Closer to seven thirty?"

"Okay."

"See you then. Ciao, ciao," she whispered and dropped the phone.

Marc clicked an icon and started to type.

"Hey, your typing skills are improving," Heidi, his secretary, said as she came through the door with a bunch of documents. Laughing she asked sarcastically, "What's your speed? One hundred words a minute?"

"I wish. I'm just a hunt and peck man…one finger at a time."

"Soon you won't need a secretary anymore."

"Believe it when you see it."

She dropped the documents on the corner of the desk. "More arguments from lawyers on the aluminium case."

Marc's mind was elsewhere. "Did you hear the news?…I'm getting the computer investigation."

"Congratulations."

"Thank you and because it's so important I can pick my own team."

"*Where* does that leave me?" she asked.

"Where do you think? Here with me, of course. No change...that is, if it's okay with you?"

"Yes, provided I get a trip to some exotic location!"

Marc raised his head, smiled and then refocused on the screen.

"I've already pulled together a dream team - a mixture of lawyers, economists and accountants. Elena Schmidt will be my legal assistant for the case."

"Is that because she's pretty?"

He laughed. "It never entered my head but now that you mention it..."

"Really?"

"Well, she's young and eager with plenty of energy. She's been to the European Court many times and has her finger on the pulse when it comes to court precedents."

"So you want her to draft the law. Make your life easy?"

"She could help especially with the international literature, particularly all those articles published on the other side of the Atlantic...invaluable if we want to rebut arguments from American-based law firms."

Heidi smiled. "She's the one then?"

"Yeah. And what's even better she does the social circuit with the young lawyers too. We'll know what's going on out there in the law firms."

"Are you sure you'll get her?"

He smiled up at her. "Kaufmann said I've a free hand and I'm going to use it. I've also talked to Henkel. He's eager to join the team. Invaluable for all the econometric modelling."

"Sounds like you're picking the best."

"Hmm...yeah...that's what a chief's supposed to do." In ten minutes he had named every member of his new team. Heidi nodded appropriately and emphasised to him that everyone would have to look after his own filing.

"Agreed. But remember, the chief investigator has to have

72

some privileges in that area."

"Maybe if you take me on an exotic mission sometime. Bangkok sounds interesting!" She smiled and walked towards the door.

"Yes, Moneypenny," came the reply, the Sean Connery immitation accent flawless.

He held the list up at eye level and laughed, "Dream Team versus the Asian Tigers. No challenge."

He went downstairs, grabbed a can of Coke from the dispenser and took a gulp. This was going to be the case of the decade demanding the best team of investigators in the ETB, he was certain.

WHEN LAURA ARRIVED at the James Joyce pub Marc was already standing at the bar talking with Pierre Chantall, a friend who worked as an administrator in the European Parliament. Pierre slid off the barstool to greet her. "Hi Laura, I was just giving Marc some advice on how to improve his squash technique."

"Really, Pierre, it must be difficult to give advice when you *are* the underdog," Marc shot back before she could speak.

"Maybe the underdog but catching up fast, you'll see. What about the last game for example?"

"Just a freak. I was a little off form."

Pierre raised an eyebrow. "Off form?"

"Stop, stop," Laura called out. "I can see you guys have been on the juice for a while. Do you always have to be so competitive?"

"He couldn't be competitive if he tried," Marc teased.

Using sport to play out the primeval male ritual of the jungle, she thought as she ensconced herself on the stool that Pierre had vacated. Marc beckoned to the bartender shouting his order for drinks above the din of the bar. They pulled over a couple of stools and flanked Laura, each with an elbow leaning on the counter.

She turned towards Pierre. "Okay... so who's having affairs in the European Parliament, any scandal?"

"Hardly, that lot of parliamentarians are too busy working out their expenses to have affairs. It takes energy to do *that*. Of course, I imagine there are a few energetic ones who can combine both," Pierre said as he reached for the glass of Guinness.

Marc drew back on the stool. "What about all those fact-finding trips to sun-drenched places?"

"They certainly like to have a broad global view of things so that they can make the right judgement on things like the proper shape of the banana. European consumers wouldn't forgive their parliamentarians if they didn't check the bend on the banana. You know how fussy people are."

Laura and Marc laughed at the cynical wit of Pierre.

"You say these things with such a serious expression," she chipped in.

"And what's more, the Euro Parliamentarians from Britain spend most of their time checking the meat content of their sausages in case the Europeans try to standardise them. Imagine the average Brit waking up some morning to find that what he always held dear was not a sausage but a frankfurter."

Laura bent over double with laughter. "Back home we call them hot dogs."

Marc raised the palm of his hand towards Laura in feigned admonition. "You shouldn't poke fun at our Euro politicians. They have to move from Brussels to Strasbourg every other week. A job in itself. Nothing could be more stressful."

"Must be exhausting," Laura said dryly.

Chapter Seven

March 1999
Hong Kong
THE SHORT FLIGHT from Brussels to Amsterdam Airport was uneventful. After disembarking Laura and Verbiest immediately boarded the KLM 747 for Hong Kong. She took the window seat and Verbiest slid into the aisle seat. The aircraft pushed back from the stand and began to turn on the apron. Ten minutes later it lifted off gracefully from Amsterdam Airport bound for Hong Kong and disappeared into the midday sky.

Verbiest turned towards Laura. "Before jet-lag sets in let's just go over the details for the meeting. We'll arrive around seven o' clock in the morning. We'll call as planned to the office at say, eleven."

"Fine," Laura said as she handed him a copy of the computations with the graphical illustrations. "There's no easy way to portray it. A forty per cent duty will shoot prices up at the retail level by around fifty per cent. Their independent distributors will go crazy."

Verbiest studied the figures in silence. After about fifteen minutes he flung the folder down on the meal tray and sighed deeply.

"We'll keep emphasising that we'll fight hard on their behalf. They've put so much investment into China they won't easily walk away."

He opened his briefcase and slid the documents inside. Leaning back, he pulled at his collar, turned and grinned at her. "It's time we relaxed. All this tension is making me thirsty." He called the stewardess.

"A Jameson please, ice and a dash of water."

He immediately turned to Laura and said, "Ever thought about the criminal side? You'd make a brilliant defence counsel."

"Not for the moment. Who knows…maybe later."

"Never appealed to me." Verbiest said as his drink was served. He waved the glass disdainfully. "It's all about the sordid side of life…defending murderers, paedophiles and drug peddlars. You see," he continued, "that's the good thing about the civil side of law. What we do here is all big picture stuff. Our decisions affect countless thousands of lives. We can change livelihoods in…" he snapped his fingers, "…in a flash. Those criminal lawyers …they just try to keep some down-and-out bum out of prison."

"Very true, Erik," she readily agreed reaching for the airline magazine in the seat pocket. Verbiest took another sip and promptly picked up the headphones to listen to a classical music channel.

TWELVE HOURS LATER, the cockpit crew made final preparations for landing at Chek Lap Kok, Hong Kong's new airport built on a man made island, thirty-four kilometres from the centre of the city. While the captain was preparing the pre-landing checks Laura was awakening from a fitful slumber. She looked at her watch and then at the monitor. It showed the aircraft above the Indian continent.

An hour to go, she thought. The business class cabin was silent. Verbiest's eyes were closed. She pushed up the plastic shutter and peered out through the window. The sun had climbed well above the horizon, the brightness stinging her eyes. She pulled down the shutter and stared at the monitor, thinking about a warm cup of coffee. The aircraft began its descent and flawlessly landed in the morning sunshine. After clearing immigration and retrieving their luggage they followed the signs for level five and boarded the train for Kowloon.

Two hours later they had checked in to their rooms on the sixth floor of the Sheraton hotel.

THE TAI PO INDUSTRIAL ESTATE was situated in the New Territories area of Hong Kong close to the Chinese border. The Falcon Tech operation nestled among a sprawl of drab concrete buildings where the renowned free-enterprise culture was born decades earlier; its dullness contrasting sharply with the glitzy, high rise steel-and-glass buildings depicted on postcards of Hong Kong.

Shortly after eleven they entered the Falcon Tech building. The receptionist greeted them with an oriental smile and phoned upstairs. As they waited in the reception area Verbiest played with his fountain pen, shifting uneasily on the seat.

"Hi. Good to see you guys," boomed a voice from the top of the stairs.

Lindell walked down the curved stairs, denim from head to toe. They stood up as his right hand thrust forward, his other hand enveloping Verbiest's shoulder.

"This is a pleasant surprise. You guys have business in the area?"

"Not really. We thought we should take the opportunity to brief you on developments in Europe," Verbiest replied hesitantly.

Lindell spun around, leaned towards Laura and welcomed her with a firm handshake. "Good to see you again, Laura."

He ushered his visitors upstairs and called Newman to join them in the small functional boardroom.

"Coffee for everybody?" He didn't wait for a reply. He lifted the phone to his secretary. "Can you bring coffee to the boardroom please, Lai?"

Newman entered, closely followed by a Chinese man in his mid-twenties. "Let me introduce our new financial accountant. Mr. Lau joined us last week."

After the handshaking Newman motioned them towards the boardroom table.

Lindell flicked through a copy of last year's annual report. Beaming he said, "You've got our accounts for last year. Impressive eh! Almost thirty percent market share in Europe and already very profitable. We're going to whup the asses off those boys in Europe. In two years' time they won't exist."

Laura glanced at Verbiest, his eyebrows now furrowed. Newman continued the upbeat tone. "Who said trading in China is difficult. They're more helpful than in the West. That empty premises in Shenzhen was almost tailor-made for us. You'd think the Chinese knew in advance."

The longer they talk like this the more difficult it will get, she thought. *Will Erik move early to diffuse the hoopla?*

Verbiest waited patiently for his opportunity.

"And we're not forgetting our lawyers. The advice you gave us was the best...really the very best. I doubt if an American law firm would have been as helpful. I guess you guys know the Far East better."

"Well it was the best option," Verbiest replied faintly.

He did not like the way the conversation was going. Not one bit. He had news to convey - bad news - that would deflate these up-beat executives really hard. He would be talking real pain on the bottom line. He tried to get his mind clear. There was no sense in postponing it until lunch. The Falcon Tech people talked a lot about the Chinese operation, almost as a gesture to say 'thank you' to Petersson Knightley Verbiest and Saatchi for the good advice. After what seemed like an eternity, Verbiest cleared his throat with his customary semi-suppressed grunt.

"Gentlemen, we at PKV&S are proud of your undoubted achievement, all achieved in such a short time. But then it's clear you have a strong team here able to turn out the best computers at prices the customer likes. I don't think I've seen such a rapid start-up in any sector. I'm sure head office in California is celebrating its good judgement in you Dylan...in fact the whole team."

"There's no question about that," Lindell chuckled. "Puts us firmly on course for the stock launch without a doubt."

Verbiest ignored his intervention. "However, there is one dark cloud looming on the horizon. You see, this is complicated to explain but the European Commission has received a complaint from some European manufacturers...I gave you a brief outline on the phone, Dylan. They are complaining about Asian exporters selling cheap into Eur-"

"Yes, we didn't understand," Newman cut across. "What did you mean by that?"

"Well it's like this. The European computer manufacturers are complaining about cheap computers from the Far East."

"But that's not possible. They're not talking about us?"

"I'm afraid Falcon Tech has been mentioned."

"So what does that mean? Does it affect our trade?" Newman asked.

"It could mean duty...anti-dumping duty. A sort of customs duty."

Lindell threw a puzzled look in the direction of Newman. "Goddamn - what duty? Nobody mentioned this before."

"You've got to remember it's just an allegation. These Europeans are being crucified by competition. At least that's what *they* think. It's just that they're not efficient."

"That's their problem. They should get their costs in order and-"

"Well, it's more complex than that. An allegation is investigated by an agency of the European Commission, the European Trade Bureau and they more or less have discretion to decide."

Lindell was searching for clarification. "But surely they will decide that the Europeans are inefficient...costs too high."

Verbiest explained that it was not entirely about costs and that the Europeans can allege that Asian imports are too cheap leaving the exporters in the dock.

"What the hell kind of thing is that? Anyway, we won't worry. We sell covering all costs and we make a profit."

"Dylan, just let me clarify a bit more. It's not about selling under cost. It's even more complex. You see when the Trade Bureau investigates, it compares the export price of the computers against a thing called the normal value - a fair value."

"What's the bottom line here?" Newman snapped.

Verbiest leaned forward and put his right elbow on the table, deliberately dropping an octave.

"They could hit you for 40 per cent on the landed cost into Europe..."

The CEO sprang to his feet, seething.

"What are you talking about? What the hell are you saying? This can't be. We trade by the book. It's a goddamn joke..."

"No, I'm afraid not. If it happens we'll fight all the way," Laura added.

"But it-"

The phone rang. Lindell barked at Lau. "Tell Joanne to hold

all calls...meeting's going to overrun."

A moment of silence followed. Shock seemed to be setting in. Newman was becoming angry too. He hit out, "Is this why you guys flew all the goddamn way here. To tell us that we could be hit with some kind of penalty for trading efficiently? What the hell are the Europeans playing at?"

Verbiest tried to diffuse the impact. "Well, the Europeans signed up to the World Trade Organisation rules just like the United States and Japan. Unfortunately, all countries play the game to suit domestic pressures from their industries."

"But, look, we plan to ship two billion dollars worth of computers into Europe next year. What will this thing mean on that?"

Verbiest pretended to do some mental arithmetic. "Well, on those volumes, it would mean, at a straight forty per cent, say, eight hundred million dollars per year."

"What the hell are you talking about – eight hundred million dollars on the landed cost. No way...it can't happen. It's just unreal."

Verbiest tried to stay cool. "If the investigation goes that way then it's big money I'm afraid."

"That's a non-runner. We don't have that kind of money to pay."

"Well, it's the European importer who will have to pay," Erik meekly replied.

"It's the same sonofabitch thing. When the price goes up we sell less. You are our lawyers. You've got to solve this one."

"But Dylan it may not be easy to avoid it. These investigations tend to go in favour of the European industry."

"For Chrisssake, you'd better fix it so that our price doesn't move. We're going to have a discounting scheme next year - you know, on volume of sales. This will throw out all our projections."

"We can fight for you with the Trade Bureau during the investigation. Technical things - discounts, physical differences, additional features - all kinds of arguments for adjustments that could shave some percentages off."

"Look, you get us out of this. Our business is not going to

be ruined by inefficient Europeans. If you don't we'll kick ass big time."

"We'll do our best. Let's just try to make rational judgements."

Newman was not impressed with the somewhat casual style of Verbiest. He started to probe. "This problem was not mentioned before...when we were setting up the manufacturing plant. Is it because we located in China specifically?"

"No. All Asian, well mostly all Asian, exporters are likely to be hit."

Lindell jumped up and rushed to the phone on the small table in the corner of the room. He lifted the receiver, pressed a few digits and said, "Get Wong here immediately."

He dropped the phone and walked back to the table.

"He may have something to contribute on this. Right - start from the beginning. I want the whole sequence of events. Timeframes, the lot. San Jose will have to be told today."

Verbiest went through the story again. The American boys took notes, lots of notes. They stopped him several times to clarify. Laura sat back and listened. Half an hour later a knock on the door signalled the arrival of Wong.

"Thanks for coming. You may be able to help. It seems Falcon Tech could be facing a problem in Europe." Lindell riveted Verbiest's eyes, then continued, "Not of its own making I might add. We're going to have to find a solution and we're going to have to goddamn find it *now*."

Verbiest had known Wong for two years now. Their mutual client brought them into occasional contact. Even though Wong had only dealt with a few trade cases the word was out that he had secured very favourable deals from the Federal Trade Commission for his textile clients. In legal circles he was considered more of a lobbyist than a trade lawyer.

The blunt facts, as Lindell knew them, were told to Wong. He sat in the chair, listening carefully, his eyes blinking rhythmically as he digested each piece of information. When Lindell finished they each threw out ideas, bits of solutions as they saw it onto the table. In the end the two-hour-long discussion produced very little to help Falcon Tech. The executives found it difficult to come to grips with it.

Newman gasped. "Eight hundred million dollars in customs duty, every year for the next five years…"

"Well, yes at a forty per cent rate of duty," Verbiest proffered confirmation. The enormity of the impact left them almost speechless.

"Look, we have a business to run. We can't spend any more time on it. You guys will have to resolve it," Lindell barked.

There was a moment's silence and then Lindell snapped, "Get back here tomorrow with a solution. Batista will have to be told."

"May I make a suggestion, Mr. Lindell?" Wong asked.

"What?"

"I'll make a reservation at the Indian restaurant at the Sheraton for tomorrow evening."

"We could discuss options there," Verbiest added.

"Options? Verbiest, I want solutions - not options. That's what I want right now. It's not as if you're being asked to solve Fermat's Last Theorem. *You hear me,* no ifs and no goddamn buts."

Before Verbiest or Laura could speak they found themselves outside Falcon Tech's offices in the Tai Po industrial estate waiting for a taxi.

"What do you make of that mess? Lindell is sure calling the shots. Any further ideas Laura?"

"Just keep fighting for them during the investigation. As I said, shave a few percentage points off here and there. Good legal arguments…that kind of thing."

"He won't buy that line. You've heard him yourself. He's out for blood on this one."

"It doesn't look good, I agree."

"I think we're going to lose the account."

"Maybe."

"Damn it. Our best catch since the practice started. And if they move the other American corporations may follow."

"Huh, nasty."

He rubbed his chin and sighed loudly. "You bet, Laura. You bet."

THE FOLLOWING EVENING VERBIEST made his way to the Indian restaurant situated off the foyer in the Sheraton Hotel. He had spent the day combing through all the options but found little scope to gloss over the harsh reality. Falcon Tech had a zero chance of escaping a hefty duty on its computers. He now faced the biggest challenge of his career. If the Falcon Tech account were lost, he alone would be held responsible. A twenty-year unblemished record would be broken. He played the facts around in his mind. The unwritten rules were clear.

Never lose a client.

And this was the premier one. It was now as good as it was going to get. As he entered the restaurant the head waiter acknowledged the reservation and directed him to the table. He eased into the seat and propped his elbows on the surface, supporting his head with his hands. He felt the early stages of a headache across his forehead and, reaching for the jug of water, washed back two Valium.

Wong entered and made his way to the table.

"Good evening, Mr. Verbiest," he said in unaccented English, the five years spent in a Catholic school in Hong Kong and a further three at university in the States evident in the flawless delivery. Wong's command of the language allowed him to display middle class urbanity as the occasion demanded.

"And a good evening to you too, Mr. Wong," Verbiest replied. Now was definitely not the time for pleasantries. He cut to the chase without delay.

"Any further ideas about a solution before the FT people arrive?"

"I think we should go through the usual ones. But really there's nothing that can help Falcon Tech. Of course, if all else fails we could suggest a little bit of leverage."

"Leverage? What do you-"

Verbiest stopped abruptly in mid sentence as he spotted the Falcon Tech executives coming towards the table.

"Hi," Lindell muttered under his breath. Newman just about nodded.

Batista pulled out a chair and sat down. "Gentlemen I've travelled from California to hear your solution. So we'll order now and listen to your plan on how to get Falcon Tech out of this mess."

Before Verbiest could start Laura approached the table, agitated.

"Sorry. The receptionist queried my credit card. Took me twenty minutes to explain that my name was not Hudson. I couldn't get through to the crazy girl."

Lindell rose from his seat and pulled the chair back for her. "It's okay. We haven't ordered yet."

The menus were perused and Indian curries chosen. Lindell poured a glass of sparkling water from one of the bottles and started off, his voice tinged with sarcasm, "Well, gentlemen you are our lawyers. Let's hear solutions."

"There are no quick-fix solutions. This investigation is a legal process and the-"

"Damn it, Erik, don't give us that legalese bullshit." Batista snarled before Verbiest could finish the sentence. "Dylan says you've been playing that line since you've arrived here. How many times do we have to say it? Your law firm advised us to go to Asia. Now get the finger out. The goddamn launch is going ahead next February regardless. Do you guys understand that?"

"Well look, we can try hard to influence the Member States' governments around Europe. They have the final say about duties."

Newman moaned. "Just tell us the pressure points in Brussels. Who do we lean on to make things happen?"

"You could start a cacophony of complaints, you know, drum up support from consumers organisations about high prices. It just might swing enough Ministers' votes against duties."

"So what are we waiting for. Let's get active."

"Hold on, Dylan. I must warn you that there are no guarantees. Remember, the biggest push will come from the other side…from the European computer manufacturers. They have more political clout than you have. Factory closures leave politicians' nerves very frayed…all that kind of stuff."

"Is there a senate we can appeal to?"

"We've got the European Parliament but it has no real power."

"You mean a talking shop with no balls?" Lindell guffawed.

"That's one way to express it."

The waiter came with the curries. Without formality they started to eat. Newman swallowed hard. "So come down to the wire on this. Where does this thing leave us?"

"We'll fight the Bureau hard and-"

"Just shut the fuck up," Batista shouted as anger smouldered in his eyes. He stabbed his fork across the table and exploded. "I want a damn solution. Over half a billion dollars are tied up in plant and equipment in Shenzhen."

Verbiest recoiled.

"*You* Verbiest. *You* suggested we put the plant in Asia. Now get us a solution fast!"

Wong coughed in a suppressed way and then nodded towards Batista as if looking for permission to speak.

"As Mr. Verbiest said, there are no ideal solutions. A few games have been played in the past in other investigations but what you're looking for is a watertight solution."

"What games?" Lindell demanded.

"Well, it's possible to try to circumvent the duty. Ship the computers from a country not subject to the investigation... Pakistan for instance."

"Pakistan?" Newman asked incredulously. "You mean ship them there for onward shipment to Europe. More damn costs."

"Yes, it's theoretically possible but the Customs and, eventually, the Trade Bureau will smell a rat through the trade statistics. That's the risk."

Batista dropped his glass of water and banged his fist on the table, his voice seething with anger.

"Look, in less than a year Falcon Tech will be wheeled out as a showcase of how to bring a technology company to the stock market. Neither you lawyer leeches, nor the Europeans are going to stop that. Everything's at stake. Our reputation and our hard-earned money from the launch. So get your fucking heads together and come up with a solution. Falcon Tech is not going to carry thirty or forty per cent duty on its computers. Is that clear?"

A shocked silence descended around the restaurant. Conversations stopped, a few heads turning towards the table. Wong winced. After all, he had a reputation to uphold. An appalling outburst of invective in a restaurant was not the way to do business but, thanks to his wisdom, he had suggested Indian, far removed from the culinary tastes of his friends and associates. Verbiest's face turned red. A client had never spoken to him like that. Never. He was about to reply in kind but the PKV&S Hippocratic oath once more started to dance in his mind.

Never lose a client.

Never lose a client now echoed louder in his ears.

Never.

Eventually the other diners turned their heads and continued eating.

"I hear what you are saying Albert," came the muted response.

"You'd better hear it loud and clear. If you don't find a solution fast we'll sue your ass for wrongful advice. You hear me Verbiest? Now let me finish dinner without listening to this nonsense."

Again an awkward silence descended around the table. Verbiest started to push the curry around the plate, his appetite rapidly vanishing. He was sitting with his back to most of the other diners, mainly Western businessmen cutting deals with the textile sweatshops of the capitalist enclave. He didn't dare look around. Wong's face remained inscrutable, his head tilted forward, continuing to eat sloppily. He was more comfortable with chopsticks.

Batista finished eating, excused himself and walked from the table. Newman and Lindell followed on his heels. When they were out of sight Wong pulled his head back from the plate, looked at Verbiest, and smiled.

"He's going to shaft you, Mr. Verbiest. You can be sure of that. He'll go the whole way if he doesn't get satisfaction. The lawsuit is not a bluff. I can see it dancing in his eyes."

Verbiest furtively glanced over his shoulder. "Yes, but everything we advised was above reproach."

"Indeed it was but he's out for retribution 'cause he's got a lot to lose."

A voice came over the loudspeaker. *Paging Miss Harrison. Miss Harrison to the reception desk please.*

Laura raised her eyebrows, excused herself and left the restaurant. Verbiest leaned forward and asked, "By the way, what did you mean earlier about leverage?"

"Look Mr. Verbiest, there's no point in beating about the bush. You could try a bit of pressure on the investigators. Probably the chief investigator, whoever he is. Help him to find in the company's favour."

"Hell no. That would backfire immediately."

"Believe me, it has worked well in the past with some American and Canadian cases here in Asia."

Verbiest was in pensive mood, his hands supporting his chin, pondering deeply.

"Really. What kind of leverage?"

Wong leaned across and whispered. "Get the investigator into a compromising position and try a bit of bribery. If it doesn't work then have a little bit of evidence waiting…kind of stuff that puts a career in tatters and ruins a marriage or family life."

Verbiest drew back and squirmed. "You *are* serious?"

The Oriental lawyer shrugged. "There's no alternative. I tell you, it's the only way out of this for you. Couldn't be simpler. I know an organisation that specialises in this kind of thing."

"But if something goes wrong you're talking about highly illegal stuff…conspiracy. The worst form of crime. Goddamnit, we're lawyers, not some back street gang trying to rob an old lady."

"*Mr. Verbiest, nothing can go wrong.* The people who carry out the work are all anonymous faces. They just disappear into thin air afterwards."

"Who do you mean?"

Wong beckoned the waiter. "First tell me what you think of it as an option. Look, order some coffee. Give yourself time to think."

Verbiest nodded.

"Two coffees," Wong called out as he took a cigarette from

the packet. He lit it, inhaling deeply. Moments later his shoulders sagged as drafts of smoke funnelled through his nostrils. The coffee arrived. The occasional cough from Wong - a wheezing raucous sound - punctuated the silence. Verbiest sat contemplating for several more minutes. The Oriental shifted on the chair and half-subdued a sigh, a clear sign of irritation. Eventually he broke the silence.

"Tell you what. Why don't you sleep on it overnight and give me a call first thing in the morning?"

"Yes, I think I'll do just that. But who are these anonymous people you mentioned?"

"Look Mr.Verbiest, think it over. If you go for it you can trust your life with them…no trace. Nothing."

They finished the coffee and stood up.

"Put it on the bill. Room number 639."

"No Mr. Verbiest I insist. It's my treat."

He turned to Wong and said, "Thank you. I'll talk to you in the morning. Good night."

Wong responded with emphasis in his voice. "Call me before eight. I've an appointment downtown after that."

"Okay."

"And Mr. Verbiest, remember one thing, we're lawyers. We've got to protect our own livelihood. That's what this game's all about. Everybody needs a slice of the action, remember? Good night."

Verbiest was agitated, thinking hard. "I know. I know. Good night." He headed out into the foyer. Laura came rushing towards him, her eyes filled with tears.

"What's happened…what's wrong?"

"Something terrible," she sobbed. "My father's had a car accident. I must get back home."

"Sorry Laura. I'm really sorry," he said. "Look I'll arrange with the airline. You sit down there and I'll get some coffee."

Wong observed the two Europeans for a moment and then quickened his pace as he made towards the main door, the inscrutable expression on his face softening. He stood outside on the street, pulled out his mobile and hastily punched the redial button. A burst of Chiu Chow chatter ensued for half a minute and then the phone was quickly back in his pocket. His eyes glinted and he chuckled as he made off into the sultry night air of downtown Hong Kong.

THE SEVEN O' CLOCK ALARM CALL woke Verbiest from a fitful sleep. His throat felt raw and dry. Wong's proposal had been sloshing around in his head during the night. Exhausted, he lay still on the bed and tried to focus yet again on the problem. The facts did not change. It was a win-lose situation as he saw it. If Falcon Tech wins, PKV&S wins. If Falcon Tech loses, PKV&S loses - big time. It was *make-your-mind-up time.* That was for sure. Lose Falcon Tech and maybe the other American clients and go back to ambulance chasing for a living. And maybe a bruising law suit with one Erik Verbiest on the slag heap at forty-eight years of age, never having been managing partner and no prestigious post as chairman of the Law Society. Or...

Or, he thought, *play the Wong card. Let little Mr. Wong's helpers help. A duty of maybe eight to ten per cent. Falcon Tech smiling at the other Asian exporters. A stock market launch in the offing. And one Erik Verbiest, the saviour on the day.*

Listen to what Wong has to offer. This was the best option. The best by far, he was now sure. At last everything was clear. Perfectly clear. Erik Steffan Verbiest was not going to be the fall guy. He lifted the phone and dialled.

WONG WAS AT HIS DESK preparing for a property deal in the New Territories when the call came through. He drew back from the keyboard and began to tap on the edge of the desk, the anxious expression on his face melting. Verbiest had uttered the words he wanted to hear. His eyes glinted with delight as he dropped the receiver. Cheng was summoned immediately.

"Things are turning out just as I expected," Wong said. "Our friend is eager to try an alternative solution so an urgent assignment needs to be carried out right away."

"Last night's phone call has already put me on alert."

"Our client will have to be helped to make a decision."

"Indeed, the right decision."

"Call Feng in Beijing. Have him call the Village Committee. Get them to visit Falcon Tech in Shenzhen. Pull out the agreement that they signed. Remind them how expensive it would be to renege on the deal - seizure of all the computers and equipment. Compensation for the six thousand workers in the factory, not to mention those village set-ups. Let them know that a deal is a deal in China. Refresh their memory on *all the conditions*."

"I know what you want, Mr. Wong."

"Assure the Falcon Tech people that the Village Committee does this every two years...orders from Beijing. Toeing the Party line. Trying to be helpful so that there's no confusion about the agreement."

"Certainly."

"Tell our friends to be diplomatic, but above all be firm. And make sure they give them that inscrutable Chinese smile. They have to know that there's real pain if they try to backslide and pull out."

"I will do it now."

"This should really help Falcon Tech to make up its mind...to come to a sensible decision. And I want it wrapped up within three days. Is that clear?"

"Yes Mr. Wong."

"If this goes well, there may be significant new activity coming the way of the brotherhood."

"We're just a phone call away," Cheng said as he made for the door.

Wong returned to the legal paperwork. It was his way of knowing where the best deals were happening so that his Yangtze Triad could move in at the earliest stage to secure a percentage. He flicked a button on the computer and began drafting the title deeds for the property. But concentration eluded him. He walked towards the big window, lit a cigarette and surveyed the Hong Kong skyline from his tenth floor hideaway.

"Interesting times," he muttered. "Very interesting times."

Brussels

THE ONCE-A-WEEK lunchtime rendezvous took place in a cafe off Avenue Louise. Laura wanted to discuss the dilemma with Marc but knew that it would be unethical. She slipped onto the stool at the counter and, moments later, he came alongside and pecked her cheek. She talked about her trip concentrating on the peculiar things that had happened.

"The mix up about the credit card is understandable but the phone call about my dad was weird. Imagine it took me two days to get through to home to find out that everybody was okay."

"Could have been a genuine mix-up with the names. It's not easy for them to recognise the differences."

"Still my name was up on screen," she said perplexed.

"At least your luggage didn't go astray," Marc reassured her. Laura laughed and they moved on to he usual chit-chat. Lover talk and lawyer talk. A cocktail of what was topical, but neither was forthcoming about current cases. So today it was more lover than lawyer.

Chapter Eight

February 1999
Brussels & Hong Kong
THE ANTEROOM TO THE DIRECTOR'S office was the nerve centre of the Trade Bureau. Access to Kaufmann was controlled by Janet Wachter, a high-maintenance blonde secretary. His appointment schedule was meticulously planned by her but some days it fell into disarray as a steady stream of investigators competed with well-connected lobbyists and lawyers who dropped in unannounced, anxious to get the ear of the Director. By late morning a queue was not unusual, turning the nerve centre into a trading exchange for the latest gossip on the international trade scene.

Marc arrived shortly after eight am, eager to avoid the surge of people and nodded towards the Director's door.

"He's on the phone, you'll have to wait."

Several minutes of silence ensued, her eyes glued to the screen, effectively ignoring him. He moved as far away as possible from her desk and stared through the window at the rust coloured rooftops. A light flickered on her console. "You can go in," she said without lifting her head.

Kaufmann stood up and, beckoning Marc towards the soft seats around the low table, joined him. He took the document and flipped through the pages.

"You will have to publish the legal notice within two weeks to show that the investigation is starting. The European computer industry has put more pressure on the Commissioner to take action immediately."

"The case can be up and running once I get the green light from you."

Kaufmann glanced down again. "I see you've put a good group of investigators together – at least on paper. Quite an eclectic bunch. I approve. Now get moving."

"Sure."

Kaufmann rose and picked his raincoat from the stand. They walked down the corridor to the lift. Marc stepped out at the fourth floor and made his way back to the office. He opened up Microsoft Word and went directly into the dedicated L drive, scanning the standard legal texts. He clicked the mouse on the file marked – 'draft notice of initiation of the investigation', copied it and began modifying the text to suit the detail of this proceeding. By noon the final document was ready. The print icon on the screen was pressed and, minutes later, the final version was in Windsor's hands.

"It's fine by me. Have it published in the Official Journal and then the real game starts," Windsor said with an air of excitement in his voice. Marc went directly to Heidi's office on the way back from Windsor.

"I've got the okay for the notice of initiation. Here's the computer file reference. Send it by e-mail to Luxembourg for printing. Ask for publication on Tuesday next, the fifteenth."

As the new chief investigator returned to his office Rousseau was hard on his heels.

"So, whose ass did you lick to land the role of chief investigator?" he blurted out in a menacing tone. "What the hell age are you anyway? A case like that requires experienced people who know the technology sector…who know how to negotiate, not some upstart who thinks it can be done in a clinical textbook way."

Marc calmly walked to his desk, then turned and said, "Look Jacques I have a day's work to do. So leave my office right now."

"Schuman, watch what you say 'cos we can make it very difficult for you. Technology industries are our territory. We've always handled the sensitive cases around here," Rousseau said, pointing a finger across the desk as if it were a gun. Marc tilted up his head and straightened his shoulders so that he was now staring down at Rousseau. "Okay, so I got this investigation. You can't control everything with your henchman Kotler."

"Just watch it because believe me, we'll shaft you if you make one mistake," he hissed as he made for the door, his index finger still wagging in the air. "One mistake."

Marc slumped in the chair and sighed. "It seems all the

pressure on this one will come from within. Well, I will prove my worth, damn them!"

ON FRIDAY MORNING AN E-MAIL message flashed on the team's computer screens. It was the clarion call to the first team briefing later that morning. It would be a *get-to-know-you* morale-boosting session that would help to build up an *esprit de corps,* the usual drill when it came to difficult cases.

At eleven thirty Marc stood up in the meeting room. "This case is complex," he started off, "Coming as it does when there's a big push to have computers freely available for everybody. The market will grow exponentially by the early part of the next century. The European manufacturers want protection in the form of a duty imposed on the Asian exports. If they don't succeed then it's goodbye to a European computer industry."

Baker raised his hand. "So you're talking protection. Preventing competition?"

"These terms are emotive. I have an open mind. We do the investigation and then draw conclusions. Clear?" He again paused briefly to let his words sink in.

"Okay. That's just one side of the coin. Any attempt to impose duty on computers and make them more expensive will have a backlash from the consumers groups. They are well organised and will create a storm if the price goes up."

He stopped briefly to look at his notes.

"And remember, the big American and Asian manufacturers wield a lot of economic power. They'll lobby Member States governments hard and orchestrate pressure campaigns by encouraging consumers to speak out against higher prices."

He paused to take a drink from the glass of water.

"For the record, it's not my style to stitch up a result to suit the politicians and keep a cosy cartel for the Europeans. We'll draw conclusions on the basis of the facts. If pressure comes on, there may be a temptation to interpret the figures differently. You all know that from previous investigations. We just keep our heads and, above all else, we talk to nobody about how the case is progressing. You know how leaky this organisation can be at times."

"Everything by the book?" Baker asked.

"Yes. Facts and facts alone…" The chief investigator's voice trailed off.

"Are you saying that if we turn up squeaky clean prices from the Far East we close the case then?" Baker continued to probe.

"Yes, that's the way it's going to be as far as I am concerned."

"And?"

"And what?"

"And what if the people upstairs don't like it and start twisting arms?"

"Look, it's a sensitive case. That's no secret. But as long as I'm chief investigator everything will be done by the book all the way to the end. We have to be able to stand over our work whether before the Commissioner or a court of law in Luxembourg."

Baker pursued the point. "Look, I'm around here long enough now to know that we investigators have a wide margin of discretion. Interpretation, judgement, call it what you will. Putting a spin on weak facts to suit the occasion."

"The rules are the rules and we are sticking by them. Is that clear? Any grey areas of interpretation are to be left to me alone."

Schmidt had a question.

"I know I'm relatively new around here but sometimes I hear the seasoned investigators talking. They say things like a duty is a weapon to use in the international trade game. That doesn't sound like the language you use to describe something that's supposed to be fair. Is it?"

"That's just in-house jargon. It shouldn't be taken literally."

And then Henkel started.

"But has nobody asked why the Asians are selling cheaper computers? I'll tell you why. Because the prices of memory chips and microprocessors inside the computers are falling. The Asians get their hands on these things earlier and immediately reduce prices."

"Well that's something for the investigation. We won't pre-empt anything at this stage. I want to move on to the housekeeping, so to speak. Firstly, we will attempt to cut down on paper as much as possible. Notices of meetings and all reporting among the team will be by e-mail. Information from exporters and the European industry will have to be on computer tape or micro disk. Absolutely essential that we do not accept any hard copy information…except brochures, technical specifications. Otherwise they'll kill us with paper and we'll lose control."

Heads nodded in agreement. Marc had set the tone. It was an appropriate time to bring the meeting to a close.

AN HOUR BEFORE the routine partners' meeting, Verbiest stuck his nose through Saatchi's door. It was an unusual visit as partners watched their own patch and left discussion to the management meetings or the issues-of-principle meetings. And it was a long-standing rule of the partnership that any business decision or arrangement had to have the full agreement of all the partners. They had signed up to the idea that cosy little deals behind closed doors by one or two partners, were definitely off limits.

What was troubling Verbiest's mind was not for discussion in open forum but he had the feeling that he could go towards the limit with Saatchi. After twenty years of working together he knew his *modus operandi*. Verbiest felt that the Italian understood how the big bad world worked.

"Lorenzo have you got a moment?"

"Yes, yes come in."

Closing the door he walked towards the chair in front of Saatchi's desk.

"Problem to chew on. I'm in a difficult situation with the American client, you know Falcon Tech."

Saatchi leaned back on the chair and grinned. "Well, Erik, you've often heard me say that we're not just lawyers here. We run a business. That means giving the client a solution for every problem. Now sit down and let's hear it!"

Verbiest reran the details of the meeting in Hong Kong

explaining that they were turning up the heat. Saatchi smirked. "But you gave them the best advice available at the time."

"They don't think so. They're talking about suing if I don't make it harmless."

"Shit - suing the firm? It would have to be heard in a Belgian court. I'm damn sure they would lose."

Verbiest ventured a rare display of honesty admitting that he may have underestimated the repercussions. "Maybe it was bad advice to set up in China. The Bureau will hang tough, especially if they believe that Falcon Tech is using children in those village set-ups to assemble parts. A lot of emotional heartstrings will be pulled. You see that allegation is stitched into the formal complaint. The Europeans are alleging that they are even using the *laogai* to assemble the printed circuit boards."

Saatchi sat straight up in the chair. "The forced labour camps for dissidents who don't toe the party line. Hmm...a really powerful allegation."

"But it's not true in FT's case. At least that's what they tell me."

"Have we any leverage here?"

"Leverage?"

"Do the boys in the Bureau owe us any favours that we can call in?"

"Maybe but we haven't got time to pursue anything like that 'cause Batista wants results right away. He says we've got to deliver on the five-million-dollar fees we've bagged so far. The whole pressure is coming from the stock launch. While they know it's very serious I don't think they know that it spells disaster in Europe."

Saatchi rocked back in the chair. "Erik this is more than a knotty problem - it's a crock of shit."

"It sure is and that crock's going to be stirred up pretty fast and land right at our noses."

Saatchi started to play with a paper clip. "I don't know what to suggest. Just let me think...are they absolutely results-driven? Eh, you know what I mean...end justifies the means?"

"I would say so. All they talk of is bottom line this...bottom line that. Lindell and Newman are in for something close to one hundred million dollars each when the company launches on Wall Street. Batista gets some kind of bonus on top of that."

"Worth fighting for. Let's think this one out. What's the last thing they would want to happen on the eve of a flotation?"

"Some kind of uncertainty about profitability?"

Saatchi flicked the paper clip across the room. "Legal proceedings. It would ruin a stock launch. They would have to disclose it in the prospectus…contingency over a court case. It would scare the institutional investors."

Verbiest rubbed his chin. "You know something, you're right."

"So, the court case is a non runner. I'm sure of it. They're bluffing. Next thing is how can we help them with this little problem?"

Verbiest moved closer to the desk. "Well, strictly between ourselves, I talked to Wong in Hong Kong. He's on for trying a bit of shady stuff…said it worked before with some of the American and Canadian cases. So I phoned Batista in San Jose this morning and filled him in on the alternative solution, so to speak. He seemed strangely receptive to the idea. Said he'd think about it. A total contrast to Hong Kong last week."

"Sounds very interesting. Roll it out and I'll see what I think of it."

Verbiest sketched out the Wong scenario. When he finished Saatchi laughed loudly and tapped the table with his fingers.

"Ingenious."

The Belgian smiled. "I thought you'd like it. What d'you think? Wong's idea is just brilliant, isn't it? Apparently he has friends in the Triads willing to do the sleazy work." He paused for a moment. And then continued, "…for a fee, of course."

Saatchi guffawed. "In that case they must be lawyers."

"The tactics are similar."

"Amusing."

"Listen Lorenzo, if it works Falcon Tech could keep marching until it has sixty or seventy per cent of the market in Europe."

"You know, this is not much different from the solution to the cartel problem in the eighties really. When the Commission was going gung-ho on busting the big European cartels, we just had to play along. There was nothing we could tell the clients...certainly not legally anyway but other little tricks worked just as well. When some of the big European monopolies had to open up their national markets - at least on paper - strategies were devised. Indirect ways of holding on to markets. Detective agencies just got the dirt on port managers and owners of shipping companies. Sordid stuff like cheating on their wives. Then these guys used it as leverage to block trade. It was just as effective."

Verbiest got up and walked over to the window. He rubbed his chin with his right hand and muttered, "interesting". He turned around, retraced his steps and sat on the edge of the desk, his voice now down to a whisper. "If we go down that road it throws up another problem."

"I don't quite follow."

"You see, if I play along I'll have to get Harrison out of the way. I can't afford to take a risk that she will find out."

"Erik, I definitely can't take her. Throw her back to Petersson. Tell him she'd done all she can on the trade side. Make it sound convincing by giving him the old career development bullshit thing."

"No, he'd kill me. I've played that card once too often." Verbiest grinned and then continued. "Especially not after that fast one I pulled by holding on to her. Besides Knightley's also fed up with my poaching. Even I know that there's a limit."

"Throw her another client or two. Give her some complicated trans-frontier taxation issue that'll keep her tied up for months."

"That's the problem Lorenzo. My department's so efficient there's nothing like that around at the moment. No...if I move her off the case now she'll know there's something going on. After all she's been to Hong Kong and seen round one with the Falcon Tech boys. Harrison knows they're starting to box below the belt. Believe me it wasn't exactly a tea party over there."

Saatchi stretched his arms in the air and then quickly pulled them down to stifle a yawn. He began to tap the edge of the desk. "You've got me, Erik. I can't think of anything."

Verbiest's body tilted further towards the Italian, his palms pressed against the surface of the desk. "Hmm. I was…" He hesitated for a moment and then started off again. "I was thinking… you see, I was thinking what if…"

"What if 'what'?"

"What if she were to be absent for a few months."

"You're talking unpaid leave? Knightley won't buy that."

"No, no Lorenzo." He slid off the desk and came around close to Saatchi's chair.

"What if Harrison were to have an 'accident'." He wiggled his index fingers in the air when he said the word accident. Saatchi drew back in affected horror.

"An 'accident'." He paused and then mimicked Verbiest's finger gesticulation.

"An accident? You're serious."

"I've just said what if…just an idea."

Saatchi's disbelief melted. "You *are* serious, like a car accident?"

"Well, maybe not quite a car accident…something that would put her out of action for a few months. Now that she's lured the Americans I don't really need her anymore. I figured if Wong's friends were going to provide a service, they might as well provide the full service, in a manner of speaking. I'm sure the Oriental could come up with some ideas."

Saatchi threw a fake punch in Verbiest's direction. "*Verbiest,* twenty years of working with you and I never knew you were so Machiavellian."

"Twenty years of watching you in practice," he retorted. "Something's bound to rub off eventually, you know."

Saatchi leaned back and grinned broadly. "I would never be so devious…never."

San José

THE MEETING AT THE FALCON TECH headquarters one week later did not last long. Lindell and Newman arrived at San Francisco Airport in the afternoon and took a taxi directly to the office.

Batista outlined the problem as he saw it. He told them about Verbiest's phone call and confirmed that the Brussels lawyer had assured him that the Trade Bureau would not accept price undertakings from manufacturers in China because they were too easy to circumvent.

"So, what's his alternative solution that you mentioned?" Lindell asked.

"Well Verbiest said that Wong apparently knows some guys in Hong Kong that have influenced investigators by catching them in a compromising position...he's talking leverage."

"No way. It's a crackpot scheme. That asshole, Verbiest will have to come up with something realistic," Lindell snorted.

"We're not exactly in a strong bargaining position. Verbiest says it could get the duty down to under ten per cent. A special outfit can handle it with no connection to anyone around this table."

Newman's ears pricked up. Something like this could help. "But where's the downside? There's got to be a downside."

"The risk is negligible according to Verbiest. The organisation in Hong Kong takes care of everything."

Newman rubbed his chin. "You mean clean and neat?"

"That's what he said. Straight and simple."

"What do you say Dylan?"

"We're caught between a rock and a hard place. That goddamn visit from the Village Committee doesn't help either. They'll screw us if we try to move. Practically every clause of that agreement is in their favour. Commitments about employing people for years. We would end up writing off every cent."

"Yeah," Batista muttered in support. "Two hundred, maybe three hundred million dollars in compensation. We could kiss goodbye to the stock launch. And anyway we'd never get started again."

"Either way," Newman said. "Kimble-Sinclair will have our heads on a platter unless we can make this duty thing harmless."

"So let's clarify all of this again," Lindell urged.

Batista replayed the conversation with Verbiest. Finally he

said, "it may keep us on target for the launch. After all, that's still the immediate prize."

"You could be right, Albert. We must hold the European market at all costs. It's the icing on the cake for Wall Street. What do you say Tom?"

"Well, if we can't cut a deal to get out of China it's probably the only thing left."

"Right," Batista said. "We've got to neutralise this duty thing. Anyway it's only some daft European thing to protect a few small computer companies."

Newman threw a document onto the table, frustrated. "If we don't it's our necks that are on the line...our goddamm necks. We just can't let something like this get in the way."

Batista walked towards the window and then spun around, a finger wagging in the air. "Dead right. That scheme may be our only way out of this mess. If we decide to run with it, I want everything watertight. We'll send Verbiest to Hong Kong to check out how it might work...stuff we know nothing about. We'll need to cover our asses real good."

Lindell and Newman nodded as he continued, "Not one word of this conversation is to be shared with anyone. Is that clear?"

"Absolutely," echoed around the room.

March 1999
Hong Kong
VERBIEST FURTIVELY GLANCED up and down Shanghai Street. He went inside and, as instructed, took the lift to the sixth floor offices of the Great Wall Street Investment Corporation. The door opened and the receptionist greeted him. "Mr. Cheng is expecting you. Go right through."

Wong was already seated at a table. He introduced Verbiest at a distance and beckoned him towards the table. Verbiest sat down, looking distinctly uncomfortable. He started off in a low whisper.

"Batista phoned me last Friday. Seems they're willing to run with plan B, so to speak but they're paranoid about secrecy etc.

I must be assured of complete confidentiality. There are risks in this for all of us."

Wong straightened himself up and nodded towards Cheng.

"Be assured Mr. Verbiest. Mr. Cheng is a lodge father in the most secret society in the world. Its tentacles reach far and wide but leave no trace…nothing to incriminate clients."

"We know what you want is different," Cheng said. "I understand you have an American client but it's not a white powder job."

"I don't follow you."

Wong smirked. "Mr. Cheng means drugs. Heroin."

Verbiest acknowledged the clarification and then outlined the complicated trade problem that his client was facing. Finally he said, "Mr. Wong told me that your organisation might be able to help with a little leverage. Basically it would help if the Trade Bureau investigators saw it our way…if they were persuaded to use their discretion and judgement."

Cheng listened intently. "Yes, indeed," he responded.

"These investigators," Verbiest said, "…eh well you see, they get a tax-free salary and tax-free car and all that jazz. Why, they even get tax-free alcohol and cigarettes. They're very smug and comfortable, not easily lured by extra money."

"Everyone has a price. A million dollars could still be very tempting."

Wong smiled. "Indeed but just in case, we need something more persuasive…the ultimate incentive."

Verbiest readily agreed. "It's true money may not work but it's worth trying. As Mr. Wong says we need something with a bit of emotional anguish attached."

"That's no problem. Mr. Wong knows our record. Isn't that so?"

"Haven't had a complaint from a single client."

Verbiest relaxed a little as they started discussing details. Cheng liked to know everything. Particularly how the system worked. He asked detailed questions about the investigations. How many investigators? Do they visit the factories or just the head offices? And the type of hotels they stay in? Verbiest had accompanied Trade Bureau investigators around the Far East for fifteen years. He knew the routine well.

Cheng lit another cigarette and exhaled a plume of smoke. "This is straightforward. There's just one thing. The negotiation with the investigators in Brussels. That will be tough. I have a proposal to make. Why don't we engage a few free lance guys, say ex-CIA to handle that end?"

"CIA?" Verbiest asked, puzzled.

"Yes CIA for three reasons basically."

"I'm listening," Verbiest said.

In a few sentences Cheng outlined that these operatives are burly, intimidating types but nevertheless highly trained with several languages and a knowledge of bureaucracies. "Our operatives are mostly coolies," he said. "They would be too conspicuous. They're better for the background work."

"Where do you pick these guys up?" Verbiest asked incredulously.

Cheng assured him that the organisation had good relations with the CIA since the days of the Vietnam War. "Besides," he said, "they would be doing a favour for an American company."

"I see," Verbiest acknowledged.

"We have a list of 'friendly' operatives who are doing a bit of freelancing now that the Soviet threat has diminished. A phone call will reactivate them. Anyway most of them crave to be back in the game."

Verbiest was impressed by Cheng's approach. He signalled agreement by pressing his fingers and thumbs together, a gesture to emphasise a closed loop. "The main thing is secrecy. Incidentally I have some details that could already be useful. Chief investigator's a guy called Schuman. Marc Schuman… six, maybe seven years, in the Trade Bureau…thirty-four years of age…doctorate in law. Very sharp investigator with an excellent reputation inside the Bureau. Seen as a rising star and our lawyers who dealt with him consider him straight, very fair."

"Leave it with me," Cheng said confidently. "I'll send down my ops from Amsterdam. Study him up close to get the full picture."

Verbiest's confidence in the Triad operation was growing by

the minute. "There's just one thing I'd like to mention before we finish."

"Let's hear it, Mr. Verbiest."

"Things could get quite complicated with something like this. You see my associate back in our office, Harrison, could get in the way. She's very sharp. The whole thing would run smoother if she were…"

"I'm listening Mr. Verbiest."

"Well I mean delicate affairs like this are better handled by one person. I don't want anybody looking over my shoulder."

Wong's eyes sparkled with excitement. "So what have you got in mind?"

"Well if she were to be away from the office for a few months…"

The Supreme Lodge Father slid deeper into the chair, his eyes cold and calculating.

"Leave it in my hands," Cheng said. "Not another word needs to be said."

Verbiest stood up and made for the door. Wong sprang to his feet and accompanied him to the lift.

"You can count on Cheng. His activities can never be traced."

"I hope you're right."

"Be assured on that score. Now have a safe trip back to Brussels."

WHEN VERBIEST WAS SAFELY off the premises Wong rejoined Cheng in the office. He stared through the window towards the horizon. "Greed's a wonderful quality in a human being."

"Yes indeed, and our friend's got plenty of it," Cheng mused. "He's prepared to live on the edge to keep that client."

"It was good to get him over here. Best to lock him in early in case he goes soft when things get hot. The Shenzhen meeting obviously went very well."

"Indeed. The Village Committee handled it perfectly. It made them focus on the real choices. Now they understand how much Beijing values them and how it does not want to lose them. Lindell pushed hard to open up the Chinese market. Naturally the Committee offered help. Woo will work at the plant free of charge. He knows the ways of Beijing. Doors will eventually open…the right kind of doors," Cheng confirmed.

"I want some 438-ers active straight away."

Cheng leaned forward. "The Hong Kong branch is ready when you give the signal."

"If we can fix this trade problem for our friends in Shenzhen it will prove our credentials to Beijing by keeping a technology company in China. So I need smart operatives."

"I suggest Zhang and Ling, our recently recruited brothers. Educated in America and very eager to prove their ability and, above all, their loyalty."

The Supreme Lodge Father stood up and walked towards the window. He watched as a junk, its sails billowing, drew near to the Tsing Ma, the world's largest suspension bridge.

"We must have the right electronics capability for this assignment."

"Our new recruits are engineers."

"Perfect."

"Cash Mr. Wong? When can we expect some money? Our 49-ers are just working for the honour of Hung-Triad at the moment. This Lodge is now broke after the bust by Customs on the Laos shipment."

"You'll get an advance once the first assignment is executed. I'm sure the client must see results before he pays up. As soon as I give the green light our operatives have to move with the speed of light. Is that clear?"

"Everything will be ready. Hung-Triad honour, Mr. Wong. Nothing less."

Chapter Nine

June 1999
Brussels
INTERNATIONAL TRADE INVESTIGATIONS have to respect the protocol game. Two weeks before departure the Bureau issued diplomatic letters to the embassies of the Asian countries informing of the imminent arrival of European investigators. It was a routine precaution to minimise the risk of a diplomatic incident.

Marc planned to investigate five companies, starting in South Korea and working down along the Pacific Rim taking in Hong Kong, Thailand and Malaysia. Investigation of the remaining eleven exporters would be done by the other four investigators. His assistant was Carlos Montorro, a Spaniard with a pencil moustache, stocky frame, a permanent tan and the computer wizard for the case.

The frenzied activity of the past six weeks was coming to a climax. Everything now awaited the final act - verification in the industrial heartlands of Asia. Montorro came into Marc's office.

"The figures have been treble checked."

"So all the difficult questions are ready?"

He waved a micro disk in the air. "Our intelligence is here and the lap top is ready to roll. It'll be fun watching our Eastern friends come up with answers."

"You know Carlos this is the part where you get the buzz. We'll put them under pressure. So what are we waiting for?"

"Nothing apart from packing our bags, I suppose."

Hong Kong
"WELCOME TO HONG KONG, the capitalist enclave of Asia," Verbiest said with a smile as he pulled a handkerchief from his trousers pocket to wipe the perspiration from his face and proceeded to introduce the two investigators to Lindell.

"So, how was the flight?" Lindell asked.

"Fine. No problems," Montorro answered.

Verbiest told the investigators that he had booked a table at a traditional Cantonese restaurant downtown and, while acknowledging that it was late in the evening, asked if they could join them for dinner. Montorro shrugged, shooting a nod of agreement towards Marc.

They took the new motorway towards downtown Hong Kong and, after crawling through the evening traffic for almost an hour, arrived at the Sheraton. The check-in formalities were completed quickly and the bellhop carried the luggage upstairs. Half an hour later they were taken to the Red Bamboo. Wong and Batista were already seated at a table. Newman nodded towards the Oriental and then introduced the Europeans. "Mr. Wong is our lawyer for Chinese and Hong Kong affairs. Maybe you have dealt with him in Brussels."

They shook hands. Wong smiled, raised his right hand to get Newman's attention and said, "No, they would not know me. I've only dealt with some US and Canadian trade cases…and an Australian one but," he added, "of course, I'm always willing to learn the ways of the Europeans."

Batista interjected, "Believe me, Mr. Wong, we Americans have not learned the ways of the Europeans and you won't either."

"Oh…," Wong cautioned, then paused for effect. "Oh Mr. Batista, I would not quite say that. We have a lot in common. Chinese and European civilisations go back a long way. A very long way. You see, America is young and …well…still virginal."

Wong's trying to ease the tension, trying to be the genial host in his town, Verbiest thought. The European investigators chose to make no comment. Marc scanned the menu finally deciding on fish. It was now late in the evening and a heavy meal did not appeal to him.

"So who's for an aperitif?" Verbiest asked as he started off about the changes now occurring around them in Hong Kong. White wine was chosen and glasses were filled. Lindell raised his glass in the air to get attention. "Here's to a good outcome in this messy trade thing."

Marc and Montorro did not rise to the bait. Instead they

slowly sipped the wine. "Beijing's committed to keeping Hong Kong firmly capitalist." Wong interjected in an attempt to deflect the conversation away from the investigation. And then, without warning, Batista set the tone for the evening, cutting straight to the heart of the issue.

"There's no point in being capitalist if we can't export our products. We've got very lean operations in China and Hong Kong with tight control of costs, and look what's happening." He stared at Schuman. "We don't want to be penalised for efficiency just to protect those European manufacturers. This so-called trade investigation is flying in the face of world free trade."

Wong winced. This was a bad opening line especially before the investigation even got under way. These occasions were always billed as 'get-to-know-you-sessions'. Irritating the investigators was not a part of the game plan. He had an understanding with the FT people that a softly, softly, schmoozing approach was the order of the day. *Play the game so that nobody loses. At least, not immediately. No arguments, especially over dinner. Polite conversation about anything but the case in hand. Politics. The future of Hong Kong. Currency crises. Butter them up and send them home happy. Anything short of that could jeopardise the end game. Batista, the hot-head, must be controlled.*

Wong caught Verbiest's eye, sending him a coded message. A furtive movement of the eyebrows was the signal to take control of the situation. Verbiest seemed uneasy, sensing too that things were about to go belly up. But before he could speak Marc interjected.

"Gentlemen, this is a legal proceeding. The investigation is done in line with international law...rules that all the major trading blocs have signed up to, including the US."

He threw a glance in Verbiest's direction and then shot the next comment down the table towards him. "It's covered by the World Trade Organization's rules." And then his eyes riveted Batista's. "I'm sure Mr. Verbiest has explained that many times."

Confrontation was welling up. It was time to do something

about it. The end game was going straight down the toilet if the sniping continued. Verbiest coughed to deflect attention. "I think we should leave the investigation until tomorrow. Let's enjoy the evening. Taste some exotic cuisine and…relax. There's plenty of time over the coming days to argue the philosophical issues and-"

"Erik, the point needs making. This case is about protecting inefficiency and state-of-the-ark technology."

"Yes, Albert. We've already made those arguments in a formal submission. And we can make them again direct to the European manufacturers at the confrontation meeting in Brussels later. There's plenty of time yet for rebuttal."

Wong caught Batista's attention. He made a gesture as if to say 'let me handle this'.

"Hong Kong has much to offer the tourist. Perhaps we can make some time for a small sightseeing tour later in the week, say, when the investigation work is finished. We could take you by the old funicular railway to the Peak for a view of the city. It's spectacular…unforgettable really. Or even a trip on a junk around the Harbour."

"Thank you. That would be pleasant if we can find the time," Montorro responded, reciprocating the spirit of the offer.

Wong's smile was gracious. "So, let's order now. I can tell you a little about the history of Hong Kong while we wait for the best that Chinese cooking has to offer."

Everybody was in agreement, at least for now. Batista glowered but the tension eased a little. The Oriental lawyer settled into his genial host mode, recounting his favourite anecdotes about Hong Kong and the peoples of the mainland. A *pot pourri* of Chinese history over the dynasties. Dining was over by eleven thirty. When the coffee cups were drained the two investigators thanked the hosts and excused themselves.

"I will collect you at eight fifteen and we will drive out to Tai Po," Verbiest said as he stood up to walk the guests to a taxi.

When they were safely on their way back to the hotel he returned to the table.

"Albert you have to understand how these investigations

work," Verbiest said as he sat down. "The rules are the rules. They are carrying out an investigation. There's really no place at this stage for philosophical arguments. We should treat them nicely. Remember they don't owe us anything. And maybe they'll let a figure fall the right way. Margin of discretion and all that kind of thing."

Wong backed him up. "Look, there's a lot at stake. We all want this plan to work. If you antagonise Schuman it could ruin everything."

Batista looked across at Newman. "Okay Tom, you and Dylan do all the liaising with these guys from now on."

Newman nodded. "That's probably in our best interest."

"Mr. Batista," Wong said. "Let's just deal with this very calmly from here on. Nobody gets a bonus if you have a flaring row with those guys. You'll be the loser in the long run. Treat it as a game for the present." Wong now gritted his teeth. "And the ideal outcome is a win-win for everyone." And then grinned. "...Apart from the European manufacturers."

Batista exhaled a sigh of acceptance. "Okay. But the Europeans are not going to fuck with us. The flotation is going ahead next year. No bunch of neanderthal computer companies is going to mess up the launch. Is that clear?"

"Yes Albert," Verbiest replied. Wong's acknowledgement came as an imperceptible bow of the head.

FIVE DAYS OF INTENSIVE investigation out in the Tai Po Industrial Estate followed. The offices were buzzing by nine and activity didn't slow until late in the evening. Most of the time was spent combing through accounts and poring over documentation. The contentious issues mainly revolved around deferred discounts and adjustments for technical differences of Falcon Tech's computers compared to the European manufacturers' models. Endless documents and computer printouts were heaped in piles on the boardroom table with the heavier binders strewn on the floor.

With no air conditioning in the building, the boardroom invariably became a steamy cauldron of humidity by early afternoon, creating beads of perspiration from head to toe. Wong was on standby in his downtown office. Verbiest hung around waiting to be consulted, playing the consummate lawyer role. He made it clear he was not an accountant - not a figures man. The complicated transactions in the accounts of the company were for the FT people. He would not, therefore, be sucked into the eye of the storm. He would only argue on issues of principle - legal issues.

Batista stayed away from the frenetic activity, allowing everything to run smoothly. By the final day, the boardroom was awash with paper and everybody was in compromising mood, making agreement on the last few outstanding issues easier. A final trawl through the bank records turned up a document with Chinese characters on it. Marc asked for an interpretation. Lau, the accountant, gave a vague reply that it related to transport costs from the factory in Shenzhen province to Tai Po in the New Territories. Marc scrutinised the characters, putting his evening course in Mandarin at the Free University of Brussels to good use. He had a hunch and continued to probe. It could not relate to transport costs. And finally the admission came that it was under-the-counter commissions to export trading houses in Hong Kong. Marc was happy. He had found something they were trying to hide. And it meant another two per cent duty on Falcon Tech's computers.

"So," Newman said, "You never mentioned that you could read Chinese."

"I can decipher many things," Marc replied with a grin. "Especially when someone tries to tell me differently."

Newman let it pass.

"That about wraps it up. Thank you again for your cooperation. And also the kind hospitality."

"I hope you enjoyed your brief stay in Hong Kong," Newman said.

They said their farewells and accepted Verbiest's offer to drive them back to Chek Lap Kok airport.

Bangkok

IT WAS NOW WEEK THREE of the investigation. Before arriving in Hong Kong they had finished a five-day investigation at Wantoe Electronics in Seoul. It had gone well. In traditional Korean style the management was anxious to please; every question was answered, every doubt dispelled. It was their way of doing business. And the social side was also well organised. Evenings were spent high up in the hills above Seoul, seated on a restaurant floor, savouring kimshi and other exotic dishes in time-honoured Korean tradition.

Visits to companies in Thailand and Malaysia remained. The Thai Airlines 737 landed smoothly at Bangkok's Don Muang Airport and taxied across the apron to Gate 22. The two investigators headed for the carousel, picked up their luggage and cleared Customs and Immigration without delay. They slumped into the back seat of the air-conditioned Lakoo Computers limousine, happy to take refuge from the sticky heat and were shepherded away like VIP's direct to the Holiday Inn. Even though the sun had set, the temperature hovered above the nineties, the humidity oppressive. As the driver edged his way through the heavily congested streets Marc gazed out through the window in silence. He was looking forward to seeing the street life of Bangkok again.

The same investigation routine was applied at Lakoo Computers making it a straightforward verification. Larry Ellison, a stocky American lawyer represented the company. He said very little. In fact he was adrift when it came to the international trade scene. Marc figured that the Thai company had felt that they should have some legal representation at the investigation. And so they called in a hot shot corporate lawyer from New York. More to do with image than substance. Ellison spent his time stretching his braces in a lawyerly sort of way, grabbing them and pulling down and out and then gently letting the elastic draw his hands back to his chest. He looked pompous and bloated and he irritated Marc. But the investigation was going as planned leaving no reason to become entangled in argument with the East Coast lawman.

After the first day Marc turned to Mr. Kanjana, the manager

of the Thai company, and said, "Tomorrow we'll need to check a random selection of your sales invoices to customers in both Thailand and Europe. And, of course, the bank statements."

"We will have everything ready for you in the morning," the Thai said.

Marc stood up, stuffed the files into his briefcase and moved around the table. As they shook hands Kanjana said, "We invite you to explore our beautiful city this evening."

"Thank you Mr. Kanjana."

"We have the company car pick you up at eight o' clock."

As they walked out of the boardroom Ellison came across the room, handed his card to Marc and said, "We handle a lot of Fortune 500 corporations, mostly restructuring and takeovers."

Marc took the card, briefly studied it and said, "Huh, very interesting."

Half an hour later they were back at their hotel. Later that evening, the company car from Lakoo Computers arrived. The hotel porter opened the door and the investigators climbed into the back seat. The driver sped off down the ramp and out onto the main thoroughfare. A few minutes later they were alongside the Chao Phya river. The car pulled up and the driver pointed towards Kanjana who was standing on a jetty wearing a colourful patterned shirt and cream coloured slacks.

"Good evening, Mr. Kanjana."

"Nice of you to come. We bring you on a sampan along the klong," he said pointing to the tiny craft moored to the jetty. "Come down this way to board."

"The klong, Mr. Kanjana. What's that?" Montorro asked.

"I think you call them canals. I go to Holland five or six times a year on business. They have klongs there too but smaller. Just be careful. Watch the step."

They boarded the sampan. "Where are our oars? Do we have to row?" Marc joked.

"No oars. Look we've got outboard motor." Mr Kanjana took up his position at the back and tilted the handle to control the rudder. The craft eased away from the jetty as he dipped the propellor into the water. They entered a world unseen from the road as he guided the sampan along the water.

"You like our transport system?"

"Very impressive," the Spaniard shouted from the bow. Kanjana guided the flat-bottomed sampan under overhanging branches along a narrow stretch of water. And then he eased it out into the centre, picking up speed. They passed a line of teak homes built on stilts, a necessary precaution, the host explained, against the ravages of the monsoon season. Two women were stooped precariously over the edge of a makeshift jetty washing clothes. A short distance away, small children waved from the window of a house while others jumped into the water and splashed about as the sampan approached, delighted at the attention from the passers-by.

Kanjana continued to talk proudly about his city and the waterways as they glided through the still, muggy air. Further along the waterway several roofed boats were moored to wooden poles on the bank. As their sampan sailed by, an old lady waved and the waft of spicy cooking drifted across their path. Kanjana accelerated away from the boats leaving a trail of blue smoke and skimmed the surface for another five minutes in silence. He turned into a broader expanse of water where small craft zig-zagged their way between the big rice barges queuing up to off load their cargo. And now the wash from water-buses, as they sped past, rocked the sampan.

"Don't worry. It can survive bigger waves than that!" he joked.

He was now standing up like a true captain as the tiny engine spluttered along with the aid of the current.

"Mr. Schuman, I hope you will not push us out of the European market. We sell all our computers at a fair price. Bear in mind that we are a small company. If our European importers have to pay duty of ten per cent they will not survive in the market place. It's different for those big Korean exporters. You should help the small companies."

"Mr. Kanjana, we cannot give special treatment. We must treat every producer fairly. We will review all the information back in Brussels and then decide on the basis of the evidence."

"We want to stay in business. We need the European market to survive. Please remember that when you get back to Brussels."

Marc was sympathetic but had to be impartial. "I can assure you, Mr. Kanjana, we will give you a fair hearing."

Kanjana sat down again and steered the sampan towards a big river boat moored to enormous teak beams. He tied up the craft and helped his guests onto the gangway.

"And now, gentlemen, this is what the French call the *pièce de resistance. Sanuk* (pleasure) all the way."

The riverboat moved away from the jetty and glided down river. Kanjana played the consummate host for the next three hours. As dusk fell, he pulled down the shutters and amused them with stories of the traditions and culture of Thailand.

The investigators were happy to listen. And to their relief he did not stray onto trade issues making it indeed *sanuk* all the way. By midnight the big riverboat had edged its way back up river and slowly came alongside the jetty.

"Thank you very much, Mr. Kanjana. It was very enjoyable." The Thai bowed and pointed towards the waiting taxi.

WEDNESDAY WAS THE WRAP-UP DAY at the company. The margin of difference between the export prices and the local sales prices on the Thai market averaged around thirty per cent. Differentials of that magnitude would make a good duty penalty. By five pm briefcases were packed with enough evidence in case of doubt or dispute later.

As arranged, the Europeans were whisked back to their hotel by taxi. It was Montorro's first time in Thailand. He was curious about Bangkok's reputation as the nightlife capital of the world. He wanted to experience it firsthand, he declared to Marc several times. Marc agreed easily, happy to go along with his wishes. They were becoming tired of living out of suitcases and making business talk and polite social talk in interminable meetings and over long drawn-out dinners - and they still had to fly to Malaysia in the morning.

They met in the foyer and headed down a street towards the city centre. The evening was humid and sulphurous and a peel of thunder rumbled in the distance. After a few minutes Marc spotted a McDonald's sign. "It beats rice...rice...rice!"

Montorro said. "McDonald's is everywhere now. Probably more outlets than stars in the sky," Marc replied.

After they had finished eating Montorro stood up and declared, "Why don't we go to see some of the night life in the Pat Pong district. It's supposed to be quite unbelievable."

The Pat Pong area consisted of two parallel streets running about three hundred metres in length and lined with bars and massage parlours. Around the clock, traders and tourists mingled in this red light citadel but after dark the streets became particularly congested.

Marc felt relaxed and mellow. "Fine, but we won't stay late. Remember our flight to Kuala Lumpur is at eleven."

"I know. I know." Montorro motioned towards the street and stood up. "Come on, let's take one of those three-wheeled things like James Bond in…oh, I can't remember the name of the film."

"Oh, the trishaw?"

"Yes, whatever! Let's get going."

They left the restaurant and hailed the first three-wheeled taxi that came along.

"Pat Pong's," Montorro shouted above the distinctive 'tuk tuk' sound of the spluttering engine. The driver acknowledged and edged out into the evening traffic. The street was awash with vehicles and the air dense with the pollution of exhaust fumes. The pavements were lined with stalls selling T-Shirts and jewellry. As he manoeuvred through the tangle of chaos, the Europeans sat back and watched the street traders haggling, mostly with Western tourists, about the price of a piece of silk clothing or a Buddha statue. Eventually, the tuk tuk stopped abruptly and the driver turned around in his seat, immediately dishing out cards to his passengers.

"Oriental Delight. Best massage in town," he said, tapping the cards before he handed them over. He lifted his head and grinned as he pointed. "Good for fucky, fucky too. Hundred metre down street on right."

They took the cards. "Is this the Pat Pong area?" Montorro asked.

The driver again pointed towards the side street. "Yes. Pat Pong."

Marc pulled one hundred baht from his wallet and thrust it into his hand.

"That *tuk tuk* is an easy way to get around the busy streets of Bangkok. Strange it never caught on in Europe," Marc laughed, stepping back from the edge of the footpath, and watched as it pulled away.

The neon-lit street throbbed with life. Western couples meandered up and down, occasionally stopping at stalls to look at the Thai silk or gaudy jewellery. Other tourists haggled with pedlars as music blared from the strip bars and brothels. Young Thai girls hung around the doorways, trying to entice unaccom-panied foreigners inside. Someone tugged at Marc's sleeve.

"You want see naked girlie show. Come."

They ignored the boy and continued down the street. For a brief moment Marc thought about the life of that eight-year-old out scouring the streets to drum up business for some perverted godfather lying on a beach far from the seedy nightlife of the city.

"Let's try one of these floor shows," Montorro said eagerly.

"Why not." Marc pointed to a large flashing neon light but Montorro firmly took charge.

"No. Walter Horst told me about the best one. The GI's Good Time Bar. It's a hangover from the Vietnam War days. Let's see if we can find it."

"Sounds okay. What's good enough for Uncle Sam must be good enough for us," he laughed, the words tinged with sarcasm. After another few paces along the street a young Thai girl approached Montorro.

"Two hundred baht, I smoke your cigar."

He threw a glance in Marc's direction, a puzzled crease lining his forehead. Shrugging, he said, "But the problem is, mine is only a cigarette."

They both burst into laughter. Suddenly Montorro shouted, "Look that's it ...there. Right there."

He eagerly pointed to the façade of a wild west saloon, a neon-lit figure of a cowboy with a lasso in his hand strategically mounted above the door. They stood outside the entrance for a few moments, watching the enticing sign flashing on and off. The lights of the lasso pulsed in sequence creating the illusion of the cowboy throwing it out and then reeling back in his prey.

Montorro smirked. "Come on. Let's try it. It kept the GI's happy for ten years."

Marc laughed, tapped Montorro on the shoulder and said, "Lead the way, investigator. Lead the way."

THE WAKE UP CALL shook him out of a deep slumber. He lifted the receiver and immediately let it fall back down on the cradle. He tried to open his eyes but the lids felt heavy, felt as if they were glued together. Eventually a ray of light pierced through and he groaned loudly. He rolled and twisted towards the edge of the bed and his head felt heavy and now slumped over the side. The blood immediately pounded in his brain as the first deep breath was drawn. He turned over, crumpled up the pillow and tried to drift into a sleep but he felt disorientated and strange. Marc crawled out of bed and stood up, his head now throbbing fiercely in a funny way.

He staggered towards the shower and allowed the hot water to cascade over his body. After ten minutes he stepped out and squinted into the mirror. "What a hangover! That damn Thai beer!… Probably some locally-brewed mash made with rice. Never touch the stuff again," he muttered. Towelling off he walked gingerly back into the bedroom.

Hong Kong
THE PHONE RANG in Cheng's office. He took three quick paces towards the desk, lifted the hand piece and listened. The voice started off. "Mr. Cheng, instructions carried out to the letter. Our friend knows how to relax. He likes a beer or two. It made it so easy."

"Good."

"And he'll have a bit of trouble remembering how he got amnesia last night."

A grin broke across Cheng's face. "Excellent work."

He threw the handset onto the cradle, slumped back into the chair and chuckled out loud. Moments later he rose to his feet and made for the door.

"Just a few more pieces of the jigsaw to be put in place," he muttered, as he made his way down Shanghai Street towards Wong's tenth-floor retreat.

"Wong Wing Zu is expecting you. Go right through," the receptionist said, putting family name first and then the given names in the traditional Chinese way.

Hu Hei bowed as he opened the door for Cheng. Wong was staring through the big floor-to-ceiling glass window out over Hong Kong bay, slowly inhaling on a cigarette in his customary fashion.

"It's good news, I take it?"

"Everything went well. We can expect a special delivery tonight from Bangkok."

Wong chuckled to himself almost as a compliment for his good judgement. "So they found Mr. Schuman's weak spot?"

"Yes. His Achilles heel by all accounts. Schuman's commitment to our plan is now written in blood." He reflected for a moment. "Well…well almost in blood. The next best thing, I suppose." His eyes became dark and sinister. A smile lit Wong's face.

"Now that we have our little insurance policy it's time to take care of our man." He leaned forward, pressed the button and said to his secretary, "Call Verbiest. Tell him that the signed and sealed affidavit is arriving from Bangkok tonight. All that remains is to have it delivered."

"So that means we call in our American friends to do the stalking around Brussels."

"Yes but not too fast, Cheng. We need to take it very easy. Gradual pressure built up until he bends…and I mean slowly."

"Yes." Cheng gestured a bending movement with his hands. "Just like a bamboo."

A touch of glee crossed Wong's face. He was enjoying the anticipation. "Yes, just like a bamboo…force it and it breaks. Gentle but constant pressure and it bends nicely. Properly shaped, it has many uses."

"Many uses." Cheng echoed Wong's words.

The Supreme Lodge Father continued to stare through the window. "We can't afford a debacle with this one. With the new attitude of Beijing and the freeing up of the mainland economy we must be ready to give our occidental customers the best service. The full treatment. The kind of treatment they should expect from their Chinese partners."

"Yes. If we do this right it will prove our credentials to Beijing."

Wong's face turned stern again. "Nothing is to go wrong...nothing. Keep in mind that drugs sting with the Australian guy."

"My other lodge fathers remind me often enough," Cheng said and then continued, "I was young then and only learning the methods of the Hung-Triad brotherhood. But now? Now it's different."

"Indeed."

The lodge father was determined to impress Wong. "We'll make no mistakes this time. The best that Langley has to offer. Ideal operatives for the Brussels stalking."

Wong pulled another cigarette from the packet, tapped it against the side of the packet and lit it. "Those Americans know how to play a psychological warfare game." He flicked the match across the room. "And when they've done the job we just throw them to the wolves."

"I've set out the rules of engagement for *them* very clearly."

He moved away from the window. "It's time for action. I want to have more monitors around Schuman than a patient in an intensive care unit. Get Amsterdam to start surveillance as soon as he arrives back in Brussels."

"Certainly."

Wong reflected for a moment. "Yes. Uncle Sam's finest. Ex-CIA operatives doing a *cover-your-ass* job for the brotherhood. Oh, how times have changed."

"Yes, indeed. Changed utterly."

"And for the better too, Cheng. For the better too."

THEY WATCHED HIM for seven days. They knew what he ate, who he met and when he slept. Every little piece of information found its way back to the command centre in that high rise building in Hong Kong. It was studied - digested - and then directions were dispatched back to the operations centre in Amsterdam. After seven days they were happy. They knew their man. He was a creature of habit, they agreed. A prawn cracker in their eyes. Surveillance would be easy. The time was ripe to get the machinery rolling in earnest.

Chapter Ten

AMBIORIX IS a square in name only. A row of three-storey town houses forms a graceful elliptical curve around a small park making it a much sought-after location for twenty-somethings. Laura's apartment, which she shared with Sarah Macpherson - a fun-loving and spontaneous twenty-eight year old who hailed from Scotland - was situated on the second floor overlooking the tranquillity of the park. Sarah was tall, almost statuesque, with long dark hair and spoke with a softly-accented Edinburgh brogue. She was a lobbyist, hustling the European lawmakers to see things her clients' way. Over the years, she had become Laura's best friend and confidante.

Laura left her apartment before eight o' clock to meet Sarah at a gym in the centre of town and spend an hour at a gruelling workout. The twice-a-week ritual was their way of ridding themselves of the stresses and strains that inevitably came with being ambitious associates in leading professional firms.

It took Laura no more than twenty seconds to reach the perimeter of the Park. The evening scent of the roses wafted up to meet her as she entered and then cut diagonally across towards the entrance to the metro station. Suddenly she hit the ground hard, her knees taking most of the impact. Her chin slid along the sandy path, grazing the skin. It stung wildly. Her hands involuntarily shot up to her head in a protective instinct as she tasted the first asphyxiating grains of dust and grit around her lips and up her nose. Dazed and disorientated, her body started to tremble as the beginnings of a dull ache spread out across her shoulder blades.

They had come from behind and she was now face down on the path, totally at their mercy. *The bag,* she thought. *It's money they want.* She tried to release her grip from the straps so that they could take it and go. Her fingers stung as it was pulled away in a sharp movement. And now she felt her watch being yanked from her wrist. Her breathing became more laboured as the dry particles choked her lungs but she dared not move. *They have what they are looking for,* she thought. But it was not over yet. The job would be finished to specification. A powerful blow to her right arm and another from the side to her ribs sent pain shooting around her body. Suddenly the activity above her stopped, an eerie silence descending on the Park. Lying motionless in a twilight of consciousness, she began to recite a familiar prayer.

The emergency services responded to the anonymous phone call. Half an hour later she was lying on a bed in Saint Luc hospital hooked up to monitors and an IV. Visiting hours were long over when Marc arrived shortly before midnight. Sarah had phoned him immediately after the hospital called. He slid onto the only chair beside the bed and took her hand, squeezing it gently. She opened her left eye and immediately started to sob, the tears streaming down her cheeks. He pulled a handkerchief from his pocket and carefully patted them dry. Her face was badly bruised and a line of stitches pulled together a split in her lower lip. Gauze covered her chin and the flesh around her right eye was so swollen her eyelids barely parted. A nurse finished her routine with the only other patient in the ward, walked directly to the head of the bed and began taking Laura's blood pressure and temperature. Laura strained to smile and then she turned her head to watch the nurse squeezing the IV bag suspended from a hook above her. A doctor came into the ward, read the chart at the end of the bed and made a discreet head motion to the nurse. It seemed to convey that everything was fine. He turned and left the room. The nurse popped a white tablet from a vial on the trolley. "This will help you to sleep," she said. When the nurse left Marc moved closer, took her hand again and clasped it between his palms to comfort her. Ten minutes later she drifted into a deep sleep.

SHORTLY BEFORE TEN the following morning Knightley received a phone call from Sarah. He went down to the third floor to put Verbiest in the picture.

"I've...I've got some bad news, Erik. Laura's in Saint Luc.

Apparently she was mugged last night."

"What?" Verbiest gasped as he pulled back from the keyboard, carefully avoiding eye contact with the managing partner.

"Yes, mugged…she's got a broken arm and a few broken ribs."

Verbiest now averted his eyes from the screen and gasped. "Jesus Christ I don't believe it…mugged?"

"Yes, in broad daylight," Knightley said impatiently. "She was pretty messed up when they found her."

"But she's okay now. I mean eh…" Verbiest stuttered but recovered quickly. "I mean is she recovering?"

"Well her friend just gave me the bare details."

He put his hand to his head and then rubbed his forehead. "It's those damn immigrants. I'm telling you Roger, this city…it's gone to hell."

"Yes. It's…pretty bad."

"The sooner every Belgian votes for Vlaams Blok the better. Kick the immigrants out. It's the only way to clean up the place."

Knightley raised his eyebrows in sardonic amusement. The Belgian lawyer was back on his favourite hobby-horse. It was *bash-the-immigrants* time again. He was also an immigrant of sorts but that didn't stop Verbiest when an opportunity to verbally whip those foreigners presented itself. He chose to ignore the racist remarks and, instead, concentrated on the incident in the Park.

Verbiest's eyes refocused on the screen. "Aggravated assault! You know it doesn't damn well surprise me. Those thugs are high on drugs. Look…I'll arrange for flowers and drop out to the hospital this evening. You know something Roger, I'd kill the bastards with my bare hands if I caught them."

Knightley shook his head in dismay. "Indeed. Awful barbarity."

THE CINQUANTENAIRE MONUMENT - the Arc de Triomphe of Brussels - towers above the city's skyline. The landmark symbol - a turn-of-the-century, three-arched monument standing thirty metres high - is situated in nine acres of parkland that stretches from Rond Point Schuman to Avenue de Tervueren, a wide, leafy thoroughfare home to many embassies. The centre section is laid out in large symmetrical flowerbeds and neatly manicured lawns. In summer months, when the sky is blue, it fills with office workers, eager to spend an hour under the midday sun.

Marc's favourite activity was a lunchtime-run. His body was lean and trim - the muscles taut and toned - and he liked to keep it that way. He tried to fit it into his schedule, at least twice a week, and always alone. On Thursday at midday he closed down the computer, grabbed his sports bag and made his way to the shower rooms in the basement. Changing into his running gear, he headed up to street level and out into the sweltering midday sun. Although the thermometer hovered just above twenty-eight, the humidity in the atmosphere made it seem more like forty degrees.

He crossed Avenue de Cortenbergh, heading straight for the north-west entrance to the Park. Immediately inside the entrance a Mosque nestles under a thicket of chestnut trees and had, of late, become the starting point for his exercise routine.

Marc started the usual aerobic warm-up routine, stretching his muscles and breathing deeply before setting off on the four-lap. He had a record to break, a personal best to beat, his spirit now rising to the challenge. Checking his watch, he started in a clockwise direction along the perimeter pathway under the shade of a neat line of chestnut, lime and maple trees, reaching a comfortable pace in a short distance. After twenty minutes the natural adrenaline in his body had begun to take effect. He reached cruising speed, his rhythmic breathing allowing his body to be carried forward in a steady flowing movement of limbs. As he came up to the cobble-stoned section around the museum buildings that flank the imposing monument, his eyes fixed on the fountain that lay straight ahead, metres inside the eastern entrance. To distract attention from the pounding that his feet were now receiving from the unforgiving surface he concentrated on a group of children splashing their feet in the water and frolicking in and out through the fine mist blowing back from the gushing spray. The shrieks of the children faded as he entered the perimeter path again, his thoughts now turning to Laura. She would be at least one month in hospital and maybe another recuperating. Plans for a holiday would have to be put on hold.

Half an hour later he was on the final lap, again facing the Breydel building where all the big European decisions are made. He could see the flags of the fifteen member countries of the European Union hanging limply on their poles. The Union flag - twelve-gold stars in a circle against a blue background, signifying unity and perfection - took up its pre-eminent position in the centre.

In a short few months I'll probably be down there defending my case, he thought, *and pushing so that all my efforts end up in law.* At that moment he felt good about himself; success was within his grasp and, right now, romance and companionship filled his life.

Now on the final leg with about three hundred metres to go, he set a blistering pace towards the Mosque. Glancing at the watch he screeched "yes, yes" and made a gesture of satisfaction with his arm as he shaved seven seconds off his previous best.

Marc slowed for his two-hundred-metre cool-down run up the centre of the Park. He looked straight ahead, watching the black, red and yellow colours of the large Belgian flag fluttering under the centre arch of the stately monument and then slowed to a walk, eventually turning back towards the Mosque, his brain waves in harmony, in synchronisation. His breathing returned to normal and his pulse rate eased back to its normal plateau of sixty beats as he walked to a bench under the shade of the chestnut trees. He closed his eyes, benefiting from the drug-like high leaving him in a very relaxed state. After a few minutes he was conscious that somebody had joined him on the bench. He opened his eyes but didn't take much notice as his gaze momentarily followed a bird pecking at the bark of a maple tree.

"Nice day for jogging," said one of the strangers. "Suppose it's the only way to stay ahead in a competitive world."

"Yeah, not bad," Marc replied.

"Exercise is the only cure for long hours spent in the office. It brings the body back into balance," said the other.

"Yes," he replied, nodding politely but with an uncertain feeling building up inside.

He turned his head to look at them face to face. Four eyes were staring straight ahead through the trees at some point in the distance. He leaned forward to spring to his feet.

"We may have something interesting to say to you. Just sit back down a minute," the man closest said, a sharp edge to his voice.

"What do you mean?"

"Sit back and listen," the other man ordered. The accents sounded American, though Marc could not be sure.

"Do you want to sell me a new pair of Nikes or what?" Marc asked, a touch of levity in the delivery. They ignored the attempt at humour, their eyes still riveted on some point straight in the distance. Something was not right, he could tell.

"Look, we want a few minutes of your time."

Marc obeyed, easing back on the bench. The older man started off, "The name's Schuman. Marc Schuman, we believe?"

Marc turned and looked directly at him. Even though he was sitting he looked tall, probably over six feet, with dark eyes and dark brushed back hair, receding at the temples. It was flecked with grey at the sides, as was the moustache. He was probably over fifty but it was hard to tell with just a glance. Marc's attention turned to the other stranger who, in contrast, was thin and lanky and probably younger. He sat awkwardly on the edge of the bench.

"Why does it matter?" Marc asked.

"Don't play games. We know who you are so we'll cut to the chase. The job you do gives you a lot of power. We're very interested in a particular case you're handling right now. You can become a wealthy man if you were to see things our way."

A knot of tension formed in the pit of Marc's stomach and a surge of blood rushed to his head as his heart began to pound in his chest. He sprang to his feet. Just as quickly the two men were standing.

"Just sit back down please. We're not finished yet," the older man said. Marc glanced from one to the other. The thin guy now took over. "Just listen Schuman. It's very much in your interest. You know success comes in many forms but mostly in the form of cash. In a word we want to cut a deal."

Marc stared straight ahead, refusing to acknowledge the words.

"Look I don't know what the hell you two are driving at," he said, "Whatever you-"

"Calm down. Relax. We'll make it clearer. Just listen," the thin man again demanded.

Marc jerked forward. The heavy man stepped in front of him.

"If it's that important then come to my office."

"Look Schuman, listen carefully. Our client intends to remain a dominant force in the European market. So here's the deal. There's five million dollars waiting for you in a numbered bank account. All you have to do is say yes to make it a win-win for everyone involved."

"Excuse me. I'm leaving."

The taller man pointed directly into Marc's face with his index finger. "Not yet Schuman. Believe us, you have a lot to lose if you walk away. Your own personal reputation is at stake. Take our advice and don't talk to anybody in the Bureau. Think about what we're saying."

"Excuse me. I *am* leaving."

"You ain't leaving until we've finished what we have to say." They again emphasised the money and how vulnerable his reputation would be if he chose to ignore them. The words came in a rush. Marc found it difficult to absorb what was being said but the feeling was sinister. One thing he did understand was the determination with which they spoke. He jerked forward suddenly, the mask of coolness slipping a little.

"Get lost guys," he barked back over his shoulder.

He motioned a gesture with his hand to say that the conversation was over and moved away in the direction of the Mosque. They leaped forward, tailing him.

"Meet us here in the Park at one o' clock tomorrow," the thin man called out.

Who are these people? Who do they represent? Thoughts were swirling around in his head. He swung around. "Who the hell are you?"

"You'll find that out soon enough. Just turn up here tomorrow and we'll fill in the details. The deal so to speak."

They moved away swiftly towards the centre of the Park. Marc watched them for a moment, then turned and made his way out onto Avenue de Cortenbergh. He continued up the Avenue and, when the traffic slowed, weaved his way to the far side. Twenty paces later he was in his office building. He sped downstairs and dashed into the shower. As the water cascaded over his body he stood motionless, his brain in overdrive.

"What the hell was that all about?" He muttered, trying to make sense of what had just happened. "What did they really want? Bribery? Who the hell is behind it?"

He stepped out of the shower, dressed and headed for the lift. As other people entered, the words from the men in the Park echoed loudly in his ears. For a moment he felt that he was being stared at. In an instant, the faces of Kotler and Rousseau flashed across his mind.

That's it - they are trying to set me up, he thought. *Trying to see would I be tempted by whatever they want to dangle in front of me.*

He stepped out at the third floor and walked down the corridor. The tap on the door drew Rousseau's attention from the memo he was reading. Marc leaned in and said with a grin, "Good try guys, but I'm not falling for that stupid prank."

Back in his office, he clicked onto the network and started to review Schmidt's outline of the legal text that would hit the Asian computer companies where it would hurt most - in the pocket. He stared at the screen and decided that when the final law would be published the Court of Justice in Luxembourg would not easily find a flaw in it.

THEIR NAMES WERE Taylor and Johnson. They had worked for more than twenty years with the CIA, mainly in the Far East. When the winds of change blew through the bureaucracy in Langley, after the end of the Cold War, they packed their saddlebags with a fat severance and, turning towards freelancing, they made themselves available for a price.

The re-activation of the informal alliance with the Triad-controlled drug cartel in Asia would prove a fertile new departure for their experience and skills, they were certain. And for the first assignment Cheng advised them to carry a piece for their own safety but he assured them that they were very unlikely to have to use it. "This war," he emphasised, "will be played out on the psychological battlefield."

Twenty minutes after observing Schuman leaving the Park, George Taylor and Chuck Johnson drifted towards the main entrance to the Park and walked one hundred metres to the métro station at Rond Point Schuman. Taylor stood at street level while Johnson descended the steps and walked along the platform to the public telephone mounted on the wall. He inserted a call card and dialled out the number from memory. It was almost 10 p.m., Hong Kong time, when Cheng picked up the receiver. Johnson immediately recognised the Oriental's voice and started off in a businesslike, brusque manner.

"First contact made in Park went as planned. Not receptive as we expected. Held his attention long enough to get message across. Asked him to meet us again tomorrow."

"The Amsterdam cell will increase surveillance," Cheng replied. "The most important thing is not to rush him. Lose him and we lose everything. And our American client will lose out to those arrogant European bureaucrats. Is that clear?"

"Understood."

"I await your next report."

The debriefing had lasted no more than two minutes.

San José

THE DECISION TO HOLD the quarterly meeting at the Falcon Tech headquarters in San Jose was Sinclair's idea. It was important to move out of the Kimble-Sinclair boardroom - be seen to be associated with the cutting edge of technology - he stressed to his fellow board members several times. Sinclair in a hands-on pose, using the latest technology would be a great photo op, an ideal occasion for a bit of pre-launch publicity in an informal context, the kind of profile that money could not buy.

The twenty-one dark suited gentlemen of the K-S board gathered in the testing room looking through the glass walls out onto the factory floor. The assembly lines were silent since production had been moved to Shenzhen six months earlier. A few half-assembled computers lay on the lines and strewn around the floor were obsolete components and cables that didn't meet quality control when production was transferred.

Batista and Lindell came through the door accompanied by a tall, white-haired gentleman in his sixties. Batista introduced him as Alexander Kapling, professor of neuro-computing at UCLA.

Kapling took the floor and talked about the workings of the human brain. Most researchers had focused on EEG signals from the cortex picked up with electrodes placed on the scalp, he explained but these were too smeared by the skull to readily identify their components. Conventional EEG and MRI were simply going nowhere. With his help the Falcon Tech research concentrated on finding a coherent signal source that could be tapped into directly. The breakthrough came with the discovery that the thalamus area of the brain had a much more ordered set of neural signals that could be picked up with laser technology targeted directly on the synapses.

"Hence the Synaptatron," Lindell interjected anxious to keep the demonstration on schedule. "Okay gentlemen this is what you've been waiting for. You've got to put on these white coats before we go onto the floor."

He led them to a corner of the factory where a bunch of T-shirted engineers and programmers, specially flown in from Hong Kong, clustered around a bench fine-tuning the equipment so that the demonstration would be flawless. These whiz kids were tweaking an array of oscilloscopes and complex devices and jabbering on about some very high level programming - fuzzy logic and blind signal separation using algorithms - stuff that went straight over the heads of the sedate East Coast gentlemen. Lindell pulled a trolley containing a computer close to a bench and picked up what looked like a pair of headphones.

"This is what the world has been waiting for. The Synaptatron. It's the essential part of our ThinkEx computer. We've taken out eight patents on the technology in here."

He slipped the Synaptatron over his head and flicked a power button on the computer. The board members stared as the words - Mind over matter - moved across the screen.

"Very simply that's how it works. The Synaptatron picks up the tiny impulses leaving the thalamus, splits the impulses into their components, converts the relevant signal using algorithms and then reconverts. Every household item will operate by brain command in a few years."

Sinclair placed it on his head and looked solemnly at the screen. A full sentence now came up: Kimble-Sinclair leading the way into the twenty-first century.

"Absolutely amazing," he declared.

The other members of the board moved closer, vying like children for the chance to try it. All of them wanted to be the first to experiment with this funny new technology. Jefferson, easily the eldest and longest serving, quickly pulled rank.

"I want to try it now," he snapped.

He grabbed the head set and fumbled with it. The screen filled with his thoughts: Brain power means computer power.

"It's simply unbelievable," he said pulling the Synaptatron from his bald head and handing it to Rendell.

"Indeed," Sinclair responded. "What about security?"

"Specs, algorithms and bill of materials are locked in a safe in my office. I'm the only one with access," Lindell assured the gathering.

Batista teased Rendell light-heartedly as he settled the device on his head. "I'm not sure you should try it George. They say you need a brain to use one of these things."

"Smart ass," Rendell retorted as the other members of the board laughed like schoolboys. One of the group at the back interjected, "That's the end of lewd thoughts for you, George. Remember big brother could be listening with one of these gadgets."

Rendell ignored the comment. As each took his turn Lindell addressed the group.

"The possibilities are limitless. The consumer will go crazy for this, especially the teenage market. It sure will take their breath away."

The visitors were impressed. "Yes, Yes," they agreed enthusiastically.

Batista used a lull in conversation to update the board on progress. He saw no reason why the year-end target could not be exceeded with Internet sales contributing double-digit growth in Europe. "And gentlemen, since the last meeting in April, we have brought onto our management team a native Chinese. His job will be to open doors in Beijing. The Village Committee visited our factory recently, reminding us about the contract we signed. We told them we had no problem with the commitment on jobs but we wanted them to play their part too by helping to crack the domestic market. They immediately offered a marketing guy who will do just that. I'm confident that we can report positive results shortly on that front."

Sinclair smiled at his board members as if to say *told you so*.

"Use that marketing guy to keep pushing Beijing," he ordered. "It's the ultimate prize. Get a lead in there and we'll be unstoppable..."

The photographers arrived. Sinclair took back the Synaptatron and ordered his board to flank him for the photo. As Batista led the group back to the reception area George Hanson, chief executive of Kimble-Sinclair's European manufacturing operations came in step with Lindell.

"I read back a month or two ago that the European Commission has opened an investigation into Asian-made computers. Does that affect our operation at all?"

Lindell looked to his left at Batista. He didn't return eye contact. He fiddled with a folder pretending not to hear. Sinclair glanced across at Lindell. He had obviously heard the question. The awkward silence forced Lindell to be frank. Well, as frank as possible without going into detail. "Well it could. We don't really know at this point. It's true we will be covered by the investigation but we have our Brussels lawyers working on it."

Hanson smelled the scent of weakness and pursued the point. "But could it mean duty into Europe? Affect market share and profitability?"

"It's possible, but too early to say."

Sinclair peered over his glasses. "Have you built that into those projections you've just shown us? Surely it's a major contingency in next year's budget?"

"No. Not until something crystallises. After all, it's just an investigation."

The president took off his glasses as he continued walking, swivelling them in his right hand.

"If we've trouble with the Europeans I'll talk to the White House. After all we've sorted out the Balkans for them. They owe us one."

Bastista shook his head vehemently. "I'm afraid trade investigations can't be sorted out that simply Howard. Kosovo's hardly a bargaining chip."

"You might be surprised what deals can be struck behind closed doors," Sinclair responded haughtily.

Hanson sighed. He was determined to pursue the point. "What do the lawyers in Brussels think?"

Batista put on a reassuring voice to assuage any concern. "The investigation has only started. The whole thing's at a very preliminary stage. Our lawyers are confident of a satisfactory outcome. Perhaps, gentlemen, we could review this in more detail at the next quarterly meeting. We'll be in a better position to know all the facts by then."

The board of Kimble-Sinclair was not happy. Confused rather than unhappy. Jefferson, a former investment banker from New York, and personal friend of Sinclair's for more than thirty years, now joined the conversation.

"Make no mistake here. This sounds like a material contingency. I see from the figures in the folder that Europe is providing fifty-six per cent of Falcon Tech's profits and eighty per cent of its growth. A potential duty is very much a material element in the eyes of the SEC."

Batista became agitated. "But by doing that we'll be sending a powerfully negative signal to Wall Street."

Jefferson had now got the bit between his teeth and would not let go easily. "We must comply to the letter with SEC regulations if we want a trouble-free launch. It's the law. Full disclosure is absolutely essential."

Sinclair stepped in. "This is for Falcon Tech to sort out. It's up to them to ensure compliance."

There were nods of agreement.

"We'll put it on the top of the agenda for the October quarterly," he continued.

"And Albert set out clearly at that stage what action is being taken. Flag it as a priority item."

The thirty-strong contingent of men arrived at the reception area and prepared for lunch at a local restaurant.

Chapter Eleven

July 1999
Brussels
ONE WEEK LATER, Marc made his way to his sports club in the suburb of Kraainem, a ten-minute-drive from the office provided he took a circuitous route of quieter back streets instead of the ring motorway, which often remained congested until after eight. His squash game had become a ritual, a place where he could get lost in the fever of competition. A standing arrangement meant that at least one court was booked in the name of their nickname clique, 'The Invincibles'.

He swung off the road and parked his BMW under the cover of the poplar trees. He stepped out of the car and grabbed his sports bag from the boot.

"Jesus Christ," he involuntarily shouted as two figures appeared either side of him. He slammed the boot lid closed. Taylor immediately stepped forward, blocking his attempt to move away.

"You didn't keep your appointment in the Park. Remember - one o'clock near the Mosque?"

"Get lost guys. I'm not impressed by your little joke."

"By the time we're finished our conversation, believe us, you'll know that it ain't a joke."

"Please step out of my way."

"Schuman, we can call you Schuman?" Johnson called out.

Ignoring the question Marc tried to move away from the car. Taylor again stepped into his path making Marc realise that he had underestimated his size in the Park. His upper body was powerfully built with a barrel-chested torso extending across to broad shoulders making him virtually immovable. And his hands were massive and threatening.

"Please...I'm leaving."

The response was abrupt and icy cold. "We need to finish last week's conversation. Close our business and let you get on with your sports."

"I've nothing to say to you guys."

Johnson moved closer, tapping the car roof for emphasis, his voice deliberately raised for effect. "Not as far as our client is concerned. He wants results and he gets very impatient if he's kept waiting. Last week we told you what we wanted. But let us spell it out again."

A group of people emerged from the club. Johnson again tapped the roof of the car loudly. The psychology worked. Heads turned towards the car.

"Okay, sit into the car."

"You're already very sensible, Schuman."

Taylor came around to the passenger door and casually slipped into the front seat. Johnson opened the rear door and sat in. The pressure started. "You've been working very hard on that case...think you'll make a success of it and make a good name for yourself in the European Trade Bureau?" Johnson asked.

"What are you talking about?" Marc replied.

"The computer case. Duties on computers from the Far East. You call them anti-dumping duties to prevent good-value machines getting onto the European market. Am I right so far?"

Marc stared through the windscreen effectively ignoring them.

"Well then let us explain. Our client wants us to do this assignment in a business-like manner. Make a fair deal, you must understand. He gets something and you get something for your effort. And here's the deal. A one-hundred-billion dollar market for computers in Europe is emerging over the next five years and our client is already well on the way to dominating it. He simply doesn't want any *hitches*."

"Yes Schuman," Taylor said. "Extra costs will slow him down and that's where you play your part. And the market is expanding at a phenomenal rate because of this Information Superhighway plan. So are you getting the picture?"

"Look, I said in the Park that I won't help you and I still mean it. The Trade Bureau is a big bureaucracy. I'm not some dictator deciding things behind closed doors."

Taylor dropped to a mock whisper. "Here's the deal. Our client is willing to make you an offer for flexibility on the rate of duty. We hear you have the discretion so you better start using it for your own-"

Marc raised his right hand stabbing it towards him.

"Who is your goddamn client anyway? Is he afraid to come out in the open? The usual tactic of a coward."

"Watch your language and listen to what we have to say. Yes, ball park offer of around five million bucks in a numbered bank account in Liechtenstein."

"It's …despicable. I'm not for sale. Now get off my back."

"Marc we're told-"

"Don't call me Marc, you hear me," he hissed in the face of Taylor who ignored the interruption.

"…We're told that, as chief investigator you have plenty of discretion, plenty of leeway to make judgements…to interpret facts as it suits. Look, Schuman, we're not going to listen to your game of bluff. A bureaucracy is just a collection of individuals. Somebody makes the decisions. It's not spread across ten or twenty people."

"Yes," Johnson added. "And our information is that you're our man on this one. So for five million you find a way to reduce our client's rate to ten per cent and leave the others at around forty per cent. And don't ask stupid questions. You're the expert. You know how it works. We just know what buttons to press to hit the jackpot."

Smug laughter filled the car. They were getting the upper hand. Marc's stomach was churning and anger was building inside.

"Get out of my sight."

"Oh we will but before we go we've just got one final piece of advice. If you haven't decided by the next time we'll have a little incentive for you. Something to concentrate your mind. Believe us, you'll find it even more motivating than money in a Liechtenstein bank account."

They both opened the doors and stepped out. Johnson put an index finger to his lips, "A secret. Our little secret. When we meet again we expect you to have decided. Don't talk to anybody. Otherwise that little motivator will cause you a lot of pain. Believe us, a helluva lot of anguish."

139

They slammed the doors. Marc sprang from the driver's seat, grabbed his sports bag and ran towards the entrance door. Kevin O' Shea was his rival tonight. Marc could see his thin frame and wavy brown hair through the glass wall at the back of the court. He was slapping a ball against the front wall in a warm-up routine.

"Sorry, sorry I just couldn't get away from the office," Marc apologised as he came onto the court.

"You look like you've seen a ghost...you okay?"

"Yeah, fine," Marc retorted as he swiped at an imaginary ball.

Kevin slapped his ball harder with the racquet. "You're up against a formidable foe tonight so the drinks will be on you!"

"Scare tactics! I won't buckle under your taunting," Marc said as he placed the bottle of water beside the front wall.

"Ready when you are," Kevin called out. Marc nodded.

Kevin started with a lob serve into his backhand which Marc barely managed to scrape up to the front wall. Kevin quickly followed with a drop shot, centimetres above the tin leaving Marc stranded at the back of the court.

"Godverdommen," Marc muttered in Dutch and shook his head vehemently in a self-chiding way and then, determinedly gripping his racquet, faced the front wall for the next serve.

He then settled down and found his rhythm and for the next half an hour they played a tightly contested match with Marc losing the first two games 7/9, 8/10.

But the usual precision with which he played was not there: his timing was off and he seemed to hesitate at the vital moment, his pace and determination a poor imitation of the skill he consistently displayed in previous games. His luck changed briefly in the third game after an opening 5/0 lead by Kevin as he doggedly clawed his way back, point by point to even the score at 5/5. But the pressure intensified as a series of well-positioned shots lured Marc towards the front wall and then a final arcing shot died in the back corner shattering his confidence He slammed the racquet against the side wall.

"You sure you're okay?"

"Fine."

He found a late burst of energy that briefly put him back in the game but Kevin countered with a well-disguised reverse angle boast leaving him once more flat-footed. At this stage Kevin knew that Marc was off form, knew that he had the game in his pocket but chose to leave the post mortem until the match was truly over. The next shot kissed the front wall catching Marc unawares and at 8/8 all he foolishly called "set one" and with another precision lob Kevin finished the match.

Marc shook Kevin's hand. "Well done," he said as they left the court. In the changing rooms they chatted about past games. Tonight's defeat against the old adversary was now the second notch on Kevin's belt. It clearly shook Marc's confidence.

They showered and made their way upstairs for a drink at the bar. After ordering two beers they moved to the comfortable seats in the alcove. Kevin noticed that he seemed a little distracted as if something were preying on his mind but thought it might be a tiff with Laura or something. He raised his glass. "Slainte."

"Yes cheers," Marc replied. The two glasses kissed each other.

"My technique is at last nearly perfected," the Irishman said.

"I was no match tonight but there's always another time."

A few moments of silence passed as they quenched their thirst. And then Kevin kicked in with a question.

"Any more trips to the Far East coming up?"

"No, nothing. There's six months work left on the computer case. And you?"

Kevin worked for OLAF, the Commission's Fraud Bureau. He explained how they were on the verge of infiltrating a criminal gang, pirating software in the Far East and smuggling it to Europe. It was a hush-hush job that could show big results any day.

"Sounds exciting," Marc said laconically.

Kevin smirked. "Maybe that part but drafting a one-hundred-page report is hardly riveting stuff."

These words were cold comfort to Marc's ears. The game plan seemed to be the same. The parallels were there. Officialdom trying to infiltrate the criminal world and in another way the criminal world trying to control the official world. Strange thoughts were swirling once more in his head. He would prefer not to have had this conversation…would prefer to see the world in black-and-white terms right now.

"It's a game, you just pursue them relentlessly and eventually they make a mistake. Then you flap your wings like a vulture and swoop in low for the kill. Easy if you set the sting up correctly," Kevin mused.

"Sounds exhilarating."

"Yeah. That's how we did it in the Customs when chasing the hardened drug smugglers. These guys are only human. The taste of money makes them soft and they pursue a lifestyle. Eventually they get careless, make mistakes and that's when we're there to collect."

The conversation troubled him. He was becoming agitated. His squash partner never really talked like this before. In fact he rarely spoke about work.

"Kevin, I've got to go."

"Whatever you say."

Marc reached for the glass, drained it and moved towards the counter. He settled the bill and agreed a date for the return bout.

The evening was cool outside, the sky cloudless. He scanned the area and thought about the episode earlier. Just then the parallels hit him. The two heavies evoked memories of watching Laurel and Hardy as a child.

"Yes. Almost the perfect double act for Laurel and Hardy – the comedy act," he muttered.

A new moon caught his eye as he zapped the remote control to unlock the doors. He lingered, staring up at the night sky and in an instant remembered how he used to look up at the stars as a child. Awe was always the word he associated with it because he could never quite understand the concept of infinite space. But at that moment he was happy to just plain believe it. He really only stood by the car for about twenty seconds but more than a child's lifetime passed by in those fleeting moments.

Turning the ignition, he sped down the road leading to the motorway.

Five million dollars in Liechtenstein. He allowed himself to indulge the possibility. *Sailing around the Caribbean for the rest of my life,* he mused. And then he thought about Laura and their life together.

"No deal," he shouted as he clenched his hands on the steering wheel, anger welling up inside him.

'You will find it a great motivator, even more motivating than money in Liechtenstein.' Their words echoed in his head. He banged the steering wheel in frustration.

The car radio was tuned to a French station. He fumbled for a CD, any CD from the bunch stacked in the holding tray between the front seats. Without looking at it, he slotted it in. The Eagles blared out. He wanted to drive fast and lose himself in the music but it had the opposite effect as the words of Hotel California rang in his ears.

'You can check out anytime but you can never leave.' He was acutely sensitive to those lyrics right now. He saw entrapment, snaring and incarceration in the eerie words. The song was made for his situation right now. Just like an animal being stalked in the jungle he too was being chased. He ejected the CD and threw it onto the passenger seat. "The motivator," he repeated to himself. Accelerating down the motorway towards Brussels he replayed the events over and over in his mind.

HE TRIED HARD to put the episode in perspective, to make some sense of it but right now his investigative instincts were beginning to kick in. Kotler and Rousseau certainly had a motive but he supposed that they would hardly play that kind of game. He was unsure but nevertheless filed the possibility of their involvement in the back of his mind. He went to the small table in the corner of the office, picked up the Wantoe Electronics file and returned to his desk. He pushed some papers to one side and placed the file in the middle. *The best clue to motivation would be the controlling shareholding,* he thought. *Public companies would be unlikely to engage in bribery.*

No, he reflected, *it's got to be a company where the shareholders and the management are the same people.* It was time to start checking the structure of the companies, to see who called the shots. And the Korean-based exporter was the best place to start. It was controlled by the Shing family. *It's a possibility,* he thought. *They were very helpful, very nice. Maybe too nice.*

He stared out the window pondering that possibility. Marc then averted his gaze and picked up the Falcon Tech file. It was just as he had remembered. One hundred per cent owned by the healthcare giant, Kimble-Sinclair.

The Falcon Tech file was pushed aside and the details of the corporate structure of Lakoo Computers studied. The translation copy of the corporation's constitution showed the company to be privately owned and, therefore, not listed on the Bangkok Stock Exchange.

The common denominator of the three companies was their growth rates, the American Corporation emerging from a garage-style operation in the home of its founder in 1981. Wantoe Electronics' growth wasn't quite as spectacular but it did eclipse the other three Korean manufacturers in the space of five years. It was also particularly dominant in the desktop photocopier market. Lakoo Computers, the Thai operation, showed signs of aggressive penetration in the market place. It made the cheapest lap tops and sold through a web site. The annual accounts of the three companies over recent years showed them to be cash rich with a track record of paying out handsome annual dividends to their shareholders as well as pumping between seven and nine percent of annual revenues into research and development.

Marc leaned back on the chair, tapped his pen against the side of the desk top printer and reflected on the intriguing situation that seemed to be unfolding before his eyes.

The open files strewn on the desk got his attention once more particularly the key information on relative market share. The European players were just about holding on to a twenty-seven per cent share with the combined Asian exporters controlling over seventy per cent.

Just then the advice of Champenois rang in his ears. 'Back handers, under-the-table payments.'

As the events continued to dance around in his mind,

Marc was determined to keep a cool head, to adopt a *'wait and see'* approach.

Are other investigators being influenced with inducements? Maybe it's going on all around me. It goes on in politics all the time. It could be the type of crap Rousseau and Kotler get involved in. Maybe negotiation is a euphemism for this kind of trading. He clasped his hands behind his head and tilted the chair back. The more he tried to make sense of it the more understanding eluded him.

FOR MORE THAN THREE WEEKS Marc's corner office on the fourth floor had become the control centre for the case. The chief investigator's time was in heavy demand as his team sought advice or clarified the law. By late afternoon he invariably found himself in a series of interminable meetings with arrogant lawyers pleading leniency for their clients and, after he had punched a thousand holes in their vacuous arguments, they would concede defeat, smile and invite him out to dinner. He steadfastly declined every time.

The inexperienced investigators spent their days gathered around computer screens or huddled over printouts intermittently tapping figures into calculators. Usually the arguments were about a contentious discount or sales commission that could significantly influence the final duty for an exporter. The seasoned ones spent their time with phones held between the crook of their shoulders and chins hammering out compromises with those same lawyers on real issues likely to affect the outcome.

Elena Schmidt sat in a corner facing a dedicated computer screen. Her job was to transform the commercial reality of the marketplace into an appropriate legal text. She was young and enthusiastic; the lyricist of the team who composed draft after draft with flair and finesse and impeccable precision. Marc, on the other hand, used his greater experience to put music to the words, editing so that the recitals flowed consistently, a skill that blended original argument and precedent seamlessly. By Thursday morning of the third week a draft version of the law

145

was ready. Marc began to re-read it in preparation for a team briefing at noon.

Suddenly Kaufmann was at his shoulder. Marc's heart skipped a beat. "I read your report yesterday. You're talking about provisional duties by year end and wrapping it up definitively in the Spring?"

"Yes and that's if-"

Kaufmann threw the document onto the desk. "Spring's out of the question. Be absolutely clear on that. It's not acceptable…neither to me nor the Commissioner."

"But, Mr. Kaufmann, we will be lucky to get through the confrontation meetings without a major hitch. It won't be easy to work out acceptable formulae for the adjustments. And of course many issues of principle still have to be tackled. There is big pressure on about the lap tops. The Asians are fighting hard to have them excluded since the Europeans don't manufacture that kind of computer. At least not the full range."

Kaufmann's hands were now in the air. "Stop. Stop. Stop. I don't have time to listen to the detail. You've got to come up with imaginative solutions. That's what you're paid for."

"But the problem is that the lap-top computer is taking over and will be the dominant segment of the market in two or three years alongside the network types. Now our-"

Kaufmann bent down almost into Marc's face and again cut in abruptly. "Listen carefully…very carefully. Some European politicians are pressurising the Commissioner to move immediately to impose duties. They think that these things can be done overnight and there's an election coming up in two Member States next year. Job losses don't win elections for governments. You know that the same as I do."

"I understand but we're moving as fast as we can. It's an enormous case and-"

"Let me give you the harsh reality around here. The Commissioner is looking for a second five-year term. So she wants to keep on the good side of all governments. Lean on the lawyers. Bring forward the confrontation meeting. Knock heads together and hammer out compromises. It's the only way. I've now given a commitment to the Commissioner that we would have this one on the statute books by October and I intend to honour it."

"But Mr. Kaufmann the-"

"No buts. A way will have to be found."

"Yes, but...everything has to be defendable. No short cuts."

The Director pulled off his glasses, his eyes glistening. "Marc, you are *chief investigator* for this case. Make no mistake, that role has its responsibilities. Drive your team. The law has to be in the Official Journal in October. That's the political commitment and I will not renege. Perfectly clear?"

"Yes."

Kaufmann strode towards the door. For a moment Marc contemplated confiding in him but the whole thing was too bizzare, too unbelievable.

The pressure is building, he thought. *Kaufmann's starting to play hardball. Everybody wants the right result but somebody's going to be disappointed.*

Chapter Twelve

THE FOLLOWING WEEK was quiet in the Trade Bureau. Most of the team had taken their annual vacation and Marc didn't object. He knew that it would ruin morale and team spirit if he hung tough. In any event the law firms did likewise. For Marc it was frenetic, preparing for the upcoming confrontation meeting in September. Preliminary findings would have to be on the table for the oral hearing. The opposing parties would seek a schedule of potential duties, keeping the lawyers for the European industry happy. They could report back that progress was being made and a duty on the Asian tigers was imminent...the kind of progress that made their fees acceptable to an ailing industry. By late Friday afternoon he had sent an e-mail to the law firms convening the confrontation meeting in the second half of September. It was now up to them. He would listen with the icy cold impartiality of Rhadamanthus. His time was about to come, his opportunity to play judge and jury.

But out there in the big bad world somebody else lurked. Somebody who wanted to play judge and jury too.

With Marc.

LAURA'S HOSPITAL STAY was over at last but doctor's orders meant that she would spend at least another six weeks resting interspersed with a strict exercise regime to get her back to full health as quickly as possible. When Marc arrived at Saint Luc Laura was waiting in the reception area. He walked towards her, kissed her on the lips and then bear-hugged her tightly for what seemed like an eternity.

"I missed you," he eventually said.

"Me too," she said squeezing his hand. A warmth grew within him and he kissed her forehead more than once, breathing in the scent of her and wondering how he lasted so long without her affectionate embrace.

Laura drew back and made eye contact. "I need to...well I'd like to see Jessica. She's had no visitors for three weeks. Could you take me to see her?"

Jessica was now in the rehabilitation clinic for over two years; her main source of contact with family being visits from Laura.

"Sure."

Marc picked up her case and they made straight for the car park. Fifteen minutes later they arrived at the clinic in Grimbergen in the northern part of Brussels. As they made their way along the corridor the ward nurse came through a door.

"Oh Laura great to see you back. Have you recovered?" she asked.

"Yes. I'm more or less over it now, thank God."

"Jessica's in the recreation room."

As Laura approached holding Marc's hand, Jessica's eyes lit up as she maneouvered the wheelchair around. Her arms reached up as Laura bent down and they hugged tightly for a long while.

"Are you better now?" Jessica asked, the sobbing making it hard to get the words out.

"Yes," Laura whispered and immediately tears appeared in her eyes.

Marc said hi and awkwardly touched Jessica's shoulder to comfort her. He couldn't find appropriate words to fill the silence.

"I've got good news," Laura eventually said. She pulled back slightly to look into her eyes, their hands still tightly clasped together.

"Your Grandma and Grandpa have sold the house in Georgetown. And guess what? They've found the cottage of their dreams in Virginia. Well apparently it's a big old rambling place. Dad says there's lots of places to hide from Mom. He says he'll have it done up right away with a ramp for this. I promise you'll be there by Thanksgiving."

Jessica's face lit up in a big smile. "It sounds humongous. I can't wait to see Grandma and Grandpa."

Marc came closer and put his hand on Jessica's shoulder and soon the tears turned to laughter as he teased her about the

Harry Potter book on her lap. Jessica looked up from the book as a beautiful teenager, with a look of helpless despair on her face, was wheeled into the room by a nurse. The nurse slipped earphones onto her head and moved her close to the television.

"She's just arrived…paralysed from the neck down." Jessica whispered. "Tetraplegic, they call it. A riding accident. She's never going to ride a horse again."

Marc, sensing Laura's obvious discomfort, said, "Laura's told me all about your paintings."

Jessica dropped the book and swung the wheelchair around towards a row of shelves. They passed an hour studying the raw vivid colours.

"That last one's more like Picasso," Marc said as he rose from the crouched position on the floor. Laura hated to leave but it was really time to go. They hugged again and said their goodbyes. As Marc and Laura walked down the corridor she looked distraught: Marc put his arm across her shoulders.

"It's affected me really bad this time."

"I know. I was thinking…," Marc whispered softly.

"About what?"

"You really need a change of scenery. Why don't we head to the South of France for a week? It'll do you good."

"When?"

"Right now! *Une semaine au Sud de la France?*" Marc repeated in an affected French accent, his eyebrows wiggling.

"You mean a week on the Riveria."

"Yeah. Look what if…?"

"I'm listening," she said, smiling.

"What if we drive to Paris, spent a few nights there and then put the car on the TGV to Marseilles."

She raised her arm and tugged the hair at the nape of his neck.

"I'm looking forward to this holiday already."

He winked. "Me too, Harry. Me too. Let's get going."

Paris

SATURDAY WAS SPENT doing the tourist bit. The Louvre in the morning and then a boat trip on the Seine. By late afternoon it was time for the Eiffel Tower. At the pinnacle they took in the breathtaking view of the sweeping Seine directly below. The tour boats plied the river returning to anchor at the quay below them to disgorge their cargo of camera-clicking tourists. They walked around the viewing platform and gazed across the metropolis. Laura organised Marc to stand against the steel railing with the Arc de Triomphe in the distance and enlisted a fellow tourist to take a photograph.

"Let's see the view from the other side," he then said, "and, this time, I'll take the photographs."

She nodded. "Okay."

"Stand there so that Notre Dame is just over your shoulder...now bend over a little."

"Why?"

"That way you can be the Hunchback!"

"Very funny."

He laughed loudly.

"It's my first time up here," Laura said. "I've been to Paris three or four times but never been up the Eiffel Tower."

"I wasn't going to admit it but me too."

"Well, it's more like something lovers do."

ON SUNDAY MORNING Laura awoke and stared at the ceiling. She got up and went straight to the bathroom. The phone rang awakening Marc. He leaned across to the locker and picked it up.

"Good morning...so you decided to take a little break from Brussels. We hope you're enjoying the sights of Paris."

"Who is this?" Marc spat out, a cold shiver running down his spine.

"You know who this is 'cause we've already met, remember? And don't forget to keep that important date we have in Brussels. We'll need an answer soon...the right answer."

"Look-"

The phone went dead. It all came flooding back. The faces of Laurel and Hardy...in the Park...at his club. He jumped from the bed trying hard to obliterate the image and walked to the window. Laura emerged from the bathroom.

"Was that the phone I heard?"

"Yeah...room service. They...ah they had the wrong room number," he said, a hint of trepidation in his voice. She reached for the remote control, zapping the television to life. CNN was doing an anniversary programme on the death of Princess Diana. Thoughts of his own paparazzi flooded into his mind. His own 'stalkarazzi'- hunting him down until he would bend to their demands.

In the emotional wave of grief conveyed by the programme he wanted to share his problem but it seemed too complicated. The similarity between his situation and Princess Diana's was real, in his mind. He too was being chased. He felt like shouting and screaming because he could empathise, could feel the scent of pursuit.

His thoughts had turned inward, plumbing the deepest recesses of his mind. One instant he was thinking of Diana fleeing photographers and, then, that image would dissolve and in a fleeting moment it would reappear. But this time as Marc Schuman, fleeing hit men out to kill him. Everything was uncertain with reality and imagination blurring with kaleidoscopic rapidity.

"Let's get breakfast," she said jolting him back into reality.

Laura caught his hand. He was reassured momentarily and again briefly thought about confiding in her. But some part of his consciousness – that little man inside his head - told him to wait.

"Okay, let's eat," he agreed. "I'm starving."

LATER THAT EVENING they drove the car onto the overnight train to the South of France and made their way to the couchettes. When they were curled up in bed Marc brought the conversation around to the attack even though he knew it was painful for her.

"I've checked with the police again last week. Still no suspects but seems they're pursuing a gang...apparently they carried out similar attacks in Louvain."

"Imagine they did this all for the sake of two thousand francs and a watch."

"It's unbelievable what they'll do to feed their habit."

"My ribs feel okay now...the exercises have really helped."

"Important thing's you're over it...and safe."

She sighed. "I won't go into parks again in a hurry..."

"It's just a one off. You were unlucky. There was an article about the whole drugs thing in the Bulletin."

Suddenly she started to sob. "Those bastards really hurt me, Marc."

A lump formed in his throat. He held her tightly. "I know... if I ever get my hands on them I'll kill them."

They were rocked to sleep by the vibrating movements of the train. Seven hours later they awoke in the South of France to that same undulating movement of the train. They left Marseilles and headed east along the Coté d'Azur.

SEVEN O' CLOCK WEDNESDAY MORNING: Laura listened to the birds chirping in the trees outside the window of the rented chalet near St. Tropez for a few minutes before folding back the duvet and sliding from the bed. Ten minutes later she emerged refreshed from the shower and slipped on a T-shirt. She took a pair of running shorts from the travel case and pulled them up over her hips. And finally a pair of canvas shoes. She tiptoed across to the bed and stroked Marc's forehead. He awoke, pulled her towards him and kissed her on the lips. She stood upright, wagging a finger at him.

"What about our early morning walk on the beach? All talk last night and look who has to wake you up," she teased.

"Okay, Harry. You've asked for it. Are you up to jogging?" he asked as he bounded for the bathroom.

"Maybe," she shouted after him.

Fifteen minutes later they were at St Tropez beach. The harbour was already coming to life. They stood for a minute watching the moored yachts being gently rocked by the undulating action of the waves, their flags fluttering as little bells tinkled on the masts. Some of the boat owners were busying themselves in preparation for a day at sea. Others carried bags of provisions to their floating hideaways so that they could party on deck under the relaxing Mediterranean sun. Out towards the horizon a few yachts tacked across the bay, their colourful sails billowing in the early morning breeze.

Marc began his warm-up exercises, extending his arms above and then swinging them slowly towards his toes. Laura gathered her hair into a ponytail and taunted him with a challenge.

"I'm off. Catch me if you can."

Barely glancing in her direction he continued his routine. When he finished he turned towards the sea and watched the waves lapping onto the beach.

One hundred graceful strides down the beach she was now an indistinct figure in the distance. Marc finished his stretching exercises and then glanced in her direction. At that moment she turned around and looked back down the deserted beach. He pretended not to hear her call to follow. After a moment he bounded straight into action, a few strides later settling into a rhythmic pace. His full attention was on the athletic figure in front of him. His eyes lingered on her curvaceous body, the sensuous images echoing in his loins.

He quickened his pace, eventually reaching his normal plateau. Moments later he came alongside her, motioning defiantly with his hand. She was close to exhaustion, droplets of perspiration forming at her temples. Her T-shirt was clinging to her, accentuating the outline of her firm breasts and narrow waist.

"You... go ahead. I'm fin...finished. I shouldn't have...sprinted," she bleated, the words coming out in panting breaths.

"We can stop now if you like."

"Yes. I'm...I'm not up to it. My...ribs are starting to ache."

She slowed to a walk, her face red and flushed. He eased off and turned to face her. And for a moment they stood, gazing out on the blue sea. He positioned himself behind her, his hands draped on her shoulders and kissed the nape of her neck. Her head turned so slightly that her cheek brushed his almost as if a butterfly had fleetingly caressed it. He caught her left hand and extended it up across her right shoulder. In an instant he slipped it on her finger – a beautiful solitaire ring.

"I love you so much. Will you marry me?" he whispered.

Her arm came down and she shrieked in surprise.

"Oh Marc it's beautiful, really beautiful," she whispered rising onto her toes in excitement. "I love you, Schu." A tear ran down her cheek.

"Well you said the South of-"

She kissed him impulsively muffling the words. His right hand moved along her jaw and stroked her ear. He cupped her face, gently massaging her cheeks with his thumbs. The kissing continued, soft and gentle at first, then her tongue explored deeper finding and tasting the sensuous, erotic sensations before he responded softly, then hungrily.

"Hmmm," she sighed, her hands tugging his hips closer. They were on his buttocks now, kneading the taut mounds of muscle. Spontaneously the swell of his manhood throbbed against her. She drew back and smiled. "I want this to last forever." He could feel the anticipation, almost hear the desire welling up deep within both of them. He moved his attention to her hair, untied it and suddenly it cascaded down around her shoulders. She glanced down the deserted beach and gazed up at him. "We…we shouldn't…" she murmured, whisper-soft, her eyes not quite in the words. She knew it was insanity to do this on the wide-open beach but she was helpless to resist. Need overcame everything, so intense and primal that self-restraint was washed aside. After all it was something she had dreamed of and, at that moment, it seemed so natural, so perfect.

His hands were now at the drawstrings of her shorts and then it was loose. They moved up, gently fondling her. He could feel the silky softness of her skin. She touched the muscles of his chest, then lower to the tautness of his stomach and finally her exploring fingers went lower again holding him in a firm grasp. He moaned with pleasure as they slowly edged down onto the sand, the sounds of desire intensifying around them, oblivious of where they were. Caressing and stroking each other until the movements became more regular, more rhythmic.

The palms of his hands dug into the sand, his body suspended above her, kissing her face and then dipping lower to her breasts, his tongue flicking around her nipples.

The sand gave way, his weight now bearing down on her. He rolled over and in an instant she was on top, rocking gently to the sound of the waves. He could feel the unstoppable surge as his stomach tightened. She responded spontaneously, her movements quickening to a peak, a low entrancing moan coming from deep within as her head tilted back. And then sated, she fell forward, collapsing onto him.

Some time elapsed before she stood up and watched the dappled sunlight dancing on the waves. Tugging at his arm she said, "let's have a swim."

"What, you mean...right now here without...?"

"Yes, c'mon. The place is deserted." With that, she sprang to her feet and ran towards the water.

"Catch me if you can."

He bounded across the sand and, grabbing her tightly by the waist, he lifted her off her feet as she reached the water.

"Hey watch my arm!"

"Water's not going to harm it."

He tried to throw her in but her arms hugged his neck and, eventually, laughing uncontrollably, they tumbled into the breaking waves.

September 1999
Brussels
CHUCK JOHNSON LIFTED the receiver, clicked a series of digits and waited.

"Good afternoon, Mr. Cheng."

"Good morning."

"No progress to report this week. Our goose has fled the nest. Took a week's vacation. Your Amsterdam ops trailed him to Paris. We put a call through at his hotel. Made him very uptight, I guess."

"Excellent work."

"Amsterdam also sniffed around the Bureau and found that

156

he won't be back till Monday."

"It's time to turn up the heat. Start tightening the noose when he returns. It's time for results."

"Yes."

"I will speak to our ops. They should also play a little more with his mind and once the motivator is handed over, they will put him under twenty-four-hour surveillance. Just in case he splits."

"I would suggest that Amsterdam make more frequent contact with us too. We don't really know when they are around. We need to co-ordinate better."

"Agreed. There must be no breakdown in communications."

"Perfect."

Cheng dropped the receiver. "Perfect-ly well," he snorted in guttural chiu chow as he busied himself with the documents on the desk. "But not perfectly well for everybody."

Chapter Thirteen

IT WAS CUSTOMARY for Marc to spend Thursday evenings downtown with a group of lawyer friends from his college days. The platform was almost empty when he arrived at the station. He stepped into the last carriage of the metro heading towards Central Station and sat down on a seat. Suddenly 'Laurel and Hardy' were racing towards the carriage, barely squeezing through as the automatic doors came together. They made their way up the carriage and sat opposite him. A couple occupied a seat at the other end. As the metro moved off in the direction of the city centre Johnson started off.

"That was very impressive jogging in the Park yesterday Schuman. Or should I say running…almost forgot you're an athlete."

Taylor picked up the conversation. "We like to keep a close eye on you. You're important to us."

"Get lost. I'm not going to listen to you."

Johnson turned to Taylor. "I think Schuman will need that incentive after all, that little motivator, without delay."

Taylor agreed. "Indeed, sooner rather than later."

"Your intimidation tactics won't work. Get the message. Just piss off."

"We ask only one question today," came the strident tone of Taylor. "Have you made up your mind to work with us?"

"I've given you my answer. *No*. Now bring it back to Mr. Asshole," he shouted, the tension of the past weeks bubbling to the surface. The couple at the other end of the carriage craned their heads, puzzled at the outburst.

"Okay, we promised you a little incentive. We call it leverage in the business." Johnson pulled a brown packet from his pocket. "Something to entertain you later this evening."

"Stuff it."

"Our boss ain't goin' to be very pleased if you refuse his gift, his little token of appreciation. He likes to think of it as

158

the ritual of initiation."

"Forget it. I'm not taking your dirty money."

Marc averted his eyes, staring out the window into the darkness of the tunnel. His outward face of indifference was turning to anger inside. He wanted to scream - even physically attack them - but knew he was really powerless to act. He certainly did not want to take the packet as that would be the first sign of weakness. But he did hear the pernicious words. He rose from the seat ignoring them and stepped out onto the platform at Gare Centrale. They followed hard on his heels. He needed time to assess his next move.

"Believe us it is in your interest to take this, Schuman. It's a video tape - a souvenir of your visit to Bangkok and a few photos for your album," Johnson said as he thrust forward the packet. Marc scurried along the platform, a feeling of dread enveloping him. He stepped onto the escalator and glanced back. They were following hard on his heels.

"Take it Schuman," Taylor shouted. Marc spun around, grabbed the packet and calmly walked over to the bin just inside the entrance to the station.

"That's what I think of your souvenir," he said as he let it drop into the bin and made for the exit. Johnson shouted, "We've got a bunch of them. Remember Kaufmann will get a copy in the morning. He'll be more than entertained by those Eastern delights and the nice determined investigator who never makes a mistake ain't goin' to look good anymore."

Marc quickened his pace towards the street. When he reached the far side heading towards the Grand' Place, he glanced back. 'Laurel and Hardy' stood motionless at the entrance to the station. He quickened his pace, turning onto a side street out of view of his pursuers and raced back towards another entrance to Gare Centrale. In fifteen minutes he was back at his apartment on Rue des Tongres. He sat on the couch for a few minutes thinking about the latest episode especially their plan to pass a copy to the Director. The determination in their voices echoed in his ears. Instantly he bounded towards the door and raced down the stairs. He was back in Gare Centrale within ten minutes, rummaging through the bin. A vagrant wandered in from the street and watched with amazement as Marc continued to search through the litter and refuse. Marc felt the hardness of the packet, retrieved it and ripped open the brown wrapping. Inside was a standard cassette and an envelope which he opened, his eyes widening in disbelief at the entwined naked bodies in the photographs. He immediately bundled everything into the wrapping. The vagrant muttered something and smiled. Marc dashed to the platform and returned to the apartment. He pulled the bunch of keys from his pocket, flung open the door and slotted the cassette into the video recorder. Two minutes passed. The tape was blank.

"Bastards," he muttered. He slumped back on the couch, relieved. Suddenly the screen lit up and images began to form.

"What the hell's this?"

A title came up, filling the screen.

Big Bang In Bangkok

with

Tom The Euro Cat

There, in full colour, was Marc Schuman coming through a door and now being led by a Thai hostess to a seat. She poured a beer, handed it to him, and began massaging his shoulders. Her hands moved down to unbutton his shirt. The scene continued for about three minutes, the movements becoming more sensual. It then faded and a close up shot of his face lit the screen. The camera panned down to show him being massaged by beautiful Thai girls.

His body, with all its recognisable contours - bronzed, rippling, muscular – and an expression of pleasure lighting his face. Here in front of his eyes half-remembered images flickered to life. The next sequence of shots were close ups, his facial expressions dissolving on screen to be replaced by sinuous movements of arms and breasts along his naked body. There were five, maybe even six Thai girls hovering around him.

They were not bluffing. A pornographic movie with sound effects. A musical score now kicked in to make it a very professional montage of shots and syncopation. Their hands touched every inch of flesh, arousing inner stirrings and it

160

showed. It became more explicit as they used their breasts to tingle the skin. One of them came close to the camera and, with her hands gesturing in the air, started to speak in broken English.

"Miss-er. Su-man like Icarus. We take 'im above cloud 'til his wings melt in heat of sun." She smiled into the camera and said, "Sanuk."

The tape played for maybe another six or seven minutes and Schuman was the star. His heart beat fast in his chest and anger welled up inside. He wanted to find them, to kill them with his own hands. He was now in an impossible position.

He thought of Laura. It would be impossible for her to forgive. And his colleagues at work.

How could I have been that stupid? he wondered.

The shame.

The ridicule.

The disgrace of it all.

His friends would shun him. He stared in a vacant way, in disbelief.

The Thai girls looked so young. One of them flicked her tongue along his stomach and down to the thighs, eventually enveloping him. They had snared him in the oldest trap known to man, the trap of passion. And he would not escape until his virility gave forth its essence…and it did.

"Oh my God." He jumped from the couch and placed his hands over his face. His heart was pounding, his legs were like jelly and his mind was close to delirium. He could not think of the next step to take. Was there even a next step? He stood on the spot, motionless. All that came into his mind were phrases like. "If only…if only."

The idea of ever going back to the office repulsed him. The place was tarnished - the files and documents. *All my moral authority swept away in a few crazy moments in Bangkok,* he thought.

He tried hard to recall that night. He could remember the early part of the evening - going to McDonald's for a hamburger and afterwards taking the three-wheeled taxi to Pat Pongs. He could remember jokingly calling it the *tuk tuk*. The distinctive sound of the engine now echoed loudly in his head.

Those bastards were watching me. Watching us all the time. I should have known. Goddamn Asia.

He was preoccupied with his own situation. And now his thoughts turned to Montorro. *Did they do it to him as well?*

He reached down to the video player and hit the eject button. When the cassette popped out he snatched it and headed towards the bedroom. It was buried deep into a box of law books in the bottom of the wardrobe. The turmoil in his mind would not subside to allow him to think straight.

He couldn't think straight. There was no straight thinking to be done. His world was now shattered and in little pieces. Nothing could bring back the innocence no matter how good the explanation. A career blossoming forth and winning the respect and admiration of colleagues in the Bureau and the tight-knit community of lawyers in Brussels. His family and friends…and his sports club.

These bastards will stop at nothing, he thought. *They will eventually write my epitaph.*

His stomach began to heave as he turned his head away and swore.

KAUFMANN'S TAPE. KAUFMANN'S TAPE. Jumbled images of Kaufmann staring at a television screen and shouting at Kelly to get Schuman up to his office right away played in his mind. The alarm had gone off half an hour earlier but Marc did not hear it. With the window shutters fully closed, the red digits of the clock radio were the only source of light. The first four hours of the night were spent twisting and turning but by 4:30 he had slipped into a troubled REM sleep as complete exhaustion set in. It was now 7:35 and he had slept late but the honking of a car horn on the street below catapulted him into reality. He opened his eyes and caught a glimpse of the time.

"Shit," he muttered. "Damn shit." He was on his feet in an instant literally running towards the bathroom. As he showered to rid himself of the patina of perspiration that had built up on his body during the night the words *Kaufmann's tape. Kaufmann's tape* continued to haunt his mind. Within five

162

minutes he was dressed. Bounding down Rue des Tongres, vague apologies were muttered as he swept past early morning commuters making their way to the metro. He ran as fast as he could towards the Park entrance, the warm summer air and the terrible tension deep inside triggering the first droplets of sweat on his temples. Marc's heart was in overdrive going *whump, whump, whump.* He felt weak and wanted to stop to lean against one of the chestnut trees but there was no time. His stomach heaved to rid itself of its nauseous contents but he forced himself to continue. He checked his watch: 7:52. *More than halfway there,* he thought. *Keep going at all costs. Keep going.* He raced along the asphalt drive running down the centre of the Park for another two minutes and then cut sharply right towards the exit at the Mosque. He diced with the traffic on Avenue de Cortenbergh and made it through the doorway thirty seconds later. Now standing at the elevator the muscles in his legs began twitching and his chest felt on fire. He checked the watch again: 7:55.

On the sixth floor he rushed down the corridor and tapped on the door. Seconds passed. No response. He gambled that Kaufmann would not be in yet. Opening the door, he saw no sign of the Director and made for the tray of envelopes. There was no packet that looked like the shape of a cassette. Marc's stomach flipped and he felt even weaker now. He breathed deeply to regain composure, to regain control. Within seconds he was on the ground floor in the mailroom. The baskets of envelopes were stacked five high. He spread them out on the floor and systematically began plunging both hands deep down, groping for something rectangular and solid. The fourth bunch of mail was being examined when the door opened. Although the *huissier* (postman) – a stocky man with a bald head - recognised him he nevertheless eyed him up and down suspiciously for a few seconds eventually asking what the hell he thought he was doing. Marc kept searching as he turned his head and nonchalantly explained that a legal document was urgently required for the Director. The *huissier* shrugged and disappeared through the doorway. Marc felt something solid towards the bottom of the fifth basket, pulled it up and saw that it was addressed to Kaufmann. The brown wrapping paper was similar and boldly marked 'strictly personal and confidential'. It felt hard and the dimensions were right. He raced out of the building and in ten minutes was back at his apartment. He inserted the tape and waited. The screen remained blank for thirty seconds and then the words – *Next time's for real* – filled the screen. At that moment he supposed that those mean bastards were probably having breakfast in a hotel somewhere in Brussels chuckling and laughing at the trick they had played at his expense. He moved towards the window and slumped awkwardly onto a chair, trying to fathom what exactly was happening while simultaneously a cathartic rage was slowly building deep within him.

BY ELEVEN O' CLOCK MARC was back in his office, his innate investigator's instincts beginning to kick in. He entered Montorro's office in a rush, ready for confrontation. Answers would be demanded to fill in the half-remembered images of that night in Bangkok. The computer was switched on and the table was strewn with documents but Montorro was not there. Marc checked with Heidi and a few of his confreres but nobody had seen him that morning. Repeated visits at intervals during the afternoon turned up no trace of the Spaniard. At five o' clock Montorro's name was punched into the computer and his home address noted. By seven Marc was standing on Rue Franklin, pressing the doorbell. Complete shock registered on Montorro's face at the sight of Marc. He fumbled his way through an invitation to come inside which Marc readily accepted.

"Don't often have visits like this. Is there a problem?"

"No, nothing much. So how was your holiday?" Marc asked as they walked to the living room. Montorro motioned towards the couch but he declined to sit.

"We spent two weeks at home in Barcelona. The children played on the beach and we visited old friends. Long evenings sipping Rioja on the terrasse."

Marc nodded. Apart from their shared mission to the Far East, they had little in common. He brought the conversation around to Bangkok and explained that he couldn't quite recall parts of the visit. Montorro seemed hesitant and tentative, the body language indicating unease. He talked about visiting the company and the trip on the klong but that was it. A long pause ensued. Marc found it difficult to figure out whether it was his usual style or if he was hiding something but conversation was definitely stilted. *This is not working,* Marc thought. He pointedly asked about Pat Pongs and the bar they visited, and while waiting for a reaction, he searched the Spaniard's eyes for evidence that he was hiding something, holding back. Montorro seemed nervous.

"We had a good time that night," he eventually responded.

"That's the problem, I don't remember it. What did we do exactly?"

Montorro turned and moved down the room. "Remember we went to McDonald's for a hamburger and then to Pat Pong's..."

"What was the name of the bar we went to?"

"Eh…well it was a bar with an American name. Can't remember it now," he said unconvincingly.

"But Carlos I remember you were the enthusiastic one. You wanted to see the nightlife."

"We only walked around, had a beer in that bar and went back to the hotel."

"You're sure?"

Montorro swallowed hard, averting his eyes from Marc's sharp gaze. "Yeah I'm sure. Look you can visit Bangkok again."

"Level with me. What happened that night?"

"Marc I can't help you. You had a lot to drink. That's probably why you have gaps in your memory. Cut down on the beer and it won't happen again. Why all this questioning?"

"I just want simple answers."

"Well I've told you all I remember. Look Marc you'll have to excuse me…got an appointment downtown."

Suddenly Marc was at his shoulder. "Something tells me you're not being honest. What the hell went on that night? Come on - level with me. What happened?"

Montorro stared down at the floor. He shifted his weight,

then moved towards the window in silence.

Eventually Marc asked, "It's trouble and it involves me?"

"Yes."

"What kind of trouble?"

"Some people are putting me under pressure…" He hesitated. Marc waited.

"…You've got to understand. It's not my fault. They got me to set you up in Bangkok."

Rage, uncontrollable rage, engulfed Marc. He lashed out, his hands swinging wildly. The first punch landed on Montorro's shoulder, knocking him side-ways. He recovered and made a pleading motion with his hands. Marc lunged forward and again struck Montorro with his right clenched fist. Dazed, his body spun around eventually stumbling to the floor. In the descent his head caught the edge of a coffee table, splitting open his lower lip. It pumped blood. Marc bore down on him, grabbing him by the throat.

"You bastard. You mean bastard."

Montorro jerked upwards with his smaller but stockier frame, forcing Marc to one side but Marc steadied himself and punched hard into Montorro's chest. The Spaniard curled up, groaning loudly. A moment later Marc was straddling him, his heart beating furiously in his chest.

"You betrayed me, you bastard. I should kill you here and now." Montorro tried to speak but he was winded. Marc wanted to pulverise him but something held him back. Staring into his eyes he could see the fear, feel the scent of terror. "Why did you betray me? Well why…?"

"They put…they put me under pressure to help them. I had run up some gambling debts. They…they promised to cover them if I got you into that massage parlour but I haven't seen a cent of it." He unsuccessfully attempted to wipe the dripping blood from his chin.

"Get up," Marc ordered.

Montorro rose to his feet. His hands trembled as he pulled a tissue from his pocket and rubbed his chin. He then pressed it firmly against his lower lip. Marc moved back and Montorro tried to regain his composure.

"So what happened that night?"

Marc's face registered complete shock as Montorro's story flickered the first images of that night to life....

Montorro moved towards the door of the Good Time bar. He was greeted by an hostess. She beckoned him to come in. And fast on her heels another hostess ushered Marc through the door straight to a seat inside. The place was smoky and dimly lit at ground level but the stage above the bar was awash with colourful shapes and shadows cast by strobe lights hanging from chrome fittings suspended from the ceiling.

"I get drink from the bar?" the Thai girl asked. She pointed a finger at herself.

"And one for me too?"

Montorro looked at Marc, shrugged and said, "I suppose a beer's fine."

"Yeah, two beers."

The Thai hostess added, "and two coke?"

Montorro nodded agreement.

The girls vanished into the dimly-lit bar area. The Europeans sat back on the seats and tried to get a clearer view of the place. In an instant the girls were back with the drinks. The hostesses raised their glasses in a toast, smiled in unison and said, "*Sanuk*." Montorro raised his glass in response.

"Where 'you from?"

"Europe," Montorro answered.

"Hol-i-day?"

"No...business."

The girls wore sarongs, their firm breasts showing through the delicate material. They had just enough English to engage the guests, key words of encouragement to help the clientele spend their money. They sat opposite them, smiling. The other clients were also being entertained by hostesses.

"Come on, enjoy yourself, Marc," Montorro shouted above the music. Marc mustered a smile. "Okay, okay. But one more beer, that's the limit. And then I'm out of here."

"Whatever you say. You're the chief."

After fifteen or twenty minutes the Western music stopped

and a male Thai voice boomed over the speakers: "Now we have the ping pong show." The stage lit up and two girls leapt up from the side, their sarongs dropping to the floor. Immediately the music - Thai music with a rhythmic beat - boomed out and the girls commenced their routine of sensuous gyrations. The first act lasted about seven or eight minutes as they writhed provocatively to the beat of the music. The pleasure-bent crowd watched as the floorshow became more sexually explicit. Any man not accompanied by his girlfriend or wife was surrounded by at least one hostess.

Montorro raised the glass to his mouth and finished his beer. One of the girls stood up and said, "I get more beer?" and walked towards the bar. The other hostess looked at Marc and said, "You not trink quickly. You keep trinkin' like friend."

Marc smiled and raised the glass to his head, draining it. His head felt hazy, his vision now blurring. Maybe it was the dark, smoke-filled atmosphere. He shook his head and rubbed his eyes. When he opened them two more beers were on the table and two glasses with a mouthwash of coke in them. Montorro picked up the glass and drank rapidly. The girl slid into the seat beside Marc and her friend came around and joined Montorro. Marc took another mouthful of beer and again looked up at the stage.

Another erotic floorshow was about to start. This time a girl stepped up on the stage and whipped off her sarong. Wearing no underwear, she picked up a cigarette from the floor and lit it. She took off her G-string and, placing the cigarette in position, succeeded in blowing several rings of smoke into the air. Montorro leaned across to Marc and said. "I thought they said they only smoked cigars." Marc laughed, appreciating the humour.

The music seemed louder and the atmosphere more sultry. The hostess put her arm on Marc's shoulder and began gently massaging his neck. He looked across at his partner. He, too, was receiving the same treatment from the other girl. Slowly her hand moved down to Montorro's thigh, squeezing it firmly. An expression of helpless submission lit his face. Winking, he leaned across.

"All part of investigative work. Hazards of the job. When in Rome do as the Romans do."

The music started again and attention focused on the new group of six girls gyrating on the tiny stage. The lithesome bodies of the dancers fully engaged the crowd especially as the gyrations become more explicit. The feeling in Marc's head had become more intense. It was a mixture of pleasure and relaxation. And his libido had increased.

One of the girls jumped up and went to the counter. Marc weaved his way through the now full, dimly-lit bar to the toilet. When he returned the table contained another round of beers and cokes. As he slid onto the seat he leaned over and said, "Who's going to pay for all this?"

"Don't worry about that, Dutchman. It's only a couple of beers. We need to relax before Malaysia tomorrow."

The floorshow continued to the pulsating beat of the music. And the attention of the Thai hostess was having its effect. Reality receding, Marc's mind was drifting into a twilight zone. The colours in the bar were now intense, psychedelic. And yet he was only on his third beer. He could hear Montorro whispering to the girl. At least he seemed to be whispering. He now felt a strange mixture of drowsiness and arousal. The hostess was massaging his neck and nibbling at his ear. An image of Laura flashed across his mind....strolling in Tiananmen Square and walking on the Great Wall. The first woman he ever really loved. His body shuddered momentarily and his stomach flipped.

He knew he shouldn't let things go further but he was helpless to stop it. Images were vague, his vision again blurring. Montorro was joking and laughing with the hostess. He leaned over and began to talk but the words were indistinct. He seemed to speak very slowly and kept suggesting that they go to a massage parlour afterwards.

The effect of the drink was increasing. It's just a relaxing massage...just a relaxing massage. Everything was coming in waves. Words he could not clearly focus on. And the music seemed loud and the colours bright and constantly changing. He wanted to stand up but he felt dizzy. And the hostess seemed to have her hands all over him.

"Come on Marc, let's go for a relaxing massage," Montorro repeated as he helped him to his feet. They moved past the stage towards the rear of the bar, Montorro's words still ringing in his ears.

The sounds were faint, again barely touching his consciousness. He was sinking into a world of his own. A warm glow enveloped his whole body, his concerns rapidly dissipating and his thoughts becoming wonderfully blissful. Nothing seemed to matter any more. He was the chief but somehow roles were reversing fast. His helper was now the leader. He was following Montorro along a narrow corridor, carefree and uninhibited. The leader went in through a door and walked up a narrow stairs. Marc stood at the bottom trying to discern the indistinct figure at the top. Something in the back of his mind told him to stop, told him not to follow but he was moving to a rhythm. Everything was floating. Gentle waves undulating in front of his eyes. He was being beckoned from above to follow. He started to move, then hesitated, trying to focus on his surroundings. The leader came back down and caught his arm.

Marc looked up again at the narrow stairs and put his right foot on the first step. All it took was a nudge to help him onto the next step towards a world full of eastern promise…

"So," Montorro said, breaking Marc's concentration on the events of that fateful night. "They approached me in Bois de la Cambre at the weekend…warned that if I talked to you about Bangkok that I could forget about the money, that I would pay for it with my life."

"But why can't I clearly remember that night?"

Montorro described how he was given a relaxant to put into Marc's drink in McDonald's and how the Triads had arranged that his beer would be laced with a philtre later. Before Marc could ask any questions he explained that it was a cocktail of drugs that increases libido and dulls memory.

"Bastards."

"And this morning I got this in my letter box." Montorro

pulled a piece of paper from his pocket and unfolded it. Marc studied it: Chinese letters inside a triangle. His face blanched. "Oh my God."

"Do you know what it means?"

"The letters stand for seven. I've a friend in the Chinese Studies Dept. at ULB. He's fluent in Mandarin. Maybe he can unravel it. I'll check it out later with him."

Marc folded the piece of paper and put it in his pocket. Rage again flared deep within him.

"And you conspired against one of your team."

"What can I say, Marc. I'm sorry. They've obviously approached you too."

"Yeah. They're trying to blackmail me with a tape. But I don't understand why you agreed to help them in the first place?"

"They put so much pressure on me. I was gambling a lot. Said they'd settle the debts if I helped. They needed to catch a big fish and I would be the bait to make it all so easy."

"Sadistic bastards."

Marc's bitterness towards Montorro subsided somewhat.

"We've got to find some way of trapping them," he said. "They think they own you now. We need time to work on a plan. I'll need your full co-operation."

After a pause Montorro laughed nervously. "I'll help in any way I can but I'll have to take a day off tomorrow. I can't turn up with my face looking like a boxer's."

Chapter Fourteen

THE TEMPORARY SURVEILLANCE centre was an office on
Rue Leonardo Da Vinci, one hundred metres from the Trade
Bureau building. Schuman's apartment was less than half a
kilometre away, making it, too, an easy monitoring target. The
ten Triad members from the Amsterdam cell worked to a strict
rotation, ensuring that they had twenty-four hour coverage.
They observed from cars or lurked in the shadows. They
trailed him everywhere and covered their tracks. Everything
ran smoothly. Everything was under control.

Montorro was not playing by the rules. Even the death
notice in his letterbox did not have the right effect. Talking to
Schuman about Bangkok had a high price. The Supreme Lodge
Father made up his mind. He would take no chances. It was
time for effective action. Montorro would pay for this and it
would help tighten the tension a little more on Schuman. He
lifted the phone and dialled out the usual Brussels number.

"Mr. Verbiest, things haven't been running so smoothly in
Brussels these last few days."

"What?"

"Montorro's talked to Schuman. Cheng thinks he should
take swift action."

Verbiest rubbed his temples. "Swift action? What've you
got in mind?"

"Montorro's losing it fast. They've taped a conversation
and he's squealed. And you were mentioned. It's time to
liquidate him."

"What?" Verbiest gasped.

"Look, Montorro's spilled everything leaving your law firm
in a difficult situation."

The Belgian held the mouthpiece closer and whispered
nervously, "My law firm? What are you talking about?"

Wong could feel Verbiest's angst and was enjoying the
heightening tension coming down the line. "Remember

Amsterdam's monitoring his conversations. He's obviously made the connection. After all you are FT's lawyers."

"Wong, this was to be all covert stuff."

"Precisely. Now let's make sure it's watertight by getting him out of the way."

The receiver twitched in Verbiest's hand. "Damn it Wong are you talking murder? This is crazy."

"Not crazy…necessary. Otherwise the whole game falls apart and you know the difficult position you're in."

Wong's implied threat raised Verbiest's heartbeat to one twenty but he resisted the temptation to slam down the receiver. He couldn't quite see an alternative. "So what are you going to tell the Falcon Tech people?"

"The truth. It's the safest thing to do. There's no room for secrets when the stakes are high. We tell them that he had to be removed from the equation."

A lovely euphemism, Verbiest thought. "Look, Wong, none of this 'we' stuff. You tell them. This whole thing's getting out of hand."

"Okay, I'll tell them. I've no problem with that. I'll say I cleared it with you. They have to be told…after all they *are* the client."

Verbiest sighed loudly into the mouthpiece. "This is criminal. Being a lawyer, I'm not comfortable with it."

Wong smiled. "That's fine. If you can live with the consequences…."

Wong's smugness was making Verbiest sweat and feel very helpless at the wrong end of a long-distance phone call. And the thought of being hauled off to jail for conspiracy now made it nerve-racking. He grabbed the vial of tablets from the drawer and fumbled two towards his lips. A mouthful of water washed them down. He was better able to cope.

"Look Wong, Cheng should do whatever he has to. Just let's get this sordid affair over as quickly as possible."

"Yes Mr. Verbiest. It's in our best interest."

Wong threw the phone back on the cradle and swung around towards the window. He allowed Verbiest's exasperation to entertain him for a few moments. *'Damn it*

Wong are you talking murder? This is crazy.'

Grinning smugly, he parodied the *gweilo's* words. "You were never meant to be happy, Mr. Smartass lawyer."

He leaned across and pressed the buzzer. The door opened and Hu Hei marched to the desk.

"Yes, Missa Wong."

"Take these documents to Mr. Kai's home on the Peak. Have him sign the title deeds."

"I unnastan' assignmen' Missa Wong," the insignificant-looking but lethal figure replied.

"Make sure he signs all three sets and bring them straight back to me."

Hu Hei's forehead almost touched the desk in an obsequious bow. "Hung-Triad o-n-a-h, Missa Wong. Notin' less."

Brussels

VERBIEST WAS A MAN accustomed to getting his own way but, somehow, somebody else was throwing a lot of weight around and calling the shots from afar. He did not like it but there was little he could do. The news from Wong shocked his system so badly that he impulsively found himself on his way to Saatchi's office, eager to share the burden.

"Lorenzo, I'm really in over my head with the FT thing. The Triads are now talking about eliminating one of the investigators in the Bureau. I'm not sure I should've got involved in this kind of stuff."

Saatchi's jaw tightened imperceptibly. "Look these things always have an element of risk but once you make sure you cover your own tracks…that nothing can be traced to you, it'll work out. Just wait and see."

"What if the chiefs in the Bureau reject Schuman's Regulation. What if they tell him to play with the figures…you know, creative accounting and all that?"

Saatchi flashed a grin. "Smart cooking of the figures? Chinese cooking in a wok? No, Erik that's not their prerogative. Look, you've seen it all before. A chief investigator has almost absolute power. The higher-ups never check a figure…never get into the detail. They'll trust him. If he says the duty for Falcon Tech is ten per cent and has the documentation to back it they'll sign up."

"I just feel that I'm out of my league. Lawyers shouldn't get involved in sleazy operations. It's not the kind of thing to hang on your c.v., is it? I just wish it was all wrapped up. I would go on a long holiday to the Caribbean."

"Don't worry your head, Erik. From what you've told me Schuman's in an impossible position, especially with all those sound-effects on that tape – orgasmic groaning, the lot. He wouldn't stand a chance in a court of law."

Verbiest reluctantly agreed. "Yes, it's pretty damning."

"So you enjoyed the tape?"

"Well let's say those Triads did a good job."

Saatchi laughed lewdly and then said, "I always knew that you were a bon viveur but now I know that you are also a born voyeur."

"Jesus, Lorenzo you always seem to see the funny side," Verbiest snorted as he made for the door.

When the door closed Saatchi smiled to himself, grabbed the phone, punched several digits and slouched back in his chair.

A TELEPHONE CALL to Marc's friend at ULB revealed the meaning of the symbol. It was the kiss of death; once issued it was never rescinded. Montorro's life was in mortal danger. Marc pondered all the possibilities and decided that he had to act fast. Phoning him at home, he arranged to meet at the Arts Loi metro station shortly after six.

Marc stepped from the metro and waited until the carriages moved off. He looked for Montorro on the platform but could not see him. Surveying the jammed mass of rush-hour commuters on the opposite platform, he eventually spotted the Spaniard. Montorro beckoned that he would come across. Down to the right the faint rumble of a metro echoed through the tunnel. People rose from the seats and moved forward to board the approaching metro. As the clicking and swishing sound of the metro became louder there was a surge in the crowd. Montorro's face suddenly flinched and, moments later, looking disorientated, he was forced forward to the edge of the platform by pressure from behind. Amid the mayhem and confusion he lunged awkwardly onto the track, his head taking the impact on the cold steel rail.

Above the shrieks of the shocked commuters the brakes of the metro screeched piercingly as it emerged from the tunnel and trundled the thirty metres along the track towards the Spaniard. A communal gasp reverberated about the station as the stunned onlookers stared down helplessly. The metro came to a halt within a metre of Montorro.

A face grinned across at Marc, then turned swiftly and eased back through the crowd. Another black-haired figure wearing an anorak and, carrying what appeared to be an umbrella, slithered his way to an open space and vanished up the escalator. Yet another moved nonchalantly in the opposite direction and, moments later, he too disappeared through an exit. The glimpses were fleeting, snatched through the throng, but Marc was certain. All three were Orientals. Marc stood frozen in a catatonic state, the colour rapidly draining from his face. The atavistic human survival instinct of flight immediately overwhelmed him. Vanish, Schuman, vanish. He made for the escalator and disappeared into the evening rush hour.

Hong Kong

THE LAUNCH WAS LESS than six months away and the trade issue had still not been resolved. Wong was summoned out to the Tai Po industrial estate to explain what was happening. As the Chinese secretary led him to the office, he could hear Lindell's voice reverberating down the corridor. Once across the threshold Lindell immediately barked, "Neither Verbiest nor you have goddamn reported anything to us in the last fortnight. What the hell's happening?"

The Oriental walked towards a chair and sat down. Before he spoke he wanted to fully assess the mood. He looked across at Newman who was leaning against a filing cabinet, his arms folded and a tense expression on his face. He then turned to face Lindell.

"The Triad leader told me this is the most sensitive stage. Rush him now and you lose everything. The hired hands have again made contact and will insist on a deal on Thursday evening. He has to-"

Lindell jumped from the chair and came around the desk. "Don't give me that crap," he snarled, his finger pointed at the lawyer's chest. Wong remained impassive, unmoved by the anger.

"The documents for the flotation will be lodged with the Securities and Exchange Commission at the end of November. And Sinclair is hyping up Wall Street and the media."

Newman homed in to within inches of the visitor. "The launch will fall apart if this thing's not sorted out. You and Verbiest got us into this mess, now get us the fuck out of it."

"It will come right but Schuman needs time. He's in the trap...it's only a matter of days."

"Now. We want it wrapped up *now,"* Lindell snapped back.

"It's going to work out fine. The Triads know what they're at."

"You hear me, Wong, I want it wrapped up."

The Oriental lawyer leaned back on the chair. It was time to put them in the picture, time to report on other developments. "There is something else," he said, matter-of-factly. "Montorro served us well but he was trying to turn up the heat. He wanted cash. And-"

"What are you goddamn talking about?"

Wong remained unfazed by the interruption. "He was becoming a little irrational...paranoid. There was a real danger that he would spill his guts to the police. They...well we - that's Verbiest and me - we decided to have him washed."

"What the hell are you talking about?" Newman spluttered.

"We decided to wash him...to eliminate him. Call it what you will."

Lindell's voice trembled in anger for the first time. "Jesus Christ, you mean you had somebody killed. Killing was never part of this."

"Montorro was unstable. He just had a little 'accident'.

Anyway, with him out of the way, it will make it easier for Schuman to accept the new figures. It's a pragmatic solution."

Lindell brushed his hair back with his fingers and bounced back to his chair. "I'm not...I'm not hearing this. This is fucking crazy."

Newman's index finger was now stabbing at Wong's chest. "Everything's lost if we go down that road."

Wong shrugged. "Are you willing to take the chance that he wouldn't spill his guts in the Bureau? International conspiracy carries a heavy penalty. I assure you gentlemen he was taken out of the equation efficiently."

Newman moved back, repulsed at what he was hearing. "This scares me. Playing hard to reduce duty is one thing but murder..."

"Tom's right. The whole thing's revolting. You and your Triad friends are depraved. What the fuck have you got us mixed up in here?"

Wong was cold and detached again. "You wanted a solution for a problem and we engineered one. But if you now want to stop, to back off then we call off the nasty business in Brussels. You get hit with forty per cent duty and..."

He paused for what he thought was just about the right length of time to keep suspense hanging in the air. "...and maybe the flotation collapses. No, Mr. Lindell, the stakes were too high. Montorro was starting to talk to Schuman. When it comes to things like this you cannot get sentimental. It pays to keep your eye on the prize. But...I mean...if you want to change tactics, you're the client."

Lindell didn't like Wong's smug analysis one bit. He wanted to draw out and plant a fist on his jaw but somehow knew that it would solve nothing.

"Dylan we've got to decide where this whole thing's going. It's getting out of hand and we...we need more control. Otherwise we're going to be squeezed between the proverbial rock and a hard place."

"Shit," Lindell muttered. As he paced behind the desk he kicked over the waste paper bin in vexation. "This whole fucking thing was a big mistake from the start."

The lawyer's countenance remained inscrutable.

"So Mr. Smart Lawyer, now you want us involved in killing. We started out looking for the best deal on the duty and you promised us a neat little solution. But now-"

Wong snapped back, his voice raised in anger for the first time. "Look, do you want a few inefficient *gweilos* and bureaucrats in Europe preventing Falcon Tech from becoming the shining light of Wall Street?"

Lindell's mind filled with images of that famous bell at the New York Stock Exchange ringing to announce the launch, confusing his thoughts. "No we don't but-"

"Well you were eager for a solution and Mr. Verbiest and I…we found one. He thinks we shouldn't take any unnecessary risks."

Newman banged the desk. "There must've been a better solution. Why didn't they shut him up with money."

The Supreme Lodge Father smiled deep inside at the thought of spending money on an expendable coolie like Montorro. Ridiculous.

"Money? As far as I know the Triads never pay their pawns money."

Lindell shot a glance at Newman and then riveted Wong. "You hear me *Wong* I want results by next week. We've had to postpone the quarterly meeting in Boston until November. Sinclair's asking questions. This mess had better be wrapped up before then. Now get outta here. We've work to do."

Wong bowed politely and made for the door, a smile breaking across his face as he walked down the corridor.

"*Americans!* They think they are the centre of the universe. I'm working so hard to reach the end game too and they don't even appreciate it," he consoled himself as he walked down the steps leading from the main door of the building.

Brussels
TWO EVENINGS LATER, Marc went to King Baudouin Stadium to see a friendly soccer game between Holland and Belgium. Picking up his ticket at the entrance he mounted the stairs to the

upper stand and took his seat. Almost immediately two Asians came down the steps and sat either side of him. A burst of phrases in heavy guttural accents came from left and right but their eyes remained focused on the verdant football pitch.

"We have message for you. We want answer, Mr. Schuman."

"Now is time *make-your-mind-up*."

"We watch you day and night."

"You must say yes."

"Time is running out."

He turned towards the one on the right. "I'm not going to be intimidated by-"

They were gone - vanished back up the steps just as quickly as they appeared.

They, too, are watching me, he thought.

He felt a flutter of nervousness in the pit of his stomach. *Relax,* he counselled himself. But their words repeated in his mind. *'We watch you day and night…We watch you day and night…'* A cold shiver ran down his spine as he tried to focus on the activity on the field below him.

This is not going to go away, he thought. *Not unless I succumb. Damn them. That I will never do.*

THE TAPE HUNG OVER Marc like the Sword of Damocles. With one week to go before Kaufmann's deadline he wanted energy and imagination to fight on. A smart idea that would give him the upper hand but time and fortune were not on his side. And, to add to the complication, Laura was getting suspicious. Her phone calls made him appear evasive and non-committal. Arrangements had been cancelled more than once. There was nothing he could tell her right now. Time was running out.

The following morning Marc arrived at the office shortly after eight, the events of the last few days still weighing on his mind. He wondered if Montorro had mentioned to his wife about meeting him at Arts-Loi. What if…? Just too many questions…too many explanations. A few minutes later the phone rang snapping him out of a montage of thoughts. It was Astrid Reynaud from the Personnel Unit on the sixth floor. He never had reason to speak to her although he did meet her at some of the social gatherings when people were leaving.

She was blunt. There was simply no other way to convey the news. "Marc I'm sorry to have to tell you but Carlos Montorro is dead."

He had expected the phone call some time during the day. It was real, not some nightmare. "Excuse me. What did you say?"

"Carlos died on Tuesday evening. Apparently he collapsed and fell in front of a metro at Arts-Loi station."

"I'm really sorry to hear that. Thank you for letting me know." He dropped the phone. There was nothing he could say. The piece of paper with the Chinese letters in the triangle was still in his pocket.

The words from his friend at ULB kept repeating in his head. *"The number seven is the mystic Chinese symbol for 'Death'."*

He put his elbows on the desk and propped his head in his hands. Half an hour passed, maybe more. He did not move. His mind was vacant and empty, devoid of thoughts. And then images of Laurel and Hardy came into focus. And the Orientals.

Heidi appeared at the doorway. She asked about the arrangements for the team briefing but he did not hear her. He was in a world of his own.

"Marc I asked about the meeting. Where's it going to be held?"

"Just a second." He lifted his head and looked at her with a vacant expression.

"Did you hear that Carlos is dead?" he asked.

"No? What…what happened?"

"I've just heard. Died on Tuesday. Apparently fell in front of a metro."

Heidi asked more questions but Marc did not hear her.

And then she said, "Marc, you look shocked? Are you all right?"

He passed it off. "Yes I am. We've lost a good colleague. Very sad."

"Yes, terrible."

There was a long silence and then she tentatively asked about the meeting again.

"We'll have to postpone it for a few days."

"Sure," she said and disappeared through the door.

Marc swung the chair around and stared through the window. *Those bastards will kill me too even if I co-operate with them,* he thought.

Chapter Fifteen

THE EVENTS OF THE PAST WEEKS weighed heavily on his mind. Marc badly needed to think about other things. On Sunday, he made his way to the cluster of museum buildings nestling - a short distance from his apartment - in the shadow of the Cinquantenaire monument. He planned on spending an afternoon at the Aircraft Museum, studying the latest additions to the military display. He picked up the guidebook at the entrance and had just reached the Russian Mig 23, half way down the centre row, when a voice called out.

"Schuman!"

Suddenly Johnson appeared from behind the Mig and took off a pair of sunglasses. Somebody whistled close by. Marc spun around as Taylor stepped from behind a large supporting steel girder.

"More comedy," he muttered. Ignoring his comment they marched forward to within metres of him. "I see Schuman's got his sense of humour back." Taylor said. They looked at each other, nodded and concluded that a sense of humour was a good thing in this kind of situation. Marc scanned his surroundings, saw that nobody was within earshot and slammed the guidebook he had just bought against the wing of the Mig.

"Now listen to me for a change. I'm doing the questioning and you'd better give me some answers. You bastards killed Montorro. I'm going to the police and then we'll see who's calling the shots."

Instantaneously their faces hardened. Taylor leaned towards Marc and said,

"Don't fuck with us Schuman."

"You don't fuck with me and I won't fuck with you."

"The photographs were only a teaser...a few stills from the movie which no doubt you enjoyed. Nothing beats home entertainment and when you're the star... well it's even better.

183

That little motivator is a real blockbuster."

"You're getting nowhere."

Johnson turned to Taylor. "Our friend Schuman is into a bit of macho posturing today."

Taylor grinned. "But I think it's really only arrogance from being a hot-shot lawyer in the Trade Bureau."

They refocused their attention on the prize. "Schuman, the time for games is over. You've seen the movie. You should be proud."

"Yes," Taylor continued. "Very proud. And at least you have the evidence…the hard evidence, to coin a phrase. You know something Schuman, there are many Viagra-popping menopausal males out there who would just love to be in your shoes…big boy."

A raucous guffaw filled the cavernous building. "…Yes big boy here's got a lot of lead in his pencil," Johnson agreed.

"I've passed the tape to the Commissioner's office. I'm moving off the case from next Monday. Good try guys but it didn't work."

"And moving into accommodation provided by the Thai government?" Johnson retorted.

"Schuman don't *lie*. Let me tell you the position you're in. First you were involved in the most repulsive sex acts with underage girls and it's there for everyone to see. We're talking a criminal offence with a long stretch in a Bangkok jail. The mood in Europe now is to catch paedophiles like you and put them away. It's already happened here in Belgium. And then what does big boy Schuman do? He sneaks off to Bangkok to continue his sex slave trade there. The public will be unforgiving and baying for your blood when this story breaks. Can you imagine the good fortune of the Belgian police hauling in a Euro cat? They can show to the world that they are professional once more and people may forget past cock-ups."

Their eyes - dark and evil - were riveted on him. A cold sweat broke out over his body. Marc felt as if his heart had crept up his oesophagus and was pulsating in his throat.

He had not quite thought about the tape like that before but what they said put a stark twist to it. It now seemed the nightmare was just beginning. He tried to remain calm and think of something to say but nothing came. Strong emotions welled up as he stared past them into a world beyond.

Taylor dragged a finger across the cold metal surface of the aircraft. "Take a good look at this craft, Schuman cause you ain't going to see one like this for a very long time…"

"…Yeah by the time those warders in the Bangkok Hilton are finished with big boy here suppose he won't have much interest in aircraft anymore. I hear they love white-skinned European asses over there. It's such a contrast for them. A young man could get the treatment every day…until he's carried out in a casket."

Johnson agreed. "…Yeah, big time investigator. And that's just the warders. The prisoners like it even better. Deranged and insane in the oppressive heat with nothing to live for…innocent men once - mostly drug couriers - manipulated by smart godfathers and then caught in the act. That adds up to a lot of revenge and bitterness but one day along comes a bit of pleasure. And what do you know? A daily quick-fix to fill that emptiness in their lives. Suddenly they have a reason to wake up in the morning again. Yippee, something to live for. Probably hold a guy down and take turns, day and night. Reckon you'd be begging for mercy in no time…"

The look of sadistic pleasure in their eyes said it all. Marc's neck was on fire with tension.

"…That's of course if most of the day ain't spent hopping from the cot to the can in that steamy cauldron. I hear they play nasty tricks on the new kid in there. Warders emptying their bladders on the rice can sure play havoc with the gastric tract."

"No court of law will accept that tape," Marc snapped. "I am innocent. I know that you drugged me with your so-called philtre."

"…That's the problem with big-headed arrogance from working in the Trade Bureau. Big-shot lawyer here doesn't realise that the mood in the world is to put guys like him away."

An overweight security man came towards them, slowed for a moment, then ambled past, eyeing them suspiciously. When he was well out of earshot Taylor moved closer and started again in a subdued monotone. "Schuman, I bet you're thinking that we are sadistic bastards. Well, you're right. 'Nam's made us that way. We know what fear and terror are like. One minute you're alive and the next? Well, the Viet Cong deliver a booby trap bomb. That's terror…that's fear. But, after a while you learn to live with it. You have to. You're eighteen and you're looking forward to a long life ahead."

There was a silence. Taylor straightened up and surveyed the line of aircraft. He then rotated his head and again fixed his eyes on Marc. "I see you're reflecting…thinking over your options…weighing up the pros and cons just like any good investigator would do. A wise thing to do, Schuman but look, time is running out. Let me tell you about our insurance policy. A bell boy in your hotel in Bangkok will testify that you paid him to procure girls to star in your movies. You see you were running a sideline business making pornographic movies and selling them in Europe. Your arrogance got the better of you so you wanted to be the star yourself. There you have it. Simple, really."

Marc wanted to hit out and strangle them with his bare hands.

"We can supply a bunch of witnesses from Bangkok who'd love to have a holiday in Europe."

"Okay, okay what if I say 'yes'."

They mentioned the money again. They explained that the coercion and pressure would stop but that the tape – their insurance policy as they liked to call it – would be ready to land on the Commissioner's desk at a moment's notice. They assured him that it was only there to keep him honest, to keep him straight. Marc stepped back and pretended to study the aircraft. "Right," he said in a low voice without lifting his eyes from the Mig. "I'll think about it."

Taylor's eyes hardened. "Of course, if you decide to refuse our offer, well that would be a pity. It would not help you and it would not help our client. For that matter, nor would it help your family and friends. They must count for something too, Schuman. The evidence is…as you no doubt realise fairly overwhelming…fairly damning."

186

He punctuated his words for what seemed like the right amount of time to let fear linger in the air and then continued. "However, if you want to roll the dice, to gamble with your life, then that's your choice but from where we're standing we now own your ass. And for you the only real way out is in."

Johnson took over. "Yes, Schuman, into the big family where you will be protected."

"Just like Montorro I suppose."

Johnson's face was instantly transformed by a wicked grin. "Your girlfriend…Laura isn't it…was quite lucky. Maybe next time…"

At the mention of Laura's name pure rage enveloped Marc. He lashed out with a punch that slapped into Johnson's neck and immediately followed through with a lightning-quick jab into his ribs sending him stumbling over the knee-high chain cordoning off the aircraft. Johnson's head crashed into the wing of the Mig. Taylor raced forward and slammed Marc back against the steel pillar. Marc felt his back ache badly but managed to bring his knee up landing it neatly on target into Taylor's groin. He groaned painfully and bent over. The commotion made the security guard turn. He stood stationary about thirty metres away, then swaggered towards the fracas, shouting that he would call the police and ordered them out of the Museum.

"You bastards," Marc exploded as he eased his back away from the pillar and stormed towards the exit.

They immediately pulled themselves together and followed. Johnson held the side of his head. Taylor yelled as he awkwardly hobbled along. "You're a smart guy. If we hand over the tape basically you're at the mercy of faceless Belgian bureaucrats and you don't have to think hard to figure out what that's like. You're a bureaucrat too, so you know the mind set. It's always nice to have a case neatly wrapped up. And it's the same for your investigation. You're the lawyer. You can make the law. A duty our client can live with. That's all we ask."

"Wrong again," Marc snapped over his shoulder. "I may be chief investigator but the law is drafted by someone else. Even if I wanted to, I couldn't influence her."

He realised what he had said and immediately regretted it. Stupid. Stupid. Smug grins lit their faces. "So," Taylor said. "Schuman's not the only hot shot lawyer on this case. We may be barking up the wrong tree."

They brushed past him and vanished through the door.

Hong Kong

CHENG WAS PUT IN THE picture within minutes. He listened to what Johnson had to say and then asked a string of questions. "So," he said finally. "There's a she lawyer in there with Schuman?"

"Seems she's in charge of some of the legal stuff. That's what he said. He blurted it out under pressure but realised he had made a big mistake."

"Okay Mr. Johnson we have to do some more research. I'll get back to you. Hold fire for now, so to speak."

Even though the Supreme Lodge Father was not in his office he was, nevertheless, in the loop within seconds. Cheng had known his penchant for relaxation and tracked him down to his favourite Suzie Wong bar in Wanchai where he was receiving his once-a-week massage. When the phone call came through Wong was lying on the bed listening to the beat of the music from the bar downstairs while enjoying the sinuous movements of the three masseuses as they gently spread suds along his back and buttocks. He immediately grabbed the phone from the petite girl and banished all three with a dismissive wave of his hand. They slipped on robes and hastily left the room. Wong wrapped a towel around his waist and moved to the couch.

Hmm, he was thinking deeply as he reached for the packet of cigarettes. *Maybe Schuman hasn't got the free hand we thought he had.* He punched the numbers rapidly and then pressed another button so that Cheng could listen in. "Mr. Verbiest, our friends tell us that Schuman isn't the only law-maker for the case. There's a 'she' in there somewhere in the system."

Verbiest was confused. "That surprises me. Normally the chief investigator drafts the law but it's always possible that

188

things have changed. Look, a phone call will clari-"

"And," Wong interrupted. "What do we do if it's true?"

"*We*," Verbiest retorted. "You're the brains behind this whole scheme. What do *you* do?"

"If there's another lawyer in there then we'll have to have her removed…just like you suggested with Miss Harrison."

The Belgian lawyer suddenly became angry and lost for words. Wong was talking out of line and it incensed him. "This is great," he exploded. "We keep eliminating everybody who gets in the way."

"The stakes are high. It's hardly the time for melodrama. If there's no way to influence her then we eliminate her. It's as simple as that. Just find out her name and as many details as possible and Cheng will push ahead."

Verbiest felt trapped. The whole affair was rapidly spinning out of control, unnerving him. He just wished that Wong would disappear. "Okay, okay. But you've got to talk to the FT people."

"Absolutely. FT must to be kept in the picture."

Wong finished the conversation and punched another button on the console.

"Verbiest's a very nervous guy. He just can't stick the tension," he chuckled down the line to Cheng.

"Way out of his depth," Cheng agreed, snorting contemptuously.

San José

THE MEETING WAS ARRANGED at short notice. Before they arrived Batista spent an hour scrutinising the quarterly management reports for the Falcon Tech operations in Europe and Asia. Every word. Every figure. Line by line. The future looked bright. The future looked rich. But a menacing thought kept interrupting his concentration. The trade investigation was still not put to bed, the latest reports from Verbiest and Wong unnerving him even more. He wondered how he had signed up to such illegal activity especially with so much scrutiny by the SEC and the Department of Justice right now.

And he did not like the Oriental's euphemism one bit. It reverberated loudly in his ears: 'Montorro had to be eliminated. He was a threat. He could have spilled his guts.'

It was murder, Batista reflected. *Plain and simple murder.* That thought haunted him. *We have all crossed the Rubicon on this one.* There's no going back. If the launch was going to be a success it should have been resolved by now. The little arrangement he reluctantly agreed to had not been delivered, not by a long shot, and it was now completely outside his control. Wong's latest assurances were not helping his bout of colitis either. In fact, that little slant-eyed chink made life more complicated, not easier. The Oriental's voice continued to haunt him.

'Don't worry. The Triads have done this before. All they're doing is giving Falcon Tech a bit of leverage with those arrogant investigators. They've got Schuman by the balls…in a matter of time his mind will follow.'

He sprang from his desk and headed for the washroom. When he returned, Lindell and Newman were standing in his office.

"Hi," he boomed. "I figure we've got some serious decisions to make…collect our thoughts, so to speak."

Lindell shrugged but said nothing. Batista paced in front of his own desk to help ease the bad sensation in his gut.

"Dylan, the more I think about this the more I realise that we've pushed out the envelope with this European business. We're going to have to come clean with Sinclair."

"Look Albert," Newman interjected before Lindell could speak, "I was never really convinced about this whole thing but we've gone so far now that it's-"

"Heard it all before," Batista snapped sourly. "Too dangerous to tell Sinclair."

"…Well, yes."

Batista made for his chair and eased into it. "I'm putting my cards on the table. He's got to be put in the picture about the killing of that official."

"Albert, you've already told him enough about the Schuman guy," Lindell cautioned.

190

"I just told him that our Hong Kong friends were helping to make sure that we got a favourable duty. Something we could live with. Sinclair knows that a little money is involved. That's all."

"And now, in one fell swoop, you are going to kiss and tell. Blackmail...bribery and..."

"Yes, I'll finish it for you *murder*," Batista replied in a low monotone.

"He'll have a heart attack on the spot. His lofty FFV values won't let him accept it as a way of doing business. It's-"

Batista stuck his right hand in the air. "No," he said vehemently. "We tell Sinclair that the whole sordid business will be wrapped up in late November and that we can then concentrate our energies on the launch."

Now Lindell started pacing. "I'm not so sure."

"Look, Dylan, if we don't tell Sinclair and this whole mess in Brussels is not cleared up by December, the launch documents will have to issue. We can't bluff that it's ten per cent if we're not absolutely sure. And if Sinclair finds out at the eleventh hour he'll dump us. He'll have no choice. And you know what that means. Bye bye to one hundred million dollars at least. By telling him, we lock him in. He has to take some responsibility too."

"Albert has a point. The more Sinclair knows the safer for us," Newman agreed.

Lindell raised his hands in objection. "I hear what you're saying but the whole fucking thing sucks big time. We're getting deeper and deeper into something that we don't have control over. And if we tell those blue bloods part of the story they're going to probe. We'll look stupid. Remember what happened at last July's quarterly? Our friend Hanson was asking a bunch of searching questions about the anti-dumping duty. Do you think he'll sleep through tomorrow's meeting?"

Batista smiled for the first time. "That's precisely why we tell Sinclair everything. It will be up to him to control our toffee-nosed English friend. After all, Sinclair *is* the chairman."

Lindell sneered. "He may succeed with him but what about those investment banking boys. Jefferson...and that other guy? They won't agree to any document that might have to be altered later."

Newman pondered on the issue for a long moment. "Albert, it's not going to be that simple. Investment bankers are a conservative lot. They'll row in behind Hanson. That's for sure."

Lindell drew in a deep breath. "You know, Tom has a point. Sinclair co-opted Jefferson onto the board just for credibility and connections for the launch."

Batista smacked the palm of his hand down hard on the table. "Well, I don't have all the solutions. Remember I wasn't that happy back in April when this whole crappy thing took off. And you know what? We were so concerned to distance ourselves from the triad skulduggery that we gave Verbiest and Wong total control. And you see what happened…they authorise killing to accomplish the end result. We made a big mistake back then. Somebody should've controlled those guys from the very beginning. The whole thing's now too complicated. We damn well never agreed to have ex-CIA guys involved."

"And, goddammit, we don't exactly know what's going on now. Problem is, all we know about is building and selling computers," Lindell exclaimed, rubbing his temples in exasperation.

"Dylan's right," Newman said. "It was a mistake which is blowing up in our faces. I think we gotta haul Verbiest in and lay down the law for once and for all. Bring Wong in too. Let them know who calls the shots."

Batista had a look of resignation on his face. "Yes. In hindsight, we should have let Verbiest sweat a little longer. All we know is that Wong has got some hit men running around Brussels bumping off people."

"Yes. And they tell us when it's too late to do anything about it," Newman agreed. "It was a big mistake to let control slip away to those chinks. What the hell were we thinking of?"

Lindell stopped pacing. "Greed…I suppose we were all greedy then. The flotation windfall on the horizon was making all our hearts beat faster."

"Okay," Batista said, "enough of the soul searching. Come on, give me ideas."

"Looks as if we go along with your earlier suggestion. You know, put the full facts to Sinclair. See how he reacts and then let him play it whatever way he wants to with the rest of the board."

"Do you go along Tom?"

"It's the best we've got. We can't hide it any longer. With a bit of luck the Brussels business will be wrapped up in a couple of weeks."

Batista rubbed his stomach. "You know this whole thing has brought my colitis back big time."

"Take it easy Albert, or you won't live to see that winery in Napa."

"Funny, smartass. Seriously, it's causing me some real problems."

Lindell reassured him. "Well look, it's up to Sinclair to stage-manage the whole affair. After all it's his project first and foremost."

"Okay," Batista said. "We'll schedule a meeting with Sinclair next week. Now let's focus on the computer exhibition in Denver on Friday."

"We're sure goin' to take the industry by storm with the launch of the ThinkEx," Lindell declared confidently.

Chapter Sixteen

THE COMMOTION STARTED shortly before midnight with the sound of sirens, immediately piercing his senses and catapulting him into consciousness. Marc awoke with a shriek and sat bolt upright, the sheet moist with sweat and knotted around his legs. The book he had been reading had slipped from his grasp as he drifted into a deep sleep. The sound was closer now and tyres squealed loudly some distance up the street. He rubbed his eyes and glanced at the clock radio. He had been in bed no more than thirty minutes. The activity intensified as several vehicles seemed to screech to a halt on the street below. The sirens blared for another thirty seconds and, then, suddenly silence. He pulled back the covers, bounced his legs out onto the floor and was on his feet bounding towards the living room. He peered through the window but immediately jerked back, jolted by the sight unfolding below him.

At least four police cars had zig-zagged to a stop. He could see two policemen scurrying around the parked cars on the opposite side of the street. They crouched down, their guns pointing across towards the apartment entrance. In the shadow of a shop entrance two more policemen lurked; their guns also pointed towards his building.

"Jesus Christ," he gasped. "They've come to arrest me." A nauseating feeling rose from the pit of his stomach at the thought that he was about to lose everything. His heart was now beating like a jackhammer. He forced himself back for another glance just to make sure.

The scene made him flinch, choking back a hard lump in his throat with a nervous swallow. He stepped back from the window. A voice started to echo in his head; telling him it's over…telling him to walk down the stairs quietly…telling him to put his hands out for the handcuffs…telling him to surrender. For a moment he obeyed and, walking across the room, he stood at the door and reached for the handle but instead banged the wall with his fists.

"Christ this is crazy," he whispered to himself. "I've really done nothing wrong…nothing." He decided he would not submit…would not capitulate because, after all, he was innocent…he was framed. There was only one option left…one way to freedom. Escape!

Contemplating his options for a moment he dashed back into the bedroom and fumbled around for his jeans. Grabbing them from the chair he hopped around the room, struggling to push his right foot down the leg, eventually toppling over. The doorbell buzzed. *They are in the foyer*. A surge of blood to his head left him disorientated and beads of perspiration began oozing out all over. He scrambled onto the bed and managed to get his other foot into the jeans. The doorbell buzzed again, this time more insistently. Marc jumped to his feet and grabbed a shirt from the wardrobe. Finally he slipped on a pair of loafers he found by the bedside locker.

He bolted back towards the window and again cautiously surveyed the activity below as the blue lights threw eerie shadows around the darkened living room. They had set up an arc light on the opposite footpath almost turning the street into a film set.

French doors led from the bedroom to a small balcony. He raced back into the room, opened them and looked down into the darkness at the rear of the building. Leaning over the railing he contemplated clambering down somehow but couldn't discern a safe landing place below. He pounded back to the living room and darted around like a caged lion with no particular idea what to do.

Dark images filled the void in his brain. He could see Kaufmann on the street below, leaning against a police car. 'God damn it Schuman we emphasised how important it was to keep your hands clean. This is dynamite. You have ruined the standing of the European Trade Bureau. The Commissioner simply had to sign the order lifting diplomatic immunity to allow the Belgian police to take over. We didn't want a fuss in the office so it's best this way. But I have just one question: Why did you do it Schuman? Why? You had it all there in front of you for the taking…a great career. You would've gone to the top, I'm sure of it. But paedophilia? Why Schuman? Why?'

The criminal trial now played out in his mind. It would be a long drawn out affair. A first for international child sex trafficking. Paraded out for everyone to see at the court hearing. The people would bay for his blood…would demand that such a heinous crime could not go unpunished - not after all that sleazy stuff in Belgium. Nobody would believe his story. The judge would pass down the toughest sentence possible for such a reprehensible act.

'Marc Hendrik Schuman - convicted paedophile. Twenty years.'

Twenty years! An exemplary sentence…a warning to others.

And now his thoughts turned to Laura. She would be scorned. Girlfriend of a sex fiend. The tabloid press would have a field day.

The doorbell buzzed longer this time. His imagination was firmly in overdrive but the shrill ring jolted him back to reality. He ran to the bedroom, pulled the duvet from the bed and yanked the sheet from the mattress. Grabbing two more sheets from the wardrobe, he tied them all together and ravelled them into one long makeshift rope. He secured one end to the parapet of the balcony and threw the lifeline over.

Footsteps floated from the direction of the landing. Moments later the pounding and banging started. *Probably the butt of a gun against the door,* he thought. His chest felt as if it were burning, his stomach in turmoil. The banging was louder now and then faint voices. He thought he heard the plaintive calling of his name.

He lunged forward and straddled the railing, staring into the darkness below. Most of his body was now over the wrought iron railing; his feet dangling loosely, trying in vain to search for a toehold along the brick wall. He grabbed the ravelled sheet with both hands, steadying himself by pressing his toes against the wall. His right foot found a firm grip in the recess between two bricks, giving him a chance to plan his next move. Suddenly he heard a door open below and a figure walked from the foyer into the garden. The beam of a torch flicked in all directions and now another figure emerged. He froze on the spot, balancing precariously as he listened and watched intently. The faint light from the foyer doorway confirmed his fears. *They're definitely uniforms. Every escape route has been covered,* he thought. Gingerly grasping the railing, he silently pulled himself up and again listened. The banging subsided and the voices started again. He crept back onto the balcony and moved cautiously towards the living room. They were louder now, shouting something incomprehensible as if breathless with excitement. He tried to understand, to make sense of it. With no other way out he walked across the room, unlocked the door and opened it. A policeman was standing there with Ricardo Ravisi by his side. Ravisi lived in the apartment a floor below him.

"Oh Marc, I knew you were in there," Ravisi exclaimed.

"What?" Marce asked, baffled.

"Come quickly with your keys. A stolen car's crashed beside yours and petrol's leaking. It could explode at any moment. The police are trying to clear the street."

Marc's chest deflated in one big sigh and his body sagged almost to the floor. He followed them downstairs in a daze, trying hard to regain his poise. The tangled wreck had hit the lamppost first and then careened into the wall beside the entrance door, within metres of his BMW.

"One of the joyriders has escaped but this one's dead," the policeman said, pointing at the front passenger seat. Marc zapped the alarm, jumped in and drove off. He parked at the first available place and ran back to the mayhem. "We're certain he escaped through the foyer to the back garden," the policeman continued. "Don't panic though…he's probably back in Saint Josse by now."

An ambulance arrived and took away the dead teenager. A few minutes later the activity died down and Marc returned upstairs. Walking straight to the bedroom, he slumped onto the bed and willed himself into a fitful doze.

Boston

FORMALITY WAS THE HALLMARK of their relationship. Miss Rockwell knew his every idiosyncrasy, his every peccadillo but never divulged anything or confided in anybody. A well-preserved lady, she had been Sinclair's secretary for more than thirty years. At precisely ten o'clock she tapped on the door, came in and greeted Sinclair.

He cleared his throat. "Morning, Miss Rockwell."

"The executives from Falcon Tech are at reception sir. Shall I tell them to come up?"

"Yes, please."

"Will you require secretarial assistance for the meeting sir?"

"No thank you. It's just a briefing on the Falcon Tech subsidiary."

"Anything else Mr. Sinclair?"

"No, Miss Rockwell. That's all for now."

A few moments later she guided the executives towards the conference table. Lindell studied the portrait of *Sinclair the first* decorating the wall opposite the president's desk. And then his eyes scanned the paintings on the other walls. He nudged Batista. "Looks like the art gallery's expanding."

Sinclair moved from his desk and joined them at the table. "Good morning, gentlemen. I take it that you've all had coffee?"

He was met with muttered yesses and nods. "That'll be all for now, Miss Rockwell."

Lindell's eyes followed as the well-rounded figure walked towards the door. *If I ever become president of Falcon Tech*, he thought, *I'll have a twenty-something tending to my needs.*

"Okay gentlemen, you wanted to see me. Let's hear it."

Batista cleared his throat. "Well, Howard, it's a follow-on to what you and I discussed a month ago."

"A month ago?" Sinclair was playing confused.

"The trade thing. You remember, the Brussels business...we spoke about-"

"Oh yes...yes. You said that you were making sure that we got the best deal on the duty. It's all wrapped up I take it."

"Well, not quite. You see, it's a bit more complicated."

Sinclair's eyebrows furrowed. "Complicated?"

Batista explained that the plan to influence the investigator had gone a bit too far.

"What...what d'you mean?"

"Look Howard, this is the way the whole thing stacks up right now. Well, for a start, they killed a trade investigator from Brussels and-"

"What did you say?"

"I said they killed a guy."

"What the hell have you been at? What's the game-"

"We're just as unhappy. It shouldn't have happened."

"Damn right it shouldn't have happened. I hope you've made sure nothing is traceable to Falcon Tech."

"The Triads leave no tracks."

Lindell tapped the table. "Excuse me, Albert, but it was the former CIA guys who eliminated him."

"No, Dylan," Newman interjected. "You're getting confused. Wong said that three Triads from the Hong Kong cell came across to carry it out. The ex-CIA guys were not involved."

Sinclair was exasperated. "Look, it doesn't matter a damn who did what. Is the whole thing sorted out now?"

Batista explained the leverage being used to get the chief investigator on board but warned that, of late, things were becoming even more complicated. Wong and Verbiest were briefing them regularly, he said, but they did not have the full picture.

"But is it working?"

"We think so."

"And?" demanded Sinclair.

"Apparently he's about to deliver. The ex-CIA guys have been working on him and at last he's about to crack. Within a month he'll push through the law giving Falcon Tech a ten per cent duty."

"Ten per cent? You said zero. This is not good for the launch."

"It's the best we can manage. It gives us a huge edge over our Far East competitors."

"That will still damage profits," Sinclair replied sharply, his exasperation barely controlled.

"No, it won't, actually," Lindell said defensively. He outlined the plan whereby Falcon Tech would suffer ten per cent duty and all the other Asians would get hit with a ball park figure of forty per cent. When all the legalities settled down secret deals would be struck with about eight or nine of the other exporters. Falcon Tech would ship their product under its brand, suffer the ten per cent and charge them another ten in commission saving them around twenty per cent overall. "And," he said, "Each of them will think that they are gaining on their competitors. The net effect is that the duty costs us nothing. The other tigers are effectively paying it for us with that commission."

"Yes but will it work in practice?"

"What can go wrong?" Batista asked. "It's the best deal for Falcon Tech. We march ahead and capture maybe sixty per cent of the market before anybody realises what's happening."

"That's your call, Albert. Nothing must damage a successful launch. Nothing," he said distancing himself from the problem.

"Howard, the alternative is stark. Our lawyers in Brussels said we were looking at forty-two per cent. Forty-two per cent! You know the same as I do what that would do to profits. The launch would have to be postponed – no – probably cancelled altogether. Nothing-"

"Nothing surer," Newman finished the sentence.

"The whole thing is a mess now. Batista, I'm holding you personally responsible for this."

"Look, Howard, I don't think we should start throwing blame around right now. What we signed up to last April was nothing more than a bit of manipulation to keep market share…nothing more than any marketing exec would do.

The president straightened himself up in the chair. "Kimble-Sinclair is a very respected health care company. We operate on trust. Governments…the public. If *they* can't trust us we're ruined."

"The whole messy saga is coming to an end. It'll be wrapped up in a few weeks but I must tell you that the deal with the investigator is that he gets a cut of a few million."

"My God, man, that's bribery. What about the Foreign Corrupt Practices Act? The Justice Department could have you arraigned."

"I told you already that was the deal – straight and simple. We can't walk away from it now."

"So this is the real reason that you postponed the quarterly. It's not a question of the accounts. It's this sleazy stuff?"

"Well, we wanted to have it wrapped up before the meeting," Batista replied.

"*Gentlemen*," Sinclair shouted, his voice angry as he pointed his index finger at the three executives in quick succession. "This is your responsibility. Falcon Tech has spent three million on the launch...money that could be in the pockets of Kimble-Sinclair stockholders. Now you people deliver. Do you hear? Deliver!"

Batista wasn't going to accept the lecture. "Howard this is not only a Falcon Tech problem. It's just as important for Kimble-Sinclair. You've got to row in and steer the next quarterly meeting. We have no magical solutions."

Cracks appeared in the presidential style of the East Coast patrician. He jumped from his chair and paced the floor. "Batista," he snarled, "You and your goddamn crew have messed this thing up big time. You get out in front of the board next month and confirm that all lights are green for the launch. You damn idiots."

Lindell wasn't about to take it in the face. "Just hold it right there. You told us to build a global corporation. That we did, Howard. That we did, and while you and your ilk were cosseted in your ivory towers here in Boston we took all the crap in China - the bureaucracy and double-dealing. All along you told us you didn't want to know the details. Well, now you damn well know. We've built this company into a ten-billion-dollar tiger and because of a little trade problem in Europe – not of our making – you want to hang us out to dry."

Batista thumped the table. "Dylan's right. A problem not of our making. Those damn Europeans want protection just because they're inefficient."

Sinclair came back towards the table and said in a calm, resolute voice, "The launch is going ahead at all costs. Now good day."

He walked back to his desk and slumped into his leather chair. The three Falcon Tech executives rose from their seats, in silence, and headed towards the door.

November 1999
Brussels
THE CONFRONTATION HEARING had been postponed twice but was now scheduled for the following Thursday. It was designed to allow both parties to meet face to face across the table, each side free to adduce arguments to rebut the opponent's case. In that way it was much the same as the theatrics of a civil court of law. On that morning Marc and his team entered the meeting-room at 8:15 and began the preparations for the scheduled four-hour hearing. Tables were laid out to form a U shape with the Trade Bureau officials taking up the top table and the opposing lawyers facing each other in true confrontational style. They could argue back and forth, eyeball to eyeball, wagging their fingers or gesticulating fiercely or whatever the moment called for.

The Smeulders & Rosenstock team of three lawyers arrived first. Dr. Rozenstock, a thin, frail man, shook Marc's hand firmly.

"I see this as no more than a mere formality. Let them have their day in court, as it were."

"Mr. Rozenstock, this case is by no means finalised. We must respect the rule of *audi alterem partem* (hear both sides)."

"Ah, mere procedure," he said, brushing a hand towards the documents on the top table. "...Anyway, we have our arguments and counter-arguments ready."

"Good for you," Marc replied.

"Think what you like but from our perspective it's an open-and-shut case. Europe cannot contemplate anything other than high duties."

"Well, today's your opportunity to prove the argument. This is precisely why we hold these kinds of adversarial hearings.

Let both sides argue the rights and wrongs in open court."

"Remember, Mr. Schuman, the European taxpayer is paying your salary. You've got to work for a good solution for the industry's short-term problems."

"Mr. Rozenstock, you know, as I do, that we conduct our investigations impartially. Now, let's just take our seats and hear the arguments in open forum."

"Fine," he muttered gruffly and walked towards his colleagues who took up positions on the right side of the U.

A few minutes later the lawyers for five Asian exporters trooped in. Mr. Nagel, from Koontz & Nagel, represented Wantoe Electronics in Korea and Mr. Ellison acted for Lakoo Computers in Thailand. Ms Smyth from Gregson White would speak for two Japanese companies while Verbiest would defend the interests of Falcon Tech and his two Vietnamese clients.

Marc tapped his Mont Blanc on the table as a judge would his gavel. The meeting room became hushed.

"Good morning and welcome. For those of you attending for the first time, I must remind you that you should confront the issues today but it should not degenerate into physical confrontation." Marc paused, smiling. The lawyers rose to the occasion, responding with half-suppressed laughter.

He continued, "Each side's opening statements will be limited to half an hour. After that, the Trade Bureau may wish to ask clarifying questions and then the rebuttals can begin. The European computer industry has, of course, made the allegation, so that side will make its opening statement first."

Dr. Rozenstock rose to his feet, opened the folder in a deliberate ritual and laid it carefully on the table in front of him.

"Good morning, ladies and gentlemen. I address my remarks to the Bureau and to the opposing parties. We are on the precipice of the twenty-first century and we still haven't got equity in world trade. The people our friends across the table represent will not play a fair game. They don't know what a fair game is." He stabbed a challenging finger across the abyss between the two sides. "And they don't even want to know the rules of the game. The book of rules - civilised behaviour allowing all to compete fairly - has been established for almost a century now. But the people on the other side of the table simply don't want to know about such things. And if they are allowed to do so they will continue to flout them."

He paused for a moment and then turned towards the top table.

"The international community, through the World Trade Organisation, drew up these laws for the orderly conduct of international trade. The European Union plays its full part in this Organisation because it believes in the principles of equity and fair play for all trading partners but our friends don't share those high ideals. They are pricing predators. Low-price predators. Just like birds of prey, they swoop into the European market with cheap prices until they kill off the competition. And what do they do next? They just do what any monopolist would do. They hike up prices once they have the market all to themselves. It's not good for business. It's not good for jobs and it's not good for Europe's citizens. We want to build a society for all our people, a social society where the unemployed are protected by social security. But the Asians don't have that social structure. Those computer manufacturers do not pay the costs that our manufacturers have to suffer. No wonder they can sell their product at a lower price. It's unfair and it should be prevented."

Rozenstock continued for another twenty minutes but there was nothing new. It had been covered in detail at the written procedure stage. Interest was waning at the top table but Marc and his colleagues wore their official facemasks for such occasions. As soon as Rozenstock concluded his statement, Marc turned towards the defending lawyers.

"So, do you wish to plead individually for your own clients or will it be a single oral pleading on behalf of all exporters?"

Verbiest rose from his seat and turned towards the top table.

"If the hearing will permit, I would like to explain the arrangements from the point of view of the defendants of this proceeding. I have been asked to represent the Asian exporters en bloc. My colleagues here with me today may, of course, wish to intervene at the rebuttal stage. But for the pleadings I will put the exporters' case forward. My client is the largest exporter, but the arguments put forward by me today equally apply to all Asian exporters."

The opposing lawyers studied the reaction of Verbiest's colleagues. They just might be able to exploit differences of opinion in the coalition making up the Asian exporters. Falcon Tech was clearly on a roll – producing cheaply in China and selling aggressively in Europe. The other Asian producers had much to fear from the Dragon - the name they jocosely called Falcon Tech - but right now the loss of the European market was the immediate threat facing all exporters alike.

Verbiest was now in full stride. "The economy today is fast becoming a global economy. Any one country does not have a monopoly on production. European video recorders are built with Asian components. Japanese household goods are made with European electronics. American cars have lots of Japanese technology in them. And the chemical and pharmaceutical industries buy ingredients from all corners of the globe. The world is trading technology...intellectual property... knowledge. That's what makes up the value of products today. Trade is less and less about the physical bits and pieces. So I say to the Bureau today to reject this complaint and embrace the information age. It's the only equitable thing to do as we enter the twenty-first century. Allow the citizens to have access to the latest technology from around the world and do not protect outdated practices. Our clients should not be punished because they have set up efficient manufacturing operations. No, most definitely not. The spotlight should be shone on the inefficient ones and they are the European producers using 'state-of-the-ark' technology. It's no wonder they are losing market share."

Verbiest continued his opening statement, pausing at intervals to allow his fellow lawyers to nod their agreement. Just as he finished and sat back in his chair Rozenstock sprang to his feet and shot a salvo across the table.

"Mr. Verbiest, your client is in no position to get high and mighty about efficiency and equity. We have evidence that Falcon Tech is using child labour...children under fourteen

205

years of age - in those village set-ups around Shenzhen. It's reprehensible child abuse and worse than that, the sub-assemblies are being done in the forced labour camps run by the army…the so-called *lao gai*."

Verbiest retorted imperiously. "Dr. Rozenstock what you've just said is nonsense. It's a canard to drum up false arguments. On a point of procedure I would remind the Trade Bureau that the opposing party is not entitled to bring emotional argument to this hearing. The economic facts are all that matter." He was now stabbing the index finger of his right hand at his opponent, his voice raised a few octaves. "You, Dr. Rozenstock, keep firing allegations across the table but you have not produced a shred of evidence. This is typical of the European manufacturers trying to characterise the Asian exporters as some kind of chimeras ready to swoop on Europe and kill off its computer industry. Nothing could be further from the truth. I would remind the Bureau that the complainants are devoid of evidence. And they are trying a most pernicious trick by bringing in emotional arguments about child labour and-"

"No, no. Not at all. It's well known what's happening. It's just that the international community simply cannot investigate in China. If we could, we would throw the evidence across the table right now."

"Well, Dr. Rozenstock, you've said it yourself." Verbiest chirped smugly. "You haven't a shred of evidence in your possession. And that's why your allegation should be struck from the record. I would respectfully ask the top table to note what the complainants have just admitted. A major tenet of their argument has collapsed and this case is-"

"I appeal to the Bureau to censure Mr. Verbiest. He clearly knows well what his client is doing behind the bamboo curtain. It's simply a fact that no investigative journalist can legitimately go into China to investigate the human rights abuses. It's the nature of things."

"Dr. Rozenstock, I suggest you put up or shut up. Come out from the comfort of your protectionist fortress and quit making wild allegations just to blacken our client."

Rozenstock banged the table. "What about the

widespread human rights breaches in China over the last fifty years? And the-"

Marc leaned forward and firmly took charge. "Gentlemen this is a confrontation hearing, not the European Court of Human Rights. Your arguments must be germane. Now, each party must commit to argue within the law as it stands. Dr. Rozenstock, let me make it very clear. We cannot take account of human rights issues and any oral allegations not backed up by evidence will be struck down. Everybody around this table is seasoned enough to know the ground rules."

There was a long silence.

"You can proceed, Mr. Verbiest, but argument must be supported by evidence. Otherwise we will disregard it."

The lawyers nodded conciliatory gestures across the table. Verbiest continued his advocacy for about fifteen minutes, relying mostly on technical arguments. Both parties politely batted back and forth until lunchtime but nothing new emerged. Rozenstock's attempts to split open the coalition of Asian exporters never really picked up speed and the human rights issue was irrelevant making it a weak performance by an experienced trade lawyer.

'Punish the inefficient, not the efficient' was the catch cry across the table.

Schmidt and Henkel listened, faithfully recording the pleadings. By one o' clock the arguments and counter arguments had been fully aired and the heat had dissipated. Marc took advantage of the lull by bringing the proceedings to a close.

THE INVESTIGATING TEAM met the following morning to review the confrontation meeting. No new arguments meant that the proposed draft law would now be scrutinised for the last time. Elena Schmidt joined Marc at eleven and they started the polishing process. Every word was double-checked, every precedent examined and every phrase sanitised to ensure that no court of law could impugn it. They were wordsmiths picking and mixing from the lexicon of law. As agreement was reached on a recital, the printer spewed out the latest version and then they moved forward to the next paragraph.

By seven o' clock the one hundred-page final draft was printed. The principles were now settled; nothing remained to be added but the ten pages setting out the duty penalties for each exporter. That would take a little longer but good progress had been made. The efforts of the past months were taking shape in one piece of legal text.

"This case will be wrapped up within weeks," she said confidently as she waved goodbye and headed towards the door. He continued scrolling the draft on the screen in a final proofing exercise but raised his head in acknowledgement. "Yes, provided that computations for the problem cases can be sorted out." He lifted his right hand from the keyboard and stuck his thumb in the air. "Thanks Elena. I'll have a final meeting with our legal department in the morning and then Kaufmann will have the draft on his desk."

Chapter Seventeen

November 1999
Brussels
THE VIDEO CAMERA had recorded the whole ritual. In the adjoining room the men pulled off the shrouds and nodded to each other. After a few minutes of silence they started to chatter in a low, guttural Chinese dialect. It was a job well done. The first Caucasian and it had gone as planned.

One of the men moved to the table, picked up the phone, pressed twelve digits in quick succession and waited.

The phone was answered.

"Our task is complete. Death By One Thousand Cuts, as you ordered," he said in chiu chow.

"Excellent work. How long did she last?"

"Fifty-eight minutes. There was life until the last."

"Good. Get that tape to Schuman straight away. And have our hired hands deliver a message to him too."

THE MEETING WITH THE legal department produced a few cosmetic changes and lasted less than an hour the following morning. Marc spent the rest of the day at the computer screen verifying the duty penalties proposed by the other investigators. By 8 pm he had become tired of the complex calculations and returned to his apartment, exhausted. He stretched his arms into the air, yawned and slumped back onto the couch, closing his eyes. Suddenly, he heard a clicking sound from the video recorder and a tape started to play. *Weird*, he thought, as he saw that the remote control was on the bookshelf where he always left it. As he stood up his attention was drawn towards an image flickering to life on the television screen.

Marc stared at the screen puzzled, but with a sickening sense of foreboding. The gruesome killing in the cellar now played before his eyes. He stared helplessly as the butchery continued; the body now awash with congealing blood from the multiple lacerations. Several times the camera zoomed in on the cold steel knife poised above the body of the woman. And now he gagged as a figure stepped into view and ceremonially removed the hood from her head. When the masking tape that covered her eyes was removed the camera lens homed in, filling the television screen with her face.

Marc recognised her in an instant. He gasped and his heart started to race furiously.

"Christ," he screeched, his hands covering his face, trying to blot out the horror of what was unfolding before him. He involuntarily recoiled, stumbling backwards towards the couch.

Marc's eyes started to water but he could not sob. His chest felt rigid, he could barely breathe. Rivulets of perspiration ran from his temples and then his legs folded.

His body started to shake uncontrollably and his stomach heaved. He tried to scream, to shout out, but nothing came apart from a primeval rasping groan from deep within his being. The blood pounded in his ears and nausea rose from the pit of his stomach. He made for the bathroom and leaned over the toilet. A few minutes later he rinsed his mouth and returned to the living room. The tape was still playing. He didn't know what to do. He flailed his hands in the air. It was his way of trying to stop it all. He could take no more. Lunging forward, he grabbed the remote control and ejected the tape.

He sat on the couch with his head between his hands. Another macabre twist of events. His thoughts turned to yesterday. Everything was so different then…she had just returned from her holiday in Crete full of enthusiasm to finish the case that they were working on together.

Twenty-four hours earlier Elena Schmidt was beautiful. Twenty-four hours earlier Elena Schmidt was happy.

But that was twenty-four hours earlier.

He was jolted back to reality by the shrill sound of the phone ringing. It rang for about thirty seconds, then stopped. Moments later it started again. This time he answered it.

"She was innocent."

Silence.

"You could have saved her."

Silence.

"You could have said 'yes'."

Another pause.

"Her blood is on your hands."

His hands were shaking. He slammed down the receiver, pulled the cable from the socket and flung the phone across the room.

THAT THURSDAY EVENING it had taken Elena Schmidt no more than two minutes to walk from the Trade Bureau offices, half way along the Avenue, to the post office just meters away from the junction at Rond Point Schuman. Traffic was quiet and, unusually, there were no pedestrians at the lower end of the Avenue. A transit van had pulled up at a parking space just alongside her but she was oblivious of the activity around her, thinking about her holiday in Crete.

It was the hand across her forehead that struck her first followed by the firm grip on her shoulders. The nightmare started with the asphyxiating feeling from the masking tape covering her mouth and now the taste of adhesive. They had come from behind in silence. Her mouth was completely sealed, then her eyes. It stuck to her hair but it did the job. Not a scream…not a murmur. She tried to wrest herself free, to get away from her captors but it was in vain. She was being carried and roughly flung through the side door of the van. That part of the operation took nine seconds. They had planned on twelve. The van sped away towards the lights and disappeared around the junction.

HER BODY WAS FOUND three days later. The gruesome discovery made all the news bulletins on national television and the hunt for the killers started. It took two days for the police to make a positive identification with dental records and the investigation began in earnest. Two detectives from the Brussels police called to the Trade Bureau. Her team mates, including Marc, were gathered into the conference room on the ground floor and told of the macabre find by the detectives. Marc stared into space, wondering whether to tell what he knew. He could be charged with conspiracy to cover up a murder; that much was certain. He closed his eyes and wondered if he had the courage, the strength, to pull off what he was planning.

The senior detective explained what they had found.

"The last positive identification of the victim was from a closed-circuit TV camera outside a bank at the bottom of Avenue de Cortenbergh last Thursday evening. We've never dealt with a murder case like this before. Her body was lacerated from head to toe. Her wrists were slashed, her ankles, her throat. All the main arteries severed. Every piece of flesh cut open." Everyone drew back in horror filling the room with a collective gasp. Somebody spoke out loud. "Elena Schmidt. Why? Why Elena?"

"It's baffling. We're not just looking for one maniac. One person, acting alone, could not have done this. There must have been at least four or five. She would have put up a fierce struggle. We're looking for motive here. It could be a cult – some way-out religious thing – but it's difficult to know. If anybody knows something about her private life – any lead at all – we'd like to know."

The other detective now took over. "We've requested the assistance of Interpol. The Dutch police have confirmed a few similar cases in Amsterdam but they were all Orientals – probably involved in drug dealing. Apparently those secret Chinese Triad sects carry out this kind of butchery on disloyal members. If you can think of a reason, any reason at all, why somebody would want to do this, then please come forward."

One man in the room – just one man – could have put most of the pieces of the jigsaw into place but he stayed silent. He knew more than the police but the most important piece of his jigsaw was still missing. He was determined not to move until he was in possession of that final link.

Marc left the room, leaving huddled, sombre groups whispering in disbelief. As he walked down the corridor the senior detective called out his name. Marc stopped and the detective approached.

"We understand that the victim's the second person in your team to die. Mr. Montorro also worked for you?"

"That's true. It's quite bizarre."

"Any possibility that there's a connection? Something common related to their work?"

"Not that I can see. Our work's fairly straightforward. We investigate trade cases."

"Well if you think of anything that might help, lift the phone," he said handing over his card.

"I will."

Marc returned to his office on the fourth floor.

The toll was mounting. They were now playing with other peoples lives; other innocent victims. He would have to do something. The perpetrators would stop at nothing.

Despite the visit of the detectives, Marc was resigned to signing up to a wicked blackmail scheme. It was the only way out of a very dark tunnel. He figured not doing so would bring him to certain disgrace and maybe behind bars, whereas this way might give him some leverage to reverse the roles and maybe put some of them in jail. It was a long shot, he knew.

But the most potent primordial urge of all would also have to be satisfied. The murders could not go unavenged. He had to fight back, to find a way and it would have to be something so impudent that his tormentors would never suspect.

THURSDAY ONE WEEK LATER. The early afternoon sun was still strong in the sky when Marc waved to the security guard as he drove up the ramp of the Trade Bureau building and out onto the street. The sunlight reflected off the smoked-glass buildings on the opposite side of the street, creating a mellow, late autumnal setting. He slipped on his Ray Bans, flicked the stereo button and drove thirty metres to the first set of traffic lights. A car pulled out from a parked position and abruptly came to a halt behind him. The squeal of the tyres prompted him to glance in the mirror. The driver's appearance caught his attention first. And then the passengers. They were definitely Orientals. The front passenger seemed to wave what appeared to be a knife as if trying to attract Marc's attention.

A cold shiver ran down his back. He riveted his eyes on the traffic lights, holding a firm grip on the steering wheel. Speeding away from the lights he shot a glance in the mirror and saw that the car was following at the same speed. Now accelerating towards the roundabout, he sped around it and screeched off towards the Cortenbergh tunnel. As he emerged he shot another glance in the mirror. Nobody trailing. Cool it, Schuman. Just your imagination in overdrive again.

He felt himself relax. As the speedometer hit one hundred and thirty kilometres, he threw another glance in the mirror.

Shit! A Mercedes had emerged from the tunnel and was closing fast.

Was it the same one? He couldn't be sure. He tried to match the fleeting glimpse he had caught of the driver with the faces of his 'menacing friends' from the football match in the King Baudouin stadium. There seemed to be a similarity but he could not be sure. Nothing more than a resemblance.

"Don't get paranoid Schuman…one of those coincidences. They just happened to pull out at the same time," he consoled himself.

He checked the mirror again. The car was now within thirty metres of him. He floored the accelerator, reaching the Ring motorway junction in less than thirty seconds. At the last possible moment, he swung right onto the Ring and again glanced in the mirror. The navy blue Mercedes also swept right at very high speed, swerving onto the hard shoulder and back into the outer fast lane again. He could see it rocking onto its two left wheels, virtually flipping over. And just as quickly it bounced back onto the middle carriageway.

"Christ *it is* those bastards."

The clock was pushing close to the danger zone at one hundred and eighty-five kilometres per hour but the Mercedes was keeping pace. Marc weaved in and out of the afternoon traffic, jumping lanes at every opportunity.

"Lose them Schuman," he shouted, urging himself to concentrate. "Lose them."

He did a fishtail-swishing manoeuvre past two cars but the

Mercedes copied the deft manoeuvre, keeping up the chase. Marc's blood pressure was rising. It was a matter of life and death that they would not get the upper hand. An opportunity presented itself and he took it on reflex. Changing down to third gear he zapped the pedal and swerved across to the inside slow lane, veering the BMW onto the hard shoulder in a skilful move and blasted past a truck. The pursuers tried to copy the manoeuvre but the truck driver jerked to the right making it impossible. A long continuous hooting came from the truck horn and the driver flashed his lights repeatedly, gesturing furiously to the BMW by stabbing his clenched fist in the air. The Mercedes pulled back and bolted to the outer fast lane. Marc now pushed it to the maximum, the surge of speed leaving his pursuers trailing in the distance. But decision time was coming fast. He had covered the southbound stretch of the Ring. The junction that would take him towards France was coming up. He glanced once more at the rear view mirror only to see the Mercedes speeding past the truck, again closing fast. He moved to the fast lane and accelerated into the steep dip under the bridge that would take him towards Waterloo again asking the maximum from the engine. For the next five kilometres the carriageway twisted and banked as he sped past the town of Waterloo on the right. The tyres gripped the road tightly, responding well to the rear-wheel traction giving him superb control on the tortuous surface. He swung onto a slip road and slowed to one-twenty.

"I've lost them," he screeched, gesturing with a clenched fist. A kilometre down the single carriageway he pulled into the wide expanse of car park serving Waterloo's famous tourist attraction.

The Butte de Lion - a twenty-eight-tonne, cast-iron lion - stands on a forty-metre high mound of soil, majestically surveying the surrounding landscape where the Battle of Waterloo was fought in 1815. The monument was built to celebrate the victory of the Duke of Wellington over Emperor Napoleon. A two-metre high security fence encircles the entire attraction, the only access point being through a reception building a few metres from the base of the Butte. Inside the building tourists can either browse through books on its history or watch a multimedia presentation or study a scale model of the actual battle. The energetic ones can pass through a corridor leading out to the base and climb the two hundred and twenty six steps to the viewing platform at the top.

Marc glanced up at the Lion and observed the steady two-way flow of people on the steps. Suddenly there was a screech of brakes. The Mercedes sped by, braking hard. It swung off the road onto an expanse of gravel about thirty metres further on, spraying pebbles at the sides of the parked cars. Immediately the passenger door opened and one of the passengers jumped out. He pointed in Marc's direction.

Marc glanced in the opposite direction and saw that a bus had stopped and tourists had started to disembark, leaving him no easy escape route. He jumped from the car and made towards the bus - for sanctuary - to lose himself in the crowd. As the busload of tourists moved towards the entrance, he bent down among them to avoid being seen. Once inside the ticket office, he glanced back at the door and saw that his pursuers had joined the queue. They were in no hurry. There was nowhere for him to go. He eased forward towards the counter. Just as he came to the top of the queue he heard a shriek from the entrance. In a moment of panic, he jumped the counter. The cashier yelled and backed away from the till. A tall, burly attendant lunged towards Marc certain in the knowledge that a robbery was being attempted. Marc deftly slipped past him and scrambled for the corridor leading to the Butte. Now dashing out towards the concrete steps that would take him to the top, he bumped into an old lady who had just come down the steps. She recoiled in shock. He gestured an apology with his hands and bounded towards the first step. His heart raced furiously, and his rib cage heaved with each breath as he took the first few steps. The commotion of the tourists probably gave him a head start, but he could not be sure. He staggered up the steps, taking two at a time. About half way up, he slowed and looked down. A group of people was standing at the base looking up at him. The Orientals were also there, staring up, blending in as perfect tourists.

Starting again for the top, his stomach began to churn with nerves. Breathless, he grabbed the safety support bar that ran the full length of the steps to the top. He was aware that tourists making their way down on the other side of the safety bar had stopped. They were staring at him. An elderly man asked if he was all right. He mustered a response and continued further up. The muscles in his legs began to twitch uncontrollably and, gripped by fear, he again leaned on the steel safety bar to shift the weight from his legs.

He scrambled up more steps, willing himself on. His heart pounded hard in his chest. Now on the last twenty steps and then onto the viewing platform. There was a fine view of the battlefield from the pinnacle where the statue of the Lion was mounted but he was not a tourist today. He glanced back and saw that they had begun to climb the steps. Then suddenly he realised how foolish he had been. The entrance was also the exit. One way up. One way down.

His head felt dizzy and in a moment of giddiness he muttered, "One way out really means no way out." He immediately raced to the other side of the Lion, out of sight of his pursuers. A split-second decision was needed and he made it. He dived off the platform out onto the grassy mound and started to roll down the steep surface. The forty-metre drop seemed interminable. Rolling, rolling and now careering out of control, the bone-jarring impact of the hard earth leaving him dazed. And then suddenly the bottom. A group of Japanese tourists congregated at the railing of the viewing platform, giggling and laughing, and eagerly clicking their cameras at the spectacle unfolding below them. Marc half-crawled, half-stumbled towards a security gate, climbed up and, in one quick heave, flung his body awkwardly over the serrated teeth along the top, landing on the concrete pavement the other side.

His adrenaline still flowing, he raced down the road bordering the tourist attraction and in less than thirty seconds was back in the car. The car lurched forward as the accelerator was floored, leaving a shower of dust in its wake. He had escaped from them – for now – but he wondered how long his reprieve would last. He glanced at the Butte de Lion once more and, for a moment, thought that this, too, could have been his nemesis - his Waterloo.

In less than a minute the BMW was back out on the motorway heading fast towards Brussels. It was then that he noticed the blood on the steering wheel. His hands had been cut and scraped by the serrated teeth and they started to sting.

Chapter Eighteen

HE WAS NOW PREPARING for the final meeting. After that attitudes would have to change. Laurel and Hardy would have to alter their tune.

Marc left his office and went downstairs to the reception area. He surveyed the activity on the street and then crossed to a Commission building. Flashing his identity pass at the security guard, he walked into the cafeteria on the ground floor. From now on, he was going to make himself as invisible as possible. He lifted a phone but hesitated for a moment. It seemed the only option open to him. He pressed five digits for an internal call.

"Hi Kevin."

"Oh Marc, haven't seen you since that terrible defeat. See, I told you to retire when you were winning!"

"There's always the next time."

"Idle threat!"

After the small talk, Marc suggested they meet later that evening and Kevin agreed. Marc was back in the office within ten minutes, scanning documents on the desk but his thoughts were firmly focused on his plan.

The agreed rendezvous point was an out-of-the-way place but within walking distance of the office. As he entered the dark and dingy restaurant the patron threw a quizzical look that said it all. Marc was definitely not part of the regular clientele. He was ushered to a table at the rear. Kevin joined him minutes later.

Coffee was ordered and the conversation meandered around the sports club and the fact that Marc had missed a lot of games lately. Marc agreed but did not offer an explanation. He had come here for one reason, and one reason only.

"Kevin, can I talk to you in confidence?"

"Why, sure. You're getting married?"

"No! Listen, very serious stuff."

"Very mysterious stuff," said Kevin, suppressing a chuckle.

Marc leaned across the table and said in a calm voice, "I'm

in big trouble – I'm in danger."

Kevin drew back, the open smile dissolving. Marc started a blow-by-blow account of everything that had happened in the last three months, the two stringers turning up on a regular basis to extract a deal, the Orientals following him everywhere, periscoping him day and night and the Bangkok photos and video tape. He explained that he had witnessed Montorro's "accident" in the metro station and now had a video of Schmidt's gruesome murder. Kevin drew back in horror. He then started to ask questions, trying to understand what had been said. Marc became agitated. He felt like closing the conversation. He just wanted Kevin to shut up.

"Wait until I've finished and then, maybe, you'll understand."

He took a drink and started to explain further about the Bangkok video. Kevin sat in silence, intermittently gagging, as the seriousness of the whole chain of events registered with him. After a few moments, he asked incredulously, "You talking murder?"

"Yes."

Kevin gasped. "Dynamite. So they've murdered two people already and they have a video tape of you? Very delicate with the mood here in Belgium after those kidnappings!"

"Tell me about it! The public would be unforgiving. But the worst part is the murders."

Kevin raised his cup and drank. Marc scanned the restaurant again.

"I'm planning some counter-espionage. You see, I'm thinking of going along with their plan, get them to name the company and then play them at their own game."

Kevin leaned forward and whispered, "You're not serious?"

Marc nodded vehemently. "It's my only hope."

He went on to say that he planned on using listening devices to trap Mr. Big and his cohorts, whoever they turn out to be. His plan was met with complete disbelief.

"That's high-tech stuff, way out of your league…even professionals fail at that game."

"You don't understand, I'm desperate."

"That may be, but it's crazy. Marc, you're not macho man. You're an investigator in the Bureau. You know the law, economics and things like that. But come on, espionage?"

"Look, I need listening devices and that's where I want your assistance. The Fraud Bureau must have that kind of equipment."

"It's mainly human surveillance. We do very little high-tech stuff. Anyway, spy stuff is not just about devices. It's a black art in its own right ...a bit like witchcraft. Our investigations are carried out by the customs. We're just a co-ordinating body shuffling paper from one Member State to another, you know that."

"I'm convinced I can pull it off. I desperately need those devices."

"Hold on, Marc, you ...*you* are going to take on undercover agents...and win?"

"That's about it. There's only one way out and I have to take it."

"So you intend to go sleuthing around on some extra-curricular espionage merry-go-round and what do you think your so-called friends, Laurel and Hardy, will be doing?... Waiting patiently for you to call?"

"Give me a better idea."

Kevin paused for a moment, leaned forward and whispered, "It's for the movies but, dammit, if I can help, I will."

Marc raised the cup as a gesture of thanks. After a minute or so, Kevin told Marc that his cousin ran a surveillance company in Dublin. He offered to make a phone call.

"Don't breathe a word to anyone," Marc said.

An index finger came up to Kevin's mouth and he said, "My lips are sealed."

"From now on, don't phone me at the office or the apartment. I'll call you from different locations."

"Whatever you say. You're the sleuth around here."

They paid for the coffee and Kevin left immediately. Marc stayed back for a few minutes and then slipped down the street in the opposite direction.

Always wanted to play James Bond, he thought as he made his way towards Central Station.

December 1999

EVEN THOUGH IT WAS RAINING and bitterly cold on Saturday morning, by nine o' clock the ancient cobble-stoned Square was packed with jubilant well-wishers. An air of magic and majesty filled the Grand' Place as the expectant crowd waited for the almost-medieval pageant to commence. Shortly before ten o'clock a cavalcade of limousines entered the Square at measured intervals, bringing a stream of family members to witness the civil wedding ceremony of Princess Mathilde and Prince Philippe in the magnificent gothic town hall.

All eyes focused on the bride as she stepped out of the limousine wearing a Brussels-lace veil. At first the crowd gasped and then cheered as she entered the ornate building where her prince was waiting. An hour later, even louder cheers and spirited clapping greeted the couple as they appeared on the royal balcony, waving to the crowd. The people chanted *"Vive les maries"* as the couple embraced. Fifteen minutes later they emerged down the red-carpeted steps and smiled for the photographers.

Marc was among the thousands of Belgian citizens, watching the pomp and ceremony. He had little choice; the telephone message the previous evening made it clear that he should be in the Square by nine. He found a standing position close by a lamp post but a clear view of the Town Hall was not possible. However, he could see the ritual on a large outdoor projection screen, positioned in the corner of the Flemish renaissance-style square, beside the Roi d'Espagne café. When the cavalcade moved off to the nearby cathedral for the religious ceremony, the crowd began to disperse. Suddenly Marc heard a voice behind him. "It's time to choose."

He spun around, recognised Hardy and grabbed his tie. "You bastards had Elena Schmidt killed."

"Cool it, Schuman, we don't know what the hell you're talking about."

"Well, I know what you're at. Those Triad bastards have killed Montorro and now Schmidt." He turned and pointed a finger at Johnson's chest.

"The voice on the telephone was yours. You played a part"

Johnson brushed his finger away with a firm swipe of his hand.

"Schuman, I wouldn't threaten anybody right now. You're in no position to do that, are you? Now have we got a goddamn deal?"

"I'll play ball but on my terms. Five million dollars into my hands at a place of my choosing once the Regulation has been signed by the Commissioner and ready for passing into law by the Council of Ministers."

They looked at each other. Johnson then turned to Marc and said, "Okay, now we need to know about timing. When can all this happen?"

"Within a week. Maybe a little longer...once I've got the new sanitised data."

"Is that a guarantee?"

"You have my word. Now – the name of the exporter?"

"Not so fast. We have ground rules too – our insurance policy, remember?" Taylor said.

He explained that five consignments of video tapes had been secretly stashed around various ports and airports in Europe. Any attempt to double cross would trigger an immediate tip-off to the customs and police. Basically they would find evidence of a paedophile ring, he said and went on to confirm that Schuman would be picked up in a well-publicised swoop.

"Don't forget," Johnson menacingly added, "we'll have the media tipped off. Next stage, we deluge the Bureau with complaints that the chief investigator tried a bit of extortion and messed with figures from Korea right down to Malaysia. Needless to say, all the other exporters will be delighted. The Bureau will have no option but declare a mistrial, so to speak, and by the time the investigation is started all over again, our client will have secured about sixty per cent of the market. Is our insurance policy clear?"

Marc scowled. "Just give me the name and get on with it."

Taylor pulled an envelope from his inside pocket. "Everything is in there. You'll find a complete set of discs for European sales, discounts, trading terms. A replica of what you have already got but with 'user-friendly' figures."

Marc took the envelope.

"When you're ready, we'll deliver the supporting invoices, price lists. Whatever you need, basically."

"It will take a few days."

"Schuman, this must be wrapped up within a week. Remember, you'll still be watched, day and night. If we see anything suspicious, like visits to the Commissioner or contact with the police, then your world comes crashing down around you."

"I hear you."

"Meet us at one o'clock next Friday by the Mosque. Our client will want a progress report."

The two stringers moved swiftly towards a side street.

EARLY FRIDAY EVENING Marc stood in a doorway at the top of Avenue Louise, carefully surveying the activity. His attention was concentrated on the law office of PKV&S. He had her in his sights from the time she stepped out of the building but he mainly watched behind her to see if somebody was following. He was nervous, even scared, but the sight of the sensual figure aroused the male in him and, for a moment, he allowed himself to think of something other than the wicked scheme being prosecuted around him. She approached and they kissed. Her eyes were radiant. Marc had not seen her for more than two weeks. Laura had accompanied Jessica to Virginia which she managed to stretch into a full two-week vacation to celebrate Thanksgiving with the family.

He nodded eastward and they headed for the side street where the car was parked.

"So how was your first day back at the office?" he asked.

"Great, really great."

"And Virginia?"

"It was fantastic. Jessica's really happy at the cottage. Dad's done a cool design job on her room and she's complete access with the ramp. She'll be totally independent."

"Great."

Laura had some news from the office. Marc hung on every word. She told him that the partners had offered her senior associate from January and that she was going back to the Intellectual Property Department under Petersson. He listened and nodded appropriately.

She got into the seat, pulled across the seatbelt and they sped off in the direction of Louvain.

"Looks like I'm going to win that bet…Looks like I'm going to make partner before you," she teased. His jaw tightened, "You deserve it, I'm delighted."

His hands were gripping the steering wheel so tightly that they were becoming numb and his neck felt hot and tense. He was trying to think clearly but it was impossible. Laura was chirping away like a bird in Spring. He didn't want to burst her bubble. After a while she noticed that he had become distant and quiet but mistook his silence for the fact that his male ego may have been dented.

They reached Louvain in twenty minutes. Marc parked the car in a side street. He leaned over and his left hand cupped her jaw. His fingers ran behind her ear stroking her neck gently. Then he kissed her.

"Laura, something has happened that I have to tell you."

She leaned forward, held his hand and whispered, "So you can't get it up? I understand. It happens a lot to nineties man."

"It's nothing like that," he said. His slow, deliberate tone made her realise that he was serious. He tried to explain the tape and the blackmail but it all seemed to come out in a jumble.

"So," she said, staring into his eyes, "you had a massage? No big deal!"

"They videotaped me in Bangkok and that's how they're blackmailing me."

The happy expression on her face faded. "But it was only a massage?"

"Well, a little more than massage."

"What!"

"Laura, these girls, well, they did it. I was drugged – I didn't know."

Her mood changed, her face blanching.

"Why are you telling me all of this now – how could you?"

"These guys say the girls were underage."

Marc pulled the photographs from his pocket and pushed them towards her. She stared in helpless shock at the naked bodies. Her arms drew back as she threw the photographs to the floor, her body recoiling. "No, please, I'm not seeing this. Oh shit, what's happening? I don't believe this…just let me out."

A feeling of claustrophobia enveloped her and suddenly her stomach felt sick. She needed to get into an open space for fresh air.

Underage girls, underage girls. The echo of the words kept repeating in her head.

He tried to remain calm. The moment of truth had arrived but instead of feeling relief, anguish welled up within him at the hurt in her eyes.

"Laura listen I had to tell you."

"You bastard. How could you?"

Marc reached across and grabbed her arm.

"I have to finish. It's more complicated."

"Let me go," she screamed across at him.

"Please listen Laura. My life's in danger and possibly yours."

Tears welled up in her eyes and she felt confused and light-headed.

"Laura please."

She snapped open the door, jumped out and started running along the narrow street away from the bustle of Muntstraat, where the restaurants and pizzerias were located. Her legs felt weak, like jelly and her knees almost gave way. Marc jumped out and raced after her. He held her shoulder. She turned around and pummelled him with her fists, beating fiercely on his chest. He tried to restrain her but she kept hitting him harder. A couple turned and stared and then walked on.

"I don't believe this is happening. Are you some kind of pervert? Everything was just…just right," she sobbed, "and you go…go to the far side of the world for some kind of *sordid* sex. With children."

A torrent of tears flowed down her cheeks. He tried to hold her but she wrenched herself free and continued down the street. Marc hesitated for a few moments and then followed.

"Laura you've got to listen to me. It's not what it seems. I was set up. I could do nothing about it."

When she came to the junction she hailed a taxi. She jumped in and it sped off. Marc raced back to the car and headed for Brussels. He arrived first and when the taxi stopped, he followed her to the apartment door.

"Laura, please I have to tell you who is involved. It's Falcon Tech. They're blackmailing me."

She did not respond. Her senses had shut down – her eyes staring blankly at the door while searching in the bag for the key.

"I need your help. My life depends on it and, who knows, maybe yours."

The sobbing started again. Tears flowed uncontrollably down her cheeks. At that moment he bottled up his mixture of fear and understanding. He wished he could explain a little more but he knew how he had felt when he first saw the images.

"You've ruined everything. No, I won't help you, you bastard."

"Please Laura don't say anything about this at the firm."

She fumbled the key into the lock and, once inside, slammed the door shut. Marc returned to the car and slumped forward, his head resting on the steering wheel. After about ten minutes he turned over the engine and drove back towards his apartment.

Chapter Nineteen

Brussels

CONFUSED AND EXHAUSTED, Laura headed straight for the bedroom and threw herself onto the bed, curling up in a foetal position. After a few minutes she pounded the pillow and shouted.

"What he said doesn't make sense. It's all just crap now trying to justify his filthy behaviour. To think that I trusted him totally...to think..."

A paroxysm of anger washed over her. The duvet was wet with tears and smudged with mascara. And then a momentary image of Tom, her first lover, flashed across her mind.

"They're all the same. Just when you trust them, they mess things up big time." Her head was now a jumble of thoughts - thoughts that conveyed potent images - sordid images. The room was dark and silent and it felt eerie. An image from the photographs flashed before her eyes. A video tape of children in Bangkok and blackmail. She punched the pillow and then dragged it across her head as if she wanted to smother herself. Her thoughts now drifted to the earlier part of the day and the news about her promotion.

She tried hard to regain her composure, to control her emotions and start to think rationally. Half an hour later the sound of footsteps on the stairs and then a key clicking in the apartment door.

"You home, Laura?" came the cheery voice.

"Yes, in here," she croaked.

The already-ajar door of the bedroom was pushed fully open.

"In bed already? Love sick with passion?"

There was no response. Laura was still wearing her navy office suit. Sarah's tone changed.

"Gee what's happening here? You sick or something?"

Laura relaxed her grip on the pillow and turned towards the door.

"What's going on? You're upset?" Sarah asked, looking straight into her roommate's eyes.

228

"I'm just not feeling well."

"Come on. It's me – Sarah - I know you better than that."

"I'm exhausted. Something's ...uh - well there's a problem."

"I'll make coffee. Let's come out to the living room."

Sarah went to the galley kitchen, made a pot of coffee and returned to the bedroom. She helped Laura off the bed, linked her to the couch and poured the coffee.

"It'll make you feel better."

Sarah sat on the edge of the armchair. Laura's face was streaked with eyeliner and make up, her face flushed and her hair dishevelled. She stared at some spot on the rug in front of the fireplace. After a while Sarah managed to coax her to talk.

"Are you cold? I can turn up the heat."

"No I'm fine...really. I need time."

"Why don't you take the coffee? It'll make you feel better. Really, it will."

Sarah handed her the cup. Laura put it on the floor and reached across for a tissue from the box on the coffee table. She ran it around her eyes and regained some of her composure. After a few minutes she told her bizarre story, at least the bits she remembered.

"It can't be right. Blackmail? There's got to be some mix-up?"

"He was serious. No...he really did it. Can you imagine? Knowing a guy for almost three years and then he comes up with this. I hollered at him on the street. I was in a frenzy...I punched him."

"Tried to kill him there and then, did you?" Sarah asked.

Laura smiled for the first time. "He actually thinks Falcon Tech's behind it."

"That's the company you deal with?"

"Dealt with...past tense. Verbiest has been handling their affairs since June. Can you believe it?...Falcon Tech. They may be aggressive but they're hardly into sleaze."

Sarah frowned. "What if...what if it's true? Just imagine for a moment that it is."

"I just don't believe him. Why should I?"

"Still, bizarre things go on out there in the business world. You said it yourself."

"Yes, but this?...It's far-fetched."

Sarah saw how exhausted Laura looked.

"The best thing for you right now is sleep. I'll get you one of my sleeping-"

"No, no I don't need them."

"Yes you do. A good night's sleep and you'll feel better in the morning."

Sarah went to the bathroom, popped a white tablet from a bottle and handed it to her. "Really, you've got to take this. C'mon."

She took her hand and guided her to the bedroom.

THE IMAGES FROM THE TAPE haunted Marc the following day. And now the fight with Laura. Raw emotions deep within his consciousness battled to control his mind. Aggression, fear, hate and love all trying to dominate his being and for the first time he realised that he was now thinking like them, using their language - the language of the criminal.

He picked up the phone, hesitated for a moment and then dialled. After about a minute a voice answered.

"Hello, Sarah, how are you?"

"Oh I'm fine thanks," she said.

"Uh...could I speak to Laura please?"

A moment of silence passed yet it seemed like an eternity.

"She's asleep...said last night-"

"But it's almost noon. Could you just ask her to come to the phone?"

"Look Marc, I'm telling you she's asleep."

"Sarah, I need to talk to her now. It's important."

"I can't. I'll ask her to phone you later."

Marc put down the receiver and went to the bathroom. He turned on the shower and gazed in the mirror. But soon the glass was covered in droplets of condensation and steam drifted through the doorway into the bedroom. He pushed the door shut with his foot and stepped under the cascading water. He pounded the wall with the sponge in a fit of frustration.

His love for her now overcame his fears and quelled the

turmoil deep inside.

"Damn it, I must see her. Those bastards, maybe they will trail me but I've got to do it."

Hong Kong

FOR SEVERAL WEEKS NOW pure adrenaline was running the show in the Tai Po industrial estate. Nerves frayed and tempers switched permanently to short-fuse mode as the countdown to the launch started. Following another *tête-à-tête* with the president of Kimble-Sinclair an ultimatum was issued. The trade issue was to be wrapped up immediately.

The berating that Verbiest and Wong had received during several stressful phone calls just didn't produce results. Lindell demanded a face-to-face and they arrived on schedule.

"I'm damn well not happy with the way this whole thing is dragging on."

"Look, Dylan, Brussels is a bureaucracy. Give him space," Verbiest pleaded.

"You said he would be back with a final figure and the piece of legislation in his hand within a week."

"Yes, that's true, but there are lots of procedures to go through. And remember, when he shows a rate of ten per cent for Falcon Tech and around thirty-five to forty for the rest, eyebrows will be raised. It won't be entirely convincing. It's inevitable that questions will be asked."

"But our new package of figures is water tight. He can show the back-up stuff to anyone."

"That's true," Verbiest agreed, "but remember there's a political dimension to all of this. It's not just about figures and right and wrong. It's a game…the international trade game and anti-dumping duty is just another weapon that's used in these situations. The *taipans* in the Commision will want to hang tough with China. In the end, the chief investigator gets his way but he needs space and time to argue his case."

Lindell glowered across the table and lectured the lawyers. "Batista's very nervous. All this underhand messing is bringing back memories of 'Nam. It reminds him of the Viet Cong

231

running through those underground ratruns ready to pounce at any moment. He's damn well gone off on a *cover-your-ass* exercise and talked to Sinclair in Boston. Mr. Arty knows what's going on but he wants everything at arms length. He has only one focus at the moment. Profit, profit, profit and solid growth projections into the future. And, I might add, so have we. So he wants it - the whole thing – over within days."

"Look you're asking the impossible. About ten people have to sign off on these things before it lands on the Commissioner's desk."

"I don't give a rat's ass how you deliver," Lindell exploded, "but deliver you will. Just shut the fuck up about the byzantine bureaucracy in Brussels. I'm paying for results, not a lesson in officialdom. This sonofabitch thing has to be wrapped up...so get your lawyerly asses off your padded chairs. Do you hear me?"

"Yes, yes, we're doing everything we can. Isn't that true Mr. Wong?"

The Oriental lawyer's eyes were cold and vacant. "Everything's being done. Schuman will deliver."

"We're paying you guys. Now get me a result or your asses are going to be in the dock big time. The sales strategy for next year has to be worked on now. The launch is only weeks away."

Newman paced around the office. "You mentioned China a moment ago but it's Falcon Tech that gets hit with the duty."

"That's the thing that makes this so complicated. You see, China is not a market economy. He'll have to argue that Falcon Tech's independent of the Chinese State to get a lower duty."

"I don't understand all this political stuff. Just get us a solution," Newman barked. "And start by turning up the heat a little more. Get your Triad guys to pay him a visit just in case he forgets that we have a deadline."

Wong joined his hands and gave Lindell a bemused glance. "A couple of weeks ago you were complaining that we were doing too much. Now is the time to be careful. We shouldn't do anything in haste."

"Mr. Wong's right. Hasten slowly because this is the most delicate stage."

Wong cautioned the FT executives with a slight wave of his

hand. "Remember, Schuman's bound to be nervous too. After all, he's taking a big risk. If things go wrong he could find himself on the wrong side of the law. It's not wise to put so much pressure on at this stage. He's moving as fast as possible."

Pointing a finger at Verbiest and Wong, Lindell snapped, "Wise? What's wise about this whole affair? You guys said it was a piece of cake. Now you come with nothing but claptrap caution. You got us into this fucking situation…now get us the hell out."

"Look Dylan we're all nervous. It's a high-risk game but we can't tie a noose around his neck. As soon as he circulates the draft Regulation showing Falcon Tech with a ten per cent duty then he will come to claim his reward. The whole thing can be wrapped up in twenty-four hours."

Lindell pushed back his chair, stood up and sneered.

"And Saddam Hussein will be in the Oval Office before Christmas! I'm wasting no more time on this. You've got a week. I've got a business to run. Not like you leeches sucking off our efforts."

Wong and Verbiest got up and made for the door.

"Don't come back here until you've a ten per cent duty in your pockets. You hear me?"

"Yes, yes," they muttered in unison from the corridor.

Brussels
THE OFFICES OF FABER & MONROE were situated in a ten-storey building in the Madou area of Brussels. Sarah worked in a small team led by Marcel Faber, the senior partner of the two-partner practice. Its specialist skill was lobbying the European decision-makers on behalf of cash-rich clients - mostly seeking modifications to proposed legislation on behalf of chemical and pharmaceutical corporations to make it more business-friendly - and so stave off the growing environmental agenda as long as possible. She enjoyed the complicated skills of lobbying and was the most senior associate in the practice.

Shortly before six on Monday evening she left her office and made her way towards the metro station. The man who had been standing inconspicuously beside a concrete pillar close to the entrance for more than an hour now moved into position a short distance behind her. After a few moments he moved closer and fell in step behind her. Sarah received a gentle tap on the shoulder. She spun around and saw Marc, his hands outstretched.

"Sarah!"

She abruptly pulled away, her pace quickening. Marc stayed at her shoulder.

"Please, Sarah it's me."

"Get lost!"

"You've got to help me."

"You've got some nerve after-."

"Sarah I can explain everything."

Her pace slowed. He came alongside her and continued, "You've got to get a message to Laura from me *please*."

"That's something you've gotta work out between the two of you. It's simply none of my business."

"Sarah, please. You're my only hope - my *lifeline*."

She pulled away fast. He quickened his pace and put his hand on her shoulder again.

"Leave me alone or I'll create a scene," she hissed over her shoulder. "Laura doesn't want to see you anymore."

"It's a big conspiracy...blackmail. You've got to believe me. Please, Sarah."

She kept walking. The Arts Loi Métro station was now only twenty metres away. He again attempted to grab her arm. She muttered something.

"You've got to ask Laura to talk to me. I'll wait for you here again tomorrow evening. Please have an answer!"

Sarah turned and saw fear in his eyes. She hesitated for a moment but then moved towards the rush-hour crowd funnelling their way towards the escalator. Marc stood rigid, overwhelmed by the pernicious twist that his life had taken. Six months earlier he was one of the bright young investigators destined to ascend the ladder in the Trade Bureau on sheer ability. And a future full of promise with Laura. But the spectre of disgrace and humiliation was looming.

Dejected, he spun around and headed in the direction of Rue de la Loi.

LATER THAT EVENING, he entered Ambiorix Park and took up an observation position close to the apartment. He watched the flow of traffic and took in every movement on the footpath. At 7.52 Laura entered the Square. He moved out of the Park in silence and crouched down behind a parked van a few metres from the apartment. He watched as she turned the key and opened the main door. In an act of desperation he lunged forward, bounded up the steps and raced through the doorway. She shrieked and ran towards the stairs.

"Marc just leave...you're obviously gone mad...paranoid," she yelled down as she guided the key into the apartment door, her voice trembling.

"Laura you don't understand... *please* listen. I'm in serious trouble."

She ignored him, opened the apartment door and entered. He clambered up the stairs and raced through the doorway before she could close it.

"Laura, you must listen."

"Oh really...it's over Marc. There's no going back," she exploded.

Despair welled up inside him. He thrust out his right arm, pointing towards her.

"I can't get through to you. Your life is in danger. I know it seems that I've done something terrible but-"

"Get out of here," she ordered.

"Please listen...it's a conspiracy. They - Falcon Tech - want a damn clean run at the market and they'll do anything to get it. That's why they're blackmailing me."

"Absolute rubbish ...we did our own calculations in the office back in June. We know they're going to be hammered with duty. Your wild imagination sees conspiracy in everything."

"Did you ever think that Verbiest might have wanted you off the case so that he could have total control? That mugging out there in the Park wasn't an accident. Maybe even that career development line he threw you was also a ruse?"

For the first time she heard fear in his voice, making her confused.

"Don't be ridiculous."

The tension continued at fever pitch. Marc pleaded with her, begged her to understand and finally appealed to her lawyer instincts to believe the unbelievable. He re-ran the details several times, emphasising the murder of Montorro and Schmidt's gruesome killing. He watched her closely and sensed that, with every new revelation, he could detect growing acceptance of what he was saying. After half an hour the heat of argument had spun out. Sarah sheepishly emerged from her bedroom and moved across the living room towards the kitchen in silence. She smiled. Marc's head involuntarily tilted downwards, suggesting embarrassment and shame. Laura apologised to her for the unseemly exchange.

"So," Laura asked. "Who is *they*? Every time you talk it's *they, they they*? Lindell, Newman - who the hell?"

"Guys hired by Falcon Tech or that sleazeball Wong in Hong Kong. Americans! At least they have American accents as far as I can tell. And a gang of Orientals chasing me everywhere."

"The whole thing's bizarre and grotesque."

"I couldn't help overhearing in the bedroom." Sarah interrupted, "but remember you talked lots of times, Laura, about the games big business plays and that Verbiest played his cards close to his chest with Falcon Tech."

Laura turned towards her as if to say *who asked you* but then her expression softened. "Yes, that's normal business. But this...shit, this is the stuff of movies."

Sarah pushed a little more. "Wong wouldn't deal with you. Remember last Spring? Suspicious, no?"

"Ah, how do I know. It's not connected."

"You were surprised by Verbiest's concern. Remember he was the one who told you not to rush back to the office...to take another few weeks recuperating. Does that not all sound a bit strange now?"

Before Laura could answer Marc interjected, encouraged by Sarah's scepticism.

"Damn it, Laura, it could be connected. Don't you see what they are trying to do to me?"

"Even if it's true what can you do?"

He explained what he had planned, the people he probably needed to target and the devices he needed to have. Finally he said, "I cannot do this on my own. I need help."

Waving her hands she muttered, "Go to hell. You're not sucking me into some kind of vendetta."

"Laura, please, I need your support now. If I don't try something they will just release the video."

Once more the photographs dominated her mind. "Well, you're not bringing me down with you," she snapped. "Remember you were the one caught playing that sordid game."

"I'm pleading with you Laura…look…you know there's big money involved what with Falcon Tech's exports last year running at eight hundred million, a forty per cent duty could hit them for three hundred and twenty million dollars a year. Don't tell me they wouldn't fight to eliminate that extra cost?"

"They may be tough, but they're not murderers."

"Your life, my life, can't you see both our lives are in danger."

"Look the whole thing's so confusing."

A brief image of Verbiest flashed across Laura's mind and then she reflected on her experience in the Park. She sat down on the arm of the couch, the tension easing. Maybe it wasn't so outlandish after all.

"These guys are ready to supply whatever it takes – invoices, computer printouts - anything that's needed to support a reduced duty." He pulled an envelope from his inside pocket. "They've already given me a whole new set of computer disks."

"Computer disks?"

"Yes. They want to change all the prices."

"You'd better be telling the truth. Which one lists the French sales?" Laura snapped. He shuffled them in his hands. "That's it there."

Marc and Sarah followed as Laura walked to the spare room. She hit the button on the computer and studied the writing on the disks while waiting for Windows to come up.

"I can remember most of the models and the prices for the French market. We'll soon know what's what."

"Unbelievable stuff," Sarah chirped over her shoulder.

She smiled. Marc's stomach was still churning with apprehension. A minute later the data was on the screen. She scrolled up and down, mentally noting model numbers and prices, as the two observers huddled over her shoulders. After a few minutes of study she swung the chair around.

"I don't believe it. Average prices twenty five per cent higher. I distinctly remember those sales."

"Infallible as usual," Marc said, grinning. "That old eidetic memory came in handy after all."

The comment catapulted Laura back to her childhood, reliving the experiences of her early photographic memory. She recalled her father using the expression 'photographic memory' a few times when she recounted details that others in the family had long since forgotten. But it was years later when she was sixteen that she found out about people with eidetic memories.

Laura's older brother, Howard, had come home from university that summer laden down with psychology books. Since she was twelve she had thought about majoring in psychology, her brother's books allowing her to explore that curiosity. Well, at least it gave a flavour of what real psychology might be like. Hidden away in one of those arcane tomes was a whole chapter on eidetic imagery; the term the medics use for a photographic memory. At that point she realised that she was not some sort of freak whose inner ability should be concealed. It was just another God-given talent that should be used and to her relief she was not alone. The book claimed that a tiny percentage of the adult population has an eidetic memory and more often than not it is accompanied by above-average intelligence.

Marc hit a key to close the file, jolting her out of the reverie. She swung the chair around fully and looked up at him.

"I can't believe it. I really can't believe that. Verbiest must've prepared those disks."

Marc's pulse climbed down from its one-thirty high and he began to relax.

"Falcon Tech," she whispered. "That will bring their duty down to around eight per cent."

"Ten per cent actually," Marc said, encouraged.

"So," Sarah asked, "what happens now?"

Laura shook her head in disbelief. "It's so bizarre. How do they expect to get away with it?"

"I said it before. They've simply got a lot to lose."

Laura flicked back her hair and shrieked. "And that gives Falcon Tech time to penetrate the market even more. Wait a minute…that's it. The launch can go ahead and they all come out winners. That's their game plan. I see it all clearly now."

She stood up and threw her arms around him. At that moment the pain and anguish, the terrible burden of guilt of the past months started to dissipate, to dissolve in her warm embrace.

He looked at Sarah, his eyes seeking her help. "Laura, if you agree to help, could we make all our contact through Sarah…that's if she agrees?"

"I might help but I don't come cheap. What's the commission?" Sarah probed.

He smiled. "Typical Scot. Always on the make!"

"Very funny coming from a Dutchman!" she retorted.

With that they started to laugh, the tension of the moment easing.

"I should be the one charging the fee. It's real-life drama…better than reading thrillers!" he said.

Laura scoffed at his suggestion.

"I have to know by tomorrow because I have a plan," he declared.

"A plan? You have it all worked out already. You really are a goddamn investigator at heart," she retorted accusingly.

"They can't be allowed to get away with murder."

Laura winked at Sarah. "Well, if his plan is half as daring as his attempt to get into our apartment, I know what to call it."

"What?" he asked.

"Operation Chutzpah."

"Run that past me again," Sarah said.

"Chutzpah. It means unmitigated effrontery or impudence. It's a word we use all the time back home in the States."

"Chutzpah! I like it." Marc agreed.

Laura fell silent, reflective. She seemed more receptive to the outlandish idea. Sarah excused herself and disappeared into the kitchen. After a few minutes she shouted out, "Coffee coming up."

"Look, Marc, I'll help you but you're still not off the hook. I need time to come to terms with this…there's a lot to absorb."

He nodded in silence, a thousand thoughts floating in his mind.

"Laura," he said finally, his eyes seeking her forgiveness, "I would really appreciate your help and understanding."

Laura moved to the couch and sat down. There was nothing more to say for the moment. For the first time in months Marc allowed himself to feel optimism.

Chapter Twenty

Brussels

KEVIN O' SHEA DROVE DOWN the ramp leading to the underground car park of the Trade Bureau building on Avenue de Cortenbergh. Descending to sub-level three, he parked close to the lifts and waited. Two minutes later Marc appeared with an overnight bag slung across his shoulder.

"Open the boot lid."

"The boot?…Why?" Kevin asked.

"Just open the boot."

"Okay. Okay."

"When I jump in slam down the lid. I don't want anybody around here to see me. And when you are well out of Brussels pull up at a quiet spot but make sure nobody is following you. I'll climb out then."

"Sure you know what you're doing?"

"Yes. Now hurry!"

Marc threw in the bag, scanned the car park and then climbed in.

"I don't like this. You could suffocate."

"Shhh…no debates. I'll be okay. Now slam the boot lid closed and move fast."

"If you say so…"

The Audi A4 spiralled up the circular ramp and out into the afternoon traffic. Ten minutes of fast driving brought Kevin past the Ring and onto the E19 motorway. A few kilometres past the Paris junction he pulled into a slip road where the view from the motorway was restricted by a thicket of tall evergreens. He opened the window and listened. Moments later he jumped out and opened the boot lid.

"I went as fast as I could."

"I know. I tumbled from side to side. Banged my head a few times."

They jumped in and sped off in the direction of Charleroi, a town seventy kilometres south of Brussels. Marc confirmed that Laura and Sarah were now fully on board, ready to help in any way they could. He wanted to get to the FT executives and Verbiest no matter how difficult that would be. After the meeting in the restaurant Kevin was still sceptical but his disbelief was melting fast. One thing was certain - Marc was serious and determined and ready to fight back no matter how great the odds were stacked against him.

As the Audi swung onto the approach road to the airport Kevin asked, "So, why Charleroi?"

"It's easier to give the stringers the slip. Brussels Airport is too obvious. I hope the *body-in-the-boot-trick* gives me an advantage. Anyway, Ryanair has cityhopper flights to Dublin... back tomorrow evening."

They came to a halt outside the terminal building. Marc got out of the car and grabbed the overnight bag. Kevin shouted through the window, "Give my regards to Sean. Tell him I said you're to get a good discount."

"Damn right - I'll need it."

He strode up to the check-in desk, picked up his boarding card and cleared immigration. Half an hour later he was on the evening shuttle to Dublin.

Dublin
THREE HOURS LATER at seven thirty he checked into the Jury's Inn at Christchurch in the centre of Dublin. He freshened up with a shower, studied the tourist map he had picked up earlier at the reception desk and headed towards the Temple Bar cultural quarter of the city.

The cadence of the fiddle drifted from the Oliver St. John Gogarty pub making the choice for the evening easy. Sidling up to the end of the bar, he slid onto a stool and took in his surroundings. The pub was crowded with a cacophony of Irish and foreign accents. Marc was on his most dangerous mission of all. Schuman the sleuth - the 007 of the Trade Bureau - firmly back in his role as chief investigator, at home with what came naturally...what he knew best. His imagination was fired up but thoughts of Laura broke his concentration on the game plan. Their week in the South of France and their first meeting in Beijing. And winning her back in spite of the sordid happenings. He was asking a lot of her, was asking her to risk losing the things he himself did not want to lose. If it went wrong she would lose her job and be stripped of her right to practise law - maybe even face criminal charges. He was really playing with her life.

The patrons were living in another world; a world removed from the devious plans he was hatching to get back at his tormentors. He was a novice, a total amateur who would pit his skill against the most cunning mixture of people in the world. Every detail in his action plan - the plan Laura liked to call Operation Chutzpah - needed to be treble checked, meticulously gone through and then shared only with his close confidants. After all, while it was well thought through it still smacked of improvisation. But that was all he could do right now - work with what he had - intelligence, help from his friends and a plan so outlandish that they would never dream of such impudence from one individual.

He raised the glass of Guinness to his mouth, drained it and watched as three musicians started to tune their instruments in a corner at the other end of the pub. He called another drink, shifted his stool and propped his back against a wooden support beam. Traditional music filled the atmosphere, and for the first time in months, his brain was silent and the tension, which up to this had been so palpable, had eased. He took a sheet of hotel notepaper from his pocket and scribbled down a rough timetable of the coming week's events. Suddenly a hand clasped his left shoulder.

"Who the f-"

Marc froze on the spot for a few helpless moments, wondering how they had traced him. In a frantic panic he spun around and saw a curly-haired man smiling at him.

"Do you mind if I take this?" the man asked gesturing towards the empty stool.

Marc mustered an awkward smile. "No...not at all," he said, relieved. Two hours later he left the pub and weaved his way quietly along the sweet security of the streets of Dublin back to his hotel.

"HELLO I'M MARC SCHUMAN. Kevin O' Shea sent me," Marc said, placing his hands on the counter of the electronic security store on Harcourt Street. O' Shea thrust out a big beefy hand shaking Marc's firmly.

"Hey good to meet you. Kevin said to expect you. So, what can we do for you?"

Leaning across the counter he started off.

"It's difficult because I'm not exactly sure what I'm looking for."

"What kind of job have you got in mind?"

"Well, bugging an office, sound and maybe video? Telephone tapping and some kind of mobile sound surveillance," he explained.

Sean O' Shea chuckled. "You're not asking for much, are you now?"

"Not really."

When Marc finished his description of the people he intended to catch and inevitably the places he needed to bug, O' Shea waved his hand towards three rows of shelves and smiled. "Well, if you've got the cash I've got the gear."

"Great. Give me some ideas so."

"Okay, let's start."

Brussels

THE TEMPERATURE HAD DROPPED and a frost glistened on the parked cars that lined the Avenue. Marc stood in a poorly-lit recess between two buildings giving him a clear view of the law office of PKV&S. For more than half an hour his eyes darted in all directions, up and down the busy thoroughfare and across towards the buildings on the far side. His attention was also concentrated on the shadowy movements under the tree-lined median, but he saw nothing suspicious. At nine-forty five, the light in Laura's third floor office flicked off and on three times in quick succession. Marc glanced at his watch and then swiftly moved out of the shadows and crossed the street. The door opened on cue; he slipped inside and winked at her. She returned a nervous smile and slapped the door closed behind him. He followed as she mounted the stairs in silence. At the fourth floor she shot a finger towards the boardroom. His eyes took in the detail and then he followed her down the flight of stairs to Verbiest's office. The desk came in for close examination and then the leather pad. It was lifted, inspected and left back in position. He ignored the pen set and went straight for the angle poise lamp. The plastic sticker with the manufacturer's name on it was peeled from the base of the lamp. He pulled a tube of resin from the hold all bag and placed a tiny blob of glue on the base of the device. It was eased into the recess and pressed into position. Beads of perspiration formed at his temples and his cheeks felt flushed. He sat down on Verbiest's chair, swung it at right angles to the desk and spoke.

Moments later Laura came to the door, beamed a smile and stuck a thumb in the air. He returned the gesture. He unscrewed the mouthpiece of the telephone, placed a miniature microphone and transmitter inside and immediately screwed it back. He dialled a number. Sarah's voice came down the line.

"Is that 7571495?" He asked.

"No, I'm afraid you've got the wrong number," she replied.

"I'm sorry for disturbing you. Good night."

In an instant Laura was again standing at the door.

"Clear as a bell," she whispered. He smiled back and sprang from the leather chair. In an instant he was in her office checking the recorder. It was concealed in the paper feeder of an unused computer printer. He stroked his chin, nodding his approval.

"Everything's perfect. Just one more bug and then I'm straight out of here," he whispered.

Entering the boardroom he walked the length of the table and then looked underneath checking the scalloped legs. *It would be futile,* he thought, *with directional microphones*. Wasting no time he glanced up at the chandelier at the same time slipping off his running shoes. An omni-directional microphone was pulled from his holdall. He grabbed a bunch of papers, spread them on the surface and bounced onto the table. It took no more than two minutes to wire the light cluster for sound. He stepped back to observe his handiwork, glancing from different angles. He then dismounted the table, walked full circle around it, observing the device from every possible angle. Now back on the table he put a fine thread of epoxy around the edge of the device. It would have to stay solidly in position for the foreseeable future. Ten seconds later the bond was dry and firm. As he slipped the tube of adhesive into the tracksuit pocket the phone rang in the outer office. Startled by the unexpected sound, he involuntarily jumped, forcing the papers under his feet to slide across the polished surface. He tried hard to regain his balance but his feet splayed at right angles flipping his upper body backwards. His head struck a chair first, tossing him awkwardly onto the floor, the impact making a heavy thud. The back of the antique chair had broken away and landed beside him.

Laura was in her office on the third floor waiting for the recorder to come to life. She heard the faint ring of the phone and, a split second later, the dull sound. She was in the boardroom in seconds.

"Oh my God what happened?" she said, taking in the scene in one glance.

"Are you okay?"

There was no response. He did not move.

The fall must have knocked him out cold, she thought. Bending over she put her ear to his chest. His heart was beating normally. Maybe a little faster than usual but she was no expert.

"At least he's alive," she muttered, "but what am I going to do now?" The phone kept ringing. In an impulse she moved to lift it but realised how stupid that would be. She cradled his head, examining the cut along his right cheek. The blood had run down his tracksuit and onto the Nepalese rug.

Just what I need right now, she thought. She fumbled in her pocket pulling out a paper handkerchief and wiped the blood from his face. The handkerchief was pressed against the wound until the blood stopped oozing. She ran her hands over his head and felt a large bump just above the right ear.

A nasty blow, a fractured skull maybe, she thought.

"Marc, Marc," she whispered into his ear as she rubbed his cheek. No response. Perspiration formed on her forehead, her heart thumping inside her chest. The phone stopped ringing.

"Oh, shit, Marc, come on, you've got to wake up."

She tugged in desperation at the tracksuit strings and still he wouldn't move. She shook him. "Marc, Marc, come on…wake up."

Pulling up one eyelid she stared into the pupil. She turned his head towards the light but there was no reaction to the stimulus. This time she shook him more vigorously, rolling his head from side to side. Seconds passed. Still no response. *Don't panic*, she thought. *There's got to be a way.* Five, maybe six, minutes elapsed and then in a moment of desperation she grabbed him around the shoulders and shook him violently, slapping him across the face.

"Come on Marc. Wake up."

He was now on his side and for the first time he gagged. Turning him face up she called his name over and over. His facial muscles twitched and he began to breathe through his mouth, moaning loudly. And slowly there was movement in his eyelids. She kept talking to him, bombarding him with questions. Seconds ran into minutes. It took another ten for his eyes to open fully. They were glassy and dilated. She desperately wanted him to recover.

"Do you know what you were doing right now…you know before you fell?"

Nothing but a blank stare.

"Well, do you?" she demanded.

In return she got a pair of vacant eyes staring at her. "Damn you, speak to me Schuman. Wake up. This is your damn mess. C'mon…"

Slowly his eyes focused on her. "Marc, speak to me. Do you know where you are?"

"What…what happened to me?"

"You fell. Look, you fell from the table right there."

"What?"

Laura sighed loudly. "The goddamn table."

His hands moved up to his head searching for the source of the pain. "It hurts."

"I know. It was a nasty fall. Do you know where you are?"

"No. Why?"

"Oh shit."

"What was I doing?"

She nodded towards the chandelier. "You were planting something."

"...Now I remember."

"Marc we've got to get out of here fast. Can you walk?"

"I'll have to try, won't I?"

"Okay let's see how you do. It's late and the lights are still on but first we've got to fix that chair and clean the rug."

He rose slowly, helped to his feet by Laura. In an instant she blazed along the corridor to the washroom and returned holding a wad of dripping wet toilet paper. She began cleaning the rug. After several trips down the corridor the rug was unblemished, just a circular wet stain on the spot.

"That glue is really powerful. It should work...for a while at least...until somebody sits on it," Marc said as he watched her fixing the chair. Minutes later, Laura slipped downstairs, opened the door and glanced up and down the street. "Everything's clear," she said, beckoning him down. He was still holding his head as he stepped outside and vanished into the darkness.

THE FOLLOWING MORNING, Kaufmann's secretary phoned down to the fourth floor looking for Marc.

"He's in the building somewhere," Heidi said, unsure where to start looking.

"Well, Mr. Kaufmann wants to see him right away."

Heidi checked the usual places but didn't find him. Marc was in a corner office on the first floor – a place euphemistically called the reference library - where the legal precedents were housed. The five racks of shelving were not enough to accommodate the growing volume of documents; consequently the recent cases were stacked haphazardly on the floor making movement difficult and a search for a suitable precedent a tedious and time-consuming exercise. He rummaged for an hour through the technology section ending up with a handful of useful texts. The genuine draft law was not a problem; it was already on disk and could be printed at the press of a button. But a different text was now needed; a potential law that would pass Verbiest's eagle eyes. He headed for the stairwell and, having bounded up the flight of stairs to his office, slumped into his swivel chair and booted up the computer.

"Where on earth have you been? I've searched all around the building looking for you."

Marc looked up startled. "What?"

Heidi was standing at the doorway.

"Kaufmann's looking for you urgently. You had better get up there now. Go."

"Somebody's always looking for me," he muttered as he rose from the chair and headed towards the door.

"When did Kauf phone?"

"Nine thirty. Go up right away."

This was going to be a *get-the-hell-off-the-case* meeting, that much he knew for sure but there was no way he could have a proposal for legislation ready for the December meeting of the Member States' governments. He would have to come out straight and say it. Champenois would froth at the mouth. Windsor and Kelly would lean back, smiling wryly. Kaufmann would pace around the room recalling the commitment at the last meeting that the documents would be on the table for the November meeting. He rushed down the corridor and into the anteroom.

"Go straight through. Hey, careful in there. We're not in the best of humour this morning," Kaufmann's secretary whispered, peering over her glasses.

Wachter being helpful at last, he thought. *My world is truly turning upside down.*

"Thanks for the warning."

He tapped on the door and entered. "You were looking for me, Mr. Kaufmann?"

"Yes," he said and motioned towards the conference table.

No low table with the soft seats this morning, Marc thought. *A really bad sign.* Kaufmann opened the door, giraffed his head through to the anteroom and said, "Tell Windsor and the others that Schuman's here."

He returned to the table but did not sit down. Instead he placed his hands on the back of a chair and began shifting his weight from foot to foot.

"We're not just against the wire on this one, we're sitting on

249

the wire. And it's very hot…all because I haven't got a draft law on my desk."

"Well I can-"

"There's nothing to explain at this stage." The Director moved away from the chair and was now in full stride pacing the length of the room, his right index finger wagging in the air for emphasis.

"I thought we'd cleared the air in August and again in October. Remember you promised a proposal for the Member States in September and then November. At the last meeting you said that the case would be wrapped up before Christmas. Nothing could be clear-"

There was a tap on the door. Kaufmann fell silent, his eyes focused in its direction. Windsor, Kelly and Champenois strutted in. No pleasantries were exchanged, their demeanour reflecting the mood of the moment. Kaufmann waved them towards the table.

"I have been going over the state of play…the urgency of the situation. We've fifteen cases on-going at the moment and yours, Marc…yours is the only one not meeting the deadline."

Champenois now began bellowing. "Do you or do you not understand what a political commitment means?"

Marc mustered a response. "Yes."

"There are always going to be conflicting pressures but let me make things clear. This place works on a trade-off and ultimately a deal. That part's simple, isn't it?"

"Yes."

"So that's where trust comes in. We trust investigators like you to go to far-flung places like the Far East and bring back results. Then our job is to manage those results like a ringmaster with a whip. And you know what that means? A law that levies strong duties on Asian-made computers." He pulled back from Marc's face, paused for a moment and then threw a glance at his colleagues. "Based, of course, on the evidence you've found."

Kaufmann was now pacing behind his desk. He stopped and came towards the conference table. "We on the administrative side, if we give a promise…you see *if we give a promise* we don't break it. Do you understand that? It's a kind of covenant between us and the political level. We deliver on these things and they don't poke their noses into our trough so to speak."

"It's clear? Isn't it?" Windsor chipped in.

"Yes, it's clear."

The Frenchman started off again. "Now follow these steps carefully. The Director here has committed himself to deliver a watertight law with duties to the Commissioner. The Commissioner has promised five Member State governments that their computer industries would have protection against cheap, Asian-made products…all done informally, you understand. A political deal." He tapped the table for effect. "Now two of those same governments are facing an election early next year. And guess what? Those politicians would hate to have to fight a campaign while factories were closing down around them. So it's not a question of us sitting around on our wide bureaucratic asses while Rome burns. Is it?"

Marc nodded in acknowledgement.

"No, it's damn well not. And it's certainly not a case of sitting on the result of the investigation just because you find it difficult to compare lap tops with desktops. Computers are all the same. Just find some nice legalese jargon to explain away the differences…you're a lawyer, a wordsmith. That's what you're supposed to be good at. So now, is there a problem that justifies delay?"

Many problems. Two investigators had been killed to get them out of the way. And a sordid tape was being used to blackmail him. Not to mention a bribe waiting to be collected once he said yes.

"No," he said faintly.

Kelly hissed. "That legislation has to be on the statute books by New Year. Do you hear me?"

"Yes, I understand."

"If you can't deliver, then you come off the case."

"But it's very complicated. It's not only about lap tops versus desk tops. It takes-"

"Look we don't want to know the details. Just deliver the result that keeps everyone on board."

"But it can't be done that quickly. The Competition people

and the Information Technology technocrats have made some strong arguments...very persuasive arguments, against duties. And the consumer groups around Europe are kicking up a huge fuss. They're fighting all the way against higher-priced computers. I have to take on board their arguments and find a way to rebut them in the legislation."

Windsor leaned forward towards Marc. "Look, we know well that law-making has many diverse elements to it." He paused to glance at his colleagues. "But at the same time it's a diffuse process that leaves plenty of scope for discretion."

"But everyone wants to get their oar in and it's delaying the whole process. It's part of our whole approach here...openness and transparency at every stage. I can't change the rules," the chief investigator shot back.

Kaufmann slipped into the chair and spread his hands out wide on the table. "Sometimes in these cases logic is not that important. There's scope for a lot of legal *blah blah*, if you understand what I mean. It's about balancing conflicting interests."

"Kurt's right," Windsor interjected. "Nothing's carved in stone with these cases. All that's needed is a watertight justification for duties. The other arguments can be dressed up in woolly language that nobody can decipher."

"Look, to put it another way," Kelly bombarded. "Law-making is like sausage-making. Nobody wants to look at the process but the winners can enjoy the end product."

A faint smile crossed Kaufmann's face. Windsor tittered. Marc attempted to put his case.

"But-"

"Are you telling us that you're not able to deliver?"

"No, but-"

"Marc, no buts," Champenois snapped, as he pulled a copy of an absence form from his folder. "So, if you needed time to finish the case why the hell take a week off at the end of August?"

"I needed a break. Simple as that."

Champenois grinned at his colleagues. "Needed a break?"

"It didn't affect the case."

Windsor drew in a deep breath. "Look you know well that

252

when the deadline is tight, to impose a duty calls for around-the-clock hard work."

Champenois sniggered. "I knew it. We wouldn't have this situation if we gave it to Rousseau and Kotler in the first place. They know what's expected of them."

"Okay," Kaufmann said, "can you deliver this case or not?"

"Well of course I can." His pride would allow nothing less.

"Well, then, get downstairs and write us up a good defendable piece of legislation and have it on my table in one week."

"Kurt, we can schedule the next Member States' meeting for the twenty second," Kelly confirmed. "In that way it can be on the Commissioner's desk before New Year, fingers crossed."

Marc stood up and made for the door. Kelly dispensed words of reassurance as his hand went for the door handle.

"It's nothing personal Marc. The system demands it. We keep our end of the bargain and the politicians keep theirs."

Marc glanced over his shoulder at the smug bureaucrats and then firmly pulled the door shut behind him. Champenois stood up and said, "I think he's got the message."

"Yes, he's still a bit idealistic," Kelly agreed. "But this case will mould him, I'm sure of it."

Kaufmann smiled. "I think he now understands what the *imperatives* are to survive in this jungle."

Champenois grinned. "Damn right. We all had to learn at some stage. He's blooded now and his pride won't let him walk away. That's for sure."

MARC WALKED DOWN the corridor in a daze. A few people spoke to him but he was not part of their world. The *gang of four's* words continued to ring in his ears.

I'm thinking openness and transparency and they're talking opacity and obfuscation. What a nightmare, he thought. *I've just been through a mauling with sumo wrestlers.* Banging the button he leaned against the polished steel panel, releasing a sigh of resignation. *What more can happen in this goddamn case,* he thought.

Chapter Twenty One

EARLY ON SATURDAY MORNING, Sarah drove along Avenue Franklin Roosevelt, a suburb in the south of Brussels. She located 'Heidelberg', a period house half way along the Avenue, parked the car a few metres further on and walked back towards the house. The area was surveyed for early morning activity and then her eyes homed in on the red post box across from the house. She walked towards the post box and dropped in some leaflets. One leaflet fell to the ground and, as she bent down to pick it up, she pressed a tiny device to the underside of the metal post box. Moments later she tried to move it. It was firmly bonded in place. She walked back to the car.

THAT AFTERNOON LAURA PACED the living room, going over every detail again and again. It made her apprehensive but there was no going back. Instead of being down town shopping, she was helping her mad boy friend to take on the world. A corporation on its way to becoming a global behemoth with the help of the Triads and some former CIA goons. The odds heavily stacked against them, in a no-win situation.

It sure takes chutzpah, she thought. She walked to the window overlooking Ambiorix Park and watched two elderly ladies exercising their dogs. Streaks of sunshine created a mellow glow to the afternoon. She turned away from the window, looked at the miniature device laid out on the coffee table and smiled.

AT 7:30 LAURA'S CAR SWUNG off Avenue Louise, and headed towards Avenue Franklin Roosevelt. Five minutes later it swished through the entrance to the Verbiest household bringing the familiar sight of Hazel Daner's car into sight. *At least one familiar face,* she thought as she pulled up alongside it. They had met on the cocktail circuit of the Brussels Bar and struck up a close relationship. The Bostonian was an associate in an American law firm giving Laura a fast track entree into the Washington legal maze. They traded information to their mutual benefit but kept the networking arrangement - a woman-to-woman kind of thing - low key, helping them to survive in the predominantly male environment.

Daner was an incessant talker. She would be a problem tonight. As Laura walked to the door she thought of ways to keep circulating at the party. The last thing she could afford was to have a shadow for the night. It would add an unwanted dimension to an already complicated night. The episode in the office had unnerved her. No matter how carefully it was planned the whole thing relied on improvisation for its realisation but taking the opportunity *impromptu-style* was still the only way, Marc had assured her.

She rang the bell. The door opened and Angeline, Verbiest's wife, greeted her. Laura stepped inside. At that moment Verbiest came down the hallway. Before she could begin her observations, a glass of champagne was thrust into her right hand and she was ushered towards the living room. Mozart's Eine Kleine Nachtmusik played in the background. Most of the office crew had already arrived. And now she could see Daner close by the folding doors leading to the dining room.

Suddenly Knightley was at her shoulder. "Good evening, Laura! Enjoying yourself?"

"Well I've just arrived."

"Angeline and Erik always throw an excellent party."

"Indeed. I was here last year, remember?"

He raised his left hand in a friendly gesture. "Oh yes, you're right."

"Old hand at these things you know."

He raised his glass, muttered something about enjoying the party and moved on. Laura drifted down the room towards the American. *Better to pass the pleasantries early and then leave me free to concentrate on my task,* she thought.

They covered the usual ground – office politics and relationships - the *who's-doing-what-to-whom* routine. Laura moved on. An apprehensive hour passed as the small talk continued. She circulated again as was expected and then her opportunity arrived. The waiters had emerged from the kitchen with trays of food.

"Erik, do you mind if I make a phone call? Forgot my mobile."

"Not at all."

She walked into the hall and left her handbag on the chair beside the phone. It was as she had remembered. The old-fashioned telephone handset on the hall table directly under the African artefacts mounted in mahogany cases. She set her mind to the task in hand. The receiver was brought to her ear while taking in the surroundings. Her eyes traced the telephone lead down to ground level and then followed it as it ran along the skirting board.

The hand piece now got her attention. The mouthpiece was a screw-on type. Cradling the phone between the crook of the shoulder and her ear she faced the wall and, pretending to dial a number, unscrewed the mouthpiece, sliding the device into place. Its miniature transmitter would be just powerful enough to transmit to the receiver on the post box across the street. Suddenly Verbiest came through the door. Her heart raced and her legs went to jelly. Her hand came up to cover the mouthpiece.

"Laura, you're missing all the action inside," he laughed, gliding down the hallway and into the kitchen.

"Be there in a minute," she replied, tilting her head around to keep the door in view.

"You don't want to miss the food, do you?" he shouted. Laura was now holding an imaginary conversation into a silent line. Seconds ticked away and then Verbiest re-emerged. She stuck a finger in the air to indicate that she would finish in a minute. He disappeared into the living room. She screwed back the mouthpiece, dropped the phone onto the cradle and pulled a tissue from her bag, wiping a film of perspiration from her temples. Glancing at her watch she took a deep breath and walked towards the living room door. *Mission accomplished in seven minutes. Now where's that champagne!*

THE TAP ON THE DOOR Tuesday evening didn't surprise Verbiest in the least. Of late, he had become accustomed to Saatchi's habit of appearing in his office late in the evening, when most of the stressed-out lawyers and secretaries had retreated to their homes to refresh themselves for the next day's activity.

Over the past months a special bond - a deep camaraderie - had developed between the two partners. Contact had become more frequent both inside and outside the office to a point where the relationship had become fraternal, where they were almost blood brothers. Verbiest took some comfort from the knowledge that he was not alone when it came to playing outside the rules, when it came to stepping beyond the limits of legal ethics – all in the interest of keeping a blue chip client.

Saatchi moved in silence towards the desk. Verbiest pulled back from his hunched position over the keyboard, allowing his shoulders to sag as he slouched back into his chair.

"This is getting to be a regular thing," Verbiest said. "What's on your mind?"

"Just been in Knightley's office. He's busy reviewing last quarter's billable hours for next Monday's management meeting. Petersson was there too. He's having big trouble with the Apollo account - another major dot com failure. Apparently they're about to go down in flames and he's exposed for more than one hundred thousand dollars of chargeable hours."

"That should keep old smorgasbord occupied for a while. At least he won't have time to criticise my business style."

"Funny thing, you came up in the conversation. They're really impressed with your acumen…with your ability to keep the most difficult clients. And amazed that you've held the Falcon Tech account against all the odds. Even Petersson had to agree that you just seem to know how to survive when things get tough. I assured them that it's natural flair…sheer talent. And I told them that your timing on the Falcon Tech thing was perfect as always, that the Clinton administration was now pushing hard for a free trade deal with China and with membership of the WTO in the offing Congress was likely to okay the whole deal within months. I assured them that in such a scenario the Trade

Bureau was likely to back-pedal...go soft and settle for something less than a punitive duty. The Europeans will probably sell the human rights activists down the river."

Verbiest chuckled. "Excellent. Thanks Lorenzo. So what did they say to that?"

"Petersson shook his head in amazement and said you seem to land on the winning side every time. Sheer skill and good judgement I assured them."

Verbiest straightened up in the chair and pursed his lips. "I *am* the best really Lorenzo," he declared arrogantly.

"Most definitely," Saatchi replied rising from the chair.

Hong Kong

WONG STARED PENSIVELY through the ceiling-to-floor glass window of Cheng's office on the sixth floor as Cheng explained the latest phone call from Johnson about delivery of the replacement documentation. He told him that Schuman had insisted that the handover of the money and the tape would have to be on his terms and that Wong himself and Verbiest would also have to turn up at the Atomium.

Wong directed Cheng to immediately procure a set of Trade Bureau stamps so that Schuman would have a complete set of sanitised documents with the original dates and registered numbers on them.

"I'll activate right away."

The Supreme Lodge Father turned away from the window and beckoned Hu Hei towards the desk.

"You will go to Brussels to take charge of security at the Atomium. Nothing must go wrong."

"I unnastan' assignmen' perfect' well Missa Wong," Hu Hei said.

"Everything must go like clockwork for the hand over."

"Hung-Triad o-n-a-h Missa Wong."

Wong turned to face the two young men sitting on the low seats in a corner of the room. Ling and Zhang had waited patiently for their instructions for more than an hour.

"One hundred thousand dollars could be very persuasive,"

Wong declared wistfully.

They nodded to show their agreement.

"Yes indeed," Cheng emphasised, "very persuasive."

Wong took a key from his pocket, opened a steel press door and took out a briefcase. He handed it to Ling.

"But only pamper the ten most important analysts and journalists… and then show them the colour of our money…one hundred thousand each. One million should create enough hoopla around Wall Street to get the adrenaline pumping fast through those blue-blooded veins. Banner headlines saying that Falcon Tech's worth twelve billion should ensure that all minds are focused on the launch."

Cheng grinned, the scar exaggerating the whole effect to make it look like a sinister leer.

"We will fly directly to New York tonight," Zhang said.

"And when you've finished in that part of the world take a flight to Grand Cayman. I want you to look at some property there."

"We're on our way," Ling said rising from his seat. Zhang followed him to the door.

Wong turned to Cheng. "I leave tonight for Beijing to brief the apparatchiks on progress. They seem pleased that we are fighting hard to keep a big technology company in China."

"Wouldn't surprise me if they make you an honourary member of the Communist Party."

"Remember we haven't delivered on their demands yet. There's still a long road to travel to satisfy Beijing. When this assignment is wrapped up we'll have to start looking around to see if other Western companies need our services too."

"Now that we've got to know the ways of our occidental friends we must be ready to help."

"Yes indeed Cheng, we should always be willing to help. By helping them we help ourselves in the true spirit of capitalism."

Brussels

SARAH PICKED UP her mobile and dialled out ten digits. Moments later Marc answered.

"The Heidelberg tape verified."

"Excellent. So?"

"Verbiest made two phone calls to Wong in Hong Kong. He was briefed on progress. It's guarded...nothing very explicit. But you'll probably understand it better."

"This is fantastic."

"And Laura checked the office and boardroom. Nothing significant so far."

"It figures. Verbiest probably does all his calls from home to be safe. I've just thought of something. Maybe he's keeping all of this to himself. Keeping the other partners in the dark. Mention that to Laura. See what she thinks."

"Will do. Over and out."

Boston

THE QUARTERLY MEETING had been postponed for the second time. Several formalities still remained to be completed including the lodging of a bunch of very official-looking documents with the SEC. With the launch imminent, Sinclair issued an ultimatum and summoned the FT people to Boston to hear the latest results. The board members assembled in the mahogany-panelled boardroom and dutifully took their seats behind the nameplates under the constellation of Tipperary crystal chandeliers running the full length of the table, their conversations hushed and polite. When the members were seated Miss Rockwell led the FT executives into the boardroom.

"Thank you, Miss Rockwell. We will not need secretarial service for this meeting."

His secretary walked to the boardroom door pulling it closed behind her.

"Good afternoon, gentlemen. As you know, the flotation of Falcon Tech is our first agenda item. To set the scene you will find a copy of Tuesday's *Wall Street Journal* in front of you. Those analysts are valuing FT at twelve - not ten – *twelve* billion." A hubristic smile danced across his face and, when he was sure he had every board member's full attention, added, "Who said wining and dining the right people doesn't pay off?"

260

The boardroom returned weak smiles.

"The executives are here to answer any questions you may have. But first I would like your approval of the SEC documents in front of you. Our stockbrokers have cleared them. We need board approval so that they can be printed and lodged by close of business on Friday. It's routine for this kind of sell off."

"Chairman," JD Jefferson interrupted, "surely we should hear the progress report from Falcon Tech before we approve anything."

"It's all technical stuff just to satisfy the SEC bureaucrats and time is running out. We need to meet the deadline. Otherwise the launch may have to be postponed."

"I still think it's worth hearing from Falcon Tech first."

Sinclair looked down the boardroom table. It seemed that support was going towards Jefferson's suggestion. He would not push it further.

"Okay. So let's hear the quarterly report."

Batista mounted the podium. He gave the usual upbeat talk. Again double digit growth for quarter three. Falcon Tech was weathering the Asian currency crisis better than most. In fact, sales even increased and costs came down in most markets according to Batista's prepared script. Everything was on target for the launch. He wrapped up with a glib and reassuring reference to the trade case.

"Ten per cent duty on Falcon Tech's computers in Europe. Something the company can live with. A minor setback but with the reduced cost base from the currency crisis the impact is negligible." He stepped from the podium and took his seat.

"Well, gentlemen," Sinclair said patronisingly. "You can see that we've picked a winner here. Let's get the documents approved and start to celebrate. I've laid on some pre prandial dri-"

Hanson's right hand shot up and he began to speak without waiting for the chairman to acknowledge his intervention.

"Chairman, I think we have to be more thorough than that. After all, we are a major public company so I would like clarification on a few issues. First, we don't have all the facts on this trade case. Batista assures us that a duty of only ten per cent will be imposed. Well, that's not our experience in Europe. One of our subsidiaries in the UK was hit with fifty per cent duty on a pharmaceutical material from China. It's well known that the European Trade Bureau imposes punitive duties on manufacturers in China. As we all know, it's a communist-controlled system with no market…and the human rights issue is not settled either. The duty's always much higher. So…I find it hard to believe when Albert tells us that it's as low as ten per cent."

Newman and Lindell kept their heads below the parapet leaving Batista in the dock.

"Look we've the leading law firm in Brussels representing us. We…we're being guided by them and they tell us it's going to be ten per cent. We have to believe them. They've already prepared all the figures."

Hanson looked around at his fellow board members. "Believe them? Would you believe them? Lawyers never tell it as it is. It's regularly covered in the *Financial Times*…fortress Europe and all that. The duty from China is always higher…thirty, forty and sometimes fifty per cent. No, I simply don't believe it."

"Look, we just make and sell computers. We don't pretend to know all the ins and outs of trade issues. It's all big picture stuff…political stuff. If our lawyers say ten per cent then we believe them. After all that's what we hire them for."

George Rendell, a Harvard economics professor slipped off his glasses and coughed for attention. "I believe Mr Hanson's right. Wall Street will be very circumspect about a launch where a liability has not crystallised. What did our internal due diligence turn up?"

Lights flashed in Newman's head. He pretended to flick through documents.

"Ten per cent."

"You're sure of that?"

"I'm sure."

Rendell was not satisfied. "If we lodge the SEC documents and the duty turns out higher then we're in serious trouble. All the profit projections will be flawed. The SEC will be merciless never mind the institutional investors. They'll be furious.

Seems to me we need assurance. We need certainty."

Sinclair wanted to appease his board. He looked towards Batista and interjected, "And it's up to our Falcon Tech executives to give us that certainty."

Batista was like a pressure cooker on the boil. He could contain his anger no longer.

"Look, we've delivered a twelve-billion-dollar company to you guys. It took a lot of sweat and a lot of battles. And you're all going to benefit. Every single one of you stands to fill your pockets with up to one hundred million bucks...to become multi-millionaires overnight. So you'd damn well better start sharing the risk too."

He pushed back the chair and got to his feet. He was now at the top of the boardroom table hovering above the chairman, a finger wagging menacingly.

"We're saying ten per cent because we know it's going to be ten per cent. And that's because we've had to cut *corners*." He walked past several board members. Leaning over one of them, he raised his voice in anger and thumped the table. *"Yes, corners... a lot of corners."*

Silence descended. Batista managed to contain his anger and then continued walking around the table.

"We had no choice," he said cooly. "Triads did some leverage work for us. Bottom line, they blackmailed the chief investigator in the European Trade Bureau. He goes along and gets a cut of five million bucks straight up for his trouble. That's how we can say ten per cent with certainty. Ten per cent." He again banged the table for emphasis. "Ten per cent. Are you all happy now?"

The august body of WASPish men inhaled deeply. They were staring blackmail and bribery in the face. Thoughts of the Foreign Corrupt Practices Act and a stretch in a Federal prison. Gasps of disbelief echoed in the boardroom. It could not be true. Nobody connected to Kimble-Sinclair would do such a thing. Revered and trusted for generations. The essence of propriety.

"And now that I'm on my feet, I just might as well go for full disclosure. Damn it I will. In the process our Triad friends killed two trade investigators in Europe. That's it on the chin. The whole story."

He calmly walked back to his seat. The president of Kimble-Sinclair was speechless. Whispered conversations around the boardroom grew louder as the members took in the full implications of what they had heard. To a man they turned towards their president. It was up to him to take action. Sinclair felt the penetrating stares and the menacing silence. The standard bearers of conservatism sat stony-faced and expressionless in their padded seats. The well-bred East Coast gentlemen were being lectured to by a frontier man from the Wild West. The impudence, the sheer effrontery of it. It was up to Sinclair to put a stop to it. Howard will fix him, they were sure to a man.

Sinclair looked down the table and saw through the conservative carapace, the thin veneer of propriety, deep into their souls. Each of them had a reason to cover up the transgression of the subsidiary. One hundred million dollars was reason enough! The West Coast pioneers could be sacrificed if expediency demanded it. *What could be expected from latter-day cowboys anyway?* If necessary, the board of Kimble-Sinclair would disavow any knowledge of wrongdoing and sacrifice a few gold diggers out west. After all, the board is drawn from the best - blue bloods with impeccable pedigree - the type that made America great. Real Yankees who know how to control and *to win*.

The president did not have to look down the table. He just had to look into his own heart. One of the seven deadly sins lurked there just as it lurked in all the hearts that now beat anxiously around the table. He knew it well. Avarice, plain and simple.

"Gentlemen, we cannot acquiesce in wrongdoing. Kimble-Sinclair will never condone criminal activity... never... whatever form it takes. What the Falcon Tech executives did was reprehensible but clearly no fault lies with this board."

Sinclair was now speaking with bifurcated tongue and the members of the board liked it. He turned towards Batista.

"Can you assure us that we are at the end of this whole sordid affair?"

"This business will be wrapped up in January."

"And can you assure us that nothing can be traced to Falcon Tech. The …hmm…blackmail…the bribery…the murders?" He waved his hands as he reluctantly spat out the barely audible words.

"Anything done by the Triads never leaves a smoking gun. It's the way they operate. One hundred times better than the Mafia."

The board squirmed at Batista's last comment. The thought of even using that word in these hallowed chambers revolted them. Sinclair turned his head and faced down the table.

"Gentlemen we must press ahead with the flotation. It's in the best interest of our Corporation. You can see that this sordid affair will be wrapped up in a few weeks. But to ensure that everything runs smoothly, I propose to the board that the Falcon Tech executives go to Brussels immediately to sort out this issue and get whatever assurance is necessary from those lawyers."

Discreet nods conveyed tacit approval. Sinclair was now back in command. He waved his right hand contemptuously towards the Falcon Tech people, a clear signal that they were no longer needed. They got up and walked to the door.

"The Falcon Tech executives have let us down. They should never have allowed themselves to get into such a situation. What's important is that we have unanimity on how to proceed from here. It seems to me that the board has two options facing it. Either come clean on the wrongdoing of our subsidiary and inform the Justice Department or proceed as normal towards the launch."

He paused and then added coldly. "The first will, of course, mean the collapse of the launch and over six-billion-plus profit disappearing down the drain." The board members sat frozen in their seats trying hard to absorb the shock. "And the second will, of course, allow us to enjoy the fruits of our endeavours."

Silence again filled the boardroom. "Gentlemen," he said pointedly, "I need your…well I need the board's endorsement to push ahead with the launch."

Twenty heads turned towards the top of the table and orally declared their agreement.

"Now let's have a show of hands to approve the SEC documents."

Again twenty members and the chairman stuck their right hands in the air. A unanimous result. Sinclair leaned back in his chair, relieved. After a few moments he raised an admonishing finger in the air.

"And, finally, gentlemen I don't have to remind you, not one word of what transpired here today leaves this boardroom. Not one word."

Chapter Twenty Two

LAURA SHUT OFF her computer and took the lift to the ground floor. She made her way through the lunchtime crowd, occasionally glancing over her shoulder as if she had expected somebody to be following her. Crossing at the Louise junction, she headed towards the Hilton Hotel on Boulevard de Waterloo. She stopped outside the hotel for a few moments to regain her composure and then entered, making straight for the reception counter. The wallet was opened and her identity card displayed.

"We've booked three rooms for our clients from the Far East."

"One moment please," the receptionist responded as she clicked buttons on the computer. "Yes, for three gentlemen: Lindell, Newman and Batista. Is that correct?"

"Yes. We're celebrating twenty-five years in practice this week so we wanted to surprise them with an invite to a party tonight and also to give them documentation to review for tomorrow's meeting."

"I see. I'll take it and see that it's delivered."

"Well, the invite is rather special. I'd like to arrange it in a certain way. They are long-standing clients of the firm."

"Your firm is paying for the rooms so I suppose it's okay. Here you are: 402, 406 and 412."

"Thank you very much," she said, taking the key cards. As she walked towards the lift the receptionist called out, "Miss Harrison."

Laura's heart raced.

"Don't forget to drop the key cards back here on your way out. Saves me reissuing another set."

"Sure, no problem."

She hurried down the corridor and slipped the card into door 402. It was a spacious room with a double bed. The phone was examined and the mouthpiece unscrewed. A blob of glue was dabbed on the back of the device and it was eased into position. The task was completed and the number for Belgacom, the Belgian telephone company dialled. She spoke briefly and moments later her Nokia GSM rang.

"Chutzpah loud and clear," Sarah said. Laura smiled and switched off the call. She got to work on the other rooms. The phone calls from Sarah confirmed that all lights were green. In fifteen minutes Laura was back at reception and handed over the key cards.

She exited the hotel, returned to Avenue Louise where the same operation was repeated at the Conrad Hotel. Wong would also be wired up for sound. Mission accomplished, Laura was now back on the street heading straight for a cafe. The waitress approached.

"Un café, s'il vous plait."

Drained of energy, she sat back and waited for the coffee to arrive.

LATER THAT AFTERNOON WONG descended the stairs and headed for a sofa in the foyer of the Conrad Hotel. He ordered a pot of tea and relaxed into the luxury of his surroundings. Ten minutes later Verbiest entered the foyer and eased into the seat opposite Wong. There was no time for formalities - no place for small talk. He cut straight to the kernel.

"One thing's got to be clear from the start. Our managing partner wouldn't approve of this. I've told him that we're fighting the Trade Bureau hard all the way. He just would not accept anything shady. Anyway, I'm the partner holding the baby on this one. As far as he's concerned you're here to see how we can shave a few more percentage points off the duty. Clear?"

"It's discretion all the way with me, Mr. Verbiest...*All the way*. As you say, *you're holding the baby.*"

Verbiest rose from the sofa. Wong pointed at the teapot. "There's still some in that pot. Good Chinese tea."

"No thank you," Verbiest replied. They made their way across the Avenue. Verbiest ushered Wong into Knightley's office.

"Let me introduce Roger Knightley...and this is Zu Wong, the Hong Kong-based lawyer for Falcon Tech."

They shook hands. Wong bowed reverentially and then scanned the office. "I'm in the same business but obviously not in the same league."

"Well, one thing we don't have here is *pro bono* and thank heavens for that. It's all European Union work. High-roller clients with deep pockets," Knightley exclaimed.

Wong smiled back, Chinese-style, but remained silent.

"Please," Verbiest said beckoning to the antique chairs. Wong now had a full view of the office. The oriental retreat, the associates called it. *Very hushed opulence,* he thought. As he slid into the chair his eyes settled on the display cabinet against the back wall containing vases. His countenance suddenly became cold and detached. "You're a collector of Chinese *objets d'art* I see?"

Knightley leaned back in the chair.

"In a fashion," he answered and then deliberately paused to allow Wong to absorb the full majesty before his eyes. "My great-great-grandfather was Viceroy of Burma back in the eighteen forties. One of the great standard bearers of the British Empire. The jolly old chap was a connoisseur of oriental artefacts." He nodded towards the cabinet. "Particularly those vases." He now tapped his desk with both hands. "And, of course, furniture. Burmese teak, naturally."

"Naturally," Wong rejoined.

Knightley swirled his right hand around encompassing everything in the office. "Picked up all of this. All antique now."

"Very impressive," the Oriental said. "And your bookcase here looks like it's a law library in itself," Wong said in affected appreciation.

"Oh come, come Mr. Wong. Just the complete set of Halsbury's Laws of England - leather bound - and a few other old tomes. Hardly that impressive."

Wong let it pass and instead nodded towards the glass display cabinet. "The vases? All genuine Ming I take it?"

Knightley beamed. "Yes, splendid. The best in Europe. The museums won't get their hands on this priceless collection. No way."

"Mr. Knightley, you're so cultured. If I may be permitted to say, so refined in your taste. Surrounded by the best in oriental civilisation."

"Thank you. I can see you too have an eye for the best in life."

"You could say that indeed Mr. Knightley but unlike you I have nothing to match this. Not right now at any rate."

Wong threw one final look at the glass cabinet. Then he fixed his eyes on Knightley and thought: *What a pirate! A true pirate indeed of Chinese heirlooms ensconced in his opulent sanctuary.*

Verbiest broke Wong's wistfulness. "Mr. Wong is here to work out our final negotiation with the Bureau on the Falcon Tech case. Now that you've met, I propose that we start the hard grind downstairs."

Knightley nodded agreement and stood up.

"Nice to have met you, Mr. Wong."

"And you too, Mr. Knightley."

They took the stairs to Verbiest's office. As Wong entered, his eyes focused on the marble fireplace dominating the office. It was not as luxuriously furnished but it, too, had all the trappings of wealth.

"I see you also have an eye for artefacts," Wong observed as he dropped his briefcase on the visitor's chair.

"Family treasures you could say. Ivory from the Congo. My grandfather was stationed there before Belgium pulled out of Africa. A colonel in the Army. He amassed quite a few treasures before he left."

"I can see that Mr. Verbiest."

"Unlike Roger, I keep the precious pieces at home."

"Really," he replied as he scanned the office. "Like Mr. Knightley I can see that you're also a man of taste. Impeccable taste."

"Thank you but it's really our forebears we have to thank. They risked everything in the colonial era so that we can enjoy all of this today."

"Yes, wonderful people indeed." Wong answered, his voice tinged with sarcasm. He glanced up at the ornate mantelpiece decorated with ivory carvings and then focused on Verbiest for a few seconds.

Another pirate of culture, he thought. *This time African culture. The gweilos know how to help themselves to the good things in the world.*

Verbiest settled into his chair. "Now that Batista's insisted that you come to Europe I suppose we had better do some planning."

"Indeed. Maybe you can brief me on the ways of the *gweilos* in the Bureau so that I can fill in Mr. Cheng. He will need to have a final meeting with the two American helpers to put them in the picture."

Verbiest smiled at Wong's use of *gweilos*, the term Hong Kong Chinese call Europeans. "Excellent idea. This thing will only work if everybody sings from the same hymn sheet."

THAT EVENING SARAH sat in the foyer of the Hilton hotel, sipping a sparkling water as she flicked the pages of the Bulletin, Brussels' English language newsweekly for expatriates. She lifted her head at intervals to survey the reception area. The mobile phone in her handbag let out a faint ring.

"Expect guests in five minutes."

She switched off the phone and continued to read. Minutes later Lindell, Newman and Batista walked through the revolving door. The checking-in routine was observed from her vantage point. Once again she settled back into the magazine observing everything in her peripheral vision. They walked towards the lift. It was now 9:30 and it seemed that they had turned in for an early night. She would give it half an hour more and then quit for the night. She went to the bar and stood at the counter. It was a cosy lounge with subdued lighting, a pleasant place to unwind. The bartender walked the length of the bar towards her.

"A brandy please, with a dash of ginger ale."

A moment later she caught a glimpse of her prey in the mirror. Lindell and Newman hesitated at the entrance as if deciding whether to stay out in the foyer or enter the bar. They came in and stopped half way down the counter, just out of earshot from where she stood. She continued reading while at the same time, monitoring their every movement. Lindell held a briefcase in his left hand. They were speaking in hushed tones that were, in any event, more or less drowned out by the background music.

She took a sip and felt the burning effect on the back of her throat. And a few moments later a warm glow percolated from the pit of her stomach. She felt relaxed and for a moment thought about the life of a real spy. Tonight the hunter had the victims within her sights and wasn't going to let go easily. She drained her first glass and called for another brandy. This was courage to do the impossible. Well…almost the impossible. Her hand was now in her jacket pocket fidgeting with something. She picked up the glass and walked towards them.

"Excuse me, but I wonder would you mind if I asked where you bought that briefcase?"

The conversation stopped as their attention switched. Lindell smiled. "Excuse me?"

Sarah repeated the question. "You see I'm trying to think of a Christmas present for my father. Well he's kinda got everything, if you know what I mean. Except his briefcase is looking a bit shabby."

Lindell picked up the case and tapped the sides with his fingers. "Picked it up in Hong Kong actually. Probably make a good present all right. Can take plenty of hacking especially if you travel a lot."

Sarah furtively slipped her right hand into her pocket and withdrew it just in time to take the case. She leaned forward, her low cut blouse giving way to reveal an ample cleavage. It had the desired effect; the distraction allowing her to run her hands over the leather, the accordion side panels getting her particular attention. Her fingers sought out a suitable host site while keeping the conversation going. As she pressed firmly on a panel a blob of epoxy resin bonded to the leather firmly fixing the device in place. It was virtually impossible to see with the naked eye.

"It's really nice. Must have been expensive."

"Probably." Lindell said, his attention now back at eye level.

Newman shrugged. "I don't know much about these things. Just use them to hold papers."

"I think he'd really like something like that for Christmas. Sorry for intruding on you but that was very helpful."

"It was our pleasure," Lindell replied. "Say would you

like...." He was about to ask her if she'd like a drink but she was gone too far down the bar before he could finish his invitation. Sarah walked through the foyer and out into the street. As she headed for the metro station she pressed the redial button and put the mobile phone to her cheek.

"Are you picking up anything."

"Sure am. A little garbled but okay."

"Great. I'll be home in twenty minutes."

She slipped the phone back into her bag and quickened her pace towards the metro station.

AT 7 THE FOLLOWING MORNING Marc's mobile phone rang. He stretched out and picked it up from the bedside locker.

"Good morning. Operation chutzpah accomplished." The tone in Sarah's voice said it all.

"Great. So it worked?"

"Loud and clear. All the right places are wired and ready to go."

"Perfect."

"So what's next?"

Marc chuckled. "Await instructions from Laura. Today is D-day. Kevin will remain at his desk all day."

"Fine."

"You must phone him when Laura gives you the details...by six at the latest."

BY MIDDAY THE TAPES had been verified, and Marc had been put in the picture. Sarah confirmed that Lindell had put a call through to Verbiest at home. There was no mistaking the subject matter, she assured him. And Wong talked to some Chinese person. Amsterdam seemed to be mentioned. His friend at the university would instantly decipher it, he said. Plans for the next stage were hardened up.

"Are you still available if Laura needs you?"

"Yeah. That's if my nerves stick it."

They finished the conversation and he slipped the phone

into his pocket. He re-entered the Trade Bureau building and took the lift to the fourth floor.

ACROSS ON AVENUE LOUISE the high-powered meeting with the Falcon Tech executives had started. Laura picked up the phone and hit a few digits. Verbiest's secretary answered.

"Hi Ingrid, will you let me know when that Falcon Tech meeting breaks up. I need to clarify something with Erik."

"They plan to break for lunch at one thirty."

"Fine, I'll catch him then."

At one twenty Laura positioned herself at the photocopier facing the boardroom door. She pretended to read the copies she had just made, fiddling with the buttons on the machine at the same time. The meeting broke up as anticipated. Lindell was first through the door.

"Oh Laura. Haven't seen you in ages. Where have you been hiding yourself?"

"Busy helping Europe prepare for the Euro."

"Hey that's goin' to help us big time...no more netting off of currencies. We can cut our treasury function by three quarters."

"That's the idea."

Lindell moved closer. "So when are you going to come back to deal with us? The biggest and the best computer company in the world."

"Not likely at the moment. It's intellectual property rights for the next few months."

He glanced over his shoulder at his colleagues leaving the boardroom. And then he turned and winked at her.

"Laura, we badly need an in-house lawyer. Why not come join us? You're the best."

"Californian charm won't win me over...not at the moment at any rate. I'm happy here."

A roguish smile lit his face. "We could make you a sweet offer – stock options, the lot."

"Thanks anyway but I'm happy here."

"Please think about it."

"I hear you Dylan."

"C'mon join us for lunch? We won't talk computers."

"Can't. I have a report to get out by this evening."

"Well, how about dinner later?"

"Where?"

"Oh I think it's some fancy place in the Sablon. Erik, what's the name of that restaurant we're going to this evening?"

"My favourite. L'Ecrivain."

Laura could have finished the sentence. Her heart beat fast.

"L'Ecrivain," Verbiest repeated. "Incroyable! You were there many times Laura. Don't you remember?"

"Of course," she replied nonchalantly.

Lindell continued the persuasion. "So why don't you join us."

Right now Laura preferred the office banter between them to be the limit of their exchange. "No, I'm too busy with this assignment but thanks anyway."

"Dylan our table's waiting." Verbiest called out from the lift.

Lindell rejoined Verbiest and they both headed towards the elevator. She picked up the copy on the platen, walked back to her office and pressed redial on the mobile. Sarah answered.

"It's the Ecrivain in the Sablon," Laura confirmed. "Don't know the precise time. Be there early. Make sure Kevin can make it. And, by the way, have a romantic evening..." Her voice trailed off.

"Over and out."

She took an envelope from her handbag and raced upstairs to the boardroom. Verbiest's leather folder was on the table beside a bundle of papers. The folder was opened, one of his business cards removed and replaced with a card from the envelope. She went back to her office and switched on the recording device. Back in the boardroom she spoke softly two metres away from the folder. "Do you read me?"

Dashing back to her own office, she replayed the tape. The words she wanted to hear came over loud and clear. Five minutes later she was on the Avenue where she picked up a salad baguette and a can of coke at the corner cafe and made her way back to the office. Flopping back into the leather chair, she kicked off her shoes and began eating.

KEVIN O' SHEA ARRIVED first at the agreed meeting point. When Sarah arrived they exchanged greetings and promptly left for the Sablon, the fashionable restaurant area close to the Grand' Place in the city centre.

"Table for two," Kevin said in French.

"Have you got a reservation?"

"No."

They were crestfallen. Kevin tried a different form of gentle persuasion. Using his best French, he explained that they had just become engaged and it was a very special evening. Sarah's brown eyes became sad, a well-timed sigh accentuating the disappointment. It worked. The waiter shrugged and waved the menu in the air.

"Follow me."

He led them along a corridor past a gallery on the left side and rearranged some tables.

"That's going to mean a big tip."

She smiled. "Do you always bluff like that?"

"Only when I have to. Now listen we have to play the part...."

"So this is your excuse to use celtic charm eh?"

Kevin laughed. "Right on. And there's more where that came from."

"Really."

The maitre d' returned with the menus. They studied them, ordered a bottle of Sauvignon white and told the waiter that they would decide on the food later. The restaurant filled up and the chatter became louder. The patron edged his way past the diners and placed a *réservé* sign on the table in the alcove. Sarah sat in silence. He joked her that she should make conversation or they would look like a married couple. She feigned a dry smile. The restaurant was now full apart from the alcove table.

They sipped the wine and waited. And then came the agreed signal, a tap on his foot under the table. The guests had arrived. Sarah recognised Lindell and Newman. The other Caucasian carried a folder and fitted the description of Verbiest. The Oriental had to be Wong. They settled into the alcove and ordered drinks. Kevin placed his elbow on the table

276

cradling his left ear. That helped to block out the din from the restaurant and make the tiny speaker in the ear piece audible.

"I just hope those guys don't recognise me," Sarah said.

"Hardly. The encounter in the Hilton was very brief and with your hair up you look totally different."

"I'm well…nervous."

"Even if they do it doesn't change anything," he whispered. "You're just here for a meal. Nothing unusual about that."

"I suppose," she agreed.

They called the waiter and ordered. Peeping into her handbag a facial gesture signalled that the recording device had kicked in. And now voices were becoming distinct in his ear piece.

Kevin listened attentively. He heard each one ordering from the menu. After the first bottle of wine was consumed tongues loosened. Kevin's concentration intensified on the earpiece. And then he detected someone saying something that sounded like being near the winning post.

The meals arrived.

"Now we concentrate on the launch. Sinclair will be off our backs and happy," came an American accent.

"All that's left…" The voice petered out.

And then another string of words building to a cacophony of voices. Moments later clear words came through, words that thrilled him…sentences that suggested complicity. "…It was the only way. Schuman might not have agreed. The most effective of all…concentrated his mind…who did it…frighten anyone. Schuman… guy real strong character. But we…bend in the end."

Kevin was picking up bits and pieces of sentences. There was no doubt about the subject matter. It was looking good. He smiled, a clear indication that he liked what he was hearing. The meals arrived and they ate in silence. After about ten minutes his eyebrows arched. The really incriminating stuff was starting to flow. A voice mentioned something about eliminating a person. And another voice talked about Montorro the investigator.

"…about to spill his guts…don't take chances when the stakes…high."

"Bulgarian umbrella very effective. The ricin acted in

277

seconds…one quick push…he wouldn't have felt a thing. He was dead before he hit the tracks."

The American voices were not happy. They seemed to criticise the Asian. " You didn't have to…could have paid him off…not dangerous."

And now another string of words. "…gave Schuman a free hand with Schmidt out of the way. That law is the prize, gentlemen."

It could not have been better. When the tape would be rerun Laura and Marc would recognise all the voices, he was certain. He shot another signal across the table. This time Sarah acknowledged with a wink. He leaned closer and, feigning an American accent, said, "Houston we've not got a problem. It's all there." And then he chuckled. "If the recorder has picked up what came through this ear piece then that adds up to a lot of incriminating evidence."

The alcove table was still in full swing as they finished their meals. Kevin threw two thousand francs on the table and stood up.

"Now it's playback time," he whispered.

"And payback time later," Sarah replied, her softly accented Scottish voice unmistakable among the gathering of, for the most part, French-speaking diners.

THE PHONE RANG shortly before midnight and the rendezvous point was agreed. Fifteen minutes later Marc was standing in the darkness on Rue Archimede. As Sarah approached he emerged from a doorway, his right hand dangling loosely at his side. As she passed he snatched the bag containing the tape and disappeared back into the darkness. Twenty minutes later he was in his apartment carefully listening to the recordings. By three a.m. a complete hand-written transcript of the tapes was on his bedside locker.

THE FOLLOWING MORNING Marc went straight to the sixth floor, knocked on the Director's door and entered. Kaufmann was sitting behind his desk, a copy of the *Frankfurter Allgemeine* laid out in front of him.

"Mr. Kaufmann I would like to brief you on the computer case. Something urgent has come up."

The Director lifted his head from the paper, pulled off his glasses, rose to his feet and walked to the low table.

"Come in. Come in…please take a seat."

"There was a reason…a very valid reason why I could not move faster to close the case."

Kaufmann's forehead creased, his eyes now quizzical. "What did you say?"

Marc began his unbelievable story. A barrage of comments followed and a litany of questions were asked in between the table thumping and sighs of disbelief. Kaufmann called in Windsor and Champenois and the lecture started in earnest.

"You were warned about the risks last March," Kaufmann thundered. "You've disgraced the Bureau. It's simply indefensible."

By ten o' clock tempers had cooled and rational decisions were being made and, by eleven, a covert operation had swung into action.

"You're absolutely sure about that evidence?" Kaufmann asked several times as they stood in Commissioner Calavera's office on the fifth floor of the Breydel building. "I mean can you stand over it one hundred per cent?"

"I'm positive."

"We must be very careful. From what you told us they're ruthless. They may even have a mole in the Bureau."

Marc took in the surroundings while they waited for the Commissioner to break away from a meeting with the Italian Prime Minister. Her office was large and bright. A Picasso hung behind her teak desk. A montage of photographs decorated the wall facing the large windows. She was younger then, starting out on an ambitious political career in Madrid.

Kaufmann paced the floor and then released a loud sigh.

"The only time Champenois is punctual is when he's reporting back to Quai D'Orsay."

"Pardon?"

"Ah, it's about Champenois…the French connection. Forget it."

"Huh."

Moments later Champenois appeared in the doorway.

"We've got to make her feel that she's making the decision. We'll have to play a little with her ego," Champenois said to Kaufmann.

"Yes. By the way, I'll do the talking. Don't open your mouth unless she asks you a question. Understand?" Kaufmann said.

"Yes."

Juan Gonzales, the Commissioner's *chef de cabinet(chief of staff)* came into the office. His job was to advise the Commissioner and run the day-to-day business of the office. Every Commissioner had one. He made things happen. Gonzales was late forties with a thin frame and a bald head. He stuck out a limp hand towards Kaufmann.

"Good morning. I don't think you two have met," Kaufmann said businesslike.

"Schuman…Gonzales."

"You've got a window of half an hour."

"Fine," Kaufmann replied.

Calavera came through the door. It was Marc's first time to meet her. She was heavy set, around fifty-four or five, her sallow skin and dark hair giving her classic Mediterranean looks. Her smile was momentary but friendly.

"So, gentlemen, you said urgent." She looked around her desk. "Where's the briefing material, Juan?

Kaufmann cut in. "Commissioner, we didn't have time to prepare. Anyway, what we have to say is better kept off the record. It's …well it's very delicate."

"The Japanese up to their tricks again I take it?"

The Director cleared his throat. "No Commissioner, not quite. A difficult problem with the computer case."

It took Kaufmann half an hour to detail the complete history of the case. At first Calavera frowned, then grimaced and eventually drew back in complete revulsion.

"But this should never have happened. Kaufmann, I am holding you responsible for this."

"Commissioner, these circumstances are highly unusual. I don't think we can hold the investigator totally responsible. After all, they drugged him."

"I didn't say the investigator. I said I'm holding you personally responsible as Director of the Trade Bureau."

"What happened was highly irregular, highly exceptional. Nobody could have-"

"This is not good for the image of the Commission," she snapped back. "You, Kaufmann, are being held responsible and Schuman has to get off that case immediately. Is that clear?"

Kaufmann straightened up in his chair. "Commissioner, I think we should try to find a solution and not dwell on apportioning blame. It happened. That's all we can say but first you should hear all the facts."

He nodded in Marc's direction.

"Commissioner when they tried to blackmail me I counter-attacked by taping conversations. And last Wednesday we got the Falcon Tech people and the lawyers discussing the murders."

"But this is all illegal and very damaging."

Champenois saw his opportunity to calm the waters.

"Commissioner we have a conspiracy on our hands here. I would respectfully suggest that while you may feel uncomfortable with what Schuman did, he did it with the best interests of the administration at heart. And now we can possibly crack a very serious case of attempted criminal corruption. All thanks to the ingenuity of our investigator."

She peered over her glasses and admonished. "It should not have happened in the first place."

"Yes, Commissioner," Kaufmann agreed. "But investigations in the Far East are never easy. There's always a risk that powerful companies might fight hard to hold market share. Admittedly, this case is probably the worst."

Gonzales raised a sceptical eyebrow. "Are you sure about everything you have just said? And that you have the evidence to back it up?"

"I'm certain," Marc replied.

"Commissioner I suggest that we listen to the tapes and if

the evidence is clear and watertight then we must act."

Kaufmann smiled. "If you sanction a set-up I suggest that we play along. Schuman can agree to accept the money and then we have the Belgian police waiting in the wings. Once we catch them red-handed they'll admit everything. But the only problem remaining is they will not move until they can confirm that the Regulation is on the Council of Ministers table. A Regulation that gives Falcon Tech ten per cent duty."

"And what kind of duty should they suffer?"

"Forty-two per cent."

"Why should we go down that road. Schuman just tells them that he won't accept bribery. Go ahead and publish the law with forty-two per cent for Falcon Tech."

Kaufmann raised his hands in objection. "But, Commissioner, I don't think it's that simple. It's not just the despicable video tape stuff. We have two cases of murder here…two investigators dead. They can't be allowed to get away with it."

And Champenois now rowed in behind Kaufmann. "There are several issues involved. Schuman is concerned about the tape. They have threatened that a consignment of those videotapes will be found by the Customs. If that happens an inquiry involving a senior investigator of the Bureau would have to be carried out by the police. Lifting diplomatic immunity…possibly court appearances. A lot of adverse publicity never mind-"

"Yes, that is serious," Gonzales interjected.

Champenois added in a sombre tone. "And we have a duty to stamp out attempted corruption. If companies were allowed to attempt bribery the system would collapse in no time. No, Commissioner, we have to act. And, more importantly, be seen to act."

"I hope, gentlemen, you appreciate that this is not a decision I can take on my own. It will have to be sanctioned at the highest level. I'll be obliged to bring it before the President of the Commission. And that means explaining everything. We will have to go to the Belgian Ministry of Justice to set up the surveillance. With the chaotic state of policing here, anything could go wrong."

"Commissioner," Champenois warned. "I know it's unpalatable and sordid but we must act to protect the European industry."

"While Pierre is right," Kaufmann immediately cut in, "I think we must concentrate on the immediate task. We need to catch these people red-handed, in the act."

"So, is there a deadline for this sordid affair?"

"Schuman has agreed a meeting early in the New Year. So we don't have the luxury to play around especially with the Christmas break coming up. Swift action is called for. If I may suggest I think you should get approval immediately from the President of the Commission and arrange for the police to be brought into the picture."

"Mr. Kaufmann has a point," Gonzales said. " We really can't prevaricate on this one. We must make a decision."

"I see…," the Commissioner agreed reluctantly, "I'll take up the issue with the President and get his clearance."

"I think you're making the right decision Madame Commissioner," Kaufmann said, relieved.

"Gonzales, I want you and Kaufmann to liaise on this once I've got appropriate clearance. We'll need to make sure the police know what they're doing."

She turned to face Marc, wagging a finger. "And when all of this is over you're suspended from duty."

Marc nodded. "Yes Commissioner," Kaufmann said as he walked to the door.

Chapter Twenty Three

THE ANXIETY OF the past weeks rendered Verbiest incapable of concentrating on anything and the break from the routine over Christmas simply made things worse. A round of golf at his La Tournette Club with Saatchi seemed to be the only antidote, the kind of therapy that he needed right now.

The first hole was a Par 4 and he had pulled a putter from the bag. He looked down at the ball on the tee, then tried to focus on the green in the distance. When he realised what he was holding he slammed it down hard on the grass. The beginnings of a headache throbbed across his forehead making him wonder whether it was all really worthwhile. And he swore to himself that when this sordid affair was wrapped up he would take his foot off the pedal. Lazy days in the Caribbean beckoned and a little more attention to his wife had, of late, become more appealing. Once more he began fidgeting with the clubs, eager to get advice on how to play the final stage.

Saatchi, the reprobate, is damn well never on time, he thought. The Falcon Tech affair had its price, he now knew. A rainmaker can bring more than rain. Sure the firm had been rewarded handsomely with several American blue chips following on the coat tails of the computer giant. Securing the biggie was a licence to print money. And it did just that but now his own ass was being put on the line. There was little room for manoeuvre at this stage but he was sure that Saatchi would come up with a failsafe scheme.

He could not afford his reputation besmirched, that much he was certain of. But he had an ultimatum. Verbiest was selling his soul for money, and he knew it. A Faustian pact! That thought had played havoc with his sleep for the past month and haunted his every waking moment. He watched as a 4-ball prepared to play onto the eighteenth green but the momentary distraction didn't help to take his mind off the problem.

Moments later Saatchi breezed out of the clubhouse, debonair and stylish with his brushed-back, heavily greased hair, like a twenty-year old hot rod. He wiggled his eyebrows as he drew closer and chirped, "Hey, Erik, you sounded like you were going to die if you didn't get a round of golf. I reckon I haven't been in your club since our days as rookie lawyers trying to earn a dishonest crust."

Verbiest grunted. "What a choice of words, Lorenzo. What a choice."

"C'mon Erik, what's on your mind?" Saatchi said as he pulled a driver from the bag. "I've to plan the final details of my sailing trip in the Med next month. And the Millennium celebrations tomorrow night have to be organised too."

The Belgian placed the palm of his hand on the top of the club using it as a prop. "Look, right now there are more important things than the Millennium. The Falcon Tech thing is getting to be an even bigger crock of shit."

"What's happening?" Saatchi asked stooping to place his ball.

"Schuman will do the deal okay. I've checked out my sources in the Bureau. The law is ready for publication and he's going to accept the money."

"Great. So the deal's done."

"Not quite. He wants an insurance policy so to speak. He won't go ahead unless all the Falcon Tech executives and Wong and I turn up for the hand over ceremony."

Saatchi straightened up, grinning. "So what's the problem?"

Verbiest looked around. "Well, Falcon Tech has issued an ultimatum that we turn up but what if something goes wrong, Lorenzo? We're talking …" He grimaced, his voice dropping to a whisper, "…well we're talking nasty stuff as you well know. It's all criminal…you know that…it's criminal conspiracy that we're at. Perverting the outcome of an international investigation. You know what the law's like on that."

"Yes, but you…I mean Falcon Tech has Schuman by the balls. Isn't that right?"

"Yes, I suppose, in a manner of speaking."

"So, what can go wrong. He's nervous. Wouldn't you be if you were in his shoes?"

"Hmm yeah."

"Listen Erik, all Schuman wants is to be sure he's not going to be fucked around by Falcon Tech or indeed your friends the Triads."

"Watch it there Lorenzo," Verbiest snapped. "Those guys are nothing to me. That side is Wong's problem."

Saatchi's shoulders moved fractionally. "Okay, okay. Look, Schuman is just looking for a bit of credibility from the Falcon Tech people. So you turn up. It makes him feel comfortable. That's all."

"I hope you're right."

"I know I'm right. Think about it. Just say Schuman has squealed. Imagine for a moment that he's peed in his pants with nerves…took fright and gone to the Commissioner. And they set up a sting with the Belgian police. Immediately your friends release the tapes. And one Marc Schuman's ass is hauled off to prison. No, that's not the way he's thinking. He's out to protect his own back…his own reputation. All he wants is a win-win situation. He gets his name cleared…and the money, of course. And Falcon Tech gets a duty they can live with."

"And everybody rides off into the sunset. It never really works out that way in real life, Lorenzo. Does it?"

"The smart boys always play for the right outcome. Schuman's got himself into big trouble in Bangkok. And he knows it only too well. All he wants is to walk away unhurt…assurance, that kind of thing. I'll bet on it. Anyway, when is the hand over?"

"Sunday the ninth at the Atomium."

Saatchi gestured to Verbiest to tee off first. "Think of those juicy fees, Erik. That's your motivation. How much have we milked Falcon Tech for so far?"

Verbiest took up position, his shoulders hunched as he practised a sweeping swing and then shot the ball over the water hazard, directly towards the green. He relaxed and smiled. "Over five million dollars." The lure of the money began to dominate his thoughts once more.

"And there's more to come?"

"Damn right there's more to come. That's why I'm sticking my neck out so far." In his eyes it would compensate for the restless nights. And pay for the Valium.

Saatchi's teeing-off ritual was executed like an old pro. He crouched down to inspect the tee up close. "Remember if you lose Falcon Tech, then the others would go scurrying down the Avenue to those white shoe firms. Go for it Erik. It's not as if you have to hold the bag of money."

He straightened up, then shot a final glance at the green and sent the ball shooting into the distance. It veered slightly to the left. They grabbed their trolleys and moved onto the fairway. "Yes, indeed Lorenzo. I'm no bagman for those guys. I'm a senior partner in the most prestigious law firm in Europe." He paused and then added haughtily, "for that matter in the whole world."

"You are indeed, Erik. You are indeed."

The two senior lawyers strolled into the distance, chatting animatedly, like a pair of lovebirds.

January 2000

IT WAS METICULOUSLY PLANNED. Every little detail. Verbiest was at the office by seven thirty. Lindell, Batista and Newman took a taxi from the Hilton to Avenue Louise reaching the PKV&S offices shortly before eight. Moments later Taylor and Johnson arrived and introduced themselves. Verbiest began pouring black coffee into china cups. They sat around making final plans.

"The Triad mastermind arrived last week to check out the place. He turned up nothing unusual. He's monitoring everything with the Amsterdam cell, just in case though," Johnson confirmed.

Batista creased his forehead. "Is this not going over the top?"

"Just a precaution…the Triads take no chances."

"So who's going to hand over the money?" Batista asked.

"Well, Wong suggested that we should play safe. Meet Schuman in the Atomium as agreed but then bring him out to the car park for the hand over. He says it's easier to monitor any strange activity," Verbiest answered.

"He's probably right," Newman agreed. "We should call the shots…get Schuman out and do the deal where we can see what's happening?"

287

Verbiest nodded. "It's safer that way,"

Lindell looked at his watch. "Speaking of Wong, where the hell is he?"

"Give him time. He'll be here," Verbiest reassured the group.

Ten minutes later the doorbell buzzed. Verbiest went downstairs to answer it. He returned with Wong who staggered through the doorway, a bandage around his head and dried blood stains on his clothes.

Batista jumped to his feet. "Oh my God, Wong, what's happened to you?"

Verbiest shook his head and groaned. Wong stood three paces from the doorway trying to catch his breath. "I was involved…in an accident…crossing the road last evening." He gasped for breath.

"Should have warned you. The law's only recently changed to give pedestrians priority." Verbiest said. "Belgian drivers haven't got used to the idea of stopping yet."

Wong hobbled towards a chair as four pairs of eyes stared in bewilderment. His forehead was bandaged and his chin was badly lacerated. His left arm was in plaster. Spots of congealed blood peppered his face. He gingerly lowered himself onto the chair, in obvious pain.

"I'm sorry. This is most unfortunate. I sneaked out of Saint Luc hospital just a few minutes ago to get here. They're probably searching for me right now."

Verbiest threw his arms up in the air in despair and asked, "Are you sure you're up to it?"

Wong put his hand to his head. He seemed distracted and in pain. "I'll be fine. Have you gone over the plans?"

"More or less," Lindell said indifferently.

Wong winced. "Do you have anything for a pain in the head?"

"Mr. Wong, it's a law firm, not a pharmacy," Verbiest growled.

The Oriental mustered a grin.

"So, what are we waiting for? Let's get moving." Wong stood up from the chair but immediately wavered, unsteady on his feet. And then collapsed onto the floor, his eyes rolling back in his head. "Get him some help!" Taylor shouted. "Get some goddamn help."

Batista walked to the window. "That's all we damn well need right now. A full blown comedy show."

Verbiest picked up the phone and dialled 100. "An ambulance please? ...Avenue Louise..."

He dropped the phone and came across to the body now lying on the rug in the middle of his office. The Falcon Tech executives were leaning over trying to revive him. Wong opened his eyes and attempted to rise but immediately slumped back. Verbiest grabbed a glass and darted to the corridor. He rushed back and splashed Wong's face with cold water.

"That won't work Erik," Lindell said, shaking him vigorously.

"We've got to get him conscious. Turn him on his side...otherwise it could be dangerous."

Wong lifted an eyelid and sighed. "Where am I?" he called out. "Where am I?"

"Relax. It's okay. Everything's just fine," Newman reassured him. They made a cushion with Verbiest's jacket and propped up his head.

Wong now seemed lucid again. "Ah, yes, we have a job to do." He rose to his feet.

Verbiest asked if he was okay...if he was up to the task. Wong again brought his hand to his head, steadying himself by grabbing Verbiest's arm.

"Yes I'm fine, really. Let's get the job done."

He tentatively moved towards the door and into the corridor. As he reached the top of the stairs he stumbled again.

"Watch him," Verbiest screeched. It was too late. The Oriental tumbled down the wooden stairs landing with a thud, fifteen steps below. This time he did not move, his limbs twisted like a rag doll.

"He's definitely a hospital case. The ambulance should be here in a moment," Verbiest said, taking control. They carried him to the ground floor and laid him on the chaise longue in the reception area.

"We'll just have to carry on without him. Let's get him off to hospital and concentrate on the work of the day," Batista said, searching for agreement.

Ten minutes later the paramedics put Wong on the stretcher and wheeled him towards the door. He regained consciousness once more and gestured furiously that he wanted to get off.

"We've got a day's work to do," he protested. "Let me off this thing."

"Mr. Wong, you're in no fit condition to do anything," Batista snarled.

He twisted and turned under the straps. "Let me off. We must finish our business," he pleaded.

Moments later the siren roared as the ambulance sped off down Avenue Louise.

"It's almost nine. Let's get moving. Wong wasn't absolutely necessary for the game plan anyway," Verbiest said reassuringly.

"You're right," Lindell replied. Batista turned towards Taylor and Johnson, exasperated. "I don't really know what the fuck's going on. We still have no control. And now we're going over there blind. Have you guys any idea how the Triad people operate?"

"The plan was worked out by Mr. Cheng," Johnson replied. "We just carry out his instructions."

Batista then turned towards Verbiest. "Well?"

"I'm as wise as you are. Anyway, it's all covert stuff…secret stuff."

"Well, I don't like this whole thing one bit."

"Me neither," Verbiest said. "I'm just as uptight but let's get it over with and concentrate on the launch."

Lindell walked to the window.

"Dylan have you got the 'goods'?" Verbiest asked.

He pointed to the bag. "Right here."

"So let's get moving." Verbiest urged. "Once we've made the delivery we get out of there as quickly as possible. Is everything clear?"

"Clear as muddy water at this stage," Batista growled.

Johnson and Taylor moved towards the door. "When we get to the Atomium we'll stay at a safe distance and give you a signal if we see anything suspicious," Taylor confirmed. They left for a final briefing with the Amsterdam cell.

290

The fifteen-minute drive across to the rendezvous point was made in silence. Verbiest's Saab pulled into the car park beside the Kinepolis cinema complex in the shadow of the Atomium. It was a dry and sunny morning but the air was chilly from a slight frost. The one-hundred-and-two-metre high cluster of silver-grey aluminium-and-steel spheres representing the nine atoms of iron glistened in the sunshine, dominating the Brussels skyline. The forty-year old edifice had been constructed for the EXPO World Trade Exhibition in 1958 and, even though it had lost some of its sheen, still looked impressive up close. Batista made a visor with his hand. "It's enormous."

"Yeah. Sure is," Verbiest replied indifferently.

"It's time to put our plan into operation," Newman said. "Dylan stays here with the money."

"Sure," Lindell replied.

"Everybody's agreed that Schuman must come out here to the car park for his money?" Batista asked.

"Absolutely," Verbiest confirmed.

"I'll scan the area," Lindell said. "If I see anything suspicious I'll signal immediately."

Batista, Newman and Verbiest walked down the car park and out onto the main thoroughfare encircling the Atomium. They each bought a ticket at the entrance and then went their separate ways. In the viewing tower, two Asians with cameras strung around their necks were already in position monitoring the situation.

It was now ten thirty. They rode the elevator to the viewing tower in the highest atom and waited. Verbiest slipped another Valium into his mouth and took a drink from the bottle of water stashed in his coat pocket. He stared through the viewing glass at the wide panorama of city buildings. All his contacts in the Bureau had delivered well on this one. Every little movement on the piece of legislation was reported back to him. When this mess was over favours would be repaid. Friends would not be forgotten. For a moment the tension eased. It seemed that the tablet had kicked in at last.

He turned and scanned the circular viewing tower. Batista

was now to his right looking out over the Mini Europe tourist attraction. Newman was out of sight, probably looking through the viewing glass on the opposite side. Verbiest glanced at his watch. A quarter of an hour to go. Some of the anxiety came back. Would Schuman come alone as arranged? What if...?

He tried to banish these terrible questions from his mind and recalled what Saatchi had said after Christmas.

'Schuman's got a lot to lose...a lot to lose.'

At five minutes to eleven the elevator opened and disgorged its load. Tourists walked around indiscriminately. And there, among them, was Marc Schuman, chief investigator of the computer case. He was dressed in jeans and sneakers with Ray Bans covering his eyes. He emerged from the throng beside the elevator and walked to the viewing window overlooking the European quarter of Brussels. Verbiest turned and nodded towards Batista. Batista sidled closer almost touching Schuman. Both men turned towards each other. Schuman removed his sunglasses, revealing an icy revulsion in his eyes.

"The exchange will take place down there," Batista said bluntly, nodding downwards towards the car park.

"The deal was that it takes place here. Right here."

"Well, that's all changed. It'll take place in the car park. The money's down there waiting. If you want it come and collect it."

"You're playing games," Schuman said.

"We're not playing games. You just don't expect us to come into these spherical balls and hand over money. No, you've got to come out in the open where we feel safe too."

"You'd better not be reneging."

"All you have to do is walk down and collect it."

Marc looked down, discerning a figure standing beside a car.

"Follow me," Batista said.

They headed towards the elevator. Newman and Verbiest followed. They emerged from the steel structure into the sunshine and made their way towards the car park. Batista glanced over his shoulder. Two women were walking determinedly directly behind them.

"Tom, what's happening here?"

"I'm not sure."

"Schuman, what's going on?"

"I don't know. You're supposed to be leading me."

"Okay cut through that break in the bushes." Verbiest ordered. "The car park's in there to the left."

Verbiest and Batista led Schuman through the gap directly into the car park.

They could now see Lindell waiting by the car in the otherwise empty car park. Marc, with Batista and Verbiest by his shoulders, strode onwards toward the car. Newman now emerged through the opening and glanced back over his shoulder. Startled, he bounded for the car. A police van had emerged from behind the cinema complex and was now accelerating rapidly towards them. He flailed his hands in the air to attract Batista's attention and shouted something towards him. Taylor sprang from behind an evergreen shrub and raced into the car park, a gun held out in front of him. Johnson had already crouched down on the paving, a Colt held at eye level. Lindell looked up and saw three helmets moving carefully behind the bushes, their eyes fixed on him. And then suddenly a siren was blaring and blue lights were flashing. Several policemen jumped from the van as it came to an abrupt halt.

Lindell pulled open the door and slid into the driver's seat. He glanced at Newman, then turned over the engine. The Saab lurched forward, the tyres screeching on the paved surface. Gunfire straffed the metal of the car. Lindell, now high on pure adrenaline, responded to the situation. The car shot towards the exit barrier, a single horizontal hollow steel pole. A glancing blow shot it skywards. The Saab screeched out onto the public road weaving under the pillars supporting the Atomium. Police cars emerged from all directions but he managed to elude them by swinging onto a minor road. He heard the hollow clanking ring of more gunfire hitting the metal, determinedly put the pedal to the floor and headed towards the Ring.

Back in the car park Johnson opened fire and a policeman who had been partially sheltered by the van teetered and stumbled and then collapsed, face downwards, on the paving bricks. He released a sharp wail and then his body went limp, a pool of blood forming around his head. The other policemen ran for cover behind the van. Johnson raked the vehicle with more gunfire, the glass shattering in a million pieces until every window was taken out. Batista and Verbiest stood rigidly on the spot, staring in horror, terrified to move. Newman also stopped moving, his hands now in the air in a submissive gesture. Marc threw himself to the ground praying that the police would not mistake him in the confusion. More sirens wailed some distance along the road and a voice called out through a loudhailer to drop all guns. Suddenly Taylor lunged forward about ten metres, pounced on Marc and kicked his legs, ordering him to his feet. As Marc rose Taylor dug the butt of the gun into his side immediately below his ribs. Marc involuntarily groaned.

"Keep quiet and do exactly as I tell you," Taylor snarled. He then swung the barrel of the gun up until it was deep against Marc's neck and started to drag him backwards with his left arm held in a firm lock around his throat. Marc's eyes registered terror as he stumbled backwards awkwardly. Taylor dragged him further until they were sheltering behind a steel refuse bin. Johnson now darted behind the bin and lay flat out on the ground, the gun pointing at the police van in a two-handed grip. The police had regrouped and huddled behind the van, planning their next move. Batista, Newman and Verbiest still stood in open view paralysed by the turn of events. The gunfire started again. This time it was more intense, more sustained. Johnson loosed off several rounds of fire, the bullets ripping into the side of the van. A policeman shrieked as a 9-mm bullet caught him in the neck spraying a momentary hose of blood in the air. Several policemen swarmed around to help him. They pulled him back out of view behind the van and attempted to stop the blood with a handkerchief. They did not return fire. A swarm of uniforms had lined up along the thick growth of shrubs and bushes that bordered the public road almost behind Taylor and Johnson, their semi-automatic guns firmly trained on them. Taylor glanced over his shoulder at them, became agitated and shouted that he wanted a car, or a bullet would lodge in Schuman's brain. The chief of police took over the loudhailer and told him that it would take time to get a car organised. Taylor called out that they had ten minutes or else. The car park became quiet again for a minute or so and then the crackling of police radios broke the silence. The wailing sound of an ambulance echoed in the distance. Taylor ran the gun deeper under Marc's jaw making him groan more loudly.

"You have five minutes," Johnson yelled. The ambulance raced towards the van. When the two policemen were safely inside it sped off, its siren blaring in the eerie stillness. Johnson again called out. This time they had one minute to deliver. The chief responded that they needed more time. Johnson forced Marc to plead, to shout out to get the car. After a minute a black Mercedes was driven down the car park. On cue the car came to a stop and the driver opened all the doors as requested. He made his way back towards the van. A scuffling sound came from behind the bin as Marc was yanked to his feet the gun now dug deeper into his neck just under his right ear. They moved slowly into the open space. Most of Marc's body shielded Taylor's, making it virtually impossible for a police marksman to get a clean shot; to pick him off without seriously injuring Marc. The gun Taylor held against Marc's neck was a Glock, a semiautomatic. It could unleash massive destruction in seconds. Johnson measured his steps as he moved forward, his gun pointed towards the police van. They were now about ten metres from the car. The police watched in silence. Marc was moving to Taylor's orders, responding to each nudge of the gun against his neck. At the car door Taylor pulled back the gun as he ordered Marc into the seat. Suddenly Marc snapped his heel back catching Taylor's shin and spun around with a massive elbow into his chest. The split-second of confusion allowed Marc to deliver an uppercut onto his chin, knocking him backwards. As Taylor stumbled Marc grabbed his arm and the gun discharged a spray of fire. Bullets ricocheted off the car. Johnson shouted at Marc to back off but the adrenaline was pumping fiercely. Marc delivered a sharp punch to Taylor's stomach, winding him and immediately kicked the gun free from his grip. He now slammed punch after punch into Taylor's chest in a savage frenzy.

"This one's for Laura, you piece of shit," he yelled as he pulverised him.

"Back off Schuman," Johnson shouted as he edged closer. "Back off you bastard."

Marc lunged wildly at Johnson, charging like a raging bull. The gun discharged hitting Marc in the shoulder.

"Drop your gun," the police loudhailer called out. "Drop your gun."

Marc clung to Johnson's leg trying to topple him but the dart of pain in his shoulder made him slump. Several policemen jumped on Johnson, bringing him to the ground face downwards. His head slapped against Marc's legs. Marc raised his head and saw that the police were already handcuffing Taylor. They now yanked Johnson to his feet.

Suddenly a burst of automatic rifle fire rang out, blowing half of Johnson's face away. The whooshing sound of the high velocity shot came simultaneously with the crunching thud of bone. Blood and flesh spattered onto the policeman's face. The impact spun him sideways and then, shocked, he staggered for a few metres before eventually stumbling to the ground. The telescopic sight of the rifle was immediately zeroed on Taylor and in a split second another shot rang out. The bullet pierced Taylor's chest, emerging through his shoulder, leaving a huge gaping wound of raw flesh. Taylor's body buckled and sagged to the ground. Several more shots rang out in quick succession until the two bodies were a mass of raw flesh and blood. Police marksmen scanned the surrounding area trying to get a fix on the source of fire. They knelt on one knee angling for a clear shot as soon as the perpetrator came into sight. Marc lay rigid in shock. It was not until a policeman approached and helped him to his feet that he saw the full extent of the carnage just metres from him.

Other officers sprang forward and circled Verbiest and Batista. At least twenty more policemen entered through the thicket of shrubs to the car park and moved in on Newman. All three were muscled to the ground and handcuffed. Sirens roared and lights flashed as police cars and vans raced down the car park and came to a stop at odd angles. Television crews seemed to materialise out of nowhere. Cameramen ran towards the scene, eager to get shots of the grotesque scene. The police turned their attention towards the intrusive reporters and cameramen, ordering them back behind the line of shrubs and cordoned off the immediate area with red and white crime-scene tape. The activity of the television crews caught the attention of drivers who slowed, eventually stopping, eager to satisfy their curiosity. Some abandoned their cars on the road and mingled with the reporters. Two television vans edged past the line of jammed cars and drove up on the grass almost into the shrubbery. Technicians immediately set about pointing a camera into the car park and maneouvered a satellite antenna into its correct position in preparation for live transmission. The crime would be beamed around the world for everyone to see.

A group of forensic technicians got to work, one began photographing the entire scene and then moved in for some close-up work on the mutilated bodies while others pulled on gloves and started examining the clothing of the dead men.

The handcuffed men were now ordered to their feet. A police officer cautioned them with a litany of French words and then began reading them their rights. And now the Falcon Tech executives and Verbiest found themselves in the glare of camera lights. CNN and the local channels were in live transmission mode. Reporters started to shout questions from behind a temporarily erected police barrier.

"Mr. Verbiest, we believe that you are charged with bribery?"

"Mr. Batista, are you guilty of corruption?"

"Mr. Newman is it true that you were trying to manipulate an European official to gain some advantage for your computer trade?"

The questions came thick and fast but they were in no position to answer in the humiliating glare of the television lights. The police marched them towards the vans. Verbiest's eyes met Schuman's.

"Schuman, you'll pay for this big time," he shouted with venom. The policeman caught his head, pushed it down and shoved him roughly into the van.

Sirens blared as the vans screeched away from the scene. The police whisked Marc to Brugmann Hospital using the twenty-minute journey to secure a statement. Every little detail was recorded for the book of evidence.

"But why did you move so quickly?" Marc asked the detective in charge. "Lindell got away with the really incriminating evidence."

"When some of our officers saw that they were leading you out into the car park we decided to move quickly in case they got away. There are several exits to that car park. Anything could have happened. Problem was that most of our officers were concentrated around the Atomium."

MARC SPENT FOUR HOURS in the casualty department. The bullet had penetrated flesh but missed bone. After a series of X-Rays and tests they gave him a pain-killing injection, dressed the wound and released him. Later that evening he mounted the steps to Laura's apartment and fell into her arms. They stood in silence in a vice-like embrace for five minutes.

"I owe you my life," he whispered as he pulled back to look at her.

She smiled. "Yes you owe me big time. Now you're my slave."

Chapter Twenty Four

LINDELL FOLLOWED the signs for the Ring keeping one eye fixed on the mirror. Two police cars were in full view some distance back. He was forced to stop at a T-junction, and now a police car was almost sitting on his bumper. There was no time to think. He jerked forward and screeched left onto the main road leaving a trail of smoke and the smell of burnt rubber. An on-coming car hooted and flashed its lights forcing the police car to wait. By this manoeuvre Lindell gained vital seconds on his pursuers.

"I've got to lose them. Otherwise it's the end of the line," he shrieked in desperation. He floored the pedal and saw the gap widening between him and the flashing blue lights. He was now out on the Ring and clocking over two hundred kilometres an hour. The sign for Brussels Airport came into view. It could be his escape route. A thought flashed through his mind: *Five million dollars and a sun drenched beach. Five million dollars!*

"Oh shit," he muttered, thumping the steering wheel. "The damn passport."

He sped along the Ring past the Airport exit at two hundred and thirty kilometres an hour. He shot a glance in the mirror. No police car. He had escaped for now at any rate.

A minute later he saw a sign for Brussels' city centre, slowed to one eighty-five, and swerved to the right onto the feeder road. The Saab sped down towards the Cortenbergh tunnel reaching Rond Point Schuman in less than a minute. He swung off towards Rue de la Loi and headed for the Arts Loi junction. A readily recognisable landmark - the American Embassy – came into sight, just across the junction on Avenue des Arts. Lindell swung left, recalling that he had once walked back from the Embassy to his hotel in this direction. After travelling through two underpasses the familiar Hilton logo came into sight. Glancing in the mirror, he saw that the road behind him was quiet with two cars in the distance. Moments later he pulled right and, hoping that the police would not be waiting, he ground to a halt outside the hotel and ran towards the entrance. Dashing through the revolving door he raced across the foyer and hit the elevator button. His heart was pumping hard and his head felt heavy and ready to explode. As the elevator opened two elderly ladies came alongside him with a laden-down trolley. He jumped into the elevator as the ladies stood, hesitating.

"Can I help you," he said leaning out and pulling the trolley into the lift.

"Oh thank you, thank you. Are you American?"

"Yes," Lindell said curtly. "Which floor?"

"Can you remember Shirley?"

"I have the key here. Let me see. Yes it's number twenty-seven. Room twenty seven."

Lindell raised his voice in exasperation. "I mean the floor number,"

"Oh yes, the floor number. Let me see." She pulled some papers from her pocket. "It's floor fourteen."

Lindell banged the buttons. The elevator started to rise.

"We're on a European trip you know…our first time. We're from Chicago. And where are you from?" Shirley asked.

"Monterey."

"Oh that's where cousin Beth's living."

"Really." The elevator stopped.

"Well, I hope you enjoy the rest of your vacation," he said manoeuvring the trolley into the corridor and then furiously punching the button for the eighteenth. As the door closed he leaned against the mirrored surface allowing his body to sag. Out in the corridor he fumbled in his pockets for the key card. Inside, he stuffed his passport and a few other things into his travel bag and raced for the door. He glanced at his watch as he hit the lift button. Seven minutes had elapsed since he entered the hotel. He threw the bag into the boot and jumped into the driver's seat. He pulled open the glove compartment, flinging documents to the floor. Finally he found a road map of Europe.

He retraced his steps until he was back out on the motorway. Slamming on the brakes he pulled onto the hard shoulder to consult the map. Flicking the pages he decided it was better to head south. Within one minute he was again back out on the motorway wending his way along the Ring. He heard a siren blaring and saw blue lights flashing but luckily it was travelling at speed in the opposite direction.

After passing the E411 interchange the pedal was put to the floor, pushing the engine to the limits. The events back at the Atomium still lingered but the five million dollars stuffed in the bag in the boot were beginning to dominate his thoughts. *It's not one hundred million. Damn right, it's not. But it would have been be if those nerds, Verbiest and Wong, had not talked us into this crazy cabal.*

A little while later it was decision time. The road signs for the town of Luxembourg came up. He was at the border. No Customs…no police. He breathed a sigh of relief. And he could stay on the motorway. The town of Luxembourg was off to the left.

The fuel gauge had edged into the red zone forcing him to pull into the next service station and fill the tank. He flicked open the wallet and stared at the American Express card.

"No choice really. 'Got to use it," he muttered to himself. He picked up some Toblerone chocolate and a can of Coke in the shop, paid the bill and quickly returned to the car. Stretching out the map on the passenger seat it was again decision time. Switzerland caught his eye. It was five, maybe six, hours fast driving. He remembered all of the Customs problems with the computer shipments into Switzerland last year. Definitely not part of the European Union. *That's an idea. A flight out of Zurich.* Plotting what looked like the most efficient route to Zurich, he folded the map and once more gunned the engine. Back out on the motorway the Sunday afternoon traffic was light. He pushed the speedometer up to one eighty and started to think about his next move. *A flight to where? Asia? No. Somewhere else in Europe? Can't. Back to the US of A. Can't. Africa?* No. He spent the next half-hour thinking. Wondering. The alternatives were limited. To break the monotony he turned on the radio. A Bob Marley and the Wailers song was playing.

"That's it. The Caribbean. Long lazy days on the beach and long nights drinking Heineken. That's where I'll have to go."

Lindell relaxed into the driving. He was now on the E25 to Metz in France. He would follow this route to Strasbourg. Close to Colmar he changed to the A35 and continued to Mulhouse. Outside Mulhouse he picked up the E60 heading for Zurich.

Another hour brought him to the outskirts of the city where he picked up the signs for the Airport. On arrival he pulled into the car park and went straight to the Swissair desk in the main terminal where he booked a business class seat on the early morning flight to Brasilia. It was time to eat and then get an early night in an hotel somewhere. Lindell drove in the direction of the city. He parked in an inconspicuous space on a side street and walked around searching for a place to eat. As he was about to enter a restaurant a young man with long hair and a backpack approached, smiled and asked directions to the youth hostel. The accent was unmistakably American. Lindell shrugged, explaining that he was also a visitor to the town. The backpacker had moved several paces down the street by the time Lindell called after him.

"Would you like to join me for a meal? It's okay, totally up front. I figure that you might enjoy something to eat."

"Sure sir. Sure."

They went inside and followed the waiter to a table. The seats were wooden with high backs. About ten other diners, mostly couples, were peppered around the restaurant. Lindell was pleased that he had invited his new companion to the restaurant. He could do with company right now.

"What's your name?"

"Aaron Burton, sir."

Lindell thought for a moment. "Well, Aaron, isn't it a little late in the season for hiking around Europe?"

"Sure, sir, but I want to see it when it's not full of tourists."

"The name's Lindell. Dylan Lindell."

"Pleased to meet you Mr. Lindell."

"It's Dylan."

The young man smiled. "Okay Dylan."

"Where are you from Aaron?"

"Alabama sir."

The waiter came along. Lindell ordered steak and french fries.

"Choose what you want."

Aaron hesitated and then said, "I'll have the same."

"And would you like something to drink?"

They both agreed on Cokes. The waiter took the details and left. "So you're staying in youth hostels?"

"Yes."

They chatted. Aaron talked about his trek through Poland and Germany and told Lindell that he wanted to see Spain and Italy but that he had a problem. He had virtually run out of cash. Lindell thought hard for a long moment. He was going to speak but hesitated, changing his mind.

"So, Aaron, what will you do when you go back to Alabama?"

"I'm going to study electronic engineering. I want to have my own computer company." The deep southern US drawl very apparent.

"Really. The computer business is tough," Lindell replied.

"Well not just have a computer company, you see I want to design a whole new technology."

Lindell just listened as the enthusiastic young man talked about his favourite subject. Before long the meals were served. Aaron ate as if he hadn't seen food for a month. Lindell watched him, reliving his own trek through the Amazon fifteen years ago. He was seventeen then and, at one stage, had gone without food for three days.

"Aaron, I have a very unusual proposition to make to you," Lindell began. Aaron stopped eating, his jaws tightening.

"Mr. Lindell if it's some funny business…that kind of queer thing, then I ain't havin' nothin' to do with it. It's against the Bible."

"Relax Aaron, I'm not suggesting anything like that. No, I may be able to help you with your cash flow problem. Just listen to what I have to say."

Aaron relaxed and started to eat again. Lindell outlined his plan step by step, including the fact that he had to leave Europe in a hurry and that Burton could drive his car to the South of France and live it up by using his American Express card.

"And how would that help you?"

"Well some really bad guys are following me for something I didn't do. They would find the car on the Riviera and then they would follow the trail of the credit card. So they would think I'm still hiding somewhere along the Mediterranean."

"But," Aaron said smiling, "they would be wrong."

Lindell grinned. "Exactly. They would be very wrong."

"You mean you want to give me a credit card?…And a car?"

"Yes, provided you are willing to abandon it in a fairly easy-to-find spot and then head into Italy or Spain. I want it to be found a couple of days from now."

"You sure the police are not involved?"

"I'm sure."

"Hey man, it sounds fine to me."

"Okay let's finish our meal. You've got a lot of driving to do tonight."

After they finished Lindell paid the bill and they left. They drove back to the Airport. Lindell exchanged some dollars for French francs, handed them to Aaron and drove off to a hotel that he had spotted earlier. He checked in, paid for the room in cash and returned to the car.

"Remember to use the motorway all the way. Plot out your course with this map. Use the French francs at those tolls. There's six thousand dollars in my account. Practise my signature and when you hit the limit tear up the card. Clear?"

"Sure man."

Lindell tapped him on the shoulder. "I hope you can do a favour for somebody someday too, computer wizard."

Aaron turned his head and smiled. "I take it that it drives just like an old pick-up."

"Yeah, just like an old pick-up! So long buddy."

Lindell watched as the car disappeared into the darkness. He then turned and made for the hotel entrance.

Amsterdam
THE SUPREME LODGE FATHER waved his hand but didn't speak. He had seen enough coverage. A 489'-er jumped up and

304

turned off the television. Everything had gone as planned at the Atomium. And now he was resting at the operations centre off Damrak Street, surrounded by a room full of young Triads, sipping his favourite drink - Chinese tea - from a small gold rimmed bowl.

He turned towards Cheng and started off in traditional chiu chow. "Seems the idea to tip off the media has paid off handsomely. We almost wrote the script for those reporters. All they had to do was let the cameras roll leaving Sinclair and his august board sweating helplessly…"

"…Yeah," Cheng agreed, "as they watched the Falcon Tech launch going down the toilet on nation wide television."

The Supreme Lodge Father clasped his left knee and began rocking. "I knew I would use it some day. Thirty years of practising Tai Chi every morning. All those graceful movements in Kowloon Park paid off very well. I went through the full routine – collapsing and passing out. I was eager to get everything started, so I led the way and again fainted at the top of the stairs. Three summersaults later I was a really convincing hospital case, this time my legs splayed at one hundred and eighty degrees. Even I was surprised by my own agility, though I had practised that manoeuvre more than one hundred times. The Falcon Tech executives were so concerned. And I tell you my brothers, I still protested when the ambulance arrived just to show my deep commitment."

"Yes," Cheng snorted. "Commitment to *your own* plan."

"Well that's always the problem when you have a singular focus and those Americans had just one thing on their mind – a successful launch on Wall Street and riches beyond their dreams…"

Cheng nodded excitedly. "It was time they learned the most important Chinese proverb of all - *They sleep in the same bed but they have different dreams*. Taylor and Johnson could have learned something from that proverb too. They thought they were doing it for the glory of Uncle Sam…protecting American interests abroad. And they did a real good job too by keeping Schuman simmering until the time was ripe but, of course, we were holding the reins…right down to Hu Hei's last rifle shot."

A shriek of oriental laughter filled the room. Cheng dampened the exuberance with a downward movement of his palms. "Woo has already taken the ThinkEx prototype and Synapatron from Lindell's fortress. Our engineers are studying them."

"Excellent," Wong said and then waved his hand to show that it was time to get to work. "It's time for war reparations big time because when I was in Brussels I saw it for myself. Those lawyers' offices were an oasis of priceless antiques plundered from around the world during the colonial era. Ming vases from China and ivory from Africa. The West is wealthy from the wars of greed over the centuries."

"Ah, Mr. Wong," Cheng said, "I know what you're thinking. The world's a globe and, at last, it may be coming full circle. Our people should also enjoy the spoils of war."

"Precisely, Cheng. Precisely. Now we can forget about Europe. It's time to stop playing ping-pong around here. The time for hard ball in America is approaching. Get the airline tickets organised."

Brussels
THE DEBRIEFING was scheduled for 8 o' clock Monday morning. Kaufmann and Champenois were already waiting in the foyer of the Breydel when Marc arrived.

"Well handled, Marc. Our OLAF boys were monitoring everything. It went so smoothly," Kaufmann said shaking Marc's hand earnestly. Champenois tilted his head from side to side and pursed his lips in typical French style. "Yes great work indeed. We've put that behind us nicely and the Belgian police handled it well apart from letting that Lindell guy escape."

Kaufmann agreed. "But not for long. They've put a red alert out for him. I'm sure Interpol will pick him up in a few days. Incidentally CNN knew a lot about the case. The coverage was quite unbelievable."

Champenois pointed towards the elevator. "Indeed. Let's make the Commissioner compliment us on our success."

They rode the elevator to the fifth. Calavera's personal

assistant ushered them straight in. The Commissioner was sitting behind the desk, her reading glasses half way down her nose. She barely moved her head, instead preferring to raise her eyes over her glasses, and then pointed towards the conference table at the other end of the office.

"Gentlemen, take a seat. I'll be with you in a moment."

They took their seats and waited. She closed the file, took off her glasses and walked to the table.

"Commissioner, I think you will judge yesterday a complete success for the Commission. Two Falcon Tech executives are behind bars, along with Verbiest."

"Well it seems from the news reports to have gone well. The television coverage certainly made us look very professional. I've already congratulated the Belgian Ministry of Justice. The journalists sure did their homework. No leaks on our side I trust?"

Champenois smiled. "No Commissioner. It's probably the police. They badly needed to be seen to make a success of something after the recent paedophile scandals. It was just good image-making for the Belgian public."

"Hmm." Commissioner Calavera then turned towards Marc. "This will be a long drawn out trial. Lots of media coverage and questions from our parliamentarians. I've taken the decision to suspend you from duty with immediate effect."

She did not wait for a response, immediately turning towards Kaufmann. "Mr. Kaufmann, I will expect you to name your two most senior investigators to wrap up the case."

"Yes, Commissioner."

"Any questions?"

"What's the timing now?" Kaufmann asked.

She waved her right arm in the air, then flexed it dismissively to show that the meeting was over. "Within two weeks. The European industry is demanding immediate protection. We must deliver."

"Yes, Commissioner."

All three stood up and, with military precision, walked towards the door and took the lift to the ground floor.

Boston

THE BROTHERS OF THE YANGTZE triad never made a mistake. Cheng had listened very carefully to Wong's instructions over the past six months and Zhang and Ling had carried out Cheng's orders to the letter, now leaving the end game in sight. For the final piece of the jigsaw it was no different. They accompanied Cheng to Wong's room on the third floor of the Marriott on Old River Road for the final briefing.

"Our work is about to bear fruit," the Supreme Lodge Father intoned solemnly. "I'll have the introductory meeting this evening. Let's call it the softening-up initiation. Sinclair may not sleep too well tonight. Tomorrow morning you turn up at the Kimble-Sinclair headquarters and start the adrenaline pumping a little more. Remember he pops those heart pills so take him gently. He's our route to the prize…we don't want to lose him."

"Yes," Cheng agreed, "it may take some time so you must be very patient. Of course if Sinclair doesn't fold we have the minds of twenty other board members to play with."

WONG WAS LED by the maitre d' to his reserved table in the centre of the Myrtle Grove restaurant in Martha's Vineyard. He took his seat and leaned back, satisfied that he had chosen well. Scanning the faces of the other diners he then fixed his eyes on the empty seats in the alcove and smiled inwardly. He had the perfect view, the perfect vantage point. There would be plenty of time to watch and to plan. The setting was right and, no doubt, his opportunity would come, that he was sure of. There was one irritation though. It was strictly a no-smoking restaurant and the Oriental lawyer liked to inhale deeply when planning his moves. He perused the menu, eventually settling for one of his favourite dishes - king-sized prawns in garlic sauce. It reminded him of his student days in the States and now he would enjoy the memories while watching his quarry.

A few minutes later Sinclair guided the executives from the Mid-West Pharmaceutical Corporation to the alcove, gesturing discreetly to the headwaiter to uncork the champagne. The alcove table, overlooking the ocean, had, over the years, become the place where he entertained important people from the arts or the business world. He always arrived in his Lear turbofan accompanied by his guests. Sinclair was on the acquisition trail and therefore would be doing the courting tonight. He was, after all, the white knight about to propose marriage and the signs looked good. The 'would be bride' was receptive to a friendly take over. In Sinclair's eyes, it was just a matter of sorting out the details over dinner. Small issues like price were always delicate but it was a key element of the mating ritual and he was prepared to give it as much time as it needed.

The activity was slow in the alcove. A long two hours passed and still the dessert stage had not been reached. Wong amused himself by chasing a prawn around the plate before stabbing it with the fork and then slowly bringing it to his mouth.

Patience is a Confucian virtue and success comes to those who wait, he reminded himself.

Sinclair drained the wineglass, excused himself and made for the restroom. The Supreme Lodge Father patted his mouth with the napkin, stood up and promptly followed. As he entered, the president was already standing at the urinal. Wong moved into position two places away in the otherwise empty restroom.

"I'm sure it must have been a big disappointment to see the launch of your subsidiary going down the tubes on national television," he started off in a friendly tone.

The president raised his head, fixing on the Oriental's reflection in the mirror. He then drew back, somewhat nonplussed.

"Excuse me?"

Wong maintained eye contact through the mirror. "Mr. Sinclair, I say it must have been a big disappointment to see your prized subsidiary going down the tubes on national television."

No response was forthcoming. Sinclair creased his forehead as if his mind were elsewhere. Wong stepped back from the urinal and rubbed his hands together. "Let me introduce myself. I'm a Hong Kong businessman and well...I've been following your run of bad luck, what with the sordid behaviour of those Falcon Tech executives over there in Europe."

Sinclair shrugged and then responded. "Well that's business." Fixing his zip he moved quickly to the wash basin. Wong's friendly tone dissolved, replaced by resolute determination. "Well, looks like the chances of a launch are slim at this stage. Tell you what, I'll buy Falcon Tech...I'll give you a good price."

Sinclair raised his head, glancing into the mirror over the basin to catch the Oriental's countenance. He then swung around abruptly and straightened up his six-foot-four frame. Now towering over Wong, he looked down disdainfully, brushing a contemptuous hand towards the diminutive figure.

"It's not for sale."

A wily smile broke across the Triad leader's face. "Oh pardon me, Mr. Sinclair, but from where I'm standing I think it very much *is* for sale."

Sinclair bounded towards the door, grabbed the handle and pulled.

"Mr. Sinclair," Wong called out, the tone now menacing. "Bribery...murder."

The threat was unmistakable. Sinclair released his grip on the handle and spun around.

"Dammit! What do you want?"

"Oh just listen, Mr. Sinclair." Wong was now in cold and detached mode. He stared directly into Sinclair's eyes. "What happened in Europe...those Falcon Tech executives...well, you see, that was criminal."

"What the hell do you know about my business?" Sinclair barked down at the tenacious terrier.

"Well let's just say it would be a real pity if all of it could be traced back to you," he said, stabbing a finger towards the president's chest. Sinclair's blue blood was reaching boiling point fast. A deal was waiting to be concluded at his table and an Oriental was sparring with him in the restroom.

"Get out of my sight," he shouted and disappeared through the door.

Wong looked in the mirror and smiled. Round one had

gone well. He took a cigarette from the packet in a deliberate sort of way and, leaning against the edge of the wash-hand basin, lit it and inhaled deeply. The ritual was his way of complimenting himself for a job well done. He had engaged his opponent without much difficulty. Turning again towards the mirror he patted his forehead with a paper towel. No contest. Sinclair would snap like a prawn cracker, he now knew.

He retraced his steps to the table, relaxed into the chair and ordered Chinese tea. For the next half-hour the Supreme Lodge Father of the Yangtze Triad watched from his vantage point as Sinclair mixed business with pleasure. He was more animated now. Maybe the good wine was working...

Or maybe the mating ritual was reaching its climax. Anyway, the time to unnerve his prey was ripe. The routine started with a smile and then a discreet wave as if they were old friends or long-standing business acquaintances. Sinclair could not but notice the attention from the middle of the restaurant. But he managed to sit it out, to ignore the subtle intimidation, to keep his veneer.

Twenty minutes later the liqueurs arrived. Now was the time to tighten the tension and maybe stir up a little indigestion. Wong rose from his chair and threw the napkin on the table.

"Well Howard..." he boomed as he strode past the other diners, "...I hope we can cut a deal."

Silence descended around the exclusive restaurant as the Boston Brahmin turned and stared, in communal bemusement, at the curious figure gliding towards the alcove. Immediately Wong turned to Sinclair's guests and apologised for the intrusion. "Howard and I...well, we go back many years." He was now standing at the president's shoulder, grinning. "You know the way it is between old business acquaintances. We always have some deal or other on the boil."

Sinclair was speechless. Wong was now at full throttle. He looked around as if he were going to pull up a chair and settle in for the rest of the evening. "I was thinking Howard, what if our financial people were to get together in your office tomorrow to go over the figures and wrap up the deal?"

Sinclair's face reddened. Here was a Chink standing at his

table calling the shots. What effrontery! Chinks were the kind you shout orders at. Fawning types who take your order, bow gracefully and back away.

"Get out of my restaurant," he demanded. Wong smiled at him, then turned towards the bemused guests.

"Believe me, Howard's a tough negotiator. Over the years I've found that you must have leverage over him if you want a bargain. So I hope you people have lots of leverage. Otherwise you will come out on the wrong side of the deal."

Suddenly Sinclair rose to his feet and shouted to the maitre d'. "Have this piece of...this person removed from the restaurant."

Two waiters came across to the alcove and clasped the oriental's arms. Wong glanced over his shoulder and flashed a triumphant smile at Sinclair as he was peremptorily escorted through the busy restaurant.

"Will be in touch Howard, when the bean counters have done their work," he shouted as the waiters pushed him through the door. Sinclair slumped back nervously into the chair and instinctively dipped his right hand into his pocket, fumbling agitatedly for the vial of tablets.

Chapter Twenty Five

Boston
AT NINE THE FOLLOWING MORNING the marble-clad atrium
of the Kimble-Sinclair headquarters was awash with employees,
all eager to start the wheels of commerce rolling. Zhang
approached the reception desk and asked for Miss Rockwell.

"Have you got an appointment sir?" the lady asked.

"Yes. It was arranged directly with Mr. Sinclair last evening
over dinner."

The receptionist phoned to the twentieth floor. Miss
Rockwell was so facilitating. She could not have been more
helpful. Zhang and Ling rode the elevator to the presidential
suite, stepped out and were greeted by the faithful secretary.

"So you're with Mid-West Pharmaceutical."

"Not directly. Financial advisers really for takeovers."

"This way please."

When Sinclair saw them his face blanched. "Miss
Rockwell, show these people to the door."

"But they said they have an appointment."

"They haven't got an appointment. Please show them off
the premises."

She dutifully turned to usher them out of his office. Zhang
raised a hand. "Mr. Sinclair you're not keeping your agreement.
We're here to do a due diligence on Falcon Tech…that's what
you agreed to. Isn't it?"

"Call security," he bellowed. "Get out of my office."

He charged around the desk towards Ling. Zhang moved
swiftly to intercept him.

"I wouldn't do that Mr. Sinclair."

Sinclair muttered under his breath and then waved
agitatedly towards his secretary. She read the signal and
promptly left. Zhang was now surveying the surroundings.
"Very comfortable office Mr. Sinclair. I bet you'd hate to lose it."

"Say what you have to and go."

"Sinclair," he said coldly. "We've been close to you now for
some time. You're a very predictable man."

The president returned to his chair but stood, leaning forward, his knuckles pressing down on the desk. "What do you damn well want?"

"Falcon Tech. Understand now? We want the whole thing and you, Mr. Sinclair, are in no position to refuse."

"No deal, you slant-eyed bastards."

The visitors were unmoved by the vitriolic outburst. Ling pulled a tape recorder from his pocket. "This will interest you, Mr. Sinclair. Listen to it. It's just a little chat between the Falcon Tech executives and yourself."

He replayed the tape of the October meeting when Sinclair was told about the planned bribery of the trade investigator and the killing of Montorro. Sinclair's face contorted. It was his voice all right. He became agitated but quickly recovered his balance. After all he was a WASP. Ling stopped the tape.

"Heard enough Mr. Sinclair? I knew you'd recognise it." Ling now moved swiftly around the office, pointing as he went along. "You see we've worked hard…cleaned this office many times." He was now at the wall opposite the president's desk. "Yes, dusted that painting there. Even your padded chair, Mr. Sinclair and of course the boardroom. When the time was right I wired everything. It was stereophonic, digital. Professional, oh yes *re-al* professional."

"Those Falcon Tech people were acting independently. Nothing…nothing was authorised by me," he blurted out.

"What if your boardroom colleagues were to receive this tape? They might think you were trying to hide something from them."

"I have nothing-"

Zhang cut in to finish the sentence. "…to hide. You see you're so predictable. We can read your mind."

"Oh Mr. Sinclair," Ling continued as he moved towards the window. "You may think you've nothing to hide from your board members. Maybe you could play the odds and try gambling with them. Worst they'd probably do is fire you but what about the law?"

Sinclair again charged around the desk towards the visitors. Zhang's hands shot out, his forearms now taut and sinewy with his fingers dangling limply towards the floor. "…Just for

314

fitness you understand," he said menacingly. Sinclair instinctively backed off, his upper lip quivering. Rubbing a bead of sweat from his forehead he returned to the desk.

"Relax and listen to this tape because the acoustics in the boardroom are excellent. Maybe even better than your own office here."

Before he could object Ling played the tape: the quarterly meeting before Christmas. Then came the juicy bit: The cover up.

Sinclair flailed his hands hopelessly in the air and slumped into the chair. Ling again pressed the button. "What you've heard there is like Watergate revisited. We're talking cover-up."

But Sinclair kept his veneer, his blueblood pedigree. He tried to ignore them by staring at some paperwork on his desk.

"Tell you what. Meet our boss at a place of his choosing and maybe nobody else needs to hear those tapes. We will be in touch."

Before he could respond they were at the door. Sinclair jumped to his feet and tried to call them back but they were moving fast down the corridor. He watched helplessly as they disappeared behind the closing elevator doors. He spun around, muttered something to himself and headed straight for the drinks cabinet in the corner of his office. The bottle of whiskey was gripped by the neck and pointed haphazardly at the cut glass tumbler, his hands shaking wildly. Most of it spilled but he managed to get a large shot on target. He brought the glass to his mouth and knocked back the contents, rubbing his lips with his hand to wipe away the residue. He moved towards the desk, picked up a file and flung it across the office, the contents fluttering towards the floor.

His secretary tapped on the open door and peered in. "Mr. Sinclair, is everything okay?"

"I'm...fi...I'm fine, Miss Rockwell," he stuttered, motioning with his hands that he wanted to be left alone.

WONG OBSERVED THE BEAUTIFUL forest setting as he drove along the avenue leading to the Westpines Country

Club. The fact that he was actually approaching Sinclair's sanctuary gave him a tremendous sense of power and he was enjoying every moment of this very different chase immensely. A mile further on, the French-chateau clubhouse, with its distinctive and imposing entrance, came into view. It possessed all the elegance and tradition of a bygone era.

He parked in the lot, admired the surroundings for a few moments, and waited. He checked his watch. Timing was everything in this game. Pounce too early and the quarry runs scared. Move too late and the prize has vanished.

A few minutes before eight he entered the grand foyer. The concierge called after him. "This is a private club. Strictly members only, sir."

Wong turned sharply and stared disdainfully. "I am a guest of Mr. Sinclair this evening."

"Certainly, sir. Enjoy your stay with us." The concierge nodded apologetically and backed away.

The Supreme Lodge Father smiled. "I will. Question is… will Sinclair?"

A peppering of members was seated in the grand reception room, sipping aperitifs. They would be called when their table was ready. Other members entered and shuffled about, nodding pleasantries at friends and acquaintances. Wong sat down and continued to observe the activity.

The president of the healthcare giant was predictable, entering the room precisely at eight. An Oriental hand shot out to greet him but he dismissed the cynical attempt at friendliness.

"Mr. Sinclair," Wong said as he eased back into the comfortable sofa. "Surely that's no way to treat a Kimble-Sinclair stock holder."

"What do you damn well want?"

"I believe you already know, so why don't we get straight down to business?"

"Don't waste my time."

"Now we're getting somewhere. We want Falcon Tech for twenty million. That's what you paid for it back in '89."

"You're crazy. You're dreaming," he snapped resolutely.

Wong sat back. "I'm afraid not. Those Falcon Tech

executives were doing the dreaming but they were dreaming the wrong dreams. Look, this is how it stacks up right now. You've heard the tapes. The smoking gun goes all the way to the top. You've covered up illegal activity. You've covered up conspiracy…and you've covered up murder. Everything really. That adds up to a lot of charges. Many laws were broken…badly broken and now they can't be mended. The Foreign Corrupt Practices Act for example that-"

A friend of Sinclair's wandered over and interrupted, chatting animatedly about a recent golf game. As the exchange continued his eyes began evaluating Wong. Sinclair shuffled in his seat, making no attempt to introduce him. When he left, Sinclair turned his attention back to Wong.

"Those Falcon Tech people were acting independently."

"Okay, if you're so sure let's just see what the Feds and the Justice Department think." He pulled a cell phone from his pocket and started clicking digits. "…They've both got twenty-four-hour confidential telephone facilities. It'll only take a minute."

Many of Sinclair's personal friends were here; people who held him in high regard. It was bad enough having a chink in your club but a chink making a phone call to the Fibbies was just too much to countenance.

"Put that away. I don't allow those things to be used in my club."

"Start talking or I'll press the little green button here."

A waiter approached.

"Iced tea." Sinclair snapped.

"And I'll have Chinese tea."

The waiter left. "You see our tastes are almost identical."

Sinclair glowered, fidgeting uneasily with a napkin ring. Wong's finger remained poised over the button. "This finger's gettin' itchy."

Perspiration now glistened above Sinclair's upper lip. He discreetly brought the napkin to his mouth, patting gently. The waiter returned with the drinks. Sinclair raised the glass and sipped. He cleared his throat and spoke with determination, his eyes fixed on the opposite wall.

"Don't try playing mind-fuck games with me, you sonofabitch. Hard-earned Kimble-Sinclair money has helped to put the present incumbent in the Oval office. In fact many powerful friends in Washington owe me favours. If you don't back off I'll have you and your kung fu friends in a Federal prison for extortion with menaces."

Wong lifted the cup towards his lips and said. "That's true Howard. We've checked you out. You have political connections - the right *guan-xi* as we call it in the East - on Capitol Hill and in the White House, but I'm talking the Feds and Justice. Altogether different, wouldn't you agree?" He paused for a few seconds. "…Since Watergate they're the real power brokers. The politicians run scared if conspiracy or murder's involved."

Sinclair dipped to a whisper. "The President will authorise the CIA to track you down and eliminate you."

"The CIA?" Wong half-laughed, half-sniggered at the pathetic threat. Sinclair brought the palms of his hands towards the surface of the table in an attempt to get the Oriental to dampen his voice.

"…Wrong again. We've worked hard for twenty years passing information to Langley on what those high-ranking Communist mandarins in Beijing are thinking and doing. You see we're also the only ones with accurate information on China's nuclear weapons."

"You're bluffing," Sinclair stuttered, "the State Department protects American interests abroad."

"That's for diplomacy but here we're talking control and domination. Think about it for a minute, Mr Sinclair. The CIA could hardly send Caucasians dressed in dark glasses and trench coats snooping around those nuclear installations in the heart of China. No, that's what we do best. Result…it gives us a lot of power in those corridors in Virginia. A heck of a lot of power."

"You motherfucker," Sinclair muttered under his breath.

The Supreme Lodge Father grinned. He was making progress. "I'm telling you Howard this finger's gettin' real itchy."

Sinclair was now very hot and very nervous. He loosened his tie.

"Where were we? Oh yes the Feds. Basically they'll come in and crawl up your ass and down your throat like a SWAT team." Wong paused briefly. "On second thoughts maybe Justice. Wouldn't surprise me if they had a turf war over this one."

Sinclair began to cough violently, his face turning beetroot red. He couldn't breathe properly. He was now gasping for air. "My tablets, my tablets." The vial came out of his pocket and Wong pushed the iced tea close to his left hand.

"There you are. Bitter pills are always hard to swallow. You must wash them down with something," he chirped sardonically.

The waiter returned. "Can I get you something, Mr. Sinclair?"

"No thanks. Just a little problem," he said pointing to his throat. He quickly regained his composure.

It was time to continue the chase. "There is an alternative. We can negotiate with the twenty other members of the board if you haven't got the stomach to cut a deal."

Sinclair couldn't countenance letting control slip away. "*I am* the president. *I* make the decisions," he blurted out.

"So do it."

Sinclair fell silent, thinking hard.

"Tell you what Howard. I'll give you exactly one week to make up your mind and secure the agreement of the board. Exactly one week from now, if you don't sell, the Feds and Justice guys will start crawling. Probably a question of who gets up there first."

"You must appreciate that it's a boardroom decision."

"But you've said it yourself. You make the decisions."

"You're crazy. Falcon Tech's worth twelve billion."

Wong grinned. "Oh yes, twelve billion to us but to you…well even in one of those minimum security Federal holiday camps you'll hardly get to spend that amount."

Sinclair played with the glass of iced tea. Wong pulled his finger back slightly and turned to face the East Coast patrician directly. "Oh, I almost forgot. We want your pet project too."

"What the…"

"I said we want the Sinclair Foundation. Those priceless works of art at the Foundation…most of those were plundered from Europe by *Sinclair the second* after the Second World War.

The way we see it Europe and America have been plundering for centuries and now it's time for war reparations…time the East received some spoils rather than giving to the West all the time. And your little Foundation's a start."

Sinclair was speechless. Random thoughts began pulsating through his head. *His standing in the art world. The exhibitions he planned on hosting and the paintings he would loan to museums across America.*

The blood drained from his face and he now felt weak and disorientated. It was time to go in for the kill.

"Even if your political connections come out with all guns blazing for you, and I'm not so sure they will after we place a few smoking-gun rumours around the corridors of power in Washington, we'll be ready to make it an international issue. Just picture the banner headlines. 'Respected American corporation attempted to cheat Europe.' It could cause a political war between the old allies."

Wong paused, his mouth opening in a wide grin. "Oh yes, we're ready to use it. The old 'divide and conquer' tactic so favoured by the West."

"Slant-eyed bastard - get out of my sight," the president muttered under his breath.

The oriental lawyer wagged a chiding finger. "Please Mr. Sinclair, decorum. Here's the plan for next week. I control some Kimble-Sinclair stock. A small but significant enough amount, Howard," he emphasised. "So watch your stock price on Monday. It'll go into free fall. I'll place rumours around the investment houses that the board was implicated in that sordid stuff in Europe while selling at the same time. It will trigger a run on the stock. And if there's no deal in sight the Feds and Justice come riding by in a week from now and the stock hits the floor. We move in and buy up every bit of it and…take control of both companies."

Sinclair stared vacantly at the wall. Somehow this was not the occasion to dictate the pace. His club was definitely not the place for an unseemly exchange. No, decorum demanded that he would sit it out.

"So," the Supreme Lodge Father said. "We need to review

progress by Friday next. You may, of course, like to meet earlier."

The Oriental stood up and, in an unambiguous display of friendliness, stretched out his hand, immediately forcing the East Coast WASP to rise slightly and reciprocate with a handshake. Wong then formally excused himself and weaved past the other guests towards the foyer.

The Kimble-Sinclair president muttered an expletive and sank back into the sofa.

February 2000
Washington
THE DECISION TO ACCOMPANY Laura to Washington came easily. In reality she encouraged him to take a break from Brussels and, in any event, he would remain suspended from duty at least until the trial. Marc spent most of the first week strolling around the city, visiting museums and photographing the famous landmarks. And the evenings were spent over dinner with Laura talking excitedly about her new job as senior associate in the thirty-partner law firm of McKensie & Prosser. It was clubbish and close-knit, she told him, and the fact that her father and old McKensie did a stint together in 'Nam might not be a barrier to advancement. Now back to her roots, she was looking forward to tasting real success and maybe making partner wasn't such a long shot after all. Marc listened, happy that he was by her side.

The second week was cold with a dusting of snow covering the city. Marc spent most days in their room at the Club Quarters Hotel, reading. By Thursday he had become bored and began surfing the channels, eventually settling for CNN. He went to the fridge and pulled out a bottle of mineral water. It was then that he heard the words 'Falcon Tech' coming from the television. The remote control was grabbed and the sound raised. The lower part of the screen showed the familiar Breaking News banner.

"And now we go over to our business correspondent in Boston at the headquarters of Kimble-Sinclair for that news conference. Kathy Greenfelt reports."

"Thank you Tom. Here at Kimble-Sinclair we are expecting at any moment now the president of the healthcare giant, Howard Sinclair, to give a news conference on its abortive stock market launch of the Falcon Tech subsidiary. As we wait for Mr. Sinclair to come to the podium let me give you the background to these dramatic developments…"

The reporter reran the details including the dramatic fall in the Kimble-Sinclair share price. The background over the reporter's right shoulder showed Sinclair mounting the podium with a single sheet of paper in his hand. The camera zoomed in filling the screen with his image.

Sinclair carefully read from the script condemning the activities of the FT executives and pledging support to the authorities in Europe to bring the issue to a close. He continued…

"…Every aspect of this issue has been considered particularly the slide in the share price. We have decided to take swift action to reassure our customers in the healthcare sector and bring confidence back to our stock market investors. Yesterday afternoon the board decided to sell off the Falcon Tech subsidiary for fifty million dollars and to devote all its energy to its core healthcare business. In this way, the jobs of Falcon Tech employees here in the US, in Europe and particularly at the manufacturing plant in China, will be safeguarded."

Marc continued to stare at the screen trying to make sense of it. When the report from Boston ended the newscaster said that their Asian correspondent had filed a report earlier in the day from Hong Kong containing an interview with the new owners of the company. He ran the report.

"As you can see, Mr. Kai is about to read out a press statement. He's accompanied by Mr. Cheng on the right of your screen who apparently runs the company on a daily basis. And to the extreme left is Mr. Wong, the company's legal adviser."

Marc gasped as the inscrutable face of Wong filled the screen.

"Mr Kai can you tell us what existing investments the Great Wall Street Company holds?"

"Our interests are mainly in property here in Hong Kong. But as you know, the property market has slumped. So it is time to diversify."

"It would seem that your investment company got tremendous value in the deal?"

"It may seem like that but our first concern was the jobs of the people in Shenzhen. This company was a ray of hope for thousands of Chinese people…their first chance to earn a decent living after years of poverty under the old regime. We wanted to help…to give the people hope. If Falcon Tech collapsed then maybe no more foreign investment would come. And that would be a tragedy for all the Chinese people…"

Marc stood transfixed, his face frozen in a vacant stare. As each stark revelation struck him the events of the last six months all fell into place and made sense. Perfect sense. He punched the pillow furiously.

"I'll get that bastard one day. He'll pay for the hell he's put me through."

When Laura returned that evening Marc eagerly told her the news and his theory that it was all a set-up from the very beginning.

"So," Laura said. "You were merely a pawn in the whole process."

"Exactly. Wong had his own agenda all along."

Laura put her arms around his waist and kissed him on the cheek. "Maybe my boyfriend wasn't to blame after all."

"Not guilty, your honour," he said. "That means I get my sentence commuted." Marc grabbed her and in a few frenzied moments bits of clothing dropped in a zig-zag pattern across the floor.

"Hold on Marc. 'Have to take a shower. It's been a long day."

She pulled away and made for the bathroom. He flopped back onto the bed, his arousal on overdrive. A delicate waft of Laura's perfume percolated from somewhere in the room and it smelled sensual and provocative. In an instant be bounded from the bed, yanked off his remaining clothes and was pushing against the light aluminium shower door. He stepped in and felt the feminine silkiness of her skin as his fingers ran uncontrollably around her body.

She responded by massaging Marc's shoulders with the sponge and then along his back, lingering awhile near his left shoulder blade.

"Ouch!" he yelled.

"Oh, sorry…forgot about that mole."

And then suddenly a flashback. She was in the car in Louvain when Marc thrust the photographs in front of her eyes. There was no mole, no blemish on the body she saw. She was certain. She had the perfect memory after all. Relief enveloped her but decided that she would not tell him – at least not yet. After all he should not have gone to that sordid den in the first place.

He wrapped his arms around her, kissing her deeply, passionately. Above the sound of the water she could hear his breathing, strong and vital. And now her breathing became deeper too, closely matching his. Moving his hands down her back, he squeezed firmly. Laura moaned and pulled him closer to her, shuddering momentarily as his firm body pressed against her soft flesh. His head now crouched down enveloping her nipples, darting from one to the other, cupping and nuzzling them with hands and tongue. She pulled back, teasing him. "No, not so fast. Slow down," she murmured. "I want this to last for ever."

He lifted his head and moved his concentration away from her breasts to her neck, flicking his tongue behind her ear. And now his movements slowed, gently stroking her back with his fingers. In time she felt her own fingers move with his rhythm, touching him, exploring until she could hardly tell the source of the pleasure as their bodies began to ignite in an intense conflagration. He felt her surrender and instantly pushed his body hard against hers. She gasped as her muscles stiffened in response to his sustained movements as they built up to a savage urgency. An overwhelming wave of ecstasy washed over her, her body free and uninhibited until, together, they reached the pinnacle of intensity.

Chapter Twenty Six

February 2000
Tobago
LINDELL SAT ON THE VERANDA of the condo he had rented, sipping a chilled Heineken. The money was safely secreted in an account in Grand Cayman - all four million, nine hundred and fifty thousand bucks.

The evening sun was shining and, hey mon, the people were happy. He picked up the *Wall Street Journal* from the table and started to scan the headlines. The side bar article caught his attention, his eyes widening in disbelief. *The sale of Falcon Tech to a Hong Kong company?* He reread the article but couldn't see the commercial angle. Averting his eyes from the paper, he scanned the white sandy beach as the story continued to play out in his mind, the pieces of the jigsaw gradually falling into place. It all made sense; Wong and his triad friends were playing a bigger game and Falcon Tech was the prize. He flung the paper to the ground.

"I won't let that low-life piece of shit get away with it," he repeated to himself several times. "I just goddamn won't…" Pursuit had not been part of the future he was sketching out but he vowed, there and then, that when the time was right he would prepare a game plan.

One hundred yards down the beach, a calypso and steel band started tuning up for the evening's entertainment at the Paradiso Bar.

"Ah what the hell," he muttered and decided it was time to start living again. He took another drink and listened to the gentle sound of the waves lapping on the beach twenty yards directly in front of him. He then tilted his head and fixed his eyes on a clipper, its billowing sails majestically powering it along the water. The distant crack of the canvas and the hum of the rigging soothed his thoughts, bringing him back to those lazy childhood afternoons spent on his uncle's yacht off the Monterey coast. The memories came flooding back as he gazed further out to sea. The sailing boats were slowly making their way across the horizon.

Draining the glass, he decided it was time to see what the rest of this lazy Caribbean island had to offer.

He got up from the seat and walked into the living room. The doorbell rang. *Shit, they've trailed me,* he thought. The bell rang again. Peering through the blinds he saw a young woman with coffee-coloured skin standing on the veranda. He opened the door.

"Mr. Lindell?"

Studying her face for a long moment he responded, "could be."

She smiled. "What's that supposed to mean?"

A mischievous grin lit his face. "Could be means…huh could be."

"In that case hi."

He stretched out his hand and shook hers.

"I'm with Alta Rentals, the people who own this block of condos. We'll have to do a new agreement if you want to stay longer than three months."

Lindell's shoulders relaxed. He stepped back and motioned with his hands.

"Please…please come in."

"Thank you."

She put the lap top on the table. "If you give me the details I can tap them in directly."

"Okay."

She got to work.

"Nice computer!" he said.

"It's brilliant. Very little paper in the office. Everything's in here."

Lindell stared at the Falcon Tech logo. *They'll probably change the name,* he thought. *Who knows, maybe to Mandarin computers?*

When the details were entered she hit the save icon and closed down the computer.

"You planning on travelling around the island?"

"Maybe."

"Well then you might think about renting a car or whatever. My brother's in the business."

326

"Really?"

"He'll see you right if you're interested."

Lindell liked what he was hearing. "I was thinking more about fishing out on that big blue sea. And even diving."

"Does that too, even surf boards." She smiled an irresistible smile, her pearl white teeth contrasting against her tanned skin.

"Maybe I should take a trip to see this brother of yours."

"I can drive you there."

Even better, he thought. *Driven around paradise by a beautiful girl. Can things get better?*

Beijing

THE SYMBOL OF COMMUNIST SUPREMACY- the Great Hall of the People - stands out boldly on the western side of Tiananmen Square. Built in the Mao era at the height of Communist fervour to accommodate gatherings of the National People's Congress when more than ten thousand people would descend on the capital to deliberate on state affairs, its carved wooden architecture was designed to display the magnificence of Chinese aesthetics.

The Year of the Dragon celebrations had already begun to mark the beginning of Chinese New Year when Wong arrived. He watched the carnival atmosphere from the comfort of the limousine as traditional culture and Western influence fused together in a spectacular fireworks display. The cavalcade edged its way along the Square, past the crowds, finally coming to a halt outside the impressive edifice. Without delay Wong was escorted towards the entrance. A lavish feast awaited him in the Banquet Hall in the northern wing. Two thousand people were seated to celebrate the New Year and the beginning of a new era. In the eyes of the revelling aparachiks the first step on the path to making China technologically great again had been taken. The top brass of the Communist machine bowed and smiled as Zhu Feng, the Military Commission chairman, invited Wong to take the seat of honour. He sat down and scanned the neatly ordered rows of bowls and chopsticks and

327

the cold starters beautifully arranged on platters in the centre of the long tables. Feng nodded towards the food.

"*Manmanchi* (eat slowly)," he said as trolleys containing fresh platters of sizzling food were wheeled between the rows of tables. Two thousand pairs of chopsticks clanked against platters as tiny delicacies were plucked from the centre of the tables to the safety of bowls and then chewed loudly sending the decibel level into the danger zone. After a satisfying helping of *jiaozi* (dumplings) Feng put down his chopsticks, cleared his throat and began in Mandarin.

"You have indeed made Mother China technologically great again. Something truly befitting Chinese ingenuity in the twenty-first century. Soon our engineers will find a way to make that ThinkEx computer work in reverse to control the human mind and then we will start a real propaganda war with the West. For this we have decided to make you an honorary member of the Communist Party. Of course membership gives you the right to live in China."

The guest smiled graciously, reflected for a moment and then responded. "Thank you. My true homeland indeed. The first thing I must do is travel up the Yangtze river to find my *laojia* (ancestral home)."

"The residence permit will allow you to settle where ever you like."

"I must find my roots. It's very important to me."

The apparatchiks nodded.

"As requested your favourite dishes will be served," Biao confirmed as he pointed towards the feast. "Peking duck, mandarin fish and lotus crabs as well as your special request: stir-fried pig's stomach and sea urchin." He swung the chopsticks in the air. "This is our way of thanking you for the *yang* you have brought us…of showing appreciation for what you have achieved…our way of saying that you and indeed all of Hong Kong are now truly part of us."

Wong smiled but did not speak. When a helping of duck was consumed Biao turned towards him. "Now that we've got Falcon Tech what do *you* do about the trade problem? Presumably it won't go away."

"No, it won't but, like everything in life, there is a solution if you look hard enough."

"A solution?"

Wong explained that the Europeans would impose forty-two per cent duty on Chinese computers but he would shift production across to Tai Po where a factory was waiting thanks to Mr. Kai, a property developer. Falcon Tech computers would then have Hong Kong origin and because of the colony's status as a Special Administrative Region within China it has its own customs rules. He smiled and said, "So we pay no penalty, no duty."

Feng plucked a delicacy from the centre plate and started to chew loudly. He did not wait to swallow before he began to speak. "We always knew you would make the *one-country-two-systems* arrangement work to our advantage some day."

"That was the idea. So if Beijing agrees," the Supreme Lodge Father continued, "most of the workers can come from Southern China to Tai Po so costs won't change. And with the other Asian tigers suffering duty, our share of the market in Europe will grow."

Biao held up his hand as a thank-you gesture. *"To become rich is glorious.* We now have a real red chip company. I think we have made the maxim of Deng Xiaoping come true."

Yinchu agreed. "Yes, Mr. Wong you have made us all so proud."

"All I ask is to serve my country."

"So," Feng said coldly. "Beijing must have ninety per cent of the profits. You can keep the rest. Every Chinese New Year you will lodge the money in our special account in the Bank of China in time for the celebrations."

Wong's eyes became distant for a moment. It was clear that Feng was the big boss. He turned to him and said, "I understand the arrangement."

The apparatchiks sat back in their chairs, pleased. Wong picked up the chopsticks and, reaching for the sea urchin, smiled inwardly.

Hong Kong
TWENTY-FOUR HOURS LATER the highest-ranking members of the Yangtze Triad assembled in Cheng's office to hear the Supreme Lodge Father explain Beijing's latest demands. Cheng's mouth opened in a loud laugh, exposing heavily discoloured teeth. "Ninety per cent?" he repeated incredulously.

"Yes, ninety," Wong replied. "They're dreaming. We'll take ninety and they can have ten. We'll do what the Americans do to reduce taxes. We'll take our sales and finance operations to Grand Cayman starting next month. We'll feed them whatever figures we like. Maybe ten per cent if they're lucky. At last we'll be in the big league of high technology. And now the world will know that we are not a crazy group of slant-eyed Orientals fighting internecine wars in Chinatowns the world over."

"So, what are we waiting for?" Cheng asked. "Let's have a big celebration dinner tonight compliments of our good friends at Kimble-Sinclair, particularly the nice Mr. Howard Sinclair III."

The room exploded in oriental laughter.

March 2000
Washington
AFTER NUMEROUS PHONE CALLS by Marc, a disciplinary review hearing was held in Brussels where he argued his case and produced the evidence in his possession. It was accepted that he was unfairly suspended without due process and offered reinstatement in the EU Embassy in Washington.

By the second weekend in March he had returned to Laura. Spring was in the air and the light traffic hardly intruded on their conversation as they made their way to the intersection of 17th and Pennsylvania Avenue. She shuddered as a cool breeze whipped up and Laura moved closer to Marc. "Way back a year or so ago, I joked about the big bad world of business. I had no idea that world was so close to us."

"Yeah, and back in Brussels everybody was talking about China as the economic powerhouse in the twenty-first century. Damn it Laura I, too, had no idea that it would happen with the help of the most secret society in the world."

They approached the White House.

"I was thinking we could buy one of those nicely kept houses with a white picket fence around the front lawn and a big back yard. Real New England living."

"You mean 1600 Pennsylvania Avenue?" He said as they peered through the railings.

"Not quite."

"This is the Forbidden City of the West. Only the rich and powerful can gain admittance here."

"I wonder are there any concubines in there?" Laura asked mischievously.

"Most definitely not. Hillary wouldn't allow it. Strictly off limits."

"And what about eunuchs?"

"Oh they keep them in a special house."

"Really?"

"Yeah, it's called Congress."

Laura bent over laughing. They walked along by the railings stopping occasionally to embrace in the cool afternoon breeze as they headed towards Constitution Avenue. He shrugged. "I guess life's crazy."

She tugged at his arm. He turned to look at her. "Maybe we'll think about making a baby, you know an all American boy with straight pearl white teeth and a clean cut image."

Marc took a deep breath, turned towards her and spluttered out. "Suppose it would be okay. I know you don't want to be a concubine in the Forbidden City for ever."

"And you would prefer to be the emperor and not a eunuch any more."

They giggled and laughed at the analogies that they were drawing from their visit to China.

"I love you, Harry. I want to spend the rest of my life with you."

"You hunk, emperor Schuman, take me to your four poster and dismiss all the servants for the night."

As they approached the intersection they saw two helicopters landing to the right of the Washington Monument.

A police car had pulled up at the junction and a policeman got out and stopped the traffic. A minute later the presidential cavalcade flanked by outriders came down Constitution Avenue. As the limousine swung onto 15th Street President Clinton waved.

"How about that! The President comes out to welcome me. I'm really going to like being back."

"You sure are," Marc replied. "You sure are."

"It will be good for both of us."

"Laura there is something I must do right now."

He moved towards the edge of the sidewalk and hailed a taxi. Ten minutes later he stood at the end of Wisconsin Avenue, dipped his hand in his pocket and, with as much force as he could muster, flung the videotape into the Potomac. Laura smiled as she discreetly opened her handbag, pulled out the bottle of perfume and, unnoticed, threw it over the wall into the river.

"I think you have now finally declared the case closed," she said, putting her arms around his neck and hugging him tightly.

Epilogue

May 2000
Sicily

HIS ANGER MOUNTING, Saatchi swore loudly, slapped on his shades and, for the fifth time that afternoon, agitatedly moved to the balcony of his hotel bedroom in Catania.

Maybe the bastard has double-crossed me, he thought as he paced the balcony, oblivious of the soothing motion of the waves breaking on the rocks directly below him. After a few minutes he heard the phone ringing and dashed into the room.

"Saatchi," he snarled.

"Good afternoon Mr. Saatchi. I hope you're enjoying your new life by the sea."

"Enjoying? Well let's say if I didn't hear from you by this weekend I was about to send out a posse of my Mafia friends."

"You shouldn't have been so worried. A deal's a deal. I never renege when somebody helps me to the prize."

The tension in his chest eased. "So where's the-"

"Check with your bank in Switzerland. We've delivered a *hong bao* (red envelope containing money) there this morning."

The Italian relaxed. "Twenty?"

"That's what we agreed."

"So what's the next step?"

"Well Beijing was very pleased. They've given me a residence permit for the mainland. I'll keep a low profile for a year or so 'till all the fuss dies down and I suggest you do the same."

"That's not a problem. The Med's a big sea...lots of places to sail to."

"But be careful," Wong warned. "The papers say that Lindell's hiding out somewhere along the Riviera."

"Don't worry on that count. I'm out on the sea most of the time. Anyway nobody can link me to anything. Incidentally I see you had to pay our friend fifty million in the end."

"We never expected to get away with twenty. Remember we got the Foundation too. Those paintings alone are worth more

333

than one hundred million. An excellent source of cash if things ever get tough."

"Yeah. If there's a Vermeer among them, I want first call."

Wong scoffed down the line. "The Mafia's hardly known for its love of art."

"Believe me, the Romans created art while the Chinese were still in the paddi fields. By the way I see the journalists are still snooping around trying to find out why Sinclair resigned."

"In the end he was pushed. The board gave him an ultimatum to go quietly into honourable retirement because of ill health."

"Must have been difficult for him." Saatchi snorted.

"By all accounts. Problem with that schmuck was that he was a WASP but when it came right down to it he just didn't have the sting. He really should've known that the sting's our speciality."

Saatchi laughed raucously. "Indeed. Almost like Verbiest. You know near the end he was so uptight I was holding his hand practically everyday."

After a moment of silence the Oriental's voice became serious again. "The operation in Grand Cayman is now up and running. In, say, one year from now you are to move there to run the legal department. A successful global corporation must have the law on its side at all times."

The mafioso sniggered down the line. "Even better if it has the law in its pocket."

"You're a devious man, Mr. Saatchi. A very devious man."

"You too, Mr. Wong. You too."

If you liked WHEN DUTY CALLS... look out for the next book by J.L. KRAMER which will be in your bookshop shortly

The Third Degree

1

"Where did we come from?"

A simple question with monumental significance; the kind Professor Kovatz loved and the thirty-seven medical students hated with a passion. They sat blankly in seven elevated rows. Immediately the atmosphere became supercharged with tension. The preying mantis was about to pounce. Outside the class room he was one of the crowd but inside made him a demon; his lecture sessions invariably intense affairs. Kovatz scanned the auditorium for a victim, settling his eyes on the back row where the mostly male students shifted in their seats and frantically struggled to keep their heads low. Eye contact could be fatal. No volunteers. For heaven's sake this was a human anatomy class - not a philosophical debating society. He would wait but not for long. Problem for the students was that once the fray was entered, there would be no let up. A heavy tome under the professor's arm now dropped loudly on his desk, the signal that he was about to choose. The pacing began.

In typical Kovatz style the question was meant to be thought-provoking, meant to kick start the first lecture of the day. But eight thirty on Monday morning was definitely far too early to even contemplate an answer to such a brainteaser. Scheduling his classes so early had become routine for him and, of course, a nightmare for most of the students. He was not popular for this reason but his subjects were interesting and, more importantly, a requirement for the award of a Master's degree.

Kovatz himself could easily have passed for a student. He was close to fifty but the full head of dark hair had not changed and a physical-fitness crusade - three mornings a week on the tennis court by seven - continued to pay dividends; his gut remaining trim and his upper torso toned to near-perfection. Four or fives marathons a year were normal. He boasted about the therapeutic effects of fitness; it led to mental alertness, he believed and, more importantly, allowed him to play the campus don to the full. Hell, he was a professor of

Functional Anatomy after all. And he made no secret of the fact that he was still in the game, ever ready for the chase when the occasion presented itself.

The professor's head swivelled to face the class and his eyes riveted Bradford in the second last row.

"Well, want to share your views?" He asked, nodding in his direction.

Bradford sighed to show his 'why me' displeasure and began rubbing the two-day growth on his face, trying hard to look serious, trying to think. His mind was somewhere back at the party the night before and the effects of the alcohol still lingered. And lack of sleep made it feel a thousand times worse. He just wanted to be left alone. Maybe in the afternoon he would be in better shape to attack that splendid conundrum but not right now at this crazy hour. He was not unique. Almost all the class had spent the weekend celebrating the Orioles win in Camden Yards. Weekend study, if any, was superficial.

"Aw...hmm. Well...the way I see it we don't really know where-"

Bradford started to mumble and the professor strained to hear. Tittering emanated from the back rows, as his fellow students began to enjoy his predicament. Kovatz had chosen well. Bradford would be the sacrificial lamb this morning and it could end in ridicule.

"Mr. Bradford are you saying you're not even a little bit curious? Darwin provides us with a splendid theory, an explanation."

Bradford became ashen-faced. The lack of breakfast added to the lethal combination of alcohol and a bad sleep deficit. He felt distinctly unwell but waded in with a few sentences criticising The Origin of Species but he was losing it fast. Finally he said trying to lighten the tension, "The only thing Darwin makes us do is check our thumbs regularly to make sure that his evolutionary idea has really worked."

"And why is that Mr. Bradford?"

"We need to check if we still have opposable ones. Otherwise we'd have to go back up the trees with the monkeys."

"Have you checked yours lately Mr Bradford?" Kovatz snapped back.

The classroom filled with laughter. A student in the last row muttered just above the silence, "Better check to see if he has a tail while he's at it."

Bradford became beetroot red. The professor smiled arrogantly and continued pacing.

Thinking of a Present ...
Here's a Novel Idea

A beautifully bound personalised copy of **When Duty Calls** ...

If you enjoyed reading **When Duty Calls** ...
you may like to know that it is now available in a
personalised format where you or a friend can play the hero/heroine
alongside the other *dramatis personae* in this thriller.

OR

For the visually impaired a copy of **When Duty Calls** ...
with easy-to-read large print can also be ordered.

All you have to do is complete the coupon below or
visit our website at **www.cappuccinobooks.com** to order by e-mail.
Cost per personalised book €25 plus €5 for postage.
Cost of easy-to-read version €20 plus €5 for postage.
Allow 28 days for delivery.

Person buying the book: _____

Name: _____

Address: _____

_____

Payment method: ☐ Cheque ☐ Postal Order

Credit Card No. ☐☐☐☐☐☐☐☐☐☐☐☐☐☐☐☐☐☐☐

Send to: **Cappuccino Books Ltd, Galway Technological Centre, Mervue
Business Park, Mervue, Galway, Ireland**

For personalised copy:
Person who will feature in the story:
☐ Hero ☐ Heroine

Name: _____

Address: _____

_____

Address where you wish book to be delivered: _____

_____

Or visit our website at: **www.cappuccinobooks.com**